The Whole Golden World

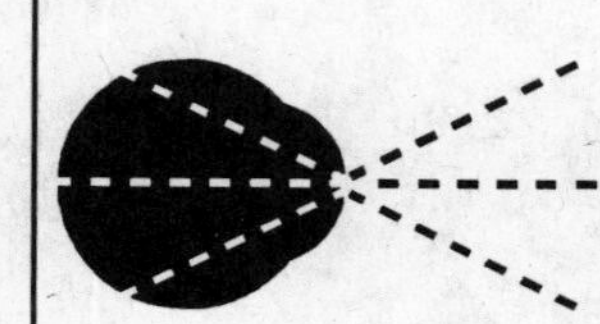

THE WHOLE GOLDEN WORLD

KRISTINA RIGGLE

THORNDIKE PRESS
A part of Gale, Cengage Learning

Detroit • New York • San Francisco • New Haven, Conn • Waterville, Maine • London

Thorndike Press, a part of Gale, Cengage Learning.

Thorndike Press® Large Print Women's Fiction.
The text of this Large Print edition is unabridged.
Other aspects of the book may vary from the original edition.
Set in 16 pt. Plantin.

LIBRARY OF CONGRESS CATALOGING-IN-PUBLICATION DATA

Riggle, Kristina.
The whole golden world / by Kristina Riggle. — Large Print edition.
pages cm. — (Thorndike Press Large Print Women's Fiction)
ISBN 978-1-4104-6602-0 (hardcover) — ISBN 1-4104-6602-7 (hardcover)
1. Teacher-student relationships—Fiction. 2. Mothers and daughters—Fiction. 3. Husband and wife—Fiction. 4. Statutory rape—Fiction. 5. Retribution—Fiction. 6. Large type books. I. Title.
PS3618.I39387W46 2014
813'.6—dc23 2013041496

Published in 2014 by arrangement with William Morrow, an imprint of HarperCollins Publishers

Printed in the United States of America
1 2 3 4 5 6 7 18 17 16 15 14

To my parents, my teachers,
my mentors throughout my teen years:
Thank you for taking me seriously,
and also for knowing when not to

ACKNOWLEDGMENTS

Thank you so much to my ally and agent, Kristin Nelson, and her team, for all the support for all these years and books together. Thank you to Lucia Macro, my insightful and wonderful editor, for understanding this book and helping me make it sing. Thanks to the many others at HarperCollins who helped bring this book to the world, including but not limited to Nicole Fischer, Jennifer Hart, Pamela Jaffee, and Mumtaz Mustafa, for that gorgeous cover.

For this book, I had to learn all about high school these days, an Elgar concerto, and the ins-and-outs of a particular type of court case. Thank you to all of my research sources for answering my questions with patience, thoughtfulness, and not a hint of embarrassment despite the occasionally awkward queries. I owe a debt of gratitude to the following (in no particular order): Larry Glazer, Carol Hendershot, Bill Castanier, Rachel Moulton, Katrina Kittle, Dan VanPernis, Kate Filoni, Scott Crooks, Marty the cellist, and as ever, my critique partner, Elizabeth Graham.

Any errors are mine, or better yet, let's assume it was poetic license.

Thank you to my family, for taking my job seriously, even though I can work in my pajamas. Love you.

Part 1

1

June 6, 2012

Dinah felt the turning away like the snap of a rubber band that's been pulled too far, finally lashing back, leaving a welt.

She had not expected Morgan to be happy. This morning she had hoped only that her children stay alive and fed, because at least this she could accomplish. Probably.

Then Morgan turned away from her, walking to the left side of the courtroom to sit behind that man.

In the low murmurs rippling in their wake, she heard the crowd registering what had just happened. Dinah reached for Joe's hand — and found only cool air.

Whether by design or accident, he'd moved his arm away just as she reached out. Dinah couldn't imagine what Joe thought when Morgan had pared herself away from them and gone to sit elsewhere. It had apparently not occurred to him to join their daughter on that side of the room. Dinah had considered it, had instinctively made to follow her as she'd done all her life, sticking close to her children like an electron does to its nucleus, before realizing how that would be received by her daughter. Before realizing what it would be like to sit that close to the man whose sick appetites had detonated in the middle of their family.

Joe had just kept moving, choosing the first row of the courtroom, right behind the prosecutor. Dinah stopped walking, feeling the equidistance of her daughter and husband immobilize her.

People nudged past Dinah without a word. No "excuse me" or even a curt, "Could you move?" It was something she'd noticed in the last months when out in public. People didn't talk to her. The river of people flowed around her like she was a fallen tree.

Dinah pressed her lips together and forced herself to walk again, the heaviness of her step recalling the newborn baby days: when you didn't think you could move one more step at 4:15 in the morning but you did anyway, to keep the baby in your arms from squalling at the cessation of motion. She joined Joe, sitting down more heavily than she'd meant to, as if someone had shoved her.

Sitting as they were, Dinah would have to turn her head entirely to the side, almost over her shoulder, to see Morgan behind the defendant's table. The table where the man would be sitting who was charged with criminal sexual conduct against her. "CSC III," the cops had called it, in their snappy jargon.

Dinah turned to look. How could she not? Was there ever a time in her life that she could not look at her beautiful girl? The buzzing overhead lights bounced off her coffee-dark hair, making it gleam. Morgan's head was bent down, exposing the back of her pale, delicate neck. This posture made her look fragile and thin. It put Dinah in mind of the way Morgan often looked down at her cello as she practiced. At performances, Dinah ignored the other musicians, her attention always drawn to Morgan's sway with the music, her arm sweeping across her cello as if coaxing out the sound.

Morgan turned like she could feel her mother's gaze. Dinah gasped at what she saw there: burning fury written in the narrowing of her eyes, in the forward jut of her chin. As if her parents had wronged her. Not the high school teacher who seduced her in a parked car, next to a highway overpass in his 4Runner.

When Dinah flinched away from Morgan and stared at her own clenched hands, she began to picture herself as she must appear to everyone else: the failed mother, whose golden child turned out to be just another girl gone bad. Schadenfreude was already in full effect, Dinah knew, from the way the other mothers fell silent when she dared step into their presence, looking at her sideways from wary, skeptical eyes.

Her own mother had exclaimed, "How could you let this happen?" when she first heard, as if Dinah had mistakenly let Morgan off her leash.

Dinah had been outraged at the time and railed at her mother for the lack of support. But in the darkest hours of the night, Dinah continued to ask herself the very same question.

The first thing that happened, when Rain saw her husband, was a leap of her heart in sadness and alarm for how he looked: haggard, frightened.

This kept happening, this Pavlovian response to the sight or thought of him. No matter what mistakes he'd made, what wrong he'd committed, Rain found herself unable to pluck out her love for him like a sliver from her finger.

He had come, with his lawyer, from some internal room in the recesses of the courthouse. Not from jail, not in a jumpsuit. Rain was grateful for that. There was, at least, that.

She glanced around the room, wondering if his parents had come, but in her darting look she did not find them.

She was not surprised. His parents had turned against their own son. Called Rain to offer their support and railed against the "disgusting" betrayal he had committed. It was good, Rain supposed, that they had reached out to her. It was perhaps better than being abandoned, and her own family could not be counted on at times like this.

Still, with her ingrained and impossible love for her husband, she died for him that everyone else had turned their backs.

He had reached the defendant's table. His eyes had been on the floor for his progress across the room. She saw in the raising of his chin and the brightening of his eyes a flicker of hope that this whole town had not forsaken him entirely. Some of them might remember who he'd been before last winter, when he'd made those crazy mistakes, for reasons unknown and unfathomable. Rain sat up straighter.

She saw TJ smile sadly. But not at her, his wife. He smiled at that girl, seated just behind his lawyer.

Her husband sat down without seeming to have noticed Rain. She saw his lawyer lean in urgently, whispering something in harsh desperation, perhaps telling him it's a bad idea to smile at the teenage girl he's said to have sexually assaulted.

"All rise," the skinny clerk ordered.

A great shuffling of feet and jackets and handbags occurred all around her. Rain would have liked to rise. Rain believed in respect.

But she remained seated, gripping the back of the seat in front of her.

Look at me, Morgan pleaded silently. *I came here for you. I'm not ruined like they all say. I'm just fine.*

He raised his head slowly, and she froze in midbreath, not daring to hope. He locked his eyes on hers, and his lips turned up in the saddest of tiny smiles. Before she could react, the lawyer yanked his arm and he turned away.

"All rise," ordered the clerk.

Morgan stood as she was told. She clasped her hands in front of herself firmly, almost as if he were the one holding her hand, steadying her. Like that day in his classroom. She'd felt an electric charge that lit her up and killed her both at once and left her nearly panting for breath.

She noticed he'd cut his hair shorter, which disappointed her. Already he looked less like himself. No doubt his lawyer had made him do it, that lady lawyer who probably thought shaggy hair made him look dangerous. Like she'd been some kind of helpless girl in a silent movie, tied to the railroad tracks while he cackled. That's what no one understood. She was no victim. She was a grown woman trapped in a body too young for anyone to take her seriously.

That quick, sad smile told her all she needed to know. Despite the courts saying it was a crime, despite her parents locking her down like she herself was a criminal, despite the gossip and vandals and spewing hate from random strangers . . . he loved her anyway. Against the odds and against all sense. She lifted her chin and straightened her shoulders, as if the orchestra conductor had just raised her baton.

The judge cleared his throat and the air in the room seemed to freeze, as everyone waited for it all to begin.

■ ■ ■ ■

"Thomas John Hill," the judge read, and his lawyer nudged him. He'd forgotten to pay attention to his full name, so seldom was it ever used.

The judge was talking, but TJ couldn't hear a thing over a voice in his head chanting, *What have you done?*

What have you done?

What have you done?

2

September 6, 2011

Rain's first thought, as the slanting light crept in through her blinds and splashed across her face: *Oh, no. Not again.*

She could feel already it was over, in the sharp tightening pressure of her abdomen. A shard of hope still caused her to think *but maybe not, maybe it's not what I think . . .*

She remained in bed, lingered in the uncertainty, though her last optimism was drying up like morning dew.

"Don't stop! Believing!" TJ's voice rang out, tuneless but with gusto, over the hiss of the shower. So Rain smiled, in spite of everything.

She decided not to tell him if it was bad news, on his first day of a new school year. Not to dampen his enthusiasm. She slid out of bed, unable to wonder any longer, and shuffled down the stairs to the spare bathroom.

In the midst of her sea-blue and sand-tan towels, the smell of sandalwood still lingering from last night's incense stick, she held her breath and looked. In spite of her earlier resolve to be strong, she cursed out loud and hot tears washed down her face. Another cycle of failure. Another month not pregnant.

Her supplies were in the master bathroom so she'd have to wait until TJ finished his shower to deal with the mechanics of her period. So she propped her elbows on her knees and sat there on the toilet, hearing TJ belt out the last lines of that corny Journey song louder than ever now that he'd shut the shower off.

"Hellooooo, gorgeous." TJ bent to peck Rain's lips, and she tried to rally to meet him in his ebullient mood.

"Hey, sexy," she answered, but her voice was limp. He busied himself with breakfast at the kitchen counter behind her. "Want some oatmeal?" he called over his shoulder as he poured coffee.

"Sure. Looking forward to today?"

"You bet. The kids haven't started hating me yet."

Rain half smiled into her coffee cup. No one hated TJ. He was probably one of the best-loved teachers in the whole place, in fact, always getting good reviews on those teacher rating websites, which most teachers claimed not to read, but Rain knew they all caved eventually. And this year he was teaching calculus to the upperclassmen, due to the unfortunate heart attack in August of Mr. Adamczyk, who'd been teaching there so long he seemed to smell of chalk dust whenever Rain had happened to see him, though the school had gone to markers and dry erase boards years ago. Though his colleague's passing was sad, TJ was thrilled to have been offered the tougher class, a huge step up from having to monitor detention and teach the basics of $x + 5 = 15$ to freshmen who never got the swing of middle school.

TJ flipped his tie over his shoulder as he poured the oatmeal and turned on the burner for the kettle. It would be the only day he would wear a tie, Rain knew. One of the last holdovers from his past track-and-field stardom was his superstition. On race day, so the story goes, he would only wear a particular pair of socks, something that earned him no end of teasing but which he regarded with utmost seriousness, along with his training regimen.

Rain allowed herself to revel in his strong

shoulders and back, obvious from the cut of his dress shirt. He turned to wink at her while the water boiled, and she let herself swoon a little and wonder how she'd won this guy.

Then her guts twisted, and she sucked in a breath.

TJ noticed her flinch. "Babe?"

Rain shook her head and screwed her eyes up.

TJ set his jaw and stared at the floor. The first few months he was consoling and sweet, plying her with chocolates, running to fill a hot-water bottle, promising it was only a small hitch, and soon enough she'd be big as a house and squeezing out a baby they would love, and cuddle, and rock, and read to. TJ would talk about how he'd teach his son to throw a football with a perfect spiral, just like his dad taught him, and when Rain teased him about his old-school gender stereotypes, he promised to teach his daughter, too.

When Rain started peeing on ovulation tests and reading books and charting her fertility signs, he'd taken to saying "Sorry, honey" and giving her shoulder a light squeeze. At last there was that day she brought home the pamphlet from Dr. Gould's, resulting in the worst fight of their marriage to date.

That night, in a hormonal, menstrual stew, she'd tearfully bemoaned his waning support, to which he replied that he felt helpless to make her happy, and that he felt like a failure himself. He'd seemed to cave in just then, curling forward on the couch and resting his elbows on his knees.

Rain had apologized for pressuring him and resolved to take her sadness to her journal, or give it up to the Universe, as Beverly was always saying.

The distance between them now — just a few feet over their laminated kitchen floor — seemed too great for her to cross, heavy with fatigue and sadness as she was, churned up with cramps as she was. She looked up and saw that he was about to move toward her, when the kettle began hissing. He turned back to the oatmeal.

The cramp began to loosen, and she turned in her chair to face her coffee again.

TJ appeared at the table and handed her the oatmeal sprinkled with brown sugar in a smiley face pattern. She ate the nose out of it and tried to be amused.

Her phone bleated out its ringtone and Rain groaned, knowing without looking it would have to be her mother. Angie did not believe in subjecting herself to the tyranny of the clock, which irritated the hell out of Rain and had a similar effect on every boss Angie had ever had. Which was why she'd had so many.

"Hi, honey." Angie started talking the moment she heard the ringing stop, not even waiting for Rain to speak. "Can you come take Dog to the vet? There's something wrong with him I think. Also, all the chocolate is missing."

Rain propped her head in her hand. "Can't Dad do it? Or Stone? I know Fawn's got the baby . . . but why can't you handle it?"

Angie guffawed. "Honey, it's not even 8 A.M. and I'm in my nightie and last night's makeup. You'll be off to work soon, right? Just take him on your way. Oh, and stop by the house sometime soon and fix Daddy's computer. That dummy has screwed it up again."

"Fine, Mom, I guess, but —"

"Love you sweet girl, bye!"

And that was that. Rain pushed away the oatmeal and rested her head on her folded arms. She could just picture them in that house so old and sideways leaning that a marble would roll if you set it down on the kitchen floor. Angie would be smoking and shouting instructions at Fawn about changing Brock's diaper, or bellowing demands at Ricky, who was tuning her out, if not shouting back. Stone — plenty old enough to be out on his own, but not inclined to move — would be blaring music into his earbuds or blaring it into the air with his guitar.

Precious little had changed since she'd escaped the maelstrom as a teenager to live with steady, stable Gran, the person she loved best in the world, who had the discourtesy to suffer a stroke and die while Rain was a college sophomore.

"Now what do the good Davidsons need you to do for them? Change the oil? Hammer down some loose shingles?" TJ rolled his eyes and snorted. "Maybe Stone needs to borrow your pee to pass a drug test."

"TJ, my darling love?" She turned her head to the side, still down on her arms. "Shut the hell up about my family, or I will hammer your shingles but good."

"I love it when you get rough with me."

"That's because you think I'm kidding."

"You have that new girl starting today, right?" TJ asked, and Rain groaned. She'd forgotten. Beverly was busy leading classes today, so she'd asked Rain to show the new girl around Namaste Yoga Center, get her settled. Rain sat up and brushed her hair out of her face.

"Is that so bad?" TJ asked, shoveling in his food, glancing at his watch. Perhaps realizing his Journey serenade had slowed him down.

"Beverly and I made a good team. You add a third person, and who knows what could happen. It shifts the whole dynamic."

"And yet, you want to add a third person to our own good team? Change our whole dynamic?" TJ raised one eyebrow, adding a half smile to show he was only kidding. Wasn't he? Sure he was. TJ adored his little second cousins and was a big hit at every faculty function with the teachers' kids, rounding up a softball game or a water balloon fight. She smiled at a memory of TJ giving his cousin's kid a horsey ride on his strong shoulders. He was going to be a terrific dad.

"That's different. I've always wanted to be a mother. It feels like . . . like I already am a mother. My child is just not with me yet, here. On earth."

"There's the hippie chick I know and love." TJ pecked her on the head. "Gotta fly, babe. Don't want to have to mark myself tardy."

"Have a nice day, Mr. Hill," she said. "Break a leg."

He waved and winked on his way out the

door, but by then he wasn't really looking at her, and his farewell landed somewhere among the books on the haphazard living room shelves.

3

The roar of the cappuccino machine drowned out what Connor had said. "What?" Dinah called.

First day of school. Her favorite day, her least favorite, her busiest.

"Britney!" she called for the girl to come get her coffee order. A slender strawberry blonde snaked her way among the round tables and scattered cushions, swaying her hips much more than necessary. Clumps of high school students filled the narrow, long space that had been the first floor of a bungalow once upon a time and had been rezoned to commercial use just before Dinah moved in, installed the restaurant equipment, and named it the Den, back when the twins had started first grade and everything still seemed shiny and possible.

Finally she turned to Connor again. "What was that, hon?"

He rolled his eyes and pulled an aggressive face, turned away from her roughly. It was the "hon," probably. She was supposed to stop calling her fourteen-year-old boys "hon" and "kiddo" and "dear" by now.

She moved to the register to take an order, now that Janine was making a smoothie. Her college student employees had vanished back to campuses, and her main employee was Janine, an aimless, ageless woman between high school and real life. Dinah had also hired a few temps whom she might keep, if they kept their hands out of the till, out of the pastries, and into the sink for proper hand washing. She needed the help today, especially. The place was jammed on the first day of school, since the Den was on the road to the high school. She knew many parents dropped their teens off on their way to work, and then the teens who had vehicles would cart the lot of them to the school after a coffee or a smoothie and a bagel.

Connor and Jared were supposed to be playing chess over in the corner in front of the fireplace — the counselor said it was good for Connor to play chess, to improve his analytical thinking — but they were horsing around with the pieces, pretending they were action figures, and creating lewd tableaux with the queen and king.

Dinah looked at the clock and wanted it to speed up so she could quit worrying about the twins' behavior in her café. She also wished she could freeze it. Soon the boys would be officially high school students. Mainstreamed into the normal high school, something she'd long prayed for, worked for, but now that it was here she felt that she was throwing her babies to the wolves.

Times like this she flashed back to their earliest days in those awful plastic boxes, with the tubes and wires coming out of them everywhere, the sum of all that equipment outweighing the boys themselves easily.

Just as well Morgan was taking them to school; Dinah might change her mind and drive them home instead when she pulled up to that huge building.

"Hi, Miss D!" chirped one of the flute girls. Dinah could never remember them all; so many of the girls in band picked the flute or clarinet.

"Hi, hon," Dinah replied. "Did you have a good summer?"

She ordered her latte, and Dinah got to work, listening to her chatter about a family vacation and a boy she met while camping and how they were texting all the time now.

Dinah handed it over and the girl — oh, was it Olivia? Maybe Olivia — skipped over to her friends on the couch in front of the fireplace. She literally skipped. It made Dinah smile. The Den kept her young, she often thought, because who could be a sour old fart among this much enthusiasm?

Dinah glanced toward Morgan and Britney, in conference in the far corner from the twins. Something seemed to be up. Britney had her hand over Morgan's, in a gesture of what . . . comfort? Commiseration?

"Miss D? Did you hear me?" asked the young man in front of her.

"Oh, sorry. Tell me again what you'd like."

She keyed in his order and shouted it to Janine, who began singing along with Lady Gaga over the speaker.

A break in the traffic occurred just then. The first school bell was coming closer. Kids walking in now wouldn't have time to drink their coffee or eat. Dinah walked around the counter, hoping to casually check on Morgan to see what might be wrong.

But in the back corner of the shop, near the stairs that led to her office on the second floor, raised voices caught her attention. No, not raised, exactly. Not loud. But urgent. Angry.

She looked in their direction and saw a young woman she remembered from the last school year. A pale little thing who favored large men's shirts and jeans. She was sitting with a boy who was glaring at her in a way that was causing her to shrink down, like she might turtle up inside that big shirt.

The angry voice was his, Dinah could see. She veered away from Morgan and headed for this couple. She'd ask if they needed anything. Her appearance alone might break whatever poisonous mood would cause this boy to look at the girl that way. Then the boy snatched the girl's wrist with the quickness of a cobra strike. She issued a small sound, just a little gasp, really, but there was pain in it, and something like fear.

Outrage crashed over Dinah like a fever. As Dinah quickened her step, she saw the boy grip her harder, and the girl turned her arm to get leverage away from him, and then he bent that wrist in a way that looked unnatural.

No, she thought, may have said out loud, but her body was taking over now, heart over head, so by the time she reached the table she bellowed, "Get out of here! You will not treat girls that way in my place of business."

The boy had raised his arms in a manner of surrender as soon as he heard Dinah's stomping footfalls. His face was all, *Who, me?*

The girl rubbed her wrist and stared between Dinah and the boy with round, wide eyes.

The boy now fixed Dinah with a sneer. She studied him, memorizing the moment. His hair was curly and shaggy, and on anyone else it might have looked endearing. Blemishes peppered his face. He had hazel eyes that were narrowed at her. He finally said, "Seriously? Really, lady?"

"Out."

"Whatever." As he stood up, he slammed his chair to the floor. He walked past Dinah just close enough for her to notice he was taller. He mumbled something as he passed. "Crazy bitch," or similar.

"Quite the big man you are, muttering things as you walk away, hurting young girls who weigh half what you do."

The music blared inanely on, but all other sounds had stopped. The boy pivoted on his heel and turned to her, slowly. "Get your eyes checked, lady. We were just talking." He started to walk away with a gliding stride, like nothing was wrong in the whole wide world.

"And don't ever come back!"

He stopped at the door, with a look like she was the dumbest rock in the garden. "Like I'd want to. Jesus."

The bells on the door jingled as it swung closed.

Dinah wanted the air-conditioning on, felt she was probably flushed in the face. She turned to the girl whose wrist the boy had grabbed.

Dinah stepped toward her, but the girl put up a hand. "Leave me alone. For serious." She turned away in her chair, then jammed in some earbuds and curled up, facing away from everyone and everything.

Chatter slowly resumed, then shortly there was a bustle as they all noticed what time it was.

She walked up to the boys, heart still rattling around in her rib cage. "Connor, Jared, get your stuff."

Jared: "I know, Mom. I can tell time."

Connor: "Mom, we're not babies."

She tried not to let Jared realize she was watching him, but she was, of course, studying his gait as he picked up his backpack and moved with his shuffling, slightly tremulous step toward the door, pushing up his thick glasses and hiking his backpack into place. The glasses, the mild palsy: lasting imprints of his early thrust into the cold world. Connor was already at the door, bouncing lightly on the balls of his feet. He, too, had lasting effects from his prematurity, but his were not so obvious. He struggled in reading and writing, had to battle his way through math, and he had no patience. What little kid would? What little kid wouldn't be frustrated and defeated by looking at all the school papers posted in the hall on Parent Night, with his own letters misshapen, his spelling garbled?

Morgan appeared behind her and popped her gum.

"Come on, Mork and Dork."

"Shut up, Morticia."

"Have a good day, guys!" Dinah called cheerily, trying to erase and write over the drama of the morning. "Love you all!"

The girl with the big shirt had slipped out without Dinah noticing, as she cleaned up behind the counter, while the rest of the kids risking tardies charged out to their cars. Dinah had to grip the cleaning rag hard to keep her hands from shaking, as her blood rush spiraled back down to normal.

When Dinah was satisfied the place was empty of customers, she turned to Janine, who was rinsing out the blender parts. "When did it become a bad thing to object to physical abuse of a girl? Have I gone through the looking glass here?"

"Well," Janine said. "Subtle is not your strong suit."

"Subtle? He was gonna break her wrist! I won't put up with bullshit like that. Not now, not ever."

Janine flipped her hair out of her face. "Okay, but Di, what's that guy gonna do at school when he sees her? You think he's gonna say, 'Oooh, I better be nice to you or Miss D is gonna get me'?"

"Hey, easy on the sarcasm. I've got teenagers at home. It's the Sarcasm Marathon on all channels already."

"Sometimes you get more flies with honey than with vinegar."

"Who says I want flies?"

The front doorbell chimed and a young mother came in with her baby. Dinah cooed at the baby, wiped counters, and prepared sandwiches for the lunch crowd. But the whole time, she kept imagining the boys having a great first day in high school, as if she could conjure such a thing into existence by force of will, the same way she felt that her fierce and terrified love kept her fragile preemie twins alive, day after day in the NICU.

4

In Morgan's nightmares, her scar opened up like a fault line and swallowed her face, then her scalp and hair, and she was left waving her hands in the blankness over her stunted neck.

Morgan knew better than to tell anyone about this, lest her parents pack her off to some shrink like they did Connor after too many playground scraps. Then she'd have to fend off their mother's hovering, and she'd be lucky if her parents let her go to college ten miles away, much less a thousand miles.

Still. Those dreams made for some unsettled mornings, and she found herself touching the side of her face, as if to check that her head hadn't actually disappeared.

This morning's variation, Morgan remembered as she sprawled on her bed, half reading the "The Summoner's Tale" for AP English, had been with Ethan. They'd been kissing — right then she knew it was a dream; she even thought, outside of her dream world yet still in it, *Oh, I'm dreaming* — and then the scar began to swallow her. She tried to back away from Ethan, but this passionate dream-Ethan wouldn't stop kissing her, wouldn't let go, in fact was almost suffocating her, and the scar swallowed them both.

She would like to be able to tell Ethan about this, but of course she could never do that. Good way to make her closest friend run off, screaming, and she had a feeling she'd need him more than ever this year, the year of senior pictures, prom, college applications, graduation. Britney always laughed when Morgan called Ethan her friend. "He's totally hot for you," she'd say, rolling her eyes. "You guys should just hook up and get it over with."

Morgan would deflect her — please, they'd been friends since sixth-grade orchestra, though Ethan long ago gave up the viola — but lately she'd been wondering if she didn't have a point about Ethan being more than a friend. Morgan looked forward to seeing him every day, thinking about him the minute she woke up. She could take or leave pretty much everyone else.

Morgan slammed shut her AP English

book. Chaucer in Middle English. Dull as shite.

From between her mattress and box spring she withdrew a spiral-bound notebook and a fine-tipped pen. She propped the notebook on her folded knees and sighed, letting all the stupidities of her day — her idiot, spoiled brothers, her dad at the assembly today with his assistant-principal gut straining his best suit, the kids mocking him — spill out onto the blue-lined paper. These days it seemed like she saw her dad at school in his suit more than he was at home, in his blue jeans, just being Dad. When he did get home finally, he always seemed too worn out to do more than say "Hey, Mo-Mo" and ruffle her hair like she was five years old.

And her mother . . . ugh. That scene at the Den where she flipped out on Justin — who, granted, was a jerkface and obnoxious — and Missy had to run around half the school day insisting she was not a battered woman or anything, they were just arguing. Morgan had tried to talk to her mom about it after school, trying to get her to cool off, that just because it's Crisis-o-Rama with the twins doesn't mean that there are epic dramas unfolding all around her. But naturally, all her mom could do was panic about all the kids abandoning the Den, before grilling her about how the boys did on the first day of school. Morgan being unofficial Deputy Mom and all.

It didn't occur to Dinah to ask how her flip-out had affected Morgan. All day long kids were going, "So I heard your mom saw Justin beat up Missy and called the cops," and she had to straighten it out about seventeen times.

She was writing semiconsciously, occasionally crossing off a word here or there, feeling the stress pour out through the tip of her pen. Morgan would never show anyone this poetry. She'd made that mistake before, in middle school, having written this weirdly dark poem about death, and though her teacher had been impressed with her "stark imagery," her mom had freaked out that she had some secret dark side and grilled her about her fears of mortality.

So it was simpler for everyone if she just hid her notebook and pretended to be as normal and straightforward as the rest of the school, cheering at football games and sneaking booze on the weekends. But turning eighteen years old in July, and finally going off to college next fall . . .

Her parents were assuming she'd go to Michigan State or U of M, or maybe Central in Mt. Pleasant. Those were the campuses they visited last summer, anyway, with Dinah more excited than Morgan about this or that dorm, about how pretty the Red Cedar River was, or how funky-cool Ann Arbor would be. She and her parents agreed (meaning: Dinah told and Morgan didn't object) to apply to those three schools and Grand Valley, too, though one in-state school or another seemed about the same to Morgan. She'd be away from home, anyway, for all of them. That counted for something.

But one bored-stiff night last summer, she'd dragged out an old map of the United States, trying to pick a better place to be. She'd run her finger down, up, and down the east coast from Maine to Florida, as cities slipped in and out of her line of sight, and stopped on Boston. She wasn't exactly Harvard material, but when she started researching, she found that Boston was in fact overrun with universities. Boston University seemed within striking distance of her academic record. Boston also had beautiful buildings, a deep and important history, and proximity to all kinds of other thrilling places. New York! Washington!

Maybe at BU she could confide in her roommate. This roommate — a worldly girl from New York, or maybe literally worldly, from France or Korea — would say *yes! I have crazy dreams, too!* Or maybe she wouldn't, but she'd nod with the sage maturity that must come from growing up somewhere way cooler than Arbor Valley, Michigan.

She hadn't exactly mentioned Boston to her parents. But once she started the online applications and had her mother's credit card at her disposal, it wouldn't be so hard just to add another to the list.

The poem began to take shape beneath her fingers; it was no more cheerful than her middle-school death verse had been.

She used to try and force herself to write something sweet and pretty, so she could show people, and teachers would hang it in their hallways and her parents would beam with pride. But those attempts resulted in her hand freezing over the paper. Morgan gave up fighting and tried to accept her unchangeable nature.

She propped up the notebook in front of her on the bed, and stretched out on her stomach, her chin in her hands, and reread some of her handiwork.

Beauty scarred
Is beauty still

But not if
The scar
Swallows up what
Is lovely pure precious
Leaving tough dead skin behind

Pounding on the door startled her. "Dammit," she muttered, and stuffed her notebook back under her mattress. She straightened the comforter and shouted, "Just a minute!"

She yanked open the door to see Connor there, frowning hard.

"What!" she demanded.

"I'm . . . Um. Mom said to ask . . ."

"Connor, spit it out."

"She said to ask you for help with my math."

Morgan let a sigh slip out.

Connor started to storm away. "Fine, be that way. I'll just go fail like I always do because it's too much trouble."

"No, stop." Morgan fought to scrub her voice of irritation. "It's fine. I'm not annoyed with you. It's not your fault . . ."

Connor stopped and slumped in the doorway. "Not my fault that I'm stupid?"

"I was going to say not your fault that ninth-grade math is hard." *Not your fault that Mom makes me take care of you.* "Come on in. Where's Jared?"

"He says he already finished his work at school."

Morgan knew the school had decided to split up the boys in different classes, so they would learn to be separate entities. The truth being, of course, that the two of them often brought out the worst in each other.

She leaned over Connor's shoulder after he perched cross-legged on the bed. As she helped explain the concepts of basic algebra — *didn't his teacher go over this?* she wondered — another part of her unbusy brain calculated the exact number of days left until graduation, then added eighty-five days for a reasonable summer vacation.

Connor smiled up at her so gratefully that she tasted a spike of bitter guilt at her secret hunger to escape.

"It would be understandable to resent your brothers," her mother had told her more than once in private moments, ticking off the reasons (as if Morgan didn't know them), like the fact their doctor appointments and tutoring and general caretaking sucked up so much of Dinah's time and energy. Morgan had learned to do her homework in her lap in waiting rooms, while the boys were being ministered to by this or that doctor or therapist or tutor.

Morgan always knew better than to cop to even a hint of resentment, though. They'd gone down that long, tortured road after the boys' wrestling match knocked Morgan into the dining room table, which shattered a vase of peonies in such dramatic fashion that a shard leaped up and sliced Morgan's face.

That day, the vase-smashing day, she'd been crying while the doctor stitched her face; it had felt like a line of fire, despite the supposed numbing medicine. Dinah had to keep reaching over and dabbing her cheek dry with a cloth so the doctor could sew. When the doctor was finished, Dinah said, "The boys just feel terrible," and Morgan shot back, "I wish they'd never been born."

Dinah's face contorted with such anguish that momentarily Morgan wished she'd been the one never born.

That was fifth grade. Just before middle school, when everyone started caring the most about physical appearance. Just when people were starting to comment how pretty she was becoming.

Dinah then launched a not-subtle-at-all campaign to convince Morgan how wonderful her brothers were by taking all of them to the park and the roller rink and the beach, forcing the boys to make handicrafts that said "We love Morgan" with painted handprints.

Everyone was more miserable than ever. Finally, Morgan made a big show of forgiving her brothers and Dinah gave it up.

"Okay," the ninth-grade Connor said, in Morgan's room. "I think I get it now."

Morgan tried not to show how relieved she was that he would finally get out of her space. "Good," she said, nodding.

He gathered his things but paused just before leaving. "Hey, Morticia?"

"Yeah, Dork?"

"Will you still help me next year? You know, on the computer? Mom said she'd get a webcam for us so we could all stay in touch."

"It's a lost cause, you know." She smirked at this. "But, sure. I'll help."

She closed the door behind him and rested her forehead against the faux woodgrain, listening to his heavy footsteps move off to the room he shared with Jared. She remained there with her head on the door, feeling smaller and smaller, as if she really were being swallowed up, like Alice in Wonderland, or Jonah, or nightmare-Morgan who ended up flailing, looking for her own head.

5

Rain took her time finding her house key as she stood on her back porch, sipping in the cool evening air that already carried the bracing hint of autumn. She felt drained in every kind of way: physically from having to teach yoga all afternoon and then hauling Dog to the vet and back; mentally by having to show around the new girl, Layla. Drained of life that might have been.

She thought she'd beaten back thoughts of her failure at conception until the prenatal yoga class trooped in, belly after happy glowing belly.

Thank God she didn't teach that one, at least.

She finally turned the key to see TJ sprawled on the couch, his tie undone, shirt untucked, the laugh track of a sitcom the only sound in the house. His five o'clock shadow was in full effect, TJ being one of those men whose face seemed determined to grow a full ZZ-Top-style beard. Rain appreciated the rugged look, less so the whisker burn on her cheek.

"Hey, hon," she said.

"Hi," he responded with a wan smile. First days could be like that, Rain had learned; depending on the makeup of the classes, he would come home feeling energized or defeated, even on day one.

"That bad?" she said, trying to smile and sound relaxed.

He smirked. "Third hour is gonna be a walk through the valley of the shadow of death."

"Oh, come on," she replied, and plopped herself down next to him. "They won't kill you. Not with anything sharp, anyway, because that's against school rules, right? What are the school rules on large blunt objects?"

By way of response, TJ leaned his head onto her shoulder for a moment.

"Did you eat?" Rain asked.

"I'm not hungry. I grabbed a snack on the way home."

"Okay, then. I'll have some leftovers."

She had her back to the living room as she retrieved leftover pasta salad from the Labor Day barbecue, so Rain wasn't sure she heard TJ right when he said, "Greg called."

"What was that?" she asked, closing the refrigerator and turning back to him.

"Greg called. Alessia sends her love," he repeated, exasperation turning his voice sour.

"Oh. What did he have to say?"

TJ slumped lower on the couch. "Just that he's still filthy fucking rich and wants to throw a party about it."

Rain stood in the kitchen, still holding her salad. "And has he registered for gifts? Maybe at Sharper Image? Radio Shack?" She tossed her hair and affected a laugh.

TJ jerked the remote at the TV to shut it off and tossed it to the floor.

Rain abandoned her pasta and came to his side on the couch. "You're still more handsome than your brother. You'll always have that."

"Till I get old and fat. I'm almost middle-aged."

"Twenty-nine hardly makes you middle-aged. Anyway, you're not going to get fat. No way," Rain said, and ran her hand along his waistband to his muscled abdomen under his untucked shirt. "Not you."

TJ snapped out of his lethargy and turned to her, crushing Rain beneath a sudden, hard kiss, tipping her back on the couch. He moved his mouth to her neck where he sucked and nibbled. His whiskers were scratching her chest, his hands kneading her breasts through her shirt, then moving down to the waistband of her yoga pants.

"TJ," she whispered. "Today isn't the best . . ."

He sat back just as suddenly as he'd pinned her to the couch. He looked at the floor and ran his hands through his hair. "I'm gonna take a shower," he blurted, and ran up the steps like he was leaping hurdles.

Rain adjusted her rumpled clothes and then punched a sofa pillow. On another day she would have rallied. She could have ignored her yoga sweat, her muscle soreness, and risen to his passion, letting him take her right there on the couch. She had done as much, any number of times, and usually enjoyed it once they got going.

Rain put the pasta away, no longer hungry.

She tried to imagine the real conversation TJ must have had. Greg probably called to invite them for dinner on the weekend. He did this often. Greg and Alessia had just built a new house with a huge dining area for entertaining and they enjoyed using it. Dr. Gregory Hill and his stunning wife would serve delectable food and amuse their guests with some hilariously disarming story, like when he met her family in Milan and Alessia's mother declared Greg in arch, accented English, to be "fugly and a hot mess" for wearing a shirt without a collar. She'd picked up the expression by reading American magazines in preparation for meeting her daughter's American boyfriend.

Everyone would laugh, and everyone would adore them, including TJ and Greg's parents, who would be as dazzled as anyone, or more so.

Rain walked up the stairs to change her clothes. She peeled off her sweaty outfit and chose a white eyelet nightgown that wouldn't cling to her anywhere. Teaching yoga meant her work clothes couldn't drape anywhere lest they fall over her face; on her off hours she preferred her clothes to swirl around her freely.

She heard the shower turn off and paused in the act of brushing out her hair in front of the vanity mirror over her dresser. The master bathroom door was visible in the mirror behind her.

TJ emerged wearing boxers and nothing else, his deep brown hair spiky-wet, his chest slick from the shower. Rain cursed her period again.

He offered her a shy smile, then a downward glance.

"Sorry, babe. I was a jerk," he said, then joined her at the mirror. He held her from behind and nuzzled her neck. She could barely hear him as he murmured, "What did I ever do to deserve a girl as great as you?"

She turned in the circle of his arms and tossed away her hairbrush, fitting herself to him. *Lucky girl,* her mother had said the day she got married, and Rain had agreed, that day and every day hence. *I'm a lucky girl indeed.*

She reminded herself how exhausting it was for TJ to be the "fun teacher," the role he had chosen for himself. All day, every day he had to be on, and up, and "dialed all the way up to eleven" as he put it, all the while maintaining a tricky balance between allowing just enough jovial fun without letting the classroom unravel into chaos. She could relate, in fact. A yoga teacher must be wise and serene and believe wholeheartedly in chakras and chanting ancient Sanskrit words, in giving up your stress to the Universe, in the one giving way to the One.

Rain always thought that kind of talk was silly; she just enjoyed the flexibility and strength and grace all twining together in a lovely physical form. She would have to stifle giggles when Beverly said something New Agey, like "lying on the floor with intention" in *savasana.*

But her students were paying for the wise, serene yogi, and so she must be, all the time, no matter how she really felt.

TJ kissed the top of her head and patted her hip in a "we're done here" dismissal. "You know, I am kind of hungry after all."

Rain's appetite was still long gone, her abdomen ached, her back cramped. But she smiled to see her husband climb out of the pit of his dark mood. "Rain's famous fajitas. Coming right up."

6

Britney leaned on the locker next to Morgan, fluffing her strawberry blond hair and slicking on shiny pink lip gloss.

"So what have you got next?"

Morgan groaned and leaned her head on her just-closed locker. "Calc. With David."

Britney paused in her glossing, then put away her makeup and stepped closer to Morgan, who was rather enjoying the hard feeling of the metal on her forehead. The sensation seemed to dull the creeping sense of anxiety that had been crawling up her spine this time of day all week, ever since she spotted her ex-boyfriend in her fifth-hour calculus class.

"So what if he's there? Walk in there looking gorgeous, so he realizes what he gave up."

Britney grabbed Morgan's shoulders, pulled her up square to face her. She reached out and started to fuss with Morgan's hair. "You know what?" She grabbed handfuls of hair and pulled it up behind Morgan's head. "You'd look fabulous with short hair. Your face is stunning but you can hardly see it . . ."

Morgan was already shaking Britney's hands off her. "Let go of me. I'm not your . . . house pet." Morgan pushed her hair back in front of her shoulders; more to the point, in front of her scar.

"I just wish you wouldn't hide yourself behind your hair."

"I like it long. Anyway, I've gotta go, we're gonna be late."

Britney shrugged and snapped her gum. "Later, then. Give my love to Mr. Hill . . ." She said this last with a wink. Morgan rolled her eyes, but smiled, too. The consolation prize for having to suffer through a postlunch advanced math class with her arrogant ex-boyfriend was her favorite teacher. Mr. Hill had taught Morgan's freshman algebra class, and his charm and enthusiasm had won over even the most cynical of kids. He was the type of teacher to high-five kids in the halls and joke around about Snooki and *Jersey Shore,* instead of acting like the kids today are on a fast train to hell, like some of the older teachers who walked around scowling most of the time. He'd been visibly nervous the first few days of calc, seeming to cringe when a student asked him a difficult question, which made her feel oddly protective of him. She wanted to cheer him on: *You can do it, Mr. Hill!* If only to see his smile, which was one of those smiles that could melt polar ice when it was big and true.

Morgan bounced around like a pinball between the larger, more brash students as she fought her way to the math hallway. She thought she felt a hand brush her ass but it might have been the edge of someone's bag, or jacket, and she didn't have time to care. The noise in the halls seemed to turn up like someone was cranking the volume knob as she approached the math corridor, and a headache started to throb behind her forehead. Sleeplessness was taking its toll; the dreams had been back in force last night, and she woke up feeling so sore and sleepy she questioned if she should bother getting into bed at all.

She edged into class as the bell chimed, slipping into her assigned seat that was not far enough away from David.

"Hey," he'd said to her the first day when she'd walked in. "How was your summer?"

Like there was nothing to it. Like they hadn't been dating all junior year and like they hadn't broken up just before prom and she had to watch him take Ashley instead.

Britney had said that clearly meant it was nothing to him, therefore he was a rat bastard and better forgotten. But Britney draped herself across the lap of every guy she ran across, so what would she know about her and David?

Morgan looked up and cut her eyes sideways, two rows over, to David. He was tapping his pencil on his notebook and looked half asleep.

Mr. Hill was taking attendance, and he had to call her name twice before she reacted, and only then because the jerkface football jock behind her poked her in the back with his pencil.

Morgan had pressed David for a reason why he broke up with her — he did this at the mall, in the food court, over a soggy eggroll and fried rice — and he would only say he didn't "feel the same" anymore. Finally he blurted, "You're so serious all the time. I want to have a little fun once in a while."

She blurted back the first thing that sprang to mind. "Sex is fun."

Morgan cringed to replay that moment. She wished with every cell in her body she'd said that flirtatiously, or at least with a smile, but instead she'd been offering it as a serious piece of evidence. *Exhibit A, ladies and gentlemen, is that we had sex at least twice a week since winter break and Mr. David Archer demonstrated and verbalized his enjoyment.*

He'd had the nerve to blush. He blushed! Morgan was still fixated on that. He was the one who urged her to get on the pill, who persuaded, reasoned, begged in fact, to have sex. He was the one who asked for oral sex and always had the courtesy to make sure he was all clean and fresh first, which at the time she took as a form of gallantry.

And there he was, blushing into his fried rice because she said sex was fun?

This was all over in about two heartbeats, because by then Morgan realized what he meant by this line of thinking: He would just have sex with other girls, who would also be fun when fully clothed.

After the initial moping and the drama of the breakup, once summer vacation started, Morgan found she didn't miss David that much. What she missed was feeling selected and favored, that out of the whole Arbor Valley High, he'd wanted to spend time with her, and hold her hand in the halls, and have her sit on his lap in the cafeteria while they joked with friends.

She hung out with Ethan and Britney all summer instead and thought she was over David. And then she walked into calculus on Tuesday and felt like someone had punched her in the chest.

Mr. Hill had been talking and her pencil had been taking notes, but she knew she'd have to reteach herself the lesson later. No big deal, as long as she had time to do so before helping one or both of the twins.

Her phone buzzed in her backpack's zipper pocket. Probably Britney texting her about plans later, though she should know better than to try that from Señora Graham's class. *Cómo se dice* "hard ass" *en Español*?

Another buzz, a few seconds later.

And another.

What the hell . . . ?

Morgan glanced over at David, and he glanced up to look back at her. He even smiled, with one corner of his mouth.

Mr. Hill had his back to the class, working out a problem on the whiteboard. Morgan was nearly at the back of the class and was sitting behind a girl named Marie who was, well, one of the bigger girls in class. Heavyset, her grandmother would say.

She slipped her phone from the backpack and thumbed across the screen.

The texts were from three different people. There was in fact one from David, saying,

glad we're in class hope we're cool ok

but the other two were from her mother and Ethan, time-stamped much earlier. Her phone must have lost service briefly and gotten the messages late.

She answered David's text so she could appear cool and worldly about it all.

Sure. Cool. Nice to see you too.

She didn't notice the shadow over her until it was too late.

Mr. Hill held out his hand for her phone. "Hand it over."

"Sorry," she said, and started to put it away. This was a teacher who had thrown paper airplanes on the first day to illustrate a point about parabolas and now he was cracking down on the first phone offense?

"Hand it to me. You can have it back at the end of the day."

She heard someone titter "Ooooooooh" in the back of the class.

What are we, in third grade? she groaned to herself before shooting a glare in the direction of the idiot.

She would start on her college applications that very night. She couldn't wait to get away from these childish morons and their stupid little sandbox-level attitudes and self-important teachers who had to act like big shots.

Getting her phone back would also make her late to meet her brothers, and late home, which meant a barrage of questioning from Detective Mom.

She put her head down on her math and wished she had her poetry notebook.

Her headache throbbed like jungle drums, drowning out whatever it was Mr. Hill was trying to tell them.

With the slam of her locker door, Ethan's face appeared from behind it, smiling at her, and waggling his eyebrows, inches from her face.

Morgan's gasp sounded disgustingly to her own ears like a mouse squeak, but any irritation dissolved in his smile.

"Student dies of prank-induced startle," she said. "Film at eleven."

"Entire school wreathed in black for mourning," he replied. "Film at eleven."

Morgan's heart continued to pound unnaturally fast for such a small thing.

"Coming to the Den?" he asked.

Morgan rolled her eyes. "Ugh. Can we not? I'm there enough, thanks."

Ethan stuck his hands into his pockets and shrugged. They began walking together toward the parking lot. He loped through the after-school crush without seeming to watch where he was going, yet never bumping into anyone. It seemed like he just knew where the crowd would part.

"Nice day," he said. "Park?"

Morgan nodded, though Ethan was a couple of steps ahead and didn't see her, but then he stopped, looked behind, didn't see her right away. His brow furrowed, eyes narrowed, and his head rotated like a searchlight; then he saw her, and everything relaxed, his smile blossomed.

Ethan held out his hand. "Here. So I don't lose you again."

Morgan slipped her hand into his and allowed herself to be pulled along, train fashion.

"Oh, crap," she said, pulling on Ethan's hand to stop him by the math hall. "I forgot, I gotta stop by Mr. Hill's to get my phone. And I can't text my brothers to tell them I'm running late. Will you go find them by the freshman door? I'll drop them off at home and meet you at the park."

"Sure. How late will you be, you think?"

Morgan rolled her eyes. "I dunno, guess that depends how much I have to grovel to get my phone back. Lame."

As she approached Mr. Hill's room, she heard voices and stopped just outside the door, allowing the kid ahead of her the dignity of the cell-phone begging, or other after-school scolding, in private. She wedged herself between the side of the adjacent locker and the doorway.

Morgan wasn't trying to eavesdrop, not really. But without her phone to amuse her for a few minutes, she found herself unable not to hear.

One voice was a boy's. It sounded kind of scrapey, like a shovel over asphalt. "I can't do it! I'm an idiot and I'll never get it."

Mr. Hill's voice, somehow both soothing and firm: "No way. None of that. We don't do 'never' and we don't call ourselves names. I wouldn't let anyone else call you an idiot, and I don't allow you to do that either."

Morgan didn't catch the next words, mumbled as they were.

Mr. Hill again. "Dude, did you think I got this the first time? I had to take calculus three times in college. No joke. . . . I swear! Ask Mr. Monetti; I told him in the job interview. It just clicked, finally, because I stuck with it, and I had a teacher who was patient enough to teach it to me three times. The third time I aced it. And I used to run in school, back in my glory days." Self-deprecating chuckle. "But at first I had skinny chicken legs and got winded after half a lap. I'm just saying, no one starts out brilliant at everything and if anyone seems like they do, they're hiding the effort to seem like a big shot. Don't feel bad, and no more idiot talk. Come back in the morning if you still don't get it tonight, and I'll walk you through it."

More mumbling, and Morgan turned away as the poor sap skittered out the door. She didn't see who it was, but she had an uncomfortable sense this could be the case of Connor in a few years.

Thinking of Connor reminded her how late and annoyed she was. She stepped into the room.

He looked up from his desk and seemed confused for a moment. He also looked pale, and like he badly needed a shave. His dark hair was spiky and mussed, as if he'd been raking his fingers through it over and over. His physical appearance contrasted so much with his soothing authority she'd heard moments ago, she briefly wondered if she'd imagined that whole exchange.

"Oh!" he exclaimed. "Right. The phone." He unlocked a drawer of his desk and held it out to her. "I assume this one's yours, and not the other in here that's covered in pink rhinestones?" He gave her a weak smile.

"Yeah. Good guess."

He pulled it back slightly just as she reached out for it. "And . . . will you be texting in my class again?"

Morgan sucked in a breath and exhaled. "No, sir, Mr. Hill," she replied, letting sarcasm slip out.

Her smart-off had a surprising effect. He handed over the phone but looked utterly defeated, like that time her sophomore year when she'd told a pimply freshman she'd never heard of that she didn't want to go out with him.

Morgan accepted the phone and glanced at it for messages. A few, none important. She stowed it in her pocket. "Hey, sorry. I had a tough day."

Mr. Hill rubbed one hand over his face. "Yeah. Me, too."

"My ex is in your class."

Morgan felt a flush climb up her face. Why had she said that?

Mr. Hill looked up, and what looked like genuine concern was written in the furrow of his brow. “Oh. That sucks. Who . . . ? No, don’t tell me. None of my business.”

Morgan was already answering. “David Archer.”

Now Mr. Hill seemed to be studying her.

“What?”

“Huh. I wouldn’t have guessed that.”

“Yeah, well, since we broke up, apparently you’re right to not guess it.”

Morgan knew she should leave. Her brothers would be getting antsy, her mom would be wondering why they were late.

Yet she said, “Look, it’s none of my business, but are you okay?”

In the pause, he’d been staring down at the surface of his desk, drumming his fingers. He startled back to life. “Huh?”

Morgan brushed her hair forward on her scar side. “You just look like you’re not . . . feeling well.”

“I’m stressed out, actually. This calculus stuff is hard.” He laughed darkly. “Probably not for you, though.”

Morgan just shrugged. It hadn’t been that hard for her so far, but she didn’t want to act smarter than him, like she was bragging.

Mr. Hill continued, “I just have to refresh myself on the details, you know? All those years teaching $x + 7 = 14$ in September have rotted my brain. And I’m worried the kids can tell. Can you tell? Is it obvious?"

She shook her head. "Nah. You seem fine to me." This was a lie, Morgan realized as soon as she said it. She'd already thought he looked nervous and unsure, his gaiety in the classroom more forced than she remembered from ninth grade. But he wasn't putting up a front with her, for some reason, which Morgan found both weird and thrilling.

He shook his head hard then, like a dog shaking off water. "Anyway, sorry. You don't want to listen to some old man groan about his job."

Morgan laughed. "Oh, yeah, old. Get out the wheelchair, Gramps. You can't be more than what, thirty?"

"I'll have you know I'm a mere twenty-nine years old. For another few months anyway. You sure know how to cheer up a person. Thanks, Morgan." He was now smiling so wide she saw his cheek tuck in with a dimple. She'd never seen that before.

Morgan felt a tingly wave of heat pouring down over her.

Her phone chimed. Her brothers, she knew without looking.

"Look, I gotta run, my brothers are expecting me. Sorry about the texting."

"Sure, Morgan. I understand. Happens to

the best of us."

Morgan had to work hard not to skip out of the room. She turned back just at the doorway and saw him watching her. She turned away and tipped her head, letting her hair fall to hide her smile.

She didn't have time to revel, though, as the phone buzzed again. Connor. *"Where the f are you? Stuck here with your fag friend."*

Morgan broke another school rule by running through the hallways so she could let her brothers know what a couple of immature jackasses they were for saying such a thing about Ethan, about anybody, but especially about Ethan.

7

Rain turned away abruptly from Layla's disappointed confusion and almost ran to the door of NYC. The new girl — lithe and young and earnest about her chakras — was under the impression everyone wanted her company every moment, and she had been trying to rope Rain into an awkward lunch in the cramped back room. Rain begged off, saying she wanted some air, and Layla had made to follow her even then. She was like a lonely puppy and in her dewy youth reminded Rain of how long ago she herself was so slender, cheerful, and fertile.

Rain shoved open the door and stole a glance into the window of the adjacent jewelry shop as she took a right turn, marching off as if with purpose, going nowhere special. Her hair was looking thin and flat, and indeed so was the rest of her, though her stomach bumped out unattractively, due to last night's garlicky pizza.

Rain bypassed her blue VW Bug parked at the end of the lot and turned away from the row of businesses toward the tree-lined neighborhood nearby.

She strode along until she found herself at the center of Arbor Valley: Richmond Park. The fanciest houses in town bordered this green, shady expanse. The founding fathers of the town had tried to echo Central Park in New York City. Known simply as "the park," it featured a fountain in the center that in fact very much resembled the Central Park fountain.

Rain settled on one of the green benches ringing the fountain space, facing inward. She and TJ — just like countless other Arbor Valley couples — had their wedding pictures taken here. In her very favorite, TJ was dipping her, and she was laughing, one arm around his neck, the other grabbing the top of her head because she feared her veil would slide off onto the pebbled ground. It was a spontaneous moment for TJ, an unguarded moment for her, and the photographer captured the exact apex of their joy.

Rain's attention was, as ever, drawn like a compass arrow to any babies or small children. Thus her gaze landed on a toddler with curlicue hair in two pigtails at the top of her head, like puppy ears. The girl was toddling in circles and giggling at her own delightful walking.

After watching for a few moments, Rain looked up to find her watchful mother to send her a smile of *isn't she adorable?*

Odd. She did not see any such watchful parent nearby. Rain began to study the adults on the benches, looking for a mother, father, nanny, big sister. No one seemed to be paying any mind.

It was about then that the toddler looked up in a searching kind of way, and her pudgy little face bunched up with confusion.

Rain left the bench and approached the girl slowly, bending over as she came so by the time she reached her, she was crouched down to her level. "Are you okay, sweetie? Where's your mommy?"

The toddler regarded her with round, wary eyes and sniffed hard. She was angling her body slightly away, as if prepared to run screaming. "Where did your mommy go?" Rain prompted again, though she knew it might be a babysitter, grandma, or dad she was with.

Rain looked around again. No one seemed to be noticing them. There were college-age kids with earbuds in, a few people reading on the benches, mothers absorbed with their own children. A jogger plodded by, his feet whapping heavily into the dirt. She looked around for an authority figure; a police officer, or even a park employee would do.

No one. Rain rose to her feet but folded over so her face was still close to the girl's. "Sweetie, let's try to find your mommy. I'll take you." She held out her hand and offered the girl a soft smile.

The girl seemed to relax at this gesture, and she slipped her dimpled hand into Rain's.

Rain started to walk toward a distant play structure, thinking that a likely place the girl had wandered from. The toddler scuffed her feet along slowly. She shifted her grasp of Rain's hand so that her tiny fingers were wrapped around Rain's pinky.

Their progress was painfully slow. Rain paused and crouched down again. "Let me pick you up, sweetie, so we can go faster. Can I do that?"

The girl didn't reply, but nor did she seem upset by the idea. Rain put her hands under the child's armpits. She didn't react or seem alarmed. So Rain stood up and propped the little girl on her hip. She smelled of strawberries and tomato soup.

A familiar pang registered in Rain's chest

at being this close to a child not her own. She looked down at the girl, those precious bouncy pigtails, and planted an impulsive kiss on the top of her head, the downy curls tickling her lips.

A shriek shattered the air.

"Let go of her!"

A woman was running toward them, almost waddling with a preschooler on her hip, the older child bouncing along crazily.

Rain set the girl down carefully, and the toddler ambled toward her mother, arms up and fingers flexing.

The mother fell to her knees and dropped the older boy at once, opening her arms for the girl. When her daughter was safely in her arms, she turned on Rain.

"What were you doing with her? Where were you taking her!"

Rain held her hands up, palms out. "I was trying to find you!"

"You were walking her toward the parking lot." The woman was half sobbing and had reached her other arm around her son, who looked to be maybe four years old, as if Rain might try to run away with him, too.

Rain replied, half pleading, "No! The playground! I thought she'd come from the playground! She was by the fountain!"

"Did you follow her there? Were you

watching for a child to wander off? I should call the police." She took out her cell phone and began to dial, but her hands were trembling and she dropped it.

The girl — who had been placid throughout her walkabout and her brief journey with Rain — began to cling to her mother and wail. The boy popped a thumb in his mouth.

"No, ma'am, please, I didn't mean any harm . . ."

Rain heard the rhythmic pounding of running feet and soon after, panting breath in her ear. Next to her was the jogger who had passed them earlier. "Ma'am?" he said, addressing the mother. "I have to say I watched this young lady with your daughter, and it's clear she was only trying to help."

He jogged in place, keeping his heart rate up.

The woman plopped down on her rear end and started to sob into her daughter's neck. "I thought she was gone . . . Joey fell, and I . . . I didn't know she could unbuckle the stroller . . ."

The jogger nodded at Rain, one curt dip of the chin, and carried on with his run. She muttered "Thank you," though he couldn't have heard.

Rain approached the woman as one might

a wounded animal. "Ma'am? Is there anything you need me to help you with? Carry that diaper bag or anything?"

The mother dried her face on her daughter's hair, her hands still locked around her children. "No," she croaked out. "Sorry. I . . . Sorry. Thank you. Sorry."

As Rain walked back down the path to the fountain, she heard the woman still muttering "sorry."

Rain walked back through the door of NYC and cringed when she saw the clock on the store's rear wall. She was a full fifteen minutes late for her next class. That meant a bunch of angry women who'd paid good money and were probably squeezing in some *ohm* before picking up school-age children or grocery shopping.

"Shit," she muttered, head down and racing past the front desk, where Beverly was sitting, before her boss had a chance to ask her where the hell she'd been.

Rain threw open the door to the studio but recoiled in shock. Instead of a roomful of angry women she found her class in full swing, everyone's butt high in the air. Layla popped her head up from her downward-facing dog and mouthed, *I got this.* Then she jerked with her head toward the door.

As Rain backed out, she saw more than a few familiar students looking back at her from between their knees, foreheads wrinkled in confusion.

Rain walked to her locker, to grab her water bottle, trying to figure out why she didn't feel grateful that Layla had filled in and spared her students the annoyance of a late class. Rain checked her phone, fumbling it just as the hysterical mother in the park had done. For the first time since she walked back in through the NYC front door, Rain noticed her own hands were shaking.

8

Morgan was so drowsy on the grass in the park, feeling the sun paint her all over with the warmth of the tailing ribbons of summer, she almost didn't open her eyes when her phone chimed with a message. It chimed again and she sighed. Mom would have the police combing the town for her remains if she didn't reply in a nanosecond.

Morgan saw it was David and turned the phone over with another snort of disgust. "Whatever." She hoped to sound casual.

Ethan was stretched out on the grass next to her, their open AP English notebooks between them, pages fluttering in a slight breeze. He cocked his eyebrow.

Morgan intoned, "High school senior commits homicide over continued texting from hypocrite ex-boyfriend. Film at eleven."

"Homicide ruled justifiable by a jury of indignant teen girls. Film at eleven."

Morgan laughed and propped up on her elbows. In the late-afternoon light flickering through the trees, Ethan looked older than she remembered. No, not older. More mature. She recalled his face earlier in the week when he thought he lost her in the crowd, and the feel of his large hand over hers, pulling her along.

"What?" he asked. "Do I have a zit?"

"Nothing," she replied, quickly. "No, you don't. Just spaced out a sec, that's all."

"So what's up with Dashing Dave? Is he trying to get back together?"

"No, at least, I don't think he is. It's like he wants to pay me just enough attention so I'll fall for him again, but not so much he has to be my boyfriend. It's screwed up."

"Yeah. That empty-headed jock didn't appreciate you anyway."

Morgan felt her face grow hot despite the shade from the trees. "Hey, he wasn't that bad." After all, she'd spent the best part of her junior year in his arms and gave him her virginity.

"It's solidarity. I thought we were hating ex-boyfriends."

"Just don't hate him so much that you cut me down for liking him in the first place."

Ethan sat all the way up, then, and turned to her with dark, serious eyes. "I'd never cut you down. Ever."

Morgan blinked under his steady gaze. She caught herself stroking her scar, so she sat up and leaned forward, allowing her hair to draw over it like a curtain. "I'm so mad at my jerk brother for what he said about you the other day. I'm sorry I told you, though. I shouldn't have even mentioned it."

Ethan shrugged and looked away toward the park's fountain. A couple was being photographed. Morgan guessed by the way the photographer kept directing her to display her left hand on his shoulder it was an engagement shot. "Whatever. No big deal."

Morgan sat up straighter. "No, actually, it is a big deal. But of course the boys acted like it was nothing and so did Mom. She was all, 'go to your room' and 'that's not nice,' like he'd said 'booger' and he's five years old."

"It's over, and it's not a big deal. Honest. I've been called worse."

"What's worse than that?"

"You don't want to know."

Morgan flopped back in the grass again. "I can't wait to get out of high school and away from these provincial, small-minded idiots."

"You think there are no idiots in college?"

"There have to be fewer idiots in college. That's kind of the point, isn't it? Maybe I'll even get into Boston U."

"While the rest of us provincial idiots toil away back here in Michigan?"

"Who says you have to stay in Michigan?"

"I don't get the grades you do."

"Your grades are good. And anyway, you don't have to go to Boston or the Ivy League to go someplace different."

Ethan pulled his knees up, propped his folded arms on them, and rested his chin there. His gaze seemed far away as he replied, "There's no place different. Not really."

"Hey, let's watch a movie on Saturday. Something hilarious and stupid. This is all getting too serious for me."

"Too serious for Morgan Monetti?"

At this he finally turned back to her, a playful smile breaking out on his lean face.

"You don't know everything there is to know about me." And Morgan risked a flirtatious smile, the same one she'd used all those months ago on David when she met him at the movies with a group of friends.

"Well. I'm intrigued then, Miss Boston."

"Don't call me that," Morgan retorted.

"You'll jinx me. I haven't even done my application yet."

"I don't believe in jinxes. A smart girl like you can't be derailed so easily."

Morgan ran her fingers along her scar, reading its familiar bumps like Braille, and said nothing.

Morgan's car wound through the slow-moving streets of Arbor Valley, and she was careful to note her speed. The cops loved nothing more than to bust a teen driver and fanatically enforced the 25 mph speed limit as a way of "preserving the peaceful residential character of our town." That's what she'd read in the paper, anyway, back when she was flirting with journalism as a career choice.

"Why not music?" she was asked all the time, because of her cello. She'd always say, "I don't want music to be my work. That would suck the life out of it." Besides, she was no Yo-Yo Ma. What would she do, teach all day? Dozens of Connors and Jareds using their bows like light sabers?

Driving away from the park took her away from the two-story brick homes with the high decorative arches and masses of sparkling windows to the southern edge of town, nearer to the commercial strip by the highway. The houses shrank as she drove along, faded aluminum siding replacing brick. The landscaping gradually faded from sharply manicured to inconsistently maintained, and now and again she spied a lawn grown long and uneven with soft wisps of seeds on top. "Gone to seed," she muttered.

She parked her car in the driveway on her mother's side, leaving her father's side of the garage accessible because he was not likely home and wouldn't be for hours yet.

Morgan opened the door to the smell of tomato sauce on the stove and knew it had been another busy day for her mother, who would throw pasta in a pot as many as four days a week. If she never had spaghetti another day in her life after she graduated, it would be too soon.

Morgan toyed with the idea of going gluten-free just to see what Dinah would do.

Dinah thumped down from upstairs then, her wavy brown hair in a messy ponytail, and her jeans riding a bit too low on her hips, revealing a sliver of red underwear. Morgan rolled her eyes and fought the urge to walk over and yank her mother's pants up, or yank down her shirt, at least.

"Oh, hi, honey," Dinah called over her shoulder. "Could you set the table, please?"

"Can I at least put down my bag first? And why, yes, I had a nice day, thanks for asking."

Dinah started chopping up lettuce after giving the spaghetti a stir. "Oh, come on, I was going to ask you. But it's close to dinnertime and I need help getting the table set."

Morgan took the plates out of the cupboard and didn't bother asking why her brothers weren't helping. They were "doing homework," which seemed to take them three times as long as it would anyone else. Morgan suspected they were probably playing their video games on low volume or playing with their laptops half the time, at least. Because whatever their parents or the school said about their ability to do schoolwork, Morgan noticed that with proper incentive — say, they wanted to go to the varsity basketball game — they miraculously found a way to get it done.

"So," her mother said, as Morgan tried not to thunk the plates down with too much force. "You had a good day, then? You were studying with Britney, right?"

"Ethan, Mom. I told you."

"Right. Sorry. How's Ethan?"

"Fine."

"Did you have a nice time?"

"Fine. Mom, your underwear is showing."

Dinah flushed and yanked on her pants, while Morgan felt a pang of regret for pointing out the underwear. What difference did it really make? "Ethan is coming over this Saturday to watch a movie. If that's okay."

Dinah paused in her dinner fixing to beam a smile at Morgan. "Well, of course! I've always liked him."

"Don't get too excited," Morgan said drily. "We're just friends."

"Well, your father and I —"

"Started out as friends, I know, I know. Just don't get . . . you know."

"How do I get?"

Morgan put a hand on her hip and paused in setting out the glasses. "Don't start picking out wedding china or anything, okay?"

Dinah raised her hands in mock surrender. "I will not be in the least supportive. In fact, I promise to hate him. Better?" She laughed so Morgan would laugh, too, and she did oblige her mother with a chuckle. She meant well, after all.

Morgan and Dinah exchanged a quizzical glance when they heard the garage. It was Thursday, the day of staff meetings and paperwork, and they never saw her dad this early.

But it was indeed him, coming in through

the garage. Morgan turned her attention back to the table and away from the strain of his blazer as it puckered at the shoulders and failed to reach around her father's middle, if he ever tried to button it, which he never did.

He hung his work bag on his appointed hook with a heavy sigh and turned to the refrigerator. He fished out a beer and with a small, silent wave to his wife and daughter he went off to the den off the living room, where his computer sat and the television was constantly tuned to ESPN.

Morgan looked up from setting the flatware to see her mother's face: grim and hard, staring into the boiling water of the pasta.

"Mom?" Morgan asked. "You okay?"

Dinah rubbed her forehead with the back of her wrist, the gesture exposing her pale forearm to the yellow kitchen lights, reminding Morgan of how seldom her mom ever saw real sunlight, between her café and their home.

"Yeah, I guess so. It's hard to be ignored, though."

Morgan nodded, adding silently: *Don't I know it.*

Dinah went on, "I can't remember the last time he and I went out somewhere or exchanged more than a few words about stuff like the twins' report cards, or your concert. Or whether there are termites eating the deck. This is not the stuff you think about on your wedding day. Termites."

Dinah had leaned back on the kitchen counter near the stove, crossing her feet at the ankles. She was looking down, her head angled and her face tight as if in concentration.

Morgan laid out napkins, and as she considered her parents' marriage, she realized it had been a good while since they seemed to have any fun together. When she was a little kid — after the boys were out of imminent danger but before they started flailing in school — there were backyard picnics and her parents' laughter as they played badminton and sailed the birdie into the bushes time and again. Her dad's imitation of Al Pacino in *Scarface* ("Say hello to my little friend," he'd say, wielding something stupid, like a pickle) would make her mom laugh until she folded at the middle. But Morgan could hardly remember her mom smiling at her dad lately, much less her dad trying to make his wife crack up.

Heck, her dad was hardly ever home for him to crack his old jokes. Even though he had the summers "off" (supposedly) he was always taking grad classes, or visiting his elderly relations back in Jersey, or working on projects like building a shed in the backyard or repainting the deck. Before he was a principal, when he'd been a science teacher, he'd taught driver's ed over the summer and regaled his family with hilarious stories of rookie drivers massacring orange traffic cones.

"So why don't you go out somewhere?" Morgan reached into the refrigerator for salad dressing. "I'm going to be staying in this Saturday with Ethan coming over. I'll keep an eye on the monsters and make sure they don't set the place on fire or take off for Vegas or something. Anyway, they'll probably just stay in their room playing their video games or whatever."

"Oh, I don't know. It probably won't make a difference."

"But it couldn't hurt. Hey, Mom, take advantage of me being here while I still am. Next year I'll be gone."

Dinah jerked her head up, seeming shocked, as if she'd forgotten. She regarded Morgan all over with one of her searching looks, like she was a suspect in a lineup.

"When did this happen?" Dinah said in an uncharacteristic voice sounding breathy and tentative.

Morgan turned away, uncomfortable with her stare, and straightened the salad dressings on the table. Britney had noticed it, too, this sudden left turn into soggy emotion that their mothers were prone to lately. Morgan could understand, sort of, but it was also fiercely irritating.

Dinah cleared her throat and Morgan heard the clanking of pans and dishes behind her, the moment snapped off, much to her relief. Then her mother said, "You know, it isn't fair that Kate talks to him more than I do. I married him, for God's sake."

Kate. Known to Morgan as Ms. Spencer, the assistant principal, who had an office right next door to her dad's.

"Okay," Dinah continued, after a pause in which she was maybe considering the proximity of Kate Spencer's office to her husband's. "Okay, we will go out. But, hon, you don't have to be in charge of your brothers. You can all be in charge of yourselves. Heck, you're all teenagers, now."

Morgan turned away to hide her smirk because she knew exactly whose ass would be on the line if the boys tore up the house while her mother was out.

Her mother looked less sad, though, now, with the prospect of her hot date. Not to mention, Morgan thought, with both parents out of the house and her brothers occupied upstairs, she would have time alone with Ethan, at least as alone as she ever got to be.

9

Ethan laughed, and the flickering glow of the television played over his face almost like flashbulbs, as if her friend was on a red carpet somewhere. He had a lean, long face that made him look — now that she was paying such close attention — nearly regal. Elegant.

Morgan shifted closer on the overstuffed den couch. She tilted her ear toward the upstairs and heard nothing from her brothers. She had swallowed her indignant pride not to bring up Connor's "fag" remark because she knew that out of sheer obnoxious stubbornness, Connor would find a way to say something like that again tonight, just to prove Morgan was not the boss of him. As her reward for not bossing the twins, they were staying out of her way. Morgan would thank them, if that were the kind of thing the three Monetti kids ever did for each other. But that would be way too weird.

Morgan yawned and scooched closer again to Ethan. The couch was so soft, and the movie so comfortably predictable with its adorable actors and wacky antics, that her insomnia was catching up to her like a freight train. Most of Friday night she'd been awake after a 3 A.M. nightmare jolted her out of bed. The details escaped her conscious mind, but the feeling of panicky suffocation had hung with her the rest of the night and most of the day.

It might not have helped that she'd swallowed about four Motrin just to beat back the headache.

Ethan stretched his arm along the back of the couch, then with his hand, gently as she'd ever been touched by any boy before, he gathered her into his side.

The movie, the house, the twins — it all swirled away as she savored the rise and fall of his chest and his enveloping warmth.

Safe. Happy. Giddy. Morgan named all her feelings and wondered if she could write a pretty poem now. If her nightmares would go away. If she could sleep again.

How had she overlooked him all last year? No matter. She'd certainly noticed him now. Someday maybe she'd ask him what took him so long to reach out for her like this.

Credits rolled. He started to reach forward for the remote, but Morgan put her hand on his chest, gently holding him back from sitting up.

"What?" he said, giving her an odd look that wrinkled up her feeling of safe happiness.

"Nothing," she said, reaching for the remote herself and stopping the credits. She arranged her hair back the way she liked it, realizing it had been pushed off her face, exposing the scar, which happened to be facing him. She'd forgotten to sit on his other side.

"Can I show you something?" she asked, and he nodded yes in a casual way, throwing in a shrug.

Out from under the couch, where she'd stashed it earlier to prevent having to trek to her room and risk an encounter with the boys, she pulled out her notebook. "I've never shown anyone this before," she said. "But I like to write."

"Cool," he answered.

She shoved the notebook in Ethan's lap to keep herself from slamming the cover shut and hiding it again.

His eyes seemed to widen, but not in horror as Morgan had feared. It was more like surprise. Even awe.

"Wow," he said, again not seeming to recoil one bit from her weirdness, even the poems about her scar. "These are great."

Morgan swallowed the boulder in her throat and dared ask, "You don't think they're sick? Like, twisted?"

Ethan paused before answering, showing a thoughtfulness Morgan instantly loved him for. How many teen boys were this genuinely thoughtful? "Not everything has to be all sunshine and flowers."

Morgan shoved the book out of his lap onto the floor and threw herself forward into his arms. He returned the embrace and chuckled softly. "You shouldn't have been so nervous. What did you think, I'd run screaming?"

"Yeah," she answered into his shoulder, chuckling herself. "Something like that."

"I'd never run screaming from you," Ethan said, and patted her back.

She tipped her face up, closed her eyes, and went for it.

He pulled back hard, as far as the couch would let him. "Morgan . . ."

Morgan recoiled, too, to the other end of the couch, her sick notebook open between them on the floor to a poem she'd titled melodramatically, "Perchance to Dream," after they'd read *Hamlet* in English last year.

"I thought . . . You seemed . . ." She stammered. She pressed her palms over her eyes. "You're my friend, and I love you and all, but . . . I'm . . . I'm . . ."

"What? You're what? Not attracted to me? Disgusted by me?"

"Not that, no! It's . . ." Ethan swallowed hard and scrunched his eyes shut. "I like guys."

Morgan leaped to her feet and snatched up her notebook. "What?" she cried.

Ethan paled. He stared at the floor between his feet and worked his hands together. "I'm sorry I gave you the wrong idea."

"How could you lie to me like this?"

"I didn't lie!" Ethan looked up sharply. "I never lied to you."

"You had a girlfriend last fall. You took her to Homecoming."

"I'm not 'out,' okay? She was just a friend. We never dated. She wanted to go and didn't have a date."

"But you pretend! You act straight!"

Ethan scowled. "What, you want me to flounce around like the fag Connor says I am? Would that make your life easier?"

"I'm your friend," she sputtered. "You should have told me. What did you think I'd do? Disown you? Do you think I'm some kind of bigot?"

"I don't think that. But I wasn't ready for all this."

"Oh, great, so instead you come to my house for a movie and snuggle up with me and let me kiss you and humiliate myself. You think I was ready for that?"

"I didn't know you felt like that about me. You never said."

"I was saying it now. Forget it. You better go."

"I don't want to leave like this."

"How do you think you should leave? I can't take back the fact that I kissed you. You can't take back that you didn't trust me enough with the truth. How do I believe you about anything, now? You probably do think my poetry is sick and disgusting but you're too good at telling people what they want to hear."

"That's not fair."

"Don't tell a soul about the poems."

"And don't tell anyone I'm gay."

"Deal. Now please go before my idiot brothers come down here and find me crying and it turns into a huge big fricking thing."

Ethan strode out past her, giving her a wide berth.

She followed him at a distance as he

walked to the front door, having always been raised to see her guests out. She clutched her notebook to her chest the whole way.

At the door he turned back to her. "Thanks for all the sympathy about being a closeted gay kid in the Midwest, by the way. Because it's a frickin' walk in the park, let me tell you."

Ethan closed the door carefully behind him, considerate as ever, even as he walked away, their friendship in shards between them.

Morgan ran to her room to hide the poetry away again, back in the dark where it belonged. On the stairs she almost crashed into Jared.

"Your boyfriend go home?"

She ignored that remark and scooted past him up the stairs. Jared spoke again, in a gentler voice. "You okay, Morticia? You look paler than normal."

She stopped, straightened her posture, and let out a shaky breath. Without turning around she answered, "Fine. Just tired. Going to go read."

Jared didn't move from the step; there was only silence. She ignored him, though, and slammed into her room, holding her notebook over her frantic heart as if her poems could slow it down.

She remained there and closed her eyes, searching her memory for clues. He wasn't in the least bit swishy, but she should know better than to stereotype, anyway. There were gay athletes, weren't there? Some NBA player? Military types, too. "Don't ask, don't tell" was about to be repealed, after all.

But shouldn't she have known anyway?

Reviewing their friendship like a highlight reel, Morgan realized how seldom Ethan spent any time around guys in a guy kind of way, jostling around in the halls, shooting hoops, whatever. He'd gone to a couple of dances with that girl last year, seen a few movies with girls — including her, of course — but had he ever held hands with a girl in the halls? Sat in the cafeteria with a girl on his lap, or gotten yelled at for kissing at school? Had he ever, even once, referred to a girlfriend?

Nor had he talked about a boyfriend, but then, he wasn't "out."

"Stupid," Morgan whispered. "Stupid, stupid."

He was her friend! And didn't tell her. She opened her poetry to him. In the past she'd confided her true feelings about her resentment of the twins, how guilty and shameful that felt. She told him things she'd never shared with another soul, and all along his whole identity was a lie.

She stuffed her notebook away and picked up her phone, texting rapidly to David.

Miss u. xoxo

She did miss him. She'd been fooling herself all summer that it didn't matter. It had only been out of sight, out of mind. Her disgust with his recent texting was only bravado. Secretly, she'd been happy to hear from him again. He must miss her, too, or he wouldn't bother, when he could have any other girl in school.

Her eyes were watering with strain as she peered at the screen, waiting for a response.

Then, finally:

thx ur sweet

She frowned. What did that mean?

She was still puzzling out her response when he texted again.

hanging out with Britney now ttyl

She quelled her first instinct to smash her phone into bits by placing it with exaggerated, trembling care on her pillow. Instead she flung open her poetry notebook, scribbling fragments of verse that zipped through her mind like darting birds.

In the forest stalking
On the plains walking
On the water gliding
On the muddy bottom, dying
~
Speak but no one hears
Gaze but you can't see
Climb but never reaching
Letting go and falling free
~
No one cares about
The bee till it stings
So why would it fly on by?

10

Rain had long since perfected the art of watching without staring, and she deployed that skill now, keeping TJ in her sights, though she was supposed to be listening to a semistranger talk about the fashion benefits of wide-leg pants.

TJ moved to the kitchen and opened another Stella Artois plucked from the drink bucket on the counter, pouring it into his glass so rapidly it glugged and foamed. In the open-plan, modern home of Gregory and Alessia Hill, Rain had all too clear a view from the living room right to him, where he propped himself against the counter, staring into his beer.

Rain nodded at a story this party guest was telling, unable to hear her, hoping this woman wasn't saying something dire or terribly amusing requiring more than a nod. The ivory living room surrounded islands of people, in clusters of three or four, who chatted and laughed, their volume making Rain think of the penguins at the zoo and how loud it is when the man with the fish comes out.

TJ looked up and met her eyes. Rain tensed; would he feel under surveillance? Guilty? Indignant?

She winked, affecting playfulness. She smiled, though she was already tired of smiling.

He returned her wink with a tight smile, stretched out across his face like a mask. When he walked back into the living room, every step seemed heavy.

Alessia was gliding toward Rain and her companion suddenly, a broad smile across her long, narrow face. "Miranda," she called, addressing the woman gabbling to Rain about pants, "your son needs you!" Miranda tut-tutted and hustled off to the rec room downstairs. Alessia put her arm around Rain's shoulders. "*Ciao bella,* how is my darling friend?"

At first, Rain had assumed such gushy phrasing was the result of inexact English, but either those habits had hardened into Alessia's speech for good, or they had always been genuine.

"Fine. So what was Miranda's kid doing? Sticking a pool cue up his nose?"

Alessia waved her hand. "Oh, I don't know. I made it up because you looked so bored I was afraid you might jump through a window. One can assume he is doing something monstrous because he is a boy, and this is what they always do."

Rain laughed, and Alessia laughed at her own joke louder yet. Rain caught TJ's gaze, and he rolled his eyes. Rain shifted so her back was to him and walked with Alessia toward the kitchen, feigning a sudden need for a beverage. Something about Alessia had annoyed TJ from the moment they met, when Alessia visited Rain in the States for the first time. Then, Alessia had the nerve to be a beautiful, exotic woman who married his rich doctor brother, and since then TJ found every reason he could conjure to disapprove of their continued friendship.

That afternoon, as they were getting ready for this party, TJ had frowned into the mirror. "Why do we even have to go?" His mood would have been sour any day, for his old insomnia monster had gotten him again. Rain had been waking up in the wee hours to find his side empty, hearing the distant *whoosh whoosh* of the elliptical as he tried to tire himself out. She couldn't sleep without him, but he never wanted company when sleepless. So they'd both lie awake, parallel but separate, in their silent house.

"He's your brother, and he loves you," Rain had answered, reaching from behind TJ to straighten his collar at the mirror. She instantly regretted the "loves you" because she knew what was coming.

"He loves showing off to me; not the same thing. Anyway, even if he does supposedly love me, that's only another thing he does better than me. Because he drives me nuts."

Rain brushed her hair again, though it already crackled with static. "Want me to tell him you have a headache? I'll go, make an appearance, make apologies, and come back. We can get some Chinese and watch a movie."

TJ was fiddling with a piece of hair that wouldn't lie flat. It stuck up like a feathery wisp. Rain rather liked it that way. There was something so boyish and appealing about how his hair would never quite co-operate.

"No," TJ grumbled. "The good Dr. Hill would just start grilling you about my symptoms and give you Tylenol 3 from his doctor stash or something. I'll just go."

TJ tossed his comb to the top of the dresser, where it slid across and landed in the small bedroom wastebasket. "Dammit," he muttered, picking it up and slamming it down in place again.

A prickly impatience swelled in Rain's chest just then, that she'd offered TJ a perfectly good way out of this night he was dreading so much, and still he refused to take it. Not for the first time she thought he got a sick satisfaction out of being the underdog brother.

He whirled away from the dresser and gathered her into a tight hug.

"Thank God I have you," he muttered into the top of her head. "I don't know why you picked me, but thank God you did."

"You picked me," Rain said, squeezing him back. "Remember? You picked me for your volleyball team."

Sand volleyball, at college, on the first warm day of spring when students had swarmed out of the dorms like ants from a hill.

"It will be fine," she'd said, her impatience melting away in his embrace. "We won't stay long. Then we'll come home and make our own fun."

He'd gotten excited at the mere suggestion, and Rain thought for a moment they wouldn't go to the party at all.

Now, standing in the living room with Alessia, seeing TJ grow red-faced and unsteady, she regretted her "make our own fun" remark. She hadn't even really felt game for sex at the time. And now . . .

Greg tapped his glass with a fork, and even Rain — who actually adored her husband's family and gave them all kinds of benefit of the doubt — internally winced at the pretension of the gesture. There weren't that many people there that he couldn't just call out if he wanted to say something. Alessia squeezed Rain's elbow, winked, and strode off to join her husband.

"We have something to announce," Greg said, once the party chatter had faded. Alessia's shining eyes swept across the room to all of them in turn.

Rain leaned back against the living room wall.

Greg continued as Alessia turned her face to him in a choreographed dance between a husband and wife who knew how to do everything right, including this.

"We figured it had been long enough, and I know our parents were getting impatient for the next big thing . . ."

TJ's mother squealed and held her hands together in front of her face like a little girl. Their father was already beaming.

Maybe they're building a new house, Rain thought. *Or moving to Swaziland to become missionaries.*

She caught TJ's eye at the other end of the room. His dark glower startled her. She gripped her glass of water so hard, she heard ice clinking around as it shook in her hand.

Alessia exclaimed, "We're having a baby!"

A happy roar exploded from the guests. Mrs. Hill shrieked and folded Alessia in an embrace. Mr. Hill was pumping his son's hand and slapping his shoulder like he'd landed one helluva trout.

Rain glanced at TJ. He'd forced the corners of his mouth up into something like a smile, but anyone who cared to look would see the deadness in his eyes.

She knew TJ's every thought. He'd be thinking that once again his brother had bested him, in even this, the most basic of human functions. He'd be thinking that once again his father's favor would be on his brother, and that Greg couldn't be satisfied with a phone call — no, he had to announce this triumph in a big spectacle.

Because of all this, she should go to his side. Take his hand.

But Rain felt herself starting to give way. The inner scaffolding that had kept her upright all week began to splinter and crack. She could almost hear it.

As fast as she could go without seeming to hurry, Rain fled to their guest bathroom and closed the door, fastening the lock and sinking down to the cool tile floor, her back against the wall next to the rack with the color-coordinated guest towels.

She folded herself into half lotus, and the tears fell before she had time to blink them away.

"Why can't I do this?" she whispered. Everyone else could. Her sister, Fawn, without even trying, without a plan, without even wanting to. Now her sister-in-law, Alessia. Teen mothers were becoming reality TV stars because they were photogenic and pregnant too soon. It was an epidemic.

She supposed it was a natural outgrowth of the wedding mania of a few years ago, when everyone was coupling up and Rain spent half her Saturdays either shopping for gifts or toasting happy couples. So it goes, she thought.

Except for her.

A burst of laughter from outside invaded her bathroom sanctuary, and she stood up so fast she got dizzy. TJ needed her — now. She peered into the mirror and used a guest towel to dab her face dry. Her eyes were still red and puffy, but that would only last a few minutes. Everyone would be so happy for Alessia and Greg that no one would look at her for quite some time, anyway.

Before she opened the door she drew in a deep, fortifying breath.

The door opened too fast, because someone was pushing it open from the outside, too.

"Rain!" Alessia exclaimed. She pushed her way in and shut the door with both of them still inside. Rain peered longingly at the door, wishing she could turn into mist and walk through Alessia and get out of there, though her friend was only concerned, as a friend should be.

Rain's one daring move all her life was to take a trip to Italy alone with some of the inheritance from Gran, and she'd befriended Alessia over late-night bottles of prosecco in that instant way some girls can click, especially girls outside of their normal lives, like at summer camp. Alessia had made good on her promise to visit Rain in the States, and in short order she had met and married TJ's brother.

Those long, prosecco-soaked nights seemed far away now.

"Are you all right?" Alessia asked, her forehead puckered up as she searched Rain's blotchy, damp face. Her near-perfect English retained a musical trill of an accent. "What's happened?"

"I'm just having a bad day," Rain forced

herself to say.

"What's wrong? Please tell me, maybe I can help."

Rain sighed and tried to imagine seizing her composure with both hands, though she knew how silly that was. One could not frantically, desperately, achieve a calm state of mind.

"I am not feeling well, and I really don't want to talk about it. But thank you. And congratulations. I'm sure you'll have a beautiful baby."

Her voice cracked over that last word, and Alessia finally stood aside.

TJ already had his coat on and was shaking hands with his brother at the door. "There you are," he said without emotion when he saw Rain and handed over her jacket.

Rain hardly had time to give her congratulations to Greg before TJ was pulling her out the door and down the long front walk to the semicircle of driveway in front of their home. He deposited her in the passenger side and slammed the door.

Rain was glad she'd pulled in her legs quickly or he might have crushed her ankle.

"Should I drive? I think I should drive," she said, aware of his charged state, the number of beers he'd had.

"No. I'm fine."

Rain unbuckled her seat belt and made to open her door. "I'll just drive. I mean what if —"

TJ revved away, having already started the engine, and Rain fell back hard into her seat. "I said I'm fine!"

Rain buckled her seat belt again, closed her eyes, and prayed. *Lord just get us home safely. Please.* Besides the risk of accident there was also the chance of getting pulled over, and he might be over the legal limit. A high school teacher with a drunk driving arrest? That would make headlines.

In fifteen minutes they were back in their driveway, and Rain slumped, trembling with released tension. *Thank you,* she prayed silently. No sirens. Scarcely another car to be seen, in fact, even on a Saturday night.

Just inside their front door, TJ seized her suddenly, pressing her back to the wall with a fierce, hard kiss. Rain almost felt as if she was drowning.

He was tugging off her jacket, then raking his hands across her breasts, down her sides to her hips. He pushed up her sundress, then hoisted her hard up against the wall. Without meaning to, Rain uttered a small cry of pain because of the pressure of him bracing her against the hard surface; the force felt crushing as he used one free hand to fumble with his own buckle.

Rain held him as much to hold herself up as from affection. Now that he'd freed himself from his pants, he went to work on her underwear, yanking them down only as far as he had to before he slammed inside her.

She cried out again and he seemed encouraged; *pain and pleasure do sound so much alike,* Rain thought then, holding her breath as TJ continued slamming her back against the wall. A glance at his face sent a chill across her skin, despite the sweat that might have been his or hers or both — he looked angry.

He shouted, sounding both furious and relieved, and then together they sank down the wall, ending up in a heap on the carpet. Rain's purse was next to her foot, her jacket by her head. She felt scraped up, sore, and burned.

"Feel better now?" she asked in her playful voice, as she gingerly put her panties back in place. "That was quite a performance."

TJ was panting and did not answer her for several long moments.

Then he said, "Let's go upstairs."

"Right now?" At this rate she wouldn't be able to walk tomorrow.

"I just want to lie down with you," he said.

He sat up, fastened his pants, and then scooped her up like a fairy-tale princess. He carried her smoothly up the stairs, sneaking looks at her face during his careful progress.

Rain was quietly thrilled at the ease with which he carried her.

He laid her down carefully on the bed and arranged the covers over her. He slid in beside her and nestled up behind her, spoon fashion.

"I love you," he said.

She took his hand that was draped over her side and squeezed it. "I love you, too."

He reached down her abdomen, his arm gliding over her hip. It was her turn, he meant. She squeezed his hand, moved it gently back to her waist. Not now. No need. She was content enough with him resting there so close to her.

He whispered in her ear, "Let's call that doctor. The one you mentioned to me."

Rain sat halfway up in the blush-orange light of dusk as it filtered through the blinds. "Dr. Gould?"

"Yeah. Her."

The fertility specialist. When she'd showed TJ the pamphlet last June, he'd torn it up, saying he was not about to make a baby "in a test tube like some lab rat," as he'd put it then. Rain's timing had been poor; he was still trying to finish grading exams. Despite this, she'd pressed on, reminding him that he'd promised to have children with her, always swore he wanted a family, too, and finally he'd just stormed out of the house and walked somewhere alone for over an hour, coming back calm but refusing to discuss it.

Now, the sentence on the tip of her tongue went something like this: *I don't want to do this because you are competing with your brother.*

But it was a fact that she'd been off the pill almost two years now and had been timing their sex for almost as long. She'd even taken Clomid for a few months, courtesy of her ob-gyn who thought that might help, claiming she used it "like water" to get her patients pregnant. All it had done was make her cranky and give her hot flashes.

TJ's willingness might be poorly motivated, but perhaps here was their chance to become parents at last, just like they'd always said they would be, going back to their honeymoon when they were making up silly baby names like Saffron and Magenta as they lay in bed for hours at a time.

Everything happens for a reason, her grandmother used to say.

"I'll call her tomorrow," Rain said, and she turned to face TJ. He pulled her close, and she felt him incrementally relax, until they were both dozing in their soft marriage bed, and Rain dreamed of tiny toes, soft cheeks, and gummy smiles.

11

Morgan shivered, tucking her hands inside the sleeves of her hoodie. Inside the school it should have been warm; most other students were running around in shirtsleeves, and some girls were wearing thin leggings and light cotton shirts. None of them seemed to feel cold.

But something about hearing the howling wind, and seeing the whirlwinds of snow through the double doors at the end of the hall, made Morgan cold down to her marrow, no matter what the inside thermometer said.

She checked her phone clock. Two forty-five. Fifteen minutes before her solo practice with Mrs. DeWitt in the band room. She hiked her backpack higher up and snaked her way through the halls. Fifteen minutes should be just enough time.

She passed Ethan in the hallway and looked down at the floor until he'd gone by.

Every time she saw him now, she flashed back to two memories: him taking her hand that day in the hall that first week of school, then him repelled by her awkward kiss, crushing himself into the far corner of her couch.

She hadn't returned the texts he sent later, trying to smooth over what had just happened with a variation on their old in-joke.

He'd sent things like,

Closeted teen misses news about gay being cool, Film at 11

Guy on deathbed from bout of terminal cluelessness, Film at 11

After each message, her thumbs hovered over her phone, trying to come up with something to say, but she simply felt empty.

Hall traffic was thinning out now. Buses outside were roaring off into neighborhoods; kids with cars had already burned rubber. A few stragglers were headed, like her, to practices and after-school meetings. The earnest types, the gold-star National Honor Society types. Or the jocks. There were some of them around, too, headed toward the fieldhouse to hit a volleyball or shoot baskets.

A couple of teachers walked by her, sharing a laugh. She recognized them as they passed. Mr. Streeter and Miss Henry, both science teachers for the underclassmen. Teachers after hours looked so . . . normal, Morgan had noticed. They could let their masks slip a bit.

This may have been one of the reasons she felt compelled to make this thrice-weekly trip, before practicing the Elgar concerto in the band room with old Mrs. DeWitt.

She knocked on the open door, softly.

He looked up and smiled genuinely to see her. "Hey there. If it's Morgan, it must be Wednesday."

"Hi, Mr. Hill."

At first, when she started coming to his classroom after school, she sat across from him, in one of the classroom desks she'd pulled up close to his teacher desk. That's when she was still bringing her classroom notes as a pretense of needing some help, but honestly she was just looking for a way to kill some time before her cello practice that didn't involve Ethan or Britney or any other high school idiot. One time he said, "This is silly, just come around here," and went to grab a spare plastic chair from the math office two doors down.

That time, she'd had a chance to stand at his desk unattended. She saw his phone vibrate and light up with an image of a very pretty, slim brunette with a high forehead and blue, wide-set eyes.

He'd come back in and she was looking at his phone, and she felt flustered, explaining she had only been looking at the picture. "Your wife?"

He'd smiled at the picture as he responded. "That's my Rain."

"She's pretty," Morgan had said, watching her teacher's face go from a warm smile to sad to something else, a frown that seemed deeper, nearly a scowl.

"Yeah," he'd said, then stowed the phone and changed the subject.

Then there was that other time a couple of weeks later. By then she'd quit bothering to even get her math notebook out of her backpack. They'd just sit for a few minutes and talk about whatever. She enjoyed hearing his stories of high school back in his day, and his early teaching foibles like the time he got stuck subbing for a Spanish teacher and had ended up sounding like Dora the Explorer.

That time — it was a Friday, Morgan remembered — he'd gotten a call from his wife and apologized for the interruption.

Morgan looked at her own phone and tried to play deaf, but she couldn't help overhearing some excited chatter spill out into the air.

He replied, "Well, that does sound good. . . . I know . . . We'll see soon, I guess." His own voice was forced and sounded thin, like he wasn't even really breathing. Then he said, "I gotta go, I have a student here. Bye, babe . . . You, too. Bye."

He hung up and looked at Morgan with a strange, searching face, and said, "You ever see someone get their hopes up a million times only to be crushed? Until you just want to crush them in advance to save them the heartache?" Then he shook his head, as if remembering where he was, who she was.

"I'm sorry," she said. "I wasn't trying to listen, but . . . that sounded tough."

Mr. Hill looked over her shoulder at his open classroom door. He lowered his voice and said, "She wants to have a baby. And so do I, but at what cost? It seems like that's all she thinks about, that her mood is dependent on things like cycles and tests . . . Not just her mood. Her whole self. So what happens if it can't happen for us ever? Do I never get my wife back? Will she stay like this forever? Or worse, because there's no hope?"

Morgan's hand was on his forearm before she even consciously formed a notion to reach out. His arm felt warm and strong through the thin cotton of his dress shirt. He glanced down at her hand with something like surprise, but when he met her eyes, she read gratitude and understanding in the way he smiled sadly. He placed his hand on top of hers.

She nearly gasped aloud, then. His touch had lit her up from inside, all the way to her fingernails and the ends of her hair.

Someone walked by the open door and laughed, and the two of them broke apart quickly.

Today, the extra plastic chair was already waiting for her, pulled up to his side of the desk. She sat down and opened up a bottle of water from her backpack.

"Here," Mr. Hill said. "I was about to open this. You can have some." It was a bag of white cheddar popcorn. He also produced some napkins from a desk drawer. "It's my weakness. It's also messy, so be warned."

The sight of the popcorn awakened Morgan's appetite, which had shriveled in the face of the school lunch offerings earlier. She eagerly shoved her hand in the bag at the exact moment Mr. Hill did, and their fingers briefly tangled. They laughed, and then both reached for the same stack of napkins, and laughed again.

Mr. Hill gestured grandly to the napkins and intoned, "After you, m'lady," tipping his head in a sort of bow.

"Why, thank you," Morgan replied in the best aristocrat voice she could muster.

"So how are things in the dog-eat-dog world of high school society?"

Morgan groaned. "I'm so over it. I can't wait to get out of here. Sitting two rows from my ex in your class, listening to Britney go on and on about who's sleeping with whom . . . what's so funny?"

He'd started chuckling as she spoke. "Just that you said 'who's sleeping with whom.' I don't know many kids who use 'whom' correctly in a sentence when complaining about their classmates."

"I'm not a kid," Morgan retorted, pointing the water bottle at him for emphasis.

"Touché, Morgan. You're really not, are you? That's the funny thing about age. It's so arbitrary. You're more mature than some adults I know. More mature than me, probably." He laughed, but the crease of his brow suggested more behind the comment than a self-effacing joke.

"Oh, I hardly think that. You're a fun

teacher, but that's good. I think it takes more work to be a fun teacher, doesn't it? Not like grumpy old Señora Graham."

Morgan's phone vibrated with a text. "Hang on," she said, and looked.

From her mother.

Jared broke glasses have to get him new ones can you come to the Den and watch the register?

"Shit," she muttered.

"What's wrong?" Mr. Hill asked, cocking his head. Morgan allowed a moment of pleasure that he didn't acknowledge her cursing.

"Oh, my stupid brother broke his glasses, so now I have to drop everything and go cover for my mom at work so she can take him to get new ones. That's me, Deputy Mom. In case of emergency, just ask Morgan. She'll do it! Of course she will!"

Her thumbs were furiously texting as she talked, reminding her mother about cello practice and Mrs. DeWitt. Her mother said she remembered but to get to the Den as soon as possible.

Jared has a terrible headache without his glasses and is pretty much blind

In other words: *Yes, I know, but don't care about your issues, hurry up already the world is ending because Jared broke his glasses.*

Morgan went to screw on the cap of her water bottle, but knocked the bottle over instead, sending the water splashing out all over her knee, causing her to jump up and spill her open backpack behind Mr. Hill's desk.

Morgan seized the now empty water bottle and flung it across the room, where the light plastic bounced off the cinder-block wall.

She knelt down to gather her things, tears snaking down her face either from embarrassment, or frustration, or the previous night's insomnia. Maybe all of it. Mr. Hill was down there, too, trying to help her. She slammed a notebook into her backpack and looked up, catching Mr. Hill's eye. His expression was soft, concerned. "Hey . . ." he said softly. "It's not so bad."

He reached out. The embrace was awkward, crouched as they both were, but Morgan found a way to rest her forehead gently on his shoulder, and for two exquisite beats she cried a couple of tears onto his white shirt.

Then she sat back, trying to recover something like that maturity he'd mentioned. As she knelt on the floor and found her English textbook, she felt Mr. Hill's hand brush her face. With his thumb he wiped away a tear.

Morgan's brief smile faded into a wave of queasy humiliation at having broken down. Some mature young woman she was, who throws water bottles when plans change.

Her embarrassment got the best of her along with her realization she was about to be late for her cello practice. She zipped her backpack roughly. "Gotta run, I'm late. Thanks, Mr. Hill, sorry about the spill."

Before he could say another word, she was sprinting down the hall faster than an assistant principal's kid ever should. By the time she made it to the band room, she was panting, and seeing stars in her peripheral vision.

Mrs. DeWitt was at the piano already, playing some other piece, and when Morgan slammed the band room door open, the teacher regarded her coldly. "I have been waiting here for ten minutes, young lady. If you're going to expect me to accompany you and practice three times a week, then have some respect for my time."

"I'm sorry. I was getting some help on my calc homework, and —"

"It doesn't matter. An assistant principal's daughter should know better. Hurry up and tune. We only have time to go through it once today. I have another engagement."

Morgan flung down her backpack and stormed off to find a school cello. Why couldn't there be another available pianist to accompany her at the solo competition? Why did it have to be rickety, dried-up old Mrs. DeWitt, the retired orchestra director who refused to go away? She kept finding reasons to come back to the school like a ghost haunts its former home.

The orchestra door opened again as Morgan was unzipping the case around the cello. Mr. Hill poked his head in. "Morgan. You forgot this." He held up her math book. It must have fallen out of her bag in her haste to go.

She walked up to get it with a grateful smile. She would have been frantic trying to find it later.

"Morgan!" barked out Mrs. DeWitt. "I asked you to please hurry."

Before Mr. Hill closed the band room door, he looked at Morgan and crossed his eyes, pulling an exaggerated face.

Morgan snickered, then rearranged her features into proper contrition, and prepared to go rosin up her bow for the Elgar concerto and Mrs. DeWitt.

12

Christmas music twinkled through the peppermint-scented air of the Den, on one of those days when a thought hummed through Dinah's head like the thrum of a purring engine: *I love my job, I love my job, I love my job.*

Her crew of college and older high school kids had clicked into place and were running it well enough so that she could escape for a few hours and Christmas shop. People were in a festive mood and ordering lots of food and drink. Soon enough Joe would be forced by the school calendar to hang up his assistant principal's hat and just hang out with them: watch football, play cards. The weather today was even cooperating: The sparkly snow danced to the ground like a little girl's glitter.

She'd donned a Santa hat in honor of her good mood. The jingle bell on the end of the hat announced her movements around the store, making her feel a little like a cat with a bell on its collar.

"Hi, Dinah!" trilled her latest customer. It was Kelly, Britney's mom. She was standing in the doorway shaking snow out of her highlighted auburn hair. Dina noted a feather extension woven near her ear. Kelly clomped up to the counter in her clunky Eskimo-looking boots that would look stupid on Dinah but somehow adorable on her. "Hey, can you talk a second?"

Dinah's instant thought: Morgan. Britney confided something about Morgan.

She nodded and asked Janine to take over for her. She led Kelly up the stairs to her office on the top floor of the converted bungalow. Most of the upstairs former bedrooms were storage, but the largest was her office. Her desk faced a circular window in the front peak of the house. Her file cabinets were tucked under the roof slant.

Dinah sank into her fancy office chair — a gift from Joe a few birthdays ago — stretching and rolling her ankles. "What's up? Is something going on with Morgan?"

"Huh? No. Or I don't think so. Brit doesn't talk about her much lately. I think it's awkward because Brit's kinda hanging out with David."

At this, Dinah sat up. "Her ex? Really?

Um, wow."

Kelly's pert face smoothed into a mask of cool detachment. "You know how kids are. They hang out and flirt with everyone. Anyway, Morgan's studying all the time, right? Did she hear from any colleges yet?" Kelly didn't wait for an answer. "Brit's probably going to U of M, or maybe as a transfer student if she has to get her grades up. I don't have much saved, but my cheating ex is coughing up some guilt money to send her. Guess I'm glad he started screwing that waitress, in the end. Ha, get it? In the end!" Kelly let loose peals of laughter.

Dinah pinched the bridge of her nose. "So what did you need to tell me, Kelly?"

"Okay, so, I was at Sereni-Tea the other day? That's a dumb name for a store, isn't it? I don't care how much tea they sell. Why not make a name out of the wine and cheese and stuff instead? In Vino Veritas, that would have been a good name."

"Kelly. What."

"Anyway, Helen came in and I overheard her talking about opening a Starbucks."

Dinah sat up in her office chair. "No. She wouldn't."

Kelly shrugged. "Sure she would. And I know your application is coming up before the Planning Commission, right? And she's got lots of friends on that commission."

"What do you mean?"

"I'm just saying. I mean, she segued right from talking about how great a Starbucks would be bordering the park — because 'adults need a place to spend time that's not a bar' she said — to the fact that the entertainment license you're asking for could theoretically be used to get a liquor license later. She was talking to Martha Wilson. And you know Martha cannot shut up about anything."

Dinah got up out of her chair and started pacing her office space, which amounted to stomping in tight circles around her chair, because of the roof slant on the second floor making the sides of the room too short.

"That's such bullshit. I'm committed to having a kid-friendly place. All I want is karaoke and poetry slams and maybe a folksinger. If I have bands, they'll be, like, local teen bands. The hardest drink I'll ever serve is espresso. And if she opens a Starbucks next to the park? The kids will go there! Especially in the summer, which is my worst season anyway. Why does she hate me so much?"

"You called her a self-righteous bitch one time, didn't you? Not that you're wrong. Because she totally is. But still."

"I didn't mean it. No, actually I did mean it. I didn't mean to say it out loud, though."

That had been back when she was first trying to get the Den approved all those years ago. Helen Demming had, for reasons Dinah could never fathom, shown up and spoken out against the parking lot plans, saying kids will be "tearing down Alton Road" to and from the Den and that the place would create traffic hazards, even though other, more intense developments sailed through without a murmur of objection from her. After the meeting when Dinah meant to confront her calmly and explain, she'd gotten a mite carried away. Then her mortal enemy went and got herself elected Chamber of Commerce president, being an owner of a downtown boutique that catered to women who had waists no bigger than those of grasshoppers.

Kelly went on, "You'd better make sure to count your votes at Planning Commission is all I'm saying."

"You think she could single-handedly sink my project?"

"Watch your back. I'm just saying. And it wouldn't hurt to have a Plan B."

"What Plan B would that be?"

"If your permit doesn't go through and she opens a Starbucks, how are you going to keep this place open? I mean, I love it, too, hon; the Den is totally quaint. But a national brand like that is pretty tough to go up against. How long did the Book Worm last after Borders opened up down the highway? Well, now they're both gone. Shame." Kelly glanced at her watch. "Oooh! Gotta run. Late for lunch. Sorry to spring this bad news on you, but I wanted you to be prepared. I'm just saying."

Kelly stood up and approached Dinah for a weird faux hug — touching only Dinah's forearms lightly with her fingertips.

"Thanks, Kell. Thanks for telling me," Dinah managed through her fog of shock and outrage at Helen's treachery. Kelly gave her a fingertip wave and then skittered down the stairs.

Dinah's cell phone rang. Only Joe ever called her cell; the kids texted, and anyone else e-mailed or called the house. So her heart was pounding before she even picked up. "Joe? What's up?"

"I just ran into Carla."

"Yeah? Did she hear about Morgan's college applications?"

"Acceptances come straight to the kids, not to her, but in a way, she heard, yeah. You bet she heard."

"What are you talking about?"

"She applied to Boston University! How the hell are we gonna afford that?"

"What? No, she didn't."

"Carla had to write her a letter and send in the transcripts and test scores, so she should know. She figured we knew, just told me offhand when we were waiting for a meeting how exciting that would be for her. And I had to pretend I knew what the hell my own kid was up to. I felt like an idiot."

"I didn't know either! She never said a word to me."

"It was your card she used to apply. Shoulda been on the credit card statement."

"I don't audit the statement, you know. I just pay it and file it."

"Look, I've got a game to go to after school and some paperwork. Talk to her as soon as you can. We gotta nip this in the . . . Oh, hell, fistfight —"

Dinah heard his phone clatter down. He'd just dropped it and gone off to break up the fight, not bothering to hang up.

Dinah pulled off her Santa hat, kneading her temples with her other hand, as the whirring of the machines and soft Christmas music from her café filtered through the floor and wove through the dry winter air around her.

■ ■ ■ ■

Dinah should have been glad that Morgan didn't scream at her. She should have been grateful for her daughter's dignified silence as she pushed back from the table and walked with a graceful, nearly gliding step up the stairs to her room. Considering Dinah had just crushed her daughter's dream of an out-of-state private university in a fascinating city. At Dinah's suggestion that Ann Arbor was a cool place, Morgan had only blinked twice.

But Dinah felt as small as the ant she now saw marching across the kitchen counter. She deserved to be yelled at. She couldn't help the reality of her bank balance, or how impractical it was that Morgan go to school so far away. And frankly, it was a pretty big lie by omission that Morgan snuck an extra school onto her list. But she should have known, should have hovered over Morgan's shoulder and followed her progress in her college applications just like she hovered over the twins' homework. Then Dinah could have told her from the beginning that they could never afford an out-of-state private school with tuition four times that of Michigan, which itself was no bargain.

But Morgan had been so eager, so excited to take the lead on her college applications, already figuring out she could use something online called "Common App" to apply to U of M, before Dinah had even heard of such a thing. Dinah had in fact secretly felt quite smug as she listened to the other moms of seniors at the Den kvetch about having to stand over their kids and harass them about applications, essays, and scholarships.

All she'd had to do was turn her competent, intelligent daughter loose and she took care of it all . . .

Well, Joe could have gotten more involved. As per usual, this was in her lap to take care of. Even though he's an assistant principal! Education should be the number one thing on his mind!

As if she'd conjured him, the garage door rattled up.

Joe shuffled in, pinching the bridge of his nose and wincing.

"What's wrong?" Dinah asked.

"I'm just tired," he groaned.

"I saved you a plate. I thought you were at the game?"

"I had a hot dog at the game, and I got tired. I stayed for a while. Kate's still there," he said, pulling a beer out of the fridge.

"We had a rough night here," Dinah began.

"Again?"

Dinah gulped hard and swallowed her first retort: *What are you saying, it's a train wreck around here every day?* "Yeah, I know. I had to tell Morgan she can't go to Boston U. I would have waited for you if I'd known you were coming home. I was twisting in the wind all alone here."

"I didn't think I'd be home, I told you. I can't believe you didn't know she wanted to go to Boston. Where'd she even come up with that? We've never been there, we have no family there . . ."

"What do you mean you can't believe I didn't know? Why didn't Assistant Principal Joe Monetti know? For crying out loud, you walk around a high school all day and you didn't think to check in with your own daughter on college plans?"

Joe tipped his head back and took a long pull of his beer. "Same old song."

"Can we not do this now, Joe? This is hard enough for me."

"Not just for you. Look, first I have to talk a teacher off the ledge, which eats up my whole lunch. That new calc teacher, TJ Hill? He's having a confidence crisis, and I have to be all soothing and shit. Then I hear Pete

Jackson is retiring."

"Isn't that good? You're next in line in seniority."

"It would have been good until they added Kate. Now, it's not good at all."

It used to be that Joe was the only assistant principal and presumptive successor to Pete Jackson, and Joe was thinking long term that he might break into administration in the district's central office. He'd even been taking classes toward his doctorate.

"But Kate is so much less experienced."

Joe huffed. "So? This isn't the union. There's no 'paying your dues' anymore. Kate is popular and pretty, and she's also Korean."

Dinah felt her hackles rising. "So?"

"Soooo." He drew the word out. "So our school is more diverse than ever, and the powers that be may decide a popular, smart dynamo of a principal who also happens to be 'diverse' herself might be just what the school needs. And Kate has no kids. The school is her life, and she shows up to everything. As I try to, which is why I'm never here, as you are so fond of pointing out."

"Just don't borrow trouble, okay? I'm sure your experience counts for a helluva lot.

Kate has only been there a year."

Joe noticed a paper on the table, a progress report from the school he could probably recognize at twenty paces, having filled out enough of them himself. As he read, he smacked his beer down.

"Now one of my kids is about to flunk English. That looks good, doesn't it? For an assistant principal's kid?" Joe jerked this thumb at the report.

Dinah snatched it back, signing it hastily on the required line so she could stuff it back in Connor's bag. "We talked about moving them to a different school other than yours, and you said no. I could turn it around and ask you, why you had to get a job in their home district?"

"I love how instead of hearing how hard of a day I had, you hear a criticism. Thanks for the support."

"And thank you, too, for that matter. You think it's easy having to be the one at home to crack the whip? While you take them to football games on the weekend? Fun Dad and Warden Mom."

"Whaddya want? Me to come home from work to paddle them?"

"Now the sarcasm to make me feel good and stupid."

"Jesus, I'm just sayin' that I don't do that

on purpose. You're here and I'm not; I can't help that. You want me to be less fun so you'll feel less bad?"

"You could be home more if you felt like it. But you hide in that office with Kate next door while I'm in the trenches here."

Joe shook his head, jutted his chin forward. "Un-frickin'-believable. I work my ass off. Come home from a bad workday, try to share it with you, and it turns out I'm the bad guy. Again. And what's this 'Kate next door' shit, eh? You jealous, now? Of her?"

He'd dropped the *R: of huh?* Joe's New York heritage was sneaking out the more upset he got. His parents had moved to Detroit from Brooklyn when he was a kid, and to this day, though he was a grade-schooler when they'd left New York, his accent would resurge when he got upset, along with a blue-collar cadence.

"Well, are you going to talk to your daughter now? And the boys?"

"Gimme a minute, I just walked in the freakin' door. I'll talk to her when I change out of my suit at least."

Joe shook his head slowly, as if his head were suddenly too heavy for his neck. He picked up his beer and left her alone at the table, walking with a heavy step past the children's doors and straight up to his room to change.

The loneliness was so familiar she flashed back to September, when they'd tried to have a romantic evening out, the night Morgan had urged them to go, saying she'd keep an eye on the boys. Joe never made reservations at nice restaurants, and they ended up at a Chili's, where Joe's eyes kept drifting to the playoff baseball highlights on a TV behind Dinah's head. Conversation evaporated, and once home, Dinah stomped to their room, tore off her pretty bra and dress, and pulled on some sweatpants, turning out the light early and alone while Joe watched more TV.

Tonight was the same: a throbbing emptiness, plus the sense of jagged edges, like a piece of paper torn roughly in half.

She rested her head on her folded arms, her face turned to the side, toward the dining room wall. On the wall in curvy script was the phrase "Family: The Heart of Every Home," which was supposed to look painted on, but from Dinah's view, the shiny edges were obvious. It was just a big tacky sticker bought for $3.99 at Walmart, after all. Not Martha-Stewart-worthy hand-painted calligraphy.

Around the words were framed photographs of the family. Connor and Jared playing flag football at a middle-school field day. Morgan and her cello last year at solo and ensemble, cropped from a larger shot of her quartet. There was just one shot of Dinah and Joe, and she realized with a start how long ago it had been taken. Morgan had taken it, and her vantage point was low, so the camera was looking up at the pair of them. They'd been at the beach. Dinah's cheeks were pink with sun and she was laughing hard, because Joe — embracing her from behind — had tickled her at the instant the shutter clicked. Then she'd whirled in the circle of his arms and tackled him to the sand, the element of surprise outweighing his strength. A familywide tickle fight ensued and carried over into the waves and became a splash fight until they were all soaked and laughing and hiccupping. Dinah squinted into the middle distance and tried to remember how old Morgan was at the time. . . . That must have been seven years ago, give or take.

Seven years ago she was laughing with her husband and family on the beach. Now, she and Joe barely talked except to discuss logistics or fight about whether he was ever helping her at home.

Though, now that Dinah was thinking of

that picture, and the years before and after, she'd have to be honest and say even before that, closeness was rare between her and Joe. That's why she'd framed the shot even though it was slightly blurry and off-center; it was such a rare, special moment.

She rewound her mental home movies of her family, the twins and Morgan shrinking down to pint-size, herself standing in the not-yet-opened Den, sweeping the scarred hardwood floors.

This took her back to the twins' fragile early days. Her chest tightened to recall the constant state of fear. Her need to control every tiny variable that might affect how the boys developed. Joe trying to help, but not able to soothe the squirmy, colicky Connor or get Jared's tiny toddler glasses to stay on right . . . Dinah tried to teach Joe, show him what she knew, but he snapped at her, accused her of treating him like a child, and she would fire back she was only trying to show him the best way . . . And he began retreating — literally is what she'd been picturing as he walked off to the home office or to some school function — but figuratively, too.

The shiny glare of the cheap sticker and the corny sentiment began to work under Dinah's skin like a sliver. She stood up so quickly that her head spun for just a moment. She took her ragged, chipped nails and went to work on a corner of the thing, until she got a piece of it, and gave a mighty rip. But only the "Fa" ripped off, leaving "mily: The Heart of Every Home," and for some reason this made her laugh, so she laughed and laughed and kept laughing as she ripped every shred of that ridiculous sticker off her wall, and she laughed even harder when she saw it had been there so long you could see a halo where it used to be and the paint was brighter.

She might have laughed her way through painting over the whole wall, except Jared and Connor started fighting, and she went upstairs to break it up, the wadded remnants of the heart of every home balled up in her fist.

13

Rain was upside down, as she was often during her workday.

"Breathe into the stretch," she was telling the class, and she was doing the same, her rear jutting up into the air in downward-facing dog, her back elongating from shoulders to tailbone, stretching the tension right out.

She almost groaned aloud with the pleasure of it; she was loose from teaching almost the full hour — they were winding down now — and it was a deep, satisfying stretch, or "juicy" as Beverly would say. "Yummy" in Layla-speak. She never could get used to that kind of language.

She prompted the class for upward-facing dog, and now her body was facedown along the floor, her legs stretched out flat behind her, up on her hands with elbows gently bent, bending up like a swoop toward the ceiling. Her chest just inside her shoulders yawned out, happily released from the hunching-over posture she fell into much of the rest of the time.

Down to the floor flat, and up again to downward-facing dog . . .

Blackness rushed into the sides of Rain's vision. She gasped quietly and went down on hands and knees, trying to breathe deeply enough so that she wouldn't crumple into a heap in front of twenty women and the retired autoworker.

The class hadn't noticed yet, she could tell. Upside down as they all were, they were looking between their legs at the back of the room.

She should have hydrated more.

Rain prompted the class to come down to hands and knees, and they did, looking at her as they did so, as if they would need help figuring out how to be on all fours. Rain walked them through the steps to *savasana,* but she did not dare lie flat, worrying she might not be able to rise. She sat in half lotus and drank from her water bottle.

Am I? she wondered. *Could I be, finally?* She could surprise TJ on his birthday on Sunday, welcome him to his thirties with the prospect of being a father, and how perfect would that be? Heading into the true adult decade together, finally on the way to being a family, more than just a couple.

But she'd been down that road so many times. So often she'd have a moment of dizziness, or nausea, or her breasts would feel sore and she'd fly to the computer and look up pregnancy symptoms, especially when she was on Clomid. Early on, she'd gone as far as to calculate her eventual due date, only to have her period arrive a few days later.

But this time was different. This time she'd had Dr. Gould and her injectable drugs on her side, and the perfected timing of medical science, so no matter what the quirks of Rain's individual uterus and hormones, they couldn't fail to get egg and sperm in the uterus together.

It had been ten days since the insemination. The longest ten days of Rain's life since Gran had died.

She prompted the class to sit up and wished them "Namaste."

She tried to keep the after-class chatter short, not having the patience for it. She just wanted to rush time forward to her next blood test with Dr. Gould, maybe the most important blood test ever.

The last student filed out, and Rain set to straightening the mats in the corner, putting away her own things. Now she just had to help Beverly behind the counter until NYC closed for the evening. With Layla off for the day, it was almost like old times.

She paused before walking out of the studio to look at the lake behind the huge glass windows at the back of the room. Snow dusted the trees around its edges. Such a lovely view, but she usually had her back to it, leading the class.

In the store area, she came upon Beverly arranging some new stock on a shelf: pretty crystals that were supposed to help your chi or whatever.

Beverly noticed her and broke into a wide grin, then immediately the grin dripped away.

"You look so pale," she said, turning a pink crystal over in one hand.

"Oh, I didn't drink enough water is all," Rain said, waving her hand through the air, but a smile snuck out anyway.

Beverly looked around quickly for customers; the last one had filed out just moments before. "Are you?" she whispered, though they were alone.

Rain allowed herself to say, "Maybe."

Beverly's round face burst into joy like a flashbulb. "So exciting!"

Rain's own smile faded as she remembered Beverly's excitement last month and how that ended. Rain hadn't been able to wait for the official doctor's test, and she took a home pregnancy test. It had given her the faintest of second lines. According to the wisdom of the Internet as she frantically searched, the test on the desk next to her, "a line is a line," meaning it didn't matter how bold or weak, that line meant she was pregnant.

She'd taken the ill-advised step of calling TJ at work, catching him helping a student after school, so he couldn't talk, really, and she couldn't gauge his reaction.

By the time he got home, it was moot. Her period had arrived with the suddenness of an earthquake. Dr. Gould allowed that it might have been an extremely early miscarriage for the test to have registered a faint second line followed by bleeding, and she said it didn't always work the first time.

"Take heart," she'd said, patting Rain's thin wrist, and Rain thought, *This is taking my heart all the time.*

She learned her lesson, in any case, about dabbling in home pregnancy tests. She would wait for the doctor's verdict. Rain realized how much happier she would have been if she'd never even known there was a faint possibility of pregnancy. If she'd only waited a few more hours, her body would have answered the question for her. Ignorance really was bliss.

Rain smiled back at Beverly, but the giddy anticipation she felt in class was gone. Instead came a creeping certainty that this cycle had failed as well. Why couldn't she just sit with the unknown? Why the wild swings from optimism to despair?

She looked at the crystals Beverly had begun to arrange once again. Rain thought she might be desperate enough to try chanting to one in the quest for inner peace. They were cheaper than fertility drugs, after all.

"How is TJ handling all this?" Beverly asked, moving on to a display of incense burners, and then heading behind the counter for her duster.

"Oh, well. It's up and down."

Rain turned away as she said it, fiddling with some folded T-shirts, which were perfectly folded already.

TJ had grown more and more stormy about the process, ever since the doctor explained to him they'd have to test his fertility, and what exactly that entailed. Then he had to "produce his sample" twice more, for the two cycles of treatment they'd tried thus far. On that day, Rain would try to be optimistic and excited about their future as parents, but TJ would stomp about the house, not speaking, slamming cabinet doors and watching sports on TV with stiff folded arms.

The day after the first failed cycle, in October with the foliage in a riot of oranges and reds, she'd gone for a drive alone, screaming in her car as she barreled along the highway to nowhere, "Do you think this is a cakewalk for me? Do you think I enjoy poking my stomach with needles? Do you think I wanted to get pregnant with my feet up in stirrups with a doctor sticking a turkey baster in my vagina? I'm so sorry you have to jerk off in a tube, but you're not the only one who hates this process, you self-absorbed sonofabitch!"

She pulled over and called Alessia from her cell phone, and her sister-in-law consoled her and mercifully omitted any information about her own pregnancy, though Rain would have liked to be able to innocently celebrate her new niece's or nephew's impending arrival without the bitter taste of envy in the back of her throat.

Then she drove home, shaky with relief and expended anger, and cooked TJ his favorite meal of turkey burgers and roasted redskin potatoes.

Rain abandoned the shirts and turned to

Beverly. "Why should this be so damn hard for me? I worried so much about getting pregnant when I was in college. I remember freaking out if my period was one day late, thinking the condom had slipped or something. And everywhere you look, people who have no money, no plan, no sense at all are getting pregnant like it's going out of style . . ." Rain cringed to hear these thoughts out loud for once, instead of just in a loop in her brain. "That's hateful talk."

Beverly nodded. "Stop being so tough on yourself. You're allowed to have feelings about it that aren't exactly politically correct. Sometimes I think you don't let yourself have feelings at all. As if you and TJ only get a ration of emotion, and he spends it all for the two of you."

"It's not like that. I like being the stable one. I grew up surrounded by people who just . . ." Rain tried to think of a way to describe Ricky and Angie. "Emoted all over everywhere, regardless of the consequences. When I moved in with Gran, I felt like I could breathe for the first time. There's nothing wrong with being reserved."

"Just make sure you don't reserve yourself until you suffocate."

"Yes, Mother Beverly," Rain said with a grin. "What do you say I count out the cash drawer? I don't see any stampeding hordes of customers."

"If you must change the subject, go right ahead," Beverly said, giving Rain a wry smirk.

"What? It's gotta be done, right?"

Rain busied herself with the money, reflecting that although she was grateful to have Beverly as a friend as well as a boss, she rather wished Bev weren't so damn perceptive.

On the drive home, Rain felt a telltale heaviness in her lower abdomen.

"No," she said out loud.

A ball of dread gathered in her chest. Without intending to, she steered the car away from her home, and TJ, whom she imagined was slouched in front of the television, though for all she knew he was working out or grading papers or waiting for her with dinner warm on the table . . .

Okay, well, probably not that last one.

She drove and let her mind wander as much as she dared while still watching the road. She took the entrance ramp onto the highway, joining the flow of cars zipping along past sleepy farms and stands of naked winter trees.

Her car passed the exit for her parents'

house. She could not deal with Fawn now, who was having trouble with a teething, cranky baby Brock. The last time she'd been there and Fawn groaned again about his fussiness, Rain wanted to grab her shoulders and scream, "Do you know what I would give?"

She took a familiar exit, figuring something inside her had been planning to go this way all along.

The roads were narrow, and Rain drove slowly, mindful of the ditches alongside filled with icy water. She passed snow-capped mounds of hay rolled into cylinders that she used to pretend were buffaloes, when she'd made this drive with her parents as a little girl.

She cut her lights as she rolled up to the road in front of an old stucco house.

Gran's house.

Not anymore, of course. Ricky and Angie hadn't wanted it when Gran died; they preferred to sell it and take the money, which they burned through rapidly, of course.

There was a light on in the kitchen. Rain rested her head against the seatback, picturing Gran with her tight coils of silver hair sipping from the stoneware coffee mug. Gran was writing letters in fluid script while

Rain did her homework at the table. The only sound other than the scratching of their pens was the crickets outside and the ticking of the grandfather clock in the hall.

Now and then Rain would share something interesting out of her history book, and Gran would nod. Or Rain would ask who she was writing to, and Gran would talk to her about her great-aunt Esther and tell some funny story about Esther as a girl, who was a tomboy and prone to coming home so covered in mud that her mother would turn the hose on her in the yard before letting her inside.

And Rain would drink in the silence, remembering the chaos of her own house where her brother and sister blared their music at all hours and Ricky and Angie came and went on no discernible schedule.

Sometimes she'd worry aloud that she was intruding on Gran's privacy, to which Gran would reply, "Never, my child. You are never a burden to me."

Gran would have been so proud and happy to see her now, with her good job, nice house, and handsome husband. None of it had come easily, but Gran always said the best things in life were worth waiting for. It took TJ a long time to sow his oats, for example, refusing to exclusively date only her in college though she was lost in him and couldn't even look at another guy.

It wasn't until his brother's opulent wedding to Alessia that he whispered in her ear he wanted to marry her. Even that wasn't the official proposal, and she had to wait another six months for the ring.

Now, they were together, and it was worth every moment of waiting, every spike of jealousy, because she'd shown him in the end that it was her constancy and fidelity that mattered. He thanked her almost daily for loving him.

Gran would have been so happy for her. If only she could have lived long enough to see the wedding.

Rain wiped under her eyes and shook her head, putting the car in reverse to head back home. No sense in crying her mascara down her face, wishing for the impossible.

"Honey!" TJ exclaimed, before she'd even put her purse down. He sounded ebullient, giddy even, and Rain's shoulders drooped with relief. This was her favorite TJ, the one she first loved back in college, who could draw in everyone's attention and love like a whirlpool.

"Hey, babe," she said, realizing just how long she'd been out driving when she glanced at the living room clock. TJ didn't seem to have noticed.

He rushed up to her and swept her up, lifting her off the floor in a hug and kissing her, sweetly, warmly. She giggled under his lips he held the kiss so long, and he finally set her down. She felt a happy swoosh in her belly and thought how lucky she was to still feel this way for her husband.

"I had a great day," he said.

"I can tell! Good for you. What happened today?"

"I don't know," he said, plopping down at the kitchen table while she rooted in the refrigerator for dinner. "I just felt 'on' today, you know? I'd been so worried that I wasn't doing well, but after talking to Joe Monetti, and then one of my kids, I felt so much better. I'd been psyching myself out. Worrying too much."

Rain paused in her preparation of the chicken. "Who, TJ Hill? Worrying for nothing?"

"This is a big deal for me, teaching this subject. I have to teach it to myself every day, practically, to make sure I can teach it to them. There was this one girl who kept coming to see me after class and I'm like, geez, if I can't teach it to her — she's one of the brainy ones, you know? — I must really be screwed up. But she's having some personal problems, it turns out, and in fact our talk made me feel better yet, like I'm doing something good for the kids besides droning on about numbers."

"Well, that's wonderful. I'm proud of you."

"A bunch of us in the math department are going out for drinks on Friday, to celebrate my final days of being in my twenties. Can you come?"

Rain mentally ran over her schedule. "Shoot, I can't; I swapped classes with Layla that day. She's got somewhere to go. I'm sorry."

TJ frowned. "It would be nice if you would come celebrate with me."

"We're going out to dinner on Sunday for your birthday, though . . . This is so last minute."

"Can't you try to get out of it? I want my fun wife back."

Rain drew up short and slammed the microwave door harder than necessary. "So I'm not fun because I can't go back on my word to a coworker? We've been over this; sometimes I work weekend days, it's the way my job is. Besides, you don't want me there, sipping my ginger ale in the corner."

"Oh, you could have a drink. One

wouldn't hurt."

Rain sighed. "I have to work. Go have fun with your pals."

TJ sighed and slumped. "You'd be bored, anyway, all that school gossip and shoptalk."

"I always like spending time with you. We'll have a nice dinner Sunday. I promise." Rain settled down into a chair and felt her abdomen pinch slightly. Tears threatened to squirt out, and she blinked rapidly. "Just . . . Be careful, okay? Take a cab if you need to. We can go get your car later."

TJ rolled his eyes. "Yes, Mother."

"I'm just saying. Teachers can't be too careful with this stuff, right?"

He nodded. "Yeah. We practically have to be monks. I remember this one girl I went to school with? Tia, remember her?"

Rain did remember. She pictured Tia's crop tops and generous bosom. TJ went on, "Tia went out to the bar for her friend's bachelorette and someone saw her out having a good time and tattled on her at the school where she was student-teaching. She didn't get the job, even though everyone there had loved her right until then. So annoying, like we're not human or something."

Rain's appetite was crumbling away with the pain in her gut. She ignored the beeping of the microwave telling her that the leftovers were done. TJ noticed her clutching her stomach.

"Oh no, hon . . . Are you? Is it?"

Rain put her head in her hand. "Dammit."

"But we haven't heard from the doctor."

She shook her head and croaked out, "I can tell. I can feel it. It's over."

TJ rose and disappeared upstairs. Rain dragged herself across the kitchen to their living room, curling up on their scratchy upholstered couch. She always hated this couch, bought when they were poorer and just starting out. If not for the fertility treatments, she might have been able to afford to replace it. But a baby was worth more than a new couch.

TJ reappeared with a hot-water bottle. He gave it to her, handed her the remote control, and went off for another minute, returning with a glass of ice water.

"Do you need anything else?" he asked, sounding like a waiter.

Rain tried to appreciate the gestures, but she could see he was forcing it. Gone was his bubbly joy at his good workday. Gone was his demonstrative affection.

She shook her head. He planted a dry peck on the side of her head and vanished upstairs.

Rain couldn't think of anything on TV she

would care to see, so she stared at her own reflection in the dark screen until the hot-water bottle turned cold and the ice in her glass melted completely away.

14

Morgan knew it was bound to happen. Though she'd tried to restrict her socializing to her orchestra friends these days, thus avoiding Britney and David, not to mention Ethan, she knew that Arbor Valley was small enough, interwoven enough, that one of these nights . . .

And there they were. In the group of kids clustered in the movie theater lobby, all having met up together with text messages flying about what to see, where to meet, and what time. Britney and David were holding hands, in the thick of the crowd.

They hadn't noticed her yet. Morgan stood between the two sets of double doors in the theater as Friday night traffic pushed past her. She pretended to be digging in her purse for something and stepped to the side.

They looked great together. Britney had that strawberry-blond hair that was almost pink, falling in soft waves meant to look natural, but Morgan knew she used hot rollers every day. David always had that kind of rugged, outdoorsy look to him with his square chin and broad shoulders. He was so much taller than Britney she looked positively elfin.

Britney shimmered. That's what she was doing. In the garish lighting of the movie theater she managed to reflect golden rays. No wonder he loved her. And Britney — whose college ambitions didn't stretch much further than going to parties and tailgates — probably never talked to David about SATs or the future. Probably never told him she didn't have time to see him because of orchestra practice.

The ripple of David's sudden boisterous laughter carried across the lobby right to where Morgan stood, as couples pushed open the door to go inside. With his laugh he pulled Britney in closer, and she laughed, too, her eyes lit up and shining, and her hand over her mouth, which was in a faux-shocked "O." Morgan knew they were talking about her. Telling some joke about that scarface freak who thought she could hang out with them, and how pathetic was that? Britney slapped David's chest weakly in a fake rebuke for whatever he'd just said.

He was probably laughing about her in

bed that first time, how she'd held her breath and scrunched her eyes, like she was getting a flu shot or something.

Morgan turned away and charged out of the theater. In a crowd that big, no one would miss her. They'd assume she didn't get the messages, and they'd probably be relieved in fact, scolding whoever had been dumb enough to include her in the first place.

She stomped through the fresh powdery snow in her silly thin flats, wishing she'd worn those fluffy boots that always seemed to look stupid on her but that other girls — smooth-skinned, confident girls — could wear anyway.

She didn't want to go home, exactly.

Her mother had blurted out last night that Boston University was too expensive, and too far away, and she would have told her right away if only Morgan had said up front she was applying there, and in fact she was annoyed at the waste of $75 for the fee. That even if her father got promoted to superintendent tomorrow — which still probably wouldn't be enough money — they didn't like the idea of her being thousands of miles from home, with no support system close by, and they weren't exactly in a position to hop on a plane at a moment's notice if she should have a problem.

What problem? she'd asked, feeling cold through and through, right to her gut, like a hard ball of ice was freezing in her center. A stomachache? A bad grade? She'd handle it.

Her mom was resolute. Too far, too far, too far. All night long those words echoed in her head.

A scrap of poem was bouncing around in her mind.

Too far gone, too far wrong, too far from what, too far from you? Too far to care, too far to ask, too far for fair . . .

The parking lot was packed, and she'd been running late, so she'd been forced to park so far away that the snowplows hadn't done a thorough job back in this section. Snow trickled in over her flats across her bare feet. Her hands began to shake with cold, as the wind whipped her long hair across her face.

She bobbled her keys, and they vanished into a pile of the fluffy snow that had been trickling prettily all day.

"Shit!"

She bent to search the snow with her rapidly numbing fingers. She started to brush over something that felt like her keychain, when she noticed she was standing over a drainage grate.

She dug with both hands until her fingers brushed metal, but then it slipped away and a moment later she heard a splash.

"No!" she cried out loud. "Dammit all to hell."

Now she'd have to call her parents for the spare keys to come to her rescue, and she'd have to explain why she didn't go into the movie, unless she made up some story about not feeling well. She stomped her foot in frustration, and it tingled with numbing cold.

This also meant she was locked out of her car and would have to go inside somewhere to wait for them or risk dying of exposure because she just had to look cute by not wearing a hat, or boots, or even stupid gloves that might have kept her hands from shaking.

"I hate this!" she shouted out loud, her voice breaking up into sobs.

"Morgan?" said a voice behind her, and she squealed a little.

"Mr. Hill?"

It was. Her calc teacher, standing there in the parking lot next to a small SUV. He was wearing jeans and a close-fitting knit sweater, a black leather coat open over the top of that. In the faded yellow light of a distant lamppost, she could see black stubble over his chin. The rest of his face seemed ruddy, like he'd been outside awhile. "Are you all right?" he asked.

"Yeah. Well, no. I dropped my keys down a sewer grate."

"That sucks."

"Yeah. I have to call my folks and wait for them, but I don't want to go in there." She jerked her head toward the theater.

"How come?"

"My ex and his new girlfriend."

Mr. Hill juggled his keys briefly between his hands, looking up in the air. Then he looked around him in both directions.

"Say, you want to wait in my car? For a while, I mean? Don't tell anybody, it's probably not really considered appropriate, but . . . You can always hop out when they're due to show up . . ."

Morgan drooped with relief. "That would be great. It's either that or wait over there at the sports bar, and I don't feel like doing that, either." She approached the car, and he escorted her to the passenger side.

"No, you sure don't. It's full of teachers right now."

He glanced around one more time, then opened the door and held out his hand.

Morgan could have pulled up using the door frame, but she went ahead and accepted his hand. She flashed on an image of a fine lady being helped into a carriage and she almost giggled. He shut the door carefully behind her and trudged around to his side.

Morgan's heart started to work a little harder, like she was out of breath.

He settled into the car, and as he closed the door, Morgan caught his scent. A spicy cologne. Her heart started to pound in earnest. In contrast to the noise of traffic and winter wind outside, it was like a monastery inside the car.

Her hands were now reddened with blood rushing back into them. Her fingers felt fat and clumsy as she bobbled the phone, screwing up the touch screen.

"Here," Mr. Hill said, cranking the engine. "Why don't you wait a minute and warm up."

The blower was cold at first, but in moments, delicious heat poured out, and Morgan held her hands in front of the vents, feeling her fingers prickle with returning warmth.

"I think I have to make a call, too," he said. "I've probably had one too many to get on the road."

Morgan actually wondered for a moment, Too many what? Until she made the connection between the sports bar and Mr. Hill's ruddy face.

"That's probably smart," she said. "Like the billboard says, a cab is cheaper than a DUI."

"Yep." He sighed heavily. "I know my wife will be pissed at me, though, if I come home in a cab. She'll get on me for drinking too much."

"She'd rather you drive yourself drunk?"

"She'd rather I not go out at all."

"Wow. Really?"

"Not exactly." Mr. Hill shook his head. "I don't want to make her sound like a battle-ax or anything. She's just not really one for going out a lot. Especially lately. Like tonight, she said she had to work. She could have gotten out of it, though, I think. She just didn't want to go out."

Morgan's curiosity perked up. "How come?"

"She's been depressed. She comes home, she doesn't talk to me, she drifts around the house with this sad face all the time. It's like, hello! I'm here, your husband, remember me?"

"What's wrong with her?"

Mr. Hill tapped his fingers on the steering

wheel to some rhythm only he could hear. He squinted across the parking lot, watching the silhouetted figures emerge from the bar. Stripes, it was called, and it was decorated outside like a referee's shirt.

"She wants to have a baby, I think I told you that before. I did, too, for a while. I like kids, and being a dad would be cool. But I didn't know there'd be doctors and drugs and needles and procedures. It's like something out of Frankenstein. Franken-baby." Mr. Hill laughed bitterly. "I shouldn't be talking like this. You don't want to hear this garbage."

Morgan shrugged. "I don't mind. It sounds like you need to get it out."

His shoulders drooped, and he briefly rested his head on the steering wheel. "I can't talk to her, because she's so deep in it. I can't talk to my parents or my brother because Perfect Greg is having a baby in his perfect house with his perfect wife. They'd never get it."

"What about friends?"

"Guys don't talk to guys about shit like this."

"Yeah."

"I wish I didn't feel like such a failure all the time."

Morgan started to reach out for his arm,

then drew her hand back . . . He was a teacher, after all. Yet, he didn't seem like Mr. Hill, slumped there in the driver's seat of his car. He was simply a person. Talking to her like a person, too.

"You're not a failure. These things happen and we can't control it. What matters is how you react. Do you curl up in a ball and cry, or do you get up and do something to make yourself feel better?"

Mr. Hill turned to her in his seat. "Anyone ever tell you how wise you are?"

Morgan smirked and shook her head. "All the damn time. Lot of good it does me."

"You're an old soul."

"I've heard that one before, too."

Morgan felt her breath go shallow under the spotlight of his sudden direct stare. His face was in shadow, but from what she could see, he wore an expression of intense interest, as if he'd never seen her before and she was the most fascinating thing he'd ever laid eyes on.

Then he reached out and stroked her hair.

Morgan felt her pulse everywhere at once: throbbing in her face, her hands, her stomach, even — yes, there too, dear God, yes. This must be what everyone was so excited about.

She reached up with her own hand and

clenched his. The connection was a jolt, and before Morgan could think, she was leaning toward him and their faces met somewhere over the emergency brake.

His mouth on hers was firm without being aggressive. He tasted like mint over the tang of beer. His tongue flicked the tip of hers, and a groan escaped her. Her body seemed to move toward him by itself, and she was all too happy to let it. The goddamn emergency brake was in the way.

A horn sounded, and she yelped and they broke apart, panting.

He looked over at his steering wheel, accusingly. He'd bumped it with his elbow. He started laughing, and so did she, also wanting to cry out to be touched again.

His mirth faded, and so did his complexion.

"Oh, God," he said. "I'm so sorry, oh God . . ."

"Don't be," she said, her voice coming out breathy and high. "I wanted you to."

"I'm in so much trouble," he said, pushing his hands through his hair, looking through the windshield to see if anyone was out there ready to jump out of the bushes and report him.

"No, you're not. No one saw us. And I'm not upset. I'm not unwilling." Morgan scarcely realized what she was saying, but she went with it anyway, her body charged and powerful, feeling more alive than she'd been in . . . Ever. More alive than ever.

She repeated. "I'm not unwilling."

Mr. Hill seemed mollified, but he rubbed his face. "We can't. For a million reasons, I mean — Christ, your dad is my boss. You'd better call your folks." He put the car in reverse. "I'll drive you back up to the theater door. Your ex probably went into the movie by now, so you don't have to run into him."

"Don't act like that was some dirty, awful thing just now. If you treat this like some dirty shame, then what does that make me?"

He paused with his hands on the wheel, not having backed out of the parking space. "I didn't mean that. You have to see how crazy that was. How wrong."

"Didn't feel wrong to me."

"Me either," he murmured, and he backed out of the parking space with exaggerated care.

Morgan didn't press him further. She could still feel the heat of his lips on hers and spent the next silent moments replaying their kiss, never doubting for a moment they were going to do that again.

"How did you drop your keys down the

sewer?" was the first thing her mother said.

She replied, as she took the spare set of keys from her mother's hand through the open window of her car, "Because I'm a terrible wretch and the worst daughter in the history of families."

"Ha, ha. Are you coming straight home? Or going out somewhere else, or what?"

Morgan paused. She had been assuming she would have to go home, but her mother was assuming no such thing.

"No, we're going out to grab some pizza or something."

"Okay, well, don't be too late. And for heaven's sake, be careful on the roads. Love you."

"Love you, too," Morgan trilled, as her mom's car pulled away.

This time she glided through the snow, hardly aware of the cold. Every part of her felt sharp and bright. The world looked distinct and dimensional in a way she hadn't seen it in months. Every dancing flake in the lamplight seemed like a star.

She cranked up the heat in her old Chevy, noting that she had a view of the front of the bar. So she waited.

She'd been listening to NPR on the way to the movies, but she shut off the British reporter relating tragedies in sub-Saharan Africa.

It was wrong, Mr. Hill had said, and Morgan knew that, obviously. He was married, she was young.

But it was once wrong for a black man to marry a white woman, too. She thought back to last week, watching *Guess Who's Coming to Dinner?* with her mother on their weekly movie night. A privileged white girl fell in love with Sydney Poitier, and who wouldn't? Morgan spent much of the movie in disbelief that their marriage should be a problem for anyone, and Dinah kept insisting that it was, especially for children they might have had, back then.

Love triumphed, of course, with a dramatic speech by Spencer Tracy, while Katharine Hepburn gazed at him with adoring, shining eyes.

She spotted the taxicab, and she knew even from that distance it was Mr. Hill climbing into it. The yellow cab was easy to follow in the snow, and follow she did, pulling to the side of the road at the end of a dark suburban block.

She watched him weave his way out of the cab and stand in the circle of his porch light, fumbling with his keys.

A shadow cast itself over her bright,

vibrant mood.

Maybe he only kissed her because he was drunk. Maybe he wouldn't even remember it tomorrow, and she'd be just a moment's indiscretion, and nothing at all to take seriously.

But no. She felt certain as the taxicab roared off and she idled slowly past his house — noting the address on a gum wrapper from her purse — that they'd shared something that couldn't exist solely on the fumes of beer.

Morgan looked at the dashboard clock. She had plenty of time to actually get a bite to eat after the movie she hadn't actually seen. She sent a text to Britney:

Sorry late for movie go out for pizza after?

Suddenly she didn't mind seeing David and Britney together. In fact, she was going to enjoy seeing them treat their silly little high school fling like it was so very important.

15

Rain curled around the hot-water bottle on the couch, torturing herself with *A Baby Story* marathon on television — the last thing she should be watching on a Saturday morning. Any morning.

She'd already had to turn the pillow over to find a dry side, having soaked the first one watching a family bring home a squirming bundle of baby after a long labor and years of infertility before that.

She'd tried to teach class for Layla the night before as promised, but the cramps knotted her up so badly she had to beg Beverly to take over, then she sat curled up and groaning behind the counter to mind the store until class dismissed and Beverly could take over the register again.

Beverly sent her home with stern instructions not to return until she felt "100 percent" and Rain thought, *What, you mean never?*

So Rain happened to be home last night when the taxi pulled up with her drunk husband inside.

She watched him feel his way up the stairway with both hands brushing along the walls, and a voice in her head asked — a voice that reminded her of the ever-practical Gran — *Would TJ still be coming home drunk if she were pregnant? Nursing a baby? Helping a grade-schooler with his homework?* Aren't we too old for this frat boy shit? Rain wondered.

Then she reminded herself of how good TJ was with his little cousins, his promise to teach his child to spiral a football. That it wasn't like he was out partying every single night and for goodness' sake, it was his birthday weekend. He hadn't driven home, and that was all she'd asked of him, really. He was allowed to cut loose once in a while.

She didn't try to talk to him. Something had been on TJ's mind already, something serious and distressing, based on the strange way he wouldn't look at her, and the way he seemed to be pale and trembling, not normally drunken traits of his.

So he'd passed out, and she'd lain awake wondering what was on his mind and dosing herself with Motrin every few hours for the terrible cramps.

The soft music swelled to a crescendo on *A Baby Story* as another mother was pushing out a new, squalling life.

Agony. But she couldn't stop trying to live vicariously, which seemed to be the best she could do. Especially if TJ refused to go through it a third time, which seemed likely.

Maybe that's what it was. He was drinking away his anxiety over whether to try again. Maybe he was torn between wanting to stop for his own sake, but not wanting to crush her hopes.

She fumbled for the remote when she heard his heavy step coming down the stairs; he'd hate to see her watching this. She flipped the television off rather than search for a new station.

TJ sat down heavily on the end of the couch, his head in his hands. "I'm a terrible human being."

"Oh, honey, no, you're not. You took a cab home, you didn't hurt anything. Maybe your own head . . ."

Rain sat up with a grimace and crawled over to join her husband. She nudged her way under his arm, the same way her parents' dog Dog did when he needed some affection.

He was draped over her as she cuddled up against him, but he wasn't responding.

Just sitting there, limp and slumped.

Rain said, "I'm not feeling well either. Tell you what. Leave your car in that parking lot today; we won't worry about it. We'll just stay here on the couch all day and watch bad TV. We'll order pizza and eat junk food and just be lazy. We won't answer the phone, we'll draw the curtains. You know how when you were little and sick your parents would spoil you? Let's spoil ourselves. Each other."

He drew her in suddenly and clenched her tight. "What did I do to deserve you?" he muttered into her hair. She could feel his lips against her scalp.

"I love you, too," she replied, happy to be distracted from her sadness and cramps.

She handed him the remote and he seemed to relax as he switched the TV on. *A Baby Story* was still playing and Rain tensed.

But he sat and watched it, instead of flipping the channel or getting upset that she was torturing herself by watching this after another failed cycle. He even chuckled when the husband got woozy in the delivery room.

Rain let herself cry a little more on TJ's shirt as another birth played out before their eyes, and he squeezed her in response.

"Hey," he said softly as the credits rolled

and the new parents cooed. "When do we have the next appointment with Dr. Gould?"

Rain turned to him and smiled with relief and surprise. "I'll call her Monday."

"Good," he said, stroking her arm as he embraced her. "Now, I definitely think we should watch something else."

"There's an Iron Chef marathon."

"Now you're talking," said TJ.

Rain let herself doze in the circle of his strong arms, not daring to question what brought about his change of attitude.

When Rain woke, the curtains were closed and she felt unmoored. She was alone on the couch, and she sat halfway up, trying to remember what time of day it was. She squinted at the clock; it was the middle of the afternoon. She'd slept through lunch.

She pulled an afghan around her against a chill and wandered the house, looking for TJ.

There was a note on the table: "Walking to get the car. Sorry about last night."

Walking? That would take him ages, and in this weather?

He was punishing himself. Trudging miles through the snow and wind with a hangover was his penance for getting drunk in the first place. Gestures like this were why she could never stay angry at him.

She picked up her phone to call, to demand that he tell her where he was, where the car was, so they could drive out and get it . . . it was pointless to go tromping around in the snow.

She heard the faint, tinny strains of "Don't Stop Believing" issue from somewhere else in the house and realized he'd left his phone at home.

Rain considered heading out into the Michigan winter white to go find him. All she'd have to do is drive the route between their house and the bar and surely she would spot him, trudging along. She could almost picture how he would look: the hangdog face, his hair wet with melted snow. He would probably argue with her about getting into the car, insisting he deserved to be cold.

Then again, he could be on his way back with the car even now; she'd been sleeping long enough. They'd miss each other, and the excursion would be pointless.

Rain shook her head and went to the yoga studio next to their bedroom, which in actual fact was the nursery, was going to be the nursery the first day they toured this house as potential buyers, only it needed a purpose before the baby. Now she referred to it as the studio to avoid a jinx. Not getting pregnant was turning her as superstitious as TJ, or Beverly with her chakras and crystals.

Rain rolled out her mat and knotted her hair roughly behind her head with one of the stray hair elastics lying around on the beat-up yard sale dresser that sat in the corner — the dresser she would surely paint fresh bright white, as soon as she had reason to.

She caught a glimpse of herself in the long mirror she'd propped up against one wall. Her face was flushed red and marred with sleep creases. Her eyes were puffy, and her hair was lank and dirty. She suddenly pictured adorable, pert Layla in her all fertile youthfulness . . . She shook her head and folded into a forward bend. Stupid to think like that. Even Layla must get sleep creases and puffy eyes sometimes.

Her abdomen felt looser, the cramps less pronounced. She breathed her way through her warm-up sun salutations until her joints slid easily in the sockets and her muscles felt long and warm, her spine long with tangible space between the bones.

Should she try it now? Well, why not?

She bent her knees into a squat, preparing

for *Eka Pada Koundiyasana I,* a hand balancing posture that would end up, if she managed it, with her weight on her hands and forearms, bent at the elbows, her body parallel to the floor. Her lower half would be twisted to the side, one leg behind her, one leg outward, balanced on her elbow.

She'd seen Beverly do this in a workshop, and she was not supposed to be jealous. Her childhood religion and her yogic study had both taught her that much about envy. The physical form was not the point. Physical achievement was not the goal, as her friend always said.

Oh stuff it, Beverly, she'd wanted to say. Easy for you to say because you can do it.

Beverly had looked at once powerful and light as air, serene and still, yet the very picture of action and vitality. Rain knew well how much strength was required to remain so very still.

Rain eased her bent knees and hips into position and was about to straighten into the pose, her forearms already shaking, trying to breathe through the burning in her shoulders and core . . .

The back door swung open. "Rain!" TJ called.

Rain fell forward, past the edge of the mat, knocking her chin on the wood floor and biting her tongue. "Shit," she muttered, untangling her limbs. She tasted the metallic bite of her own blood. She put the back of her hand to her lip and came away with a smudge of red.

She walked down to the kitchen, feeling her long, soft muscles seem to curl up tight at the very presence of her husband.

He was, as she'd predicted, wet, cold, and hangdog.

"You okay?" she asked. "I would have driven you to the car."

"It wasn't your fault I got drunk last night. I didn't want to make you go out."

She took a paper towel and dabbed her lip, and TJ finally noticed, having shrugged out of his coat and begun to make fresh coffee, that she was bleeding.

"Baby, what happened?" he said, rushing over to her as if she were hemorrhaging.

"Nothing. Fell getting into a posture, it's nothing."

"Are you sure? It looks awful . . ."

"It's nothing, I said," Rain snapped, short on patience for his outsize concern over a tiny nick in her mouth, compared to the aching hollow of being childless again, still, always.

He drew back, blinked a few times. Rain

watched as his countenance darkened, and he withdrew from her.

16

Morgan brushed her hair until it shone. She stroked lip gloss across her lips. She dabbed another swipe of concealer under her eyes.

She may have begun to feel like a different woman — awakened, fresh — after the kiss, but the nightmares refused to recede. In the one last night, the twins fell into a black pit, shrieking for her, and she reached down, down, down and couldn't reach them, but she couldn't fall, either, just stretched down endlessly, always failing to catch them.

But with the makeup, no one could even tell she was tired. Her eyes looked brighter, she thought. She turned her face slightly to one side, giving her bedroom mirror a three-quarter profile view, the same one she'd employed for her senior pictures. The photographer had tried to suggest other angles, other poses, but Morgan would just shake her head and resume her prior position. His name was Rick something, and he was gray-haired with a scowling face like a pile of rocks, all angles and furrows.

Morgan did not dignify his annoyance with an awkward explanation. She just kept the scar hidden safely away like the dark side of the moon.

Lighter, Morgan thought, regarding herself at home in the mirror. She felt lighter. That's what allowed this brighter, vibrant feeling. She no longer cared what her brothers were doing or whether her mother was upset about it. She was going to be no one's crutch anymore.

She didn't even care about her parents' verdict about Boston. When she turned eighteen, they no longer had any legal say, and if she wanted to move to Boston and wait tables until she could pay for college, she would do it and they couldn't stop her.

Or maybe she wouldn't bother with Boston, anyway. She felt like she was peeling off the old Morgan like dead skin. Or better yet: The new, adult Morgan was burning her way out, phoenix-like. The same Morgan who sat right next to Britney and David laughing at the restaurant Friday night and felt nothing, even when David let his hand drift ever farther up Britney's thigh.

She capped her lip gloss with an air of

satisfaction. She was looking forward to this Monday, yes, she was.

"Hi, David," Morgan said, swinging into her desk in Mr. Hill's calc class.

"Hey," David replied, a half smile on his face. She caught him glancing down at her hips, the shape of which today were on full view because she'd given up on the frilly peasant shirt she would normally have worn and chosen a close-fitting, finely knit sweater that she'd bought on a whim and rarely took out of the closet.

She smiled to herself and took out her notebook, turning past earlier pages with snatches of poetry in the margin. She rolled her eyes at herself and selected a fresh, new page.

Mr. Hill had not yet arrived in class, and for a moment Morgan's mood faltered. Had he called in sick? Or worse, resigned in fear of facing her again?

But no, there he was. Looking a little pale and a little scruffy, but still himself. He gave the class a wan smile and swept his eyes across the room. Morgan noticed he did not look at her.

He did not have to look at her, though, for her plan to work. The class handed their homework pages forward to the first desk in each row, and Mr. Hill collected all the papers from those kids. No one looked at anyone else's paper, why would they? And they certainly would never turn a math assignment over and look at the back as they handed it forward.

Which is why she didn't worry about anyone else seeing what she'd written on the back of her homework page, after the last problem.

We should talk, she wrote, and signed it, *M.* She'd added a cursive flourish to her initial. Then she'd carefully printed her cell number.

Mr. Hill collected all the papers and stacked them carefully on his desk. Then he slipped them into his briefcase. Of course he would likely grade them at home. His free hour for planning and whatnot was earlier in the day than this. A flutter of nerves erupted in her chest; is it possible his wife would see it?

She took a deep breath in and out. Didn't matter now. Already done. Some things you could never take back.

She caught herself running a finger down her scar, and she brought her hands back to the desk. She tried to look like any other student, just this side of bored to death.

■ ■ ■ ■

Mrs. DeWitt was pleased to see her on time in the band room.

Morgan had her cello all tuned, her bow all rosined, and she'd been rehearsing bits of her solo on her own. Her fingers seemed clumsy and fat today, her bowing arm tired, and the notes didn't trip lightly the way they should. The Elgar piece they'd chosen — Concerto in E Minor, fourth movement — was difficult, with intricate fingerings and leaps up and down the fingerboard, not to mention the musicality of the piece, from slow lush phrases to *allegro* sections. Morgan had been talked into it. Today, it showed.

In prior orchestra years, Morgan would have given into someone's pleading for a cello in their quartet and played her unobtrusive harmonies, keeping time with her toe inside her shoe while the other musicians argued about tempo or something. This time, in honor of her senior year, she'd given in to her teacher's prodding to try this difficult solo, with a little extra coaching from Mrs. DeWitt.

Today, Mrs. DeWitt's mood darkened as she got more frustrated with Morgan's mistakes, and Morgan was regretting ever attempting a solo in the first place. What had she been thinking?

The combination of retired, crotchety teacher and Morgan's own sleepless exhaustion — this was always the hardest part of the day, like a final sprint in a marathon when lungs are burning and legs are jelly — turned the atmosphere rotten.

When Mrs. DeWitt opined, "Really, you are better than this. I don't know why I bother to be here if you won't take the time to perfect the fingering at home."

"I don't know why you're here, either, if you're just going to be a jerk."

Mrs. DeWitt banged her two tiny fists on the piano keys, and the clang startled Morgan's bow out of her hand. Morgan bent to pick it up. "Well, I never!" Mrs. DeWitt exclaimed, sounding about eighty-five instead of just sixtyish. "That's it." She started stacking her music. "I'm done. This was truly a waste of time."

Morgan knew she should call her back, apologize, grovel even. Mrs. DeWitt herself lingered at the door as if waiting for such a thing. Morgan only smiled and waved her bow in a mockery of a farewell.

Mrs. DeWitt huffed one more time and stormed out, much to Morgan's relief.

"Good riddance, crusty old bitch," she muttered.

She stared at her phone, wishing it would ring, or chime for a text. Nonsense, though. Mr. Hill wouldn't risk calling her from school. What would he do, then? Make an excuse for an errand and call from the car, later tonight perhaps.

Thank God for cell phones, Morgan thought, as she readied her bow and started playing once more, her clumsy fingers already finding the music again.

Then she heard it. Her phone. She threw her bow down on the music stand and snatched up the phone.

"Hello?"

"That was quite a risk you took."

"I know. Where are you?"

"In my car in the parking lot. And, no, you can't join me."

"I wasn't going to ask." Morgan frowned. How dumb did he think she was? "But we can't just let something like that go and pretend it didn't happen."

He didn't reply. She thought she could hear him tapping the wheel.

"Because it's not just me, and it wasn't just the drinks, was it?"

Still silence. Somewhere a ticking second hand registered at jackhammer volume. The concerto was still looping in her mind, the way it should be played, not the way she'd been murdering it. She should hang up. This was insane, and she'd been a childish fool to think he'd ever —

"I can't stop thinking about you."

He'd said it in a rush, as if he'd known she was about to hang up.

Morgan let herself absorb this triumph for a moment, then started to worry for him. The stress must be tremendous. She thought of his wife and the problems he'd mentioned.

"Are you okay?" Morgan asked. "Are you . . . How are things at home?"

"Tough," Mr. Hill answered through a sigh, puffing out the word.

"That's too bad."

Silence. The line crackled.

"Hello?" Morgan said, almost shouting, fearing that if she lost the connection he'd never call her back.

"I'm here. I can't make her happy anymore. No matter what I try."

"She's shutting you out."

"Yeah," he said. The word almost a groan. Morgan wanted to fly to his side and hold him until he stopped sounding like that. "I can't go on like this. She'll barely even talk to me; it's like I'm not even there."

Morgan scowled. Okay, so she was sad, but did that give her the right to ignore her husband? As if he didn't have feelings of his own?

"I want to see you," she blurted.

After a pause in which she felt her whole new self hanging in the balance, he whispered, "How?" — the word at once a plea and a groan.

Morgan glanced around the empty room, feeling a smile play across her lips. She tried to sound appropriately mature and grave as she replied, "We'll find a way."

17

Few things in the world could stop Dinah's heart like the school's phone number on caller ID.

Such a call could mean Morgan had a stomach virus, or the boys got into a fist-fight, or that Connor was mouthing off again. The school never called to say, "Good job, Dinah. You're a great mom and your kids are awesome. We just wanted you to know."

So on this wintry Monday, when the phone yanked Dinah from work on the Planning Commission documents in her upstairs office, her first thought was, *Oh no, when we almost made it to winter break.*

She screwed her eyes shut and answered with a curt greeting.

"Hello, Mrs. Monetti? How are you?" asked Jenny from the high school office.

"That depends on what you're about to tell me."

A sigh on the other end. "Well, Mr. Jackson would like you to come down to talk about Jared."

"Jared?"

Before they left the Montessori school, it tended to be Connor who ended up in the office, usually defending his brother from some moron bully calling Jared a retard or pushing Jared in the hall hard enough to stumble. Even at their new school, Connor's frustration over schoolwork could erupt in a disrespectful outburst against the teacher and a call home.

"What happened to Jared?"

"Nothing happened to him," Jenny answered, emphasizing the "to." She went on, lowering her voice. She imagined Jenny dipping her head behind the high receptionist desk. "He was caught in the parking lot smoking pot."

"No! No way."

Jenny hastened to add, "I was just asked to call you, I don't know anything about it directly."

"I'll be right there," Dinah replied, already picking up her purse and rooting for her keys.

Principal Jackson was seated behind his desk. Jared was slouched in one of the "lecture chairs" on the other side, and Dinah took the other. Joe was nowhere around, and would not be, for this. The other principals always dealt with "faculty brats" as a matter of policy and were not even allowed to discuss it with Joe. Dinah would have to be the one to tell him about the incident, unless someone whispered it to Joe unofficially. She couldn't decide which would be worse.

"What exactly happened?" Dinah began without preamble.

"Your son was caught smoking marijuana in the parking lot this morning," Mr. Jackson said, sighing.

"Were you?" she asked Jared.

"I wasn't," he grumbled. "Some kids with me were. But I wasn't."

Mr. Jackson interjected, "He smells like Woodstock."

Dinah did notice that funny, woodsy smell. But . . . Jared? It didn't make sense.

"Mr. Jackson, could I have a minute to talk with Jared alone?"

He nodded and sighed again as if he were Atlas himself carrying the world. His eyes looked sunken and his face puffy. His hair — what remained of it — was verging from gray right into white. No wonder he was retiring. He left his own office with the remark, "I'll be back in ten minutes, and we'll talk consequences."

Jared scowled at his own crossed ankles. "I didn't do it. Scout's honor."

"What were you doing out there, then?"

"Hanging with my friends. It's not my fault that the only cool people in this school smoke weed."

Dinah wanted to lie on the floor and cry. When the boys were toddlers and throwing tandem tantrums, she'd sometimes do it. She'd get right down on the floor and start to scream and cry with them. Once in a while they'd stop their own fit and give her a look like, *What the hell . . . ?*

"If those are the kind of friends you've picked, we've got to take you out of this school. You're not ready."

Jared bolted upright in his chair, his eyes suddenly wide open and wild, glasses slipping down his nose. "No! Mom, don't, please! I'm sorry, I screwed up, but please don't take me out of this school. I don't wanna go to some special school again for retards."

"You will not use that word or so help me I'll knock you to next week. The Montessori school was not for 'retards' or special needs kids or anything. It was based on an educational philosophy, and it was a good fit for —"

"Whatever, Mom. It's not like you yanked us out of private school because we were doing so awesome."

Those were the days she'd earned her particular reputation. Jared's shuffling, awkward walk and his glasses made him a target, and his teacher kept minimizing, excusing. And those nasty little cretins were clever. They knew better than to do something obvious like stick his head in a toilet. No, they'd say vicious things under their breath when he walked by, "accidentally" bump into him in the halls so that he stumbled into the wall. Once, he fell through a doorway and cracked his head on the hard gym floor. Each time Dinah complained, and the sneaky brats made innocent faces. They were joking, or it was an accident. It would be Connor — who would throw a kid to the ground in two seconds if he saw someone pick on his twin — who got labeled a bully.

The worst day, she screamed at the teacher who'd called the twins *classic problem children* while also claiming Jared needed to "grow up and be a man about a little teasing": "You're not protecting my son!"

Okay, so maybe it hadn't been her brightest idea to throw that classroom chair. But she didn't throw it directly at Mrs. White. It was clearly thrown sideways, out of frustration only.

Every other time, a firm voice and furious glare had gotten at least some minor appeasement from the school: stricter adherence to Jared's disability accommodations, a reduced punishment for Connor once circumstances were explained. Her earliest, careful, polite requests from the school had gone ignored, so what did they expect?

Jared piped up, remembering all this, too. "You almost got arrested for throwing a chair, and then we went to the dork school. Anyway, dork school only goes up to eighth grade."

"Three months into the regular public high school and you're claiming that the stoners are the only cool people in school and cutting class to hang out with them while they get high. What am I supposed to do? Get excited about this? Congratulate you?"

Jared was back to slouching. "They all wanted to go out to that dude's car. What was I supposed to say, 'My mommy will yell at me so I can't?' They're the only friends I've ever had who don't care that I was a preemie and I have thick glasses and I can't walk normal. They're just cool."

"So what's next, then? They offer you some weed and you don't want to look like a nerd so you take it? And then what else do you do so that you can stay cool? Pot when you're a freshman and what, heroin by the time you're a senior?"

"I told you, I didn't do it."

Dinah peered hard at Jared's watery blue eyes behind his thick glasses. "Swear to me that you didn't."

He looked right at her, his lip trembling just like it used to when he was little. "I swear I didn't do it." His changing voice cracked.

She sat back in her chair and massaged her temples. Jared toyed with one of those Newton's cradle toys on the principal's desk, and they listened to the *clack-clack-clack* without speaking until Mr. Jackson came back.

He settled himself behind the desk. "Dinah, the mandatory consequence for drug use on school property is a week's suspension."

Dinah sat up straight and squared herself to face Mr. Jackson. "But he didn't do it."

He cocked his head at her. "Dinah. C'mon."

Jared grumbled, "I knew he wouldn't

believe me."

"He swears he didn't."

"I'm sure he does. You should have gotten a whiff of him when he first came in here. And his eyes were all red, and his eyelids were droopy."

"His eyes get irritated. He has allergies."

Pete Jackson shook his large head, staring down at his desk. "Allergies. Look, this is the consequence. We're not going to sit here and have a trial, and I can't take his word for it. If I took every kid's word for their innocence, it would be anarchy in here."

Dinah flushed. "I could go to the superintendent."

"If you feel you must, you have that right. But I'm telling you that he is not going to start meddling in individual student disciplinary matters. He never has, and he certainly won't now."

Dinah heard his unspoken phrase loud and clear. *Especially not for one of your boys. Everyone knows what they're like.*

She shoved back her chair. "So I may take him home now?"

Pete Jackson nodded. "Yes. He can get his assignments online. Make sure to take all his books."

"Before we go, Pete, I have to say something. You think you're being very tough and wise. You'll probably go home and congratulate yourself on how firm you were. Well, let me give you some food for thought. As much as I respect rules and order and teach my children to do the same, I'm also not afraid to call bullshit when I see it." The principal leaned back in his chair, eyebrows raised slightly, his craggy face so resigned he looked rather bored. "You have no reason to disbelieve Jared, who has never been in this type of trouble before, but you are condemning him for guilt by association and because you think you know what kind of kid he is. You are not going to define him by this." Dinah thumped her index finger into the top of his desk. "He is going to excel despite the unfairness, and someday you're going to look back and realize just how terribly wrong you were just now. Today this tirade of mine is all the confirmation you need that you're right; I can see it in your face. Must be nice, that confidence. Too bad it comes from willful blindness for everything that doesn't support your narrow, preconceived bias."

Jared sighed loudly. "Can we just go, Mom?"

Dinah opened the office door by way of answer. At the last moment she turned back to Mr. Jackson, who still wore an expression of resigned exhaustion, and said, "Happy holidays."

Dinah and Joe were squared off in Joe's home office like prizefighters.

They had retreated there and closed the door after dinner. Joe had lectured Jared through the entire meal about his dangerous path and how he would have no privileges whatsoever for the entire winter break, until Dinah tried to speak up and Joe stormed off into his office for a "talk." Only "talk" had given way immediately to "fight," and it was only with the greatest of effort that Dinah kept her voice to a hissing whisper instead of a bellow when Joe had suggested some kind of camp for rebellious teens.

"That's ridiculous," she blurted. "My God, what's wrong with you? I told you, he didn't even actually smoke it."

"Sure he didn't smoke it. And I'm the pope in Rome. It wouldn't kill him. Maybe what he needs is some damn discipline for once in his life."

"For once?"

"Yeah, for once. Your whole life you've been treating those boys like they're glass and making excuses for their every mistake."

"I've been protecting them because no

one else seems to give a shit, but I never thought I'd have to protect them from you."

"Dinah, we can't just write this off as a phase."

"And we are not sending him off to some teenage boot camp for people to scream in his face and call him names and make him run laps until he throws up."

"I'm not saying that kind of place; I'm just thinking out loud. At least I'm taking it seriously."

"And I'm not. That's what you mean."

"I'm just saying this crap has got to be nipped in the bud. Do you know how many kids I've seen walk through this door of 'just a little pot' and end up in prison? Or flipping burgers because they can't hold any other job? Wake up, Dinah."

"Oh, I'm awake. Believe me. I'm his mother, and you're not sending him anywhere."

She turned to leave.

"Dinah, so help me, don't you go and undermine me. Don't you overrule me and take back his grounding."

"Or what? You'll send me to military school, too?"

Dinah charged up the steps and into the boys' room, hearing Joe muttering behind her. She had the vague sense that her marriage was crumbling in her wake, and that to save it she'd have to turn back and snatch up the pieces before it was too far gone.

She knocked and pushed open the twins' door.

Without having to be asked to leave, Connor rose. "I'm gonna get a snack. I'm done with my homework anyway."

Jared was rubbing the lenses of his glasses in his shirt and wouldn't look up.

"Jared. Look at me."

He only shook his head. "Can't."

"Why not?"

"I'm embarrassed. I mean, Dad thinks I'm some druggie waste of space."

Dinah paused on a mental image of her throttling Joe for making their boy feel like this. "He doesn't. He didn't mean that; he's frustrated and scared for you. You've got to remember how many kids he's seen screw up their lives with drugs. Yes, I know you didn't do it, but you've got to admit that as a principal he's heard that one, too."

"He should be my dad in the house. Not an assistant principal."

Dinah sucked in a breath through her nose. He should be a dad indeed. Why wasn't he up there with her? Why wasn't he talking to Jared except to bellow at him?

Jared drew himself together, his knees up

to his chest and his arms folded tightly across. His pant legs rode up and Dinah got a glimpse of his ankles; he was so thin. So much thinner than his twin. Jared was the one born second, born thinner and weaker. He was the last one home. Dinah had felt torn asunder to have one twin at home in his crib where he belonged and the other still hooked up to machines.

She spied a tear leaking out of his eye and she wanted to leap across the bed and fold him in her arms. But she knew from experience he would shrug her off if she did. She settled for patting the top of his foot.

He croaked, "I'm sorry I made you guys fight."

"It's not your fault."

"So you always say."

"Because it's true."

After a moment's stillness, Jared unfolded and slouched back against his headboard, stretching out on the bed.

Dinah patted his shin. "But I'm worried about you, too. I don't want to have to take you out of the high school, but I can't turn a blind eye, either. If you can't figure out how to have a social life without getting caught up in a bad crowd, we'll have to think of something else."

"What? Homeschool?" Jared rolled his

eyes. “Like you could do that.”

“Hey, don’t underestimate your old mom.”

“I mean, hello? You’ve got a business to run.”

With a thud in her chest Dinah realized she could in fact homeschool the boys, if she sold the Den, which would get markedly more valuable with an entertainment license attached.

“There are private schools around. We’d think of something. But we won’t have to, right? Because you can still steer this back on course, right, Jared?”

He nodded, looking away, in his posture of wanting her to just leave now that the lecture was over.

Knowing he wouldn’t like it, she dashed over to plant a kiss on his forehead.

Dinah descended the stairs and was greeted in the kitchen by a look from her husband, who was warming up his cold dinner plate. “You make everything all better now?”

Dinah turned away from him by way of answer and threw herself down on the living room couch, listening to the clicking and scraping of Joe’s utensils on his plate, not another word uttered between them.

Part 2

18

June 6, 2012

Dinah watched as the prosecutor rose, straightened his tie, and prepared to lay out the case against TJ Hill.

She tried to shut off, unplug, and drift away somewhere else so she wouldn't have to hear it.

She came to the court because it was the thing one did when one's child was victimized. You go to court and you watch the wheels of justice turn and you applaud when the bad guy is sent to the slammer.

Only this time, her daughter's name would be dragged through the gutter.

She knew in a politically correct sense that her daughter was considered a victim, an innocent. And that the newspaper had not named her, or them, as a result of its policy to protect the identity of victims of sexual crimes.

She also knew what she'd seen and heard

around town about her daughter, what she'd read online and seen on Facebook, and she could only imagine what was said privately was worse yet. Not to mention what had happened at the Den.

As far as Arbor Valley was concerned, the two of them could go straight to hell together, the debauched teacher and his teenaged adulterous lover.

"Your Honor," began Henry Davis, unfolding his lanky frame from his chair. Dinah fixed her eyes on him and tried to call up the feeling of calm and even optimism he'd inspired when they discussed the case. She'd seen him on television before — the election of the county's first black prosecutor had been big news — but they'd never met. That first day in his office, she could have swooned from gratitude for his dignified air, considering how often she'd felt the sting of judgment and whispered titillation from the rest of the town.

"How did we get here?" Henry asked rhetorically, sweeping his arm to indicate the courtroom, the situation, everything at once. "Was this an accident of fate? A simple error in judgment? Ill-fated, star-crossed love?" Those last words Henry anointed with a whiff of irritated sarcasm.

"We are here for a specific, very clear

reason that has everything to do with abuse of authority and violation of a girl under that authority. The people will show that Thomas John Hill on numerous occasions contacted the victim by cell phone and messages exchanged through her homework papers, setting up sexual liaisons in parking lots and music rehearsal rooms."

Dinah flinched, and she heard Joe suck in a breath. Henry began to pace in front of the jury, whose faces were frozen into suitably somber expressions. Dinah could not help but wonder how thrilled they really were, how they probably were giggling to their friends which trial they'd landed.

"This was no simple crush from a teenager in some inappropriate puppy love. Couldn't TJ Hill have refused to meet her anywhere, refused to take her calls? Couldn't he have reported this unwanted attention to his superiors, in fact to the girl's very own father, his boss and assistant principal at the school? We will show that Thomas John Hill did none of these things, and instead he continued to communicate, continued to meet her, despite his supposed concern for his career and her well-being.

"Now, I know that the young lady looks very mature for her age. She's not a child with training wheels on her bike and streamers coming from the handlebars. But she is nonetheless a victim. The evidence will show that she was manipulated and exploited by a grown man who was in charge of her, had authority over her, over this young woman who, by all accounts, had always been one to respect and obey authority."

A disgusted snort emanated from Morgan. Dinah could tell it was her without looking.

The prosecutor resumed his speech. "It's June now, and a senior in high school should be graduating, celebrating, becoming Facebook friends with her college roommate. A high school senior should not have to be sitting in a courtroom watching her teacher on trial for his sexual affair with her, but here we are. And there is one person to blame for that and one person only. After we present our case, you'll find it clear that Thomas John Hill is the one responsible — the only one — and deliver a verdict accordingly."

Dinah tried to be pleased at how well delivered the speech was.

But she could only imagine all those blessedly normal things Henry mentioned — Morgan graduating with giddy pride, dancing all night at prom, bubbly with promise of a bright future — and how those simple joys were gone forever. Dinah fought to keep from throwing up all over her navy blue slacks.

Rain felt unaccountably cold.

It seemed warm in the courtroom, based on how everyone else fanned themselves and how they were all shedding jackets and cardigan sweaters.

But the prosecutor's description of TJ as a manipulative abuser of a vulnerable girl under his authority made her shake so hard she was worried she'd vibrate right off the edge of the seat.

She dared not take her eyes off the front of the courtroom to see if anyone knew who she was.

Of course they would know, though. In a town this size, someone would know, and someone would tell someone else. Hell, it was probably posted online by now, courtesy of one of the vultures following this case live, blow by blow. She could almost write the post herself. "Defendant's wife in the courtroom. Shaking and looking pale."

The defense attorney rose, and Rain sucked in a breath. Now it would get better. Alexandra would tell them how this was all just a terrible misunderstanding, laced with hysteria, the flames fanned by a troubled girl who relished the attention. Something out of Arthur Miller's *Crucible.*

Alexandra rose, her heels clicking loudly. She was tall like a basketball player, her suit smart and cut well, her hair pulled back tightly from her haughty, leonine expression.

"TJ Hill is no monster," she began. "He's no pedophile. He's a respected, popular teacher and a friend to many in the community. Yes, he made some errors in judgment. Serious errors. Perhaps it doesn't make sense for TJ to have continued to stay in contact with the girl when her inappropriate attachment became known, and we'll give you that much. But TJ's mistakes do not rise to the level of a crime, they do not make him a sexual predator. The people would have you believe that they had a sexual relationship, but this is based on, as you will see, the thinnest of so-called evidence and there's enough reasonable doubt to drive an eighteen-wheeler right through it.

"Mr. Hill tried to solve this problem quietly, on his own. He couldn't take the pressure and just wanted the situation to go away; after all, he feared this very outcome. Sure, it backfired, and with the benefit of hindsight we can see what a grievous error this turned out to be.

"But imagine if you will, this beautiful teenage girl, infatuated with him to the point she left romantic messages on his phone and on her homework! Stalked his wife online to determine her work schedule! If he went to the school administrators and said he had not encouraged a bit of this, what if they didn't believe him? What if they assumed he was guilty anyway? After all, the young lady had never taken a wrong step before, so far as anyone knew, and was in fact the daughter of an assistant principal. So he met her, tried to calm her down, tried to insist there was nothing between them and never could be, thinking if he only said the right things she would give up on him and pick a more appropriate target for her puppy love, and no one would be the wiser.

"Only, as you'll see, any attention at all was enough for her to continue pursuing him, to the point of disrobing before him. I know this is upsetting to hear. You don't want to think this way of a young woman who is a National Honor Society student. But a verdict is not delivered based on gut reactions, hunches, and stereotypes. It's delivered based on the evidence, and the evidence is just not there. We are trusting you. Mr. Hill, his loving wife, his family — we are all trusting you to put your tempers and emotions aside and look only at the facts. And you will be able to reach no other conclusion than to find my client not guilty. Thank you."

Rain felt herself relax by scant degrees. Everything made perfect sense, coming from Alexandra. It all sounded so reasonable. Believable.

Reasonable doubt, she chanted to herself, repeatedly. There is plenty of room for reasonable doubt. The jury would see. They had to. Rain would consider no other possible outcome.

Morgan imagined herself a statue. Cold marble, impervious.

It was the only way she could remain seated while she listened to the sickening lies perpetrated by both sides of this farce.

First, the prosecutor making out like she was some kind of idiot child manipulated by a mastermind.

Then, his own attorney. Morgan had known he would deny it. She was prepared for this. After all, she didn't want him to go to jail either. She knew he would say whatever it was he had to say to get himself out of trouble.

But hearing herself cast as a blend of siren, stripper, and nutcase made Morgan taste bile in the back of her throat. How could he allow this to be said of her?

She closed her eyes and conjured up his smile when he walked into the courtroom. He still loved her, of course he did. He was just following his attorney's advice. After all, if he was convicted by the salivating wolves in this hick town, not only might he go to prison — up to fifteen years! Outrageous! — he'd be labeled a sex offender for the rest of his life.

Morgan punched her thigh lightly to remember her own careless mistake: the age of consent. She'd researched it online. It was sixteen in Michigan, and she was seventeen. They should have been in the clear; she never intended this. She didn't know that there was a special legal category for a teacher and student. Didn't know it would be "criminal sexual conduct III."

Thirty-five days, she told herself. Thirty-five days and she'll turn eighteen and the trial will be over. And there would be nothing anyone could do to get in their way.

19

December 19, 2011

It was the first day of Christmas break. Students all over town were thrilled to be sleeping in, playing on Facebook, going to movies and the mall. Morgan just knew it meant two whole weeks without seeing Mr. Hill.

Unless.

Morgan said through a mouthful of toast at the breakfast table, "Oh, Mom, did I tell you? Mrs. DeWitt can't rehearse with me anymore."

Her mom paused in making coffee to look at her with a wrinkled forehead. "Oh, no! What are you going to do?"

"Actually it's already worked out. She felt bad having to quit — something about a sick relative? — so she lined up a student from the community college to help me. I can drive over to the college after school and practice with her there."

"Oh, so much more driving."

Morgan shrugged. "I don't care. It's only for a few weeks until the competition anyway, unless I go to State. Anyhow, it's not all that far. Twenty minutes maybe?"

"Oh. Well, I'm glad it all worked out then."

"We might even get to meet up over break. She said she wanted to practice with me as soon as possible so we don't lose any more time."

"Wow, that's generous. Why would she do that? Do we have to pay her?"

"She gets extra credit in her class for helping me out. Kinda like volunteering points for NHS, right?"

Morgan needed her mom to stop questioning. Thankfully, just then her dad walked into the room.

She could see her mother stiffen from all the way across the kitchen. Dad didn't talk to Mom, just reached around her to grab a coffee mug.

Morgan looked back down to her toast and hoped that if they were going to get a divorce, they'd wait until she turned eighteen in the summer to spare her the drama of visitation.

Though, she thought as she put her plate in the kitchen sink and headed back to her room, she had the kind of parents who would tough it out "for the kids." Which would be better than getting shuttled back and forth. However, if her parents were going to continue not speaking to each other, that was no laugh riot, either.

Nah, they'd keep it together for the boys, she figured. They were always acting like Connor and Jared were going to pieces at any moment, and now Jared busted for smoking pot? The last thing they would do is get a divorce. Heaven forbid.

She closed her bedroom door and very quietly pressed the lock.

Morgan had perfected a way of pushing the lock button quietly so it didn't snap into place, and when she turned the doorknob to open it, if she held the lock button down with one knuckle as she turned, it didn't snap loudly back open, either. Since her parents were kind enough to knock, they'd never have to know how often she was locking her door.

Her brothers might try to barge through, but whatever.

She licked her lips and smiled at her phone. Here goes. She started a new message to the entry in her contacts list named Teresa Jane.

Got a plan

She'd searched Mr. Hill's wife online — a name like Rain in Arbor Valley? Even with the last name of Hill, Morgan had known she'd find her — and found that she was a yoga instructor and knew what times her classes were from the website of Namaste Yoga Center. So she'd chosen to text when Rain was out of the house.

What plan?

Morgan felt a thundering gallop in her chest. He was in.

Rehearsal room at AVCC. Private, lock on the door.

Morgan had been to the community college rehearsal rooms before. They were used as warm-up spaces for competitions and performances. They were also sound dampened, to keep the practicing students from disturbing one another.

There was a window in each door. Morgan had not yet solved that problem.

Still very risky. Crazy.

Morgan paused with her thumbs over the keys, trying to think of just what she could say to make him feel better.

I have to see you. Can't just sit in class and pretend I'm just another kid. We have to talk this out. Alone.

What followed was an excruciating twenty minutes, during which time Morgan felt despair swamping back in. Like she was helpless on the muddy bottom of a drained pond that was slowly filling back up.

Her phone vibrated in her hand and she gasped.

His message said:

Time and date?

With shaking hands she typed in a rendezvous time that just happened to coincide with Rain's next class.

The halls were nearly deserted over Christmas break. But the building was unlocked, and when Morgan requested a practice room key, the bored college kid studying behind the desk of the building lobby just handed it over. He had an iPod plugged into one ear.

Morgan was, after all, nearly college age, and carrying a cello. Perfectly legitimate.

She stowed the cello in the room and then crept down a long hallway to a side exit that was locked from outside; she'd tried it already. She pushed it open and held her breath. Was it alarmed?

No sound. She slid a piece of paper between the door latch and the door frame, and let the door close. One tiny push to test; unlocked, but closed. Perfect.

Her every nerve buzzed. She felt like a spy.

She crept back into the rehearsal room and closed the door. She texted directions to that side door, and which rehearsal door was hers.

She looked up at the window in the room door. It was a high window, which was good. Cellists had to sit down after all, and Morgan wasn't very tall.

As long as they sat on the floor, anyone walking by wouldn't think anything of it. They'd have to be very tall, or stand on tiptoe, not to mention curious enough to press their noses to the window to peer inside.

She busied herself taking the cello out of the case and setting it carefully on its side next to the music stand and chair. She put her music on the stand. She rosined her bow, even, and rested that on the stand as well. This is how the room would look if someone knocked and she set her cello down to answer the door.

Footsteps in the hall. Her heart pounded harder, seemingly in rhythm with the steps. A quiet, tentative knock she could barely hear.

Morgan opened the door a crack, then flung it wide and almost yanked him inside.

"Sit down," she told him, thrilled by the command in her own voice. "So no one can see through that window."

He did as instructed and sat cross-legged along the side wall, his hands folded loosely in his lap.

She tested the lock on the door and then came to sit down next to him. She wanted to lean on his shoulder, but he seemed skittish and panicky.

"I can't believe you went to all this trouble," he said.

"It's worth it to see you alone."

"I just . . . What do you see in an old asshole like me, anyway? You could see any guy in school, and you wouldn't have to sneak like this."

"They're hardly lining up at my door. Anyway, I don't want to waste my time on them. Age is so arbitrary, you said it yourself. You know Britney? All she thinks about is boys and makeup and movies and hair. She doesn't understand the world, and worse, she doesn't care. But guess what? She's eighteen already. She can sign herself out of school for the day. She can vote, not that she'll bother. I was born a few months later, and I'm the child? Stupid. You're not even that much older than me."

"What do you want, then? What do you want from me?"

"I just want to see you. This? Right now? Is the happiest I've been in weeks. Just sitting next to you makes me feel like I could fly."

Then he turned to her. Morgan watched his eyes roam her whole face, including her scar, but she didn't flinch away, or brush her hair over it. She let him drink it all in, everything that she was.

"You're really beautiful," he said through a breath.

He drew closer to her. She smelled a minty aftershave and realized he had groomed himself for her, and she wanted to weep in happiness. His eyes were a deep, warm brown. Her breathing shallowed with his delicious proximity, and she thought she might faint and if she did, so what? He would catch her. He could save her from anything.

She opened her lips to him.

In moments he was shrugging out of his

leather jacket, stealing kisses from her as he did so. He balled up the jacket and put it on the floor behind her and while she wondered why, he was tipping her back to the floor, her head nestled in the jacket.

He pressed his body against her, and she could feel him hard through his jeans. This made her groan, as she also groaned when he raked his hands across her chest, then under her shirt.

She was exploding. No one had ever brought this out in her, and no one else ever could . . .

He lifted her head with one strong hand and pulled off her T-shirt. The room was chilly, and goose bumps raced across her arms. He reached behind her and deftly unsnapped her bra. He groaned aloud at the sight of her breasts and covered them each with kisses.

Then he was working away at her pants, and the zipper was stuck.

A spike of panic jolted through the electricity crackling between them. She had not expected to go all the way just now, she hadn't thought, he seemed so hesitant to even meet . . . He finally got the zipper down and leaned over her again, so that he nearly eclipsed all the light in the room.

She flashed on her first time with David,

when she'd been scared, and cried after.

He was whispering something in her ear.

"What?" she asked.

"Are you on the pill? I don't have any condoms . . ."

"Yes," she answered, relieved that this was true.

Her body wanted this. She could feel that wanting, dragging her to him. Yet her heart was clanging away like an alarm bell.

He'd finally gotten her pants off, and then Morgan had no more time to think.

No turning back.

Some things you couldn't undo.

The hard floor dug into her back, and the zipper from his jacket was scratching her ear. She felt her thrill fading. She tried to move to get into a better position, but he was nearly crushing her against the tile.

Soon he sucked in a sharp breath and cringed, shuddering, and then rolled off her to one side.

Morgan felt shaky, not to mention, unsatisfied.

Then he walked his hand down her abdomen, and she spied a wicked grin on his face. He reached down and touched her in a way that made her gasp out loud.

"Relax," he whispered. "It's okay."

And so she did. She closed her eyes until

her body arched and stars burst in the darkness behind her closed lids, and she heard her own voice cry out far too loud. Then his hand clapped hard over her mouth.

Her eyes snapped open. He released her, then whispered, "Sorry I did that, but you were so loud. . . ."

Then he smiled, one corner of his cheek dimpling. "You sure liked that, didn't you?"

Morgan felt like she was liquid; she could be poured into a bowl. He'd made her feel better than anyone ever had.

Given this, she failed to understand why she felt so queasy, watching him tuck his penis back into his pants and start handing her back her clothes.

They'd decided he should walk out, first, slipping out the side door.

That left her alone in the practice room. She thought about actually practicing — though she hadn't yet figured out how she'd be able to go through with performing her solo without the invented accompanist — but the brief moments she sat behind her cello felt empty. So she packed it away.

She reached for the light switch in the practice room as she was leaving and cast a glance back, staring at the spot on the floor where they had just been sprawled a few minutes ago.

She was starting down the hall toward the lobby when it occurred to her she could walk out the side door with the practice room key in her hand.

The kid behind the desk was probably supposed to take her ID or something to get the key back, but he hadn't. If she went right out that side door, which she already knew did not have an alarm . . . no one would ever know where the key had gone.

She slipped out the side door and blinked hard in the surprising bright sun; when she'd arrived, the day had been shrouded in a woolly gray.

The clouds were receding just ahead of the early winter sunset. All the power of the setting sun was pouring out through a crack between the edge of the clouds and the horizon. The light bathed everything in gold. She froze, transfixed. The word *phantasmagoric* drifted into her mind. Then, *preternatural.*

It just didn't look possible, yet there it was, right in front of her.

She hurried around the building to her car and stowed her cello in the backseat. From her backpack she retrieved a notebook and a pen and set to work in the driver's seat, before she even started the ignition.

Sun will not be restrained
bursts the seam
of the sky
spilling beneath the ashen dome
setting alight the whole golden world

20

Rain fiddled with the stem of her wineglass and threw a forced smile toward the laughing Alessia, who was running her hand over the smooth arc of her belly.

Candlelight washed over the room and symphonic versions of Christmas carols wafted through the air, courtesy of Greg's pricey sound system. A cousin teased Alessia — who was sitting cross-legged in front of the tree, handing out gifts — that next year there would be no candles, and everything would be locked down and babyproofed.

"No ornaments on the bottom branches of the tree, either!" another cousin crowed. Alessia rolled her eyes but laughed along.

Rain tried to remember which cousin that was. TJ and Greg were the only two children in their family, but their uncles and aunts all had many kids, resulting in many cousins, who were all quite a bit older, and thus all their older kids of the next generation were downstairs, tearing apart the rec room and playing pool and Wii and who knows what else.

Leaving the adults to drink their civilized wine on their civilized couches amid their civilized music.

It all made Rain want to crush her wineglass in her fist.

She took a fake sip of her wine. She'd at first intended to decline any alcohol, on her third treatment cycle now, not wanting even the slightest chance of contaminating any burgeoning life. But she knew the speculation and teasing — good-natured or not — would be unbearable.

So she decided to accept a glass. At intervals she found reasons to wander into the kitchen and spill some down the sink.

There was another gift. Among the adults, they'd all drawn names. The next gift was for Alessia, from the one who had spoken moments ago. Tammy, that was it. Her name was Tammy.

A combined gasp and "aww" erupted from the crowd as Alessia unwrapped a baby dress covered with little red strawberries. She'd just learned they were having a girl.

Alessia trilled, waggling the dress at Rain, "I can't wait to be able to pass this on to you!" The "you" was drawn out and singsongy.

Rain felt herself growing hot under her sweater. Several pairs of expectant, wide eyes turned toward her.

Rain faked a laugh, waved her hand in a gesture of, "oh you're too much." She did sip her wine for real this time, enjoying the way the smooth pinot noir rolled over her tongue. "Don't go starting rumors. No buns in this oven."

TJ caught her gaze from where he'd been trapped across the room in a discussion about the corrupt college bowl system. He crossed his eyes at her quickly, so no one else would see, and — Christmas miracle! — she felt a smile, a real genuine smile, unfold.

They could share so much through a single glance. That one funny face said to her, *I'm sorry my family is being unbearable. Here, let me cheer you up by doing something stupid.*

She smiled back at him from behind her glass, to say, *Thank you. I needed that.*

Rain set down her glass carefully before she was tempted to suck the whole thing down immediately.

She pasted on a joyous holiday smile, and let her mind wander, as she shifted her waistband so it no longer pinched her bruised injection sites.

She was long past mourning the unnatural process required to get her a baby, though she did wonder what it would be like to just wake up one day pregnant. Late period, pregnancy test, happy announcements. She imagined Alessia holding the pregnancy test and being swept into her husband's arms. Must be nice.

Rain bit her lip. She was turning into her husband, letting her bitterness and envy overtake her. TJ could never be happy for his brother, no matter now nice Greg was to him, and in fact when he was particularly nice, it was worse yet, because TJ believed Greg was patronizing him.

TJ had never been able to explain the source of the one-sided animosity. He had never revealed some great conflict in their youth, or even any favoritism as they were raised, though he certainly noticed it now that Greg was a well-to-do doctor.

Alessia herself had been so supportive and kind when Rain finally did confide in her after the first failed cycle. She really did want Rain to have that pretty strawberry dress, to share in her joy and raise cousins together.

The last present under the tree was for Rain.

She had tuned out of all sounds in the room and so had to shake herself awake, nearly, when a gift was being handed up to her.

This one was from TJ's mother. Rain pulled on the artful forest green ribbon around the cream-colored package — decked out with stylized Christmas trees — and wondered if her mother-in-law had engineered the name draw. Something about the smile on her face . . .

It was a DVD, she could tell by the size and shape. When she peeled the wrapping back, she gasped before she could stop herself.

On the cover, a round pregnant woman in a leotard was in *trikonasana.*

Mrs. Hill cried in her delighted, girlish manner, "It's a prenatal yoga DVD! We just know this year is going to bring blessings for you and TJ. We just know it."

Rain's hands would have been shaking, but she was gripping the DVD firmly to stop them from doing so. Her throat was suddenly dry, and as she swallowed, she found her breath shallow and her words simply gone.

TJ cleared his throat and noted drily, "No

pressure or anything."

"No!" protested his mother, as her hand flew to her throat. "No pressure! I just know that you're really hoping, really trying . . . We're just all really pulling for you."

Rain swallowed again. Why was she so dry? A ringing started up in her ears threatening to drown out her words. Had TJ told them about the treatments? Did they all know she'd had her legs up in stirrups with a syringe squirting his sperm into her under the bright lights of a doctor's office?

"Thank you," she croaked out, her voice in a whisper, glancing up at Alessia who was shaking her head, sending Rain a heartbreaking look of pity and mouthing *I didn't tell them.* "I appreciate the support."

TJ crossed the room to her then and held out a hand to her. She took it and allowed herself to be led from the room, upstairs. She felt them all staring holes in her back, and she knew the moment they were out of earshot, the gossip would start.

TJ led her to a guest room, one of several in this enormous house that was home to just two people.

He settled her on the edge of a four-poster bed made up in cornflower blue and indigo and returned to join her after closing the door.

"How did she know?" was the first thing Rain said. "I thought we weren't telling them."

TJ shifted on the edge of the bed. "I didn't mean to. Just that when Greg called about Christmas dinner and stuff, we got talking about the baby and he started asking questions about when we were gonna have kids. I was trying to dodge, but he was doing his lecturing voice about how we shouldn't wait forever, and fertility rates declining blah blah. You know, his 'I'm a doctor so I'm smarter than you' routine and I finally snapped that we're seeing Dr. Gould. So then he got all excited because he knows her and says her success rate is 'phenomenal.' I didn't tell you because you've seemed so touchy about this lately, I didn't think you wanted to hear it."

"I would have liked a heads-up, so I didn't walk into a sucker punch like that in front of everyone, on Christmas."

"I'll talk to Mom, tell her she shouldn't have done that."

Rain held up a hand. "No. Don't. I don't want to make her feel bad, and it's already done, anyway. I guess everyone knows now."

"I'm sorry, babe. Really."

She traced a pattern in the bedspread with her finger. It had been ages since she'd done her nails. They were ragged and uneven. She used to paint her fingers and toes all the time, given that her bare feet were always on display at work.

"Well, they are your family, and if you want to tell them about our lives, that's fine. Just clue me in."

TJ pulled her in for a hug and she let herself relax into it, trying to feel what she used to, especially since he was being so much more attentive and kind. Maybe seeing Alessia grow bigger renewed his genuine desire to be a father, for real, instead of just to compete with his brother. Stranger things have happened.

"You want to go home?" he asked into her hair.

"No," she said with a sigh. "No, just go on down ahead of me and give me a minute to collect myself. And hide that stupid DVD somewhere. I don't want to look at it."

"You got it," he said, and kissed her cheek.

On the way out, his phone chimed.

"Who's texting you on Christmas Day?" Rain asked, perplexed. His whole family was here, anyway, unless they were texting him from downstairs to hurry up.

He frowned at the screen. "Doesn't make any sense to me. Must be a wrong number. Take as much time as you need. I'll save you some ham."

Rain smiled weakly, and as he closed the door, she curled up on top of the quilt. As if she could eat anything now.

In a few minutes Rain had pulled herself together enough to descend the stairs back into the fray.

As she reached the main floor, she saw several heads turn toward her, then turn immediately away. They'd been instructed not to stare, she could imagine. Not to make her feel uncomfortable.

Too late for that.

Rain fake smiled when she happened to meet the gaze of the various cousins. They had started eating, and her spot was conspicuously empty. She squeezed TJ's shoulder as she came around to her chair, which he then jumped up to pull out for her, a ridiculously chivalrous gesture she'd never seen him deploy, even at the fanciest of restaurants.

Conversation had stalled, and they were all trying not to stare at her.

She reached for her water glass and satisfied everyone's curiosity. "We'll find out next month if our treatment cycle was successful. Thank you for your concern, everyone. Now, please let's talk about something other than my uterus."

Everyone laughed, suddenly, as if all their mirth had been contained in a boiling pot and the lid had just flown off. Some of the cousins' kids down at the end of the table looked both confused and completely grossed out. Most likely they had missed the "Don't make Rain feel weird" speech and didn't know, which suited her fine.

Conversation finally drifted to politics — the Republican primary made for some lively conversation, just on the right side of proper and civil — college bowl games, and exploits of some of the younger kids in the extended family. Cousin Will's kid Nicky had a new fascination with the word *sexy,* which he had picked up somewhere. Everyone roared with laughter when Will related how his six-year-old said at Sunday dinner when their pastor was visiting, "Please pass the sexy carrots."

Rain was starting to get her equilibrium back. This was why she loved TJ's family. Over at Angie and Ricky's house the day before, dinner had taken place at 6 P.M. instead of the advertised 2 P.M. because Angie had forgotten to properly thaw the bird, and most of the time they were treated to an off-again, on-again argument about some fight her parents had at their Walmart jobs resulting in a talking-to from their boss. They'd drop it, but then when conversation sagged an hour later, Angie would bring it up again as if they'd never stopped.

All the while, Fawn was groaning about Brock teething so much he was crying all the time, resulting in Rain searching the Internet for suggestions as Brock wailed himself into red-faced fury. Stone was half asleep for most of the day, texting and ignoring the rest of the family.

Such a refreshing contrast between that chaos and the easy camaraderie at this table.

When the pie was served and Greg remarked he'd like some of that "sexy apple," the table roared again with hilarity.

Rain laughed, too, genuinely laughed, and in a lately-too-rare feeling of spontaneous affection, she put her hand on TJ's thigh.

His phone buzzed in his pocket under her hand, and she gasped like something bit her. "What the heck? Is someone still bugging you today?"

TJ frowned. "I'd better go call them back and tell them they have the wrong number."

"Call them? Can't you just text them back and tell them to stop it? You could just shut your phone off."

But TJ was already walking away, throwing her a confused shrug over his shoulder.

People texting on Christmas. Rain shook her head and took a sip of her water. Couldn't people ever just put their phones away to enjoy a holiday?

She looked back over her shoulder to see TJ walk out to the three-season porch and close the door behind him. She could see him in silhouette through the door and watched him talk for far longer than seemed necessary for a simple wrong number.

21

Dinah swept the floor of the Den around the last two customers, two teenagers holding hands and nuzzling on the couch in the rear of the shop, near the now-cold gas fireplace.

Janine was stacking chairs on top of the tables, and they'd already shut off the music.

Dinah finally leaned on her broom in front of the couple and announced, "Okay, closing time. You don't have to go home, but you can't stay here."

The boy looked up, and Dinah almost jumped back. It was that curly-haired scary kid from back in September who'd grabbed his girlfriend's wrist. Justin something. This wasn't the same girl; this was a dishwater blonde whose hair was up in a messy ponytail, and she wore an ARBOR VALLEY CHEER shirt.

Dinah tried to act like she wasn't startled by him, but she felt her grip tightening on the broom handle. She'd gone upstairs to take a call; he must have come in then. She would have ordered him to leave. Janine must have forgotten all about that. Or she just didn't care.

He smirked at her and tipped an invisible hat. "Sure thing," he said. As he stood, he kicked over the coffee table in front of the couch.

"Oops. So clumsy of me."

The girl shrieked a giggle and clung to his arm. He refused to hurry his way out, just loping along, drawing out the moment. He knocked over a chair just before walking out the door to a fresh gale of giggles from his girl.

As the door clicked closed, Dinah whirled on Janine. "Why did you let him in here?"

"I didn't know we had a banned kids' list."

"We do. It's a list of one. Him."

"Sorry. I didn't realize." Janine picked up the chair that had fallen. "No harm done here," she said, inspecting the chair and the wood floor. "What's the matter with you?"

"You mean other than being furious that this kid comes in here and acts like that to me?"

"That's just it. The minute that coffee table went over I thought you were going to tear his head off. And then call the cops.

But you just stood there."

Dinah leaned on her broom handle. That would have been in character. She shrugged, propped the broom in a corner, and righted the table. It had a new scratch, but she'd purchased it from an antique store because she liked how it was artfully distressed in the first place.

She resumed sweeping. "Maybe I'm just tired of riding into battle all the time when nothing ever changes anyway. I mean, I turn around and instead of an army behind me, I'm all by myself. No one else cares, and I end up looking like a moron, and usually with a new mortal enemy."

"Will wonders never cease," Janine observed.

"Yeah, well. I mean, I tore into the principal for suspending Jared for pot smoking when he swore up and down to me he hadn't done it. I believed him."

"Bless your heart," Janine said, moving behind the counter to start cleaning the coffee pots.

"Don't make me feel worse. It was plausible. Only to have him confess to me that he really had taken a few puffs."

"Did you break out the rubber hose to get that confession?"

Dinah suddenly felt so bone tired she

wanted to curl up on the couch and sleep there all night, but the floor was still covered with crumbs, so she kept sweeping. "No. He heard his dad and me fighting about it again so he came clean to me. He said he couldn't stand to hear me defending him to Joe when he'd lied to me. I felt like I'd been punched in the stomach."

"Least he told you."

"Yeah. Eventually. Look, you know I don't try to be a bitch, right? It's not like I set out to be everybody's enemy number one."

"You're not my enemy number one. You're probably, like, fourth or fifth."

"Gee, thanks. I'm just saying that no one ever listened to me when I tried to be nice. You've said it yourself when you've filled in for me and tried to get the part-timers to shape up. They tune you out unless you go all General Patton on them. Running your own business is not accomplished with sweet-talking. And parenting difficult kids, yeesh. You've gotta gird your loins for those fights."

"Gird your loins? From what you've told me, sounds like the other people need to do the girding."

"Mutual girding. Girding all around. God, I'm tired. I sound like I'm drunk. But I don't like it is what I'm trying to say. I don't wake up every day setting out to make everyone hate me."

"I don't hate you. You don't pay me enough to keeping working here if I hated you."

Dinah stuck her tongue out at Janine. She needed to hire more people with a sense of humor. She should put that in a classified ad.

Dinah put the broom back in the closet and started counting the cash drawer out. The receipts were down again for the month, but at least the last two weeks of 2011 had finished strong. Maybe 2012 would improve. Maybe she and Joe would start speaking again to each other about something other than repairing the snow-blower and budgeting for Morgan's tuition.

She'd apologized to him after Jared's confession and called Principal Jackson to apologize to him, too, which tasted like wet sand in her mouth to have to admit he'd been right about her son. To his credit, he was gracious about it. "Perfectly natural impulse," he called her defensiveness, and he assured her he still thought well of Jared, who was going through the natural adolescent boundary testing.

Somehow, his kindness made her feel that much worse.

Joe was somewhat less forgiving. He restrained himself with effort from saying what was scrawled all over his face, posture, and body language. He was a living, breathing, three-dimensional "I told you so."

What he'd actually said was, "I know you meant well."

And then he'd turned on the TV and was silent the rest of the night.

"Got any plans for tonight?" Janine asked. "Gonna ring in the new year somewhere?"

Dinah sighed. "No. Just make some popcorn balls and watch the ball drop on TV. Morgan is staying over at a friend's house, but the twins are home. I keep trying to rally them for board games or something, but they just want to play Xbox all night."

"Sounds thrilling."

"You?"

"I'm going out with my boyfriend to this party at Amici's. Got a sparkly dress, tacky heels, you know the drill."

"I used to know it, anyway. Have fun, be safe. Call a cab."

"Yes, Dinah," Janine said through a sigh. "I will."

"All right, scoot on out of here. I'll finish up. Happy New Year."

Janine was gone inside of two minutes, off to go don her sparkly dress.

Dinah double-checked the locked front door, shut off all the lights, and locked the safe.

Before leaving, though, she sat back down at one of the cushioned chairs near the front of the café.

The parking lot lights filtered in through the windows and set some of the tables in a glow. It looked like the set of a play. Any moment an actor would appear in a spotlight to deliver a tender monologue.

Dinah mentally rearranged the furniture to make way for the karaoke machine in the corner. The microphone for the sensitive songwriter-guitarist, the earnest poet. The Planning Commission would be meeting soon to consider final approval of her request, and once she had that finally in hand, she'd be able to turn around the downward trend.

Things were yet going to pick up. *Roll on 2012,* she thought. *Let's do this.*

Dinah walked into her house wanting to scrunch her eyes shut. Lately, each time she crossed the threshold, she was greeted by some horrid disaster or a fight, or Joe's deep frown.

It was so . . . quiet.

"Boys? Joe?"

"Down here," she heard Joe call.

She walked to the downstairs den with a hesitant step, as if she were picking her way across thin ice.

Joe was by himself in the den. A bottle of Korbel was in a mixing bowl, apparently a quasi–ice bucket.

"Where are the twins?"

"I sent them to my sister's. They haven't seen their cousins in a while."

"You . . . What?"

Joe gave her a sideways smile. "You heard me. I sent them to my sister's. When was the last time we were home alone together?"

His New York was showing again: togeth-uh.

"Did they . . . Did they want to go? Were they glad?"

"Geez, Dinah. They whined a little bit, but they'll get over it. She has video games, too, and they like their cousin Jeff."

"They don't like Lizzie."

"Lizzie won't bother them. C'mere, sit down. They'll be fine with their aunt Sara and uncle John. She's gonna let them stay up until midnight and watch movies, and we'll pick them up tomorrow morning."

Dinah drifted over to the couch and sat gingerly next to Joe. Why wasn't she thrilled? When the kids were younger, she would have given her left tit to have all night with the house to themselves.

She pushed away her imagined doomsday scenarios: the twins breaking into the liquor cabinet while their aunt and uncle went to sleep, or slipping out of the house just for the thrill of escape, then getting hit by a car, or freezing to death in the snow.

Joe popped the cork and startled himself, then he laughed, flushing a little pink with embarrassment. Dinah found that endearing, that after all these years he could be embarrassed about anything in front of his broken-down middle-aged wife.

She smiled gamely and held up her glass as he poured the champagne too fast and it fizzed nearly over the top.

She was trying to have fun. Yet . . . her kids would be gone all night, and she hadn't known that was going to happen. With Morgan she'd given her a hug and an "I love you" before she went to work, knowing she'd have gone to her party by the time Dinah got home.

The last thing she'd said to the boys was something like, "Don't forget to put your laundry away."

"Are you in there, Dinah?"

"Yeah, sorry. I'm just distracted wondering what the boys are up to."

Annoyance flashed across Joe's face, and he struggled to recover. "They're fine. Happy New Year, baby." He clinked her glass.

She raised the glass and felt the bubbles pop against her nose and smiled at her husband, trying hard to stay in the present, with him on the couch, instead of where her heart was — with her kids, wondering if they were all okay.

Dinah woke with a start. Her heart pounded and she flailed around in a short panic before she realized she was on the couch, alone. She was wrapped in a blanket. The taste of cheap champagne plastered her tongue. The TV was off. She remembered sitting with Joe and making pleasant small talk about the New Year's Rocking Eve guests and how old Dick Clark was getting, and he had poured her another glass — or two? — and she remembered stretching out, pleasantly relaxed.

She blinked until she was able to focus on the digital clock on their old VCR. 1:30 A.M. She'd slept through New Year's.

She'd done this any number of times in the past. They weren't big on whooping it up, especially after the kids were born, and with the boys being preemie and clinging to life at first, everything fun seemed trivial to the point of insult. It took her a long time to let herself enjoy a movie, even. She just wasn't a party person anymore.

This was different, though. Joe had gone out of his way to set up a romantic evening. There would be fallout.

She crept up the stairs in search of him and found him snoring in their bed. Well, why shouldn't he go to sleep? What did she expect, he'd be naked amid strewn rose petals?

Dinah frowned. This was going to be her fault. He was going to be put out and upset, but he's the one who sprang this on her and gave her champagne when she was already tired. If she'd known, she would have tried to conserve some energy, in fact she'd have gotten someone to fill in for her at the Den . . . Or suggested another night when she would be less busy working all that day.

She could almost hear him grousing that she was ungrateful for his gesture. All she did was accidentally doze off. And he didn't even wake her. Didn't even rouse her to go to bed so she wouldn't screw up her back slouched on the sofa.

She stood there for as long as five minutes, watching him snore, frozen with indecision about climbing into bed or going back downstairs. She wished with the fervent irrationality of a child that she could spin back time, so the twins could be home where they belonged and for all four of them to have played some cards and eaten popcorn balls and gone to bed at 12:01. What was so wrong with that plan, anyway?

A glow from the hallway light cast Joe and their bedroom in a dark gray. She could make out his features well enough, and at this distance, or maybe it was her half-sleeping brain and the champagne conspiring, he looked like she remembered him when they first met. No worry lines, no middle-aged paunch — though slender was never a word anyone would have used to describe Joe Monetti.

She'd been hired to wait tables in his uncle's pizza joint, though most of the time she was on the phone taking orders, or cleaning up. The orders weren't complicated to take, and the actual delivery of the pie and the Pepsi to the table didn't take so much time. It was a good job for a girl going to junior college and trying to decide how to spend the rest of her long, unfocused life. No booze at Monetti's, so the crowd was pretty tame. Mostly neighborhood families and the kids not old enough or naughty enough to sneak off and get drunk.

Joe came home from college and his family slapped the obvious moniker Joe College on him the minute he walked into Monetti's. Dinah heard it so often that when someone asked for Joe Monetti on the phone, she first replied, "You mean Joe College?" Joe made the pizzas and sometimes delivered them, and on slow days he and Dinah would sit at the counter stools like customers, she with her Keds swinging loose instead of braced on the stool, always pushing stray pieces of her hair behind her ear because she never took the time to make a nice smooth ponytail. He would always be turned backward on the stool, facing the restaurant, elbows on the counter. She'd sip her Pepsi and listen to him tell college stories, or famous family stories about the Monettis' first arrival in New York City two generations before.

She thought of Joe then like a distant male cousin. Nice enough, that was all. But then he went back to college and every day she went into Monetti's and Joe wasn't there, her heart hurt.

He came back over Thanksgiving and confessed he'd missed her every day. Their first kiss was in the alley behind Monetti's, next to the Dumpster.

They'd had to close the place when his

dad died and none of the kids had the ability to take it, and no buyers wanted to carry it forward. Dinah had cried harder when they closed the place up than she had at Mr. Monetti's funeral, rest his soul.

She leaned against the doorjamb of their little house together, pondering all those intervening years. They fell in love accidentally, when they weren't looking. Could you fall out of love accidentally, too? Sure, she answered herself. Love is hard to find and easy to lose, same as anything small and precious.

Dinah climbed in next to him and gently squeezed his arm in case he was perhaps half awake, and then at least they could share a New Year's kiss. Joe simply turned over in his sleep to face the wall.

22

Morgan moved through the party with the mindlessness of a shark. Rumbling bass from the speakers seemed to vibrate the whole house. Most of the lights were off, though a few table lamps were still lit, and the kitchen — where the keg was, along with Solo cups and some liquor and fruit juice — was a bright halo of light, a beacon of substance abuse for the young and indestructible. Dark shapes clutching each other filled her peripheral vision, and now and then a high-pitched screech of laughter cut through the generic rap-thumping coming from somewhere.

Morgan could care less about any of it, but it was better than popcorn balls at home with her parents and idiot brothers. She was supposed to be spending the night with Britney.

Morgan only wanted to be with *him,* but they couldn't make it work.

It was just too hard for him to find a reason to be away on a holiday. As it was, they'd nearly had a disaster Christmas Day when Morgan had sent him a few texts and the phone vibrated under his wife's hand.

At first when he called her, she almost exploded with joy and delight. She'd run upstairs on the pretense of needing the bathroom immediately, only to hear him scolding her as soon as she picked up.

"You can't keep texting me today," he'd hissed.

"I wanted you to know I was thinking of you." Her voice came out as a pathetic bleat.

"Not on Christmas. And not so often."

Morgan had tightened her fist so hard she wondered if her palms might bleed from the indent of her nails. "As you wish," she'd said, suddenly remembering that was from *The Princess Bride.*

Then he'd softened his voice. "We'll see each other soon," he assured her. And just before he hung up, "I'm thinking of you, too."

Morgan waved off a random guy's offer to refresh her beer. She doubted all those hysterical stories about date rape drugs in someone's drink were actually true, but all the same, she preferred to be in control of her own consumption. She'd seen what happened to girls who constantly let guys top off their drinks. They behaved like lunatics until they passed out with puke in their hair, or disappeared with some guy in the back room and came out with their clothes on all crazy, not remembering a bit of it.

No one needed a date rape drug with enough booze around, really.

She felt a hand on her shoulder and prepared to tell the guy to get lost and found herself looking up at Ethan.

He bent down to her ear. "Can we talk?"

She rolled her eyes and looked away.

"Please," he said. "I really want to talk to you."

The bass throbbed in rhythm with a fresh pain in her temple. And Britney — who she'd been talking to for a while anyway — had gone off somewhere.

"Fine," she shouted, and led the way upstairs.

This house — she wasn't even sure whose house it was — had many bedrooms. It was one of the fancier homes in town, along the border to the park. They had to pass several locked doors before they found an unused room. There was a bed, but no sheets or pillows. Some boxes were stacked with a dust cloth over them. No curtains on the windows. A corkboard was mostly empty except for a varsity letter and a snapshot dangling from a thumbtack in one corner. A streetlight outside poured a faint glow into the room, and neither Ethan nor Morgan moved to find a light switch.

She settled on the edge of the bed, choosing a side where her scar would be facing away.

Ethan settled next to her. "I'm worried about you."

She looked at the floor and shrugged. He didn't know anything about her. None of them did.

"You don't seem like you, lately."

"What would you know about it? We haven't even talked since I threw myself at you in the most pathetic crush confession ever, which by the way, thanks for making me relive that tonight. Feels awesome."

"I see you in the hall. I watch for you when I know I'm going to see you, because I miss you lots. And you always look sad. And tired."

"Okay, first? If you weren't gay, that might be romantic, but now it just sounds creepy. Second, you can't tell about someone just by staring at them. What, you think you were so critical to my health and well-being that I'm rotting away without you?"

"I didn't mean it like that."

"I don't know how you meant it then. I'm seeing someone, actually. And I'm really happy."

"You don't look so happy."

"I'm tired. I'm having trouble sleeping. But I am happy, and I don't have anything to prove."

"Why are you so mad at me?"

Morgan slumped. He hadn't done anything wrong; he was just being thoughtful, the same way he'd always been. "I'm not. I'm feeling awkward, that's all. And tired. And wondering where the hell Britney went."

"I saw her go upstairs with a guy."

"Not David?" David was on vacation in Florida with his family.

"Apparently not. When the cat's away, I guess."

Morgan snorted. "Maybe they're not having sex. Maybe they're only getting high." She laughed through a sneer. "I just hope she doesn't abandon me here. I don't want to drive home in the middle of the night, not after this especially." She gestured with her cup, which she still held in her hand.

"You could stay at my place. I'd tell my folks your ride ditched you."

"You're not drinking, yourself?"

"Nah."

Morgan chewed on her lower lip. There was only one place she wanted to be, and it was closed off to her as sure as a medieval castle, complete with moat and alligators.

Ethan nudged her. "It's not as if I'm going to seduce you."

It was a joke, but it only brought her back to that moment again, with her poetry book lying open exposing every sick thing she was, her lips aiming for his face, his startled recoil.

Morgan stood up roughly, sloshing some of her beer on the floor. She set it down, just as the rhythmic countdown to midnight began downstairs.

"Morgan —" Ethan said, and as she turned, she saw that he'd stood up. He was holding his arms out to her. The countdown grew louder and more frenzied.

She yanked open the door and flew down the hall, down the stairs and through the crush of people to the living room.

At the unified "Happy New Year!" a random guy reached for her and plastered her face with his lips, scruffy face, and tongue. She shoved him away and found her winter coat on the back of a sofa where she'd left it, only with a beer spill down the back.

She bolted out the door of the house.

Morgan trudged along the walk, hearing

shouts and revelry from the houses, porches, and streets.

It was too far to walk home. Driving seemed like a bad idea now, and anyway, her car was parked in. The plan had been to walk to Britney's, which was only a few blocks away, and get her car in the morning.

Morgan texted her:

Can we go now? Bored.

She was surprised and relieved by the rapid text back.

Yeah, gimme a sec. Where r u?

Walking. Halfway to your house.

Wait, I'll catch up.

Morgan went to Facebook on her phone and left a falsely cheery update in case her mom checked. "Happy New Year! So excited for 2012 and graduation!" She almost added a "woo hoo" but decided that would be out of character and pushing her luck.

She went to his Facebook. He had no information publicly visible, but he did have a handsome profile picture. That jaw, those mischievous eyes. She sighed. That's when she noticed the picture was cropped from a larger one, and she could glimpse resting on his shoulder a slim feminine hand, and a diamond wedding ring.

She shut off Facebook and peered down the street to wait for Britney.

In a few minutes, Britney skipped down the sidewalk, her hair out behind her like a sail, her breath puffing out ahead of her in delicate clouds.

"Hey!" she said as she caught up. In the streetlight, Morgan could see her cheeks were flushed pink, and her makeup was smeared.

Britney linked her arm through Morgan's and started skipping. Morgan had not been drinking the rum and Cokes like her friend had been and did not join her in the skipping. In fact, she was feeling tired from the beer, not to mention the previous evening's nightmare that kept her up half the night, the classic "scar eats Morgan's head" version.

Morgan often thought such a repetitive dream should lose its power. If only.

Britney was ebullient. Morgan spelled ebullient in her head, just for something to do.

"So, David is out of favor?" she asked.

Britney stopped, pulling on Morgan's arm. "Why, you want him back?" She winked, just playing, or so it seemed.

"Hardly. I'm through with high school boys."

Britney started up again, this time walking. "Well, ooh la la, college girl."

"What are you doing after graduation?"

Britney tipped her head so far back Morgan caught her arm so she wouldn't fall. "Oh, who cares!" she shouted up to the sky, shrouded in clouds and dark. "Don't act like my mom on New Year's."

"I don't care what you do. I was just asking."

"Okay, then I'll tell you. First? I'm going to get so drunk I can't stand up. Then I'm going to get a job at Aeropostale or something where I can get a clothing discount and fold T-shirts. Then maybe I'll go to community college so my mom will shut up about what I'm going to do with my life. And I'm going to be happy. Isn't that simple? Maybe that's the secret to happiness, Morgan. Being simple."

Britney giggled and laid her head on Morgan's shoulder.

It couldn't be that easy, nothing ever was. But Morgan also knew she was goddamn tired of being complicated.

23

On a snowy January Tuesday, Rain did something she'd never before done. She'd lied to Beverly by calling in sick.

Rain turned the radio to NPR on the drive to Dr. Gould's, hoping that stories of atrocities and natural disasters would keep her mind on the road, and not the day to come.

She parked the car and drifted to the doorway of the clinic; once inside, she perched gingerly on the end of a chair, nodding to the receptionist, who made a note on a chart and knew exactly why she was there.

She'd chosen a chair facing what was labeled the "Success Wall." Dozens, maybe hundreds, of baby photos festooned the bulletin board opposite her. There were photos of wrinkled specimens in hospital-issued blankets and cherubic toddlers with first-birthday cake on their faces. Every one of them a baby helped into the world by Dr.

Gould and her colleagues.

Some days, Rain would choose a seat facing away. Today, she wanted to believe in possibility.

She hadn't told TJ she was here. He had not inquired about the particulars of the cycle after he'd performed his part, and she hadn't volunteered, because this time she wanted time to absorb what the verdict was, before having to anticipate and manage his reaction.

He'd just assumed she'd gone to work, and really, that's where she was supposed to be.

"Rain?" the nurse said, peeking around the door. "We're ready for you."

Rain was rolling up her sleeve before she even sat down.

Her name was Marta, and she knew better than to discuss the particulars of this morning's blood test. Marta, Rain knew, would act as if this blood test were nothing, just another test to monitor her various hormones.

They would never call it a pregnancy test, even though it was now well past the insemination, and now was the time.

Marta tied the tourniquet. Rain used to look away for the poke, but now she'd become inured. She watched the needle slide in, though today she did let out a small gasp. The pinch seemed harder today.

"Sorry," Marta muttered, frowning at the needle.

"Oooh, ouch," Rain said, now turning away as Marta had to dig around.

"I'm so sorry, honey, this happens sometimes, the veins can be tricky, so sorry . . . Ah. There."

Rain relaxed and could almost feel her blood spurt into the little vial.

"Are you okay?" Marta asked, pulling the needle out and putting the square of gauze on the tiny wound. Rain held it in place for her without being asked, as Marta turned to grab a piece of medical tape to stick on it. "You seem pale."

"I'm a little light-headed."

Marta patted her hand. "I'm so sorry about that; usually your veins are so easy. Let me drop this off, and I'll be back with a cup of juice. Take your time."

Marta left her in the room, and Rain put her head in her hand. She never felt faint over this. It seemed like an ill omen.

Her attention was pricked by a groaning sound from somewhere else in the clinic. As it grew in volume she recognized it as a keening of grief and trauma. Someone had just gotten some dire news. No heartbeat in the embryo, perhaps. Dr. Gould continued to see patients through the first weeks of pregnancy, so it could be a success story reversing itself. Or maybe someone's eggs were in poor shape and the couple had just learned they could not continue trying. There was no shortage of ways for this dream to be dashed.

Marta returned with juice, casting a discomforted glance behind her at the continued wail. "I'm sorry if that upsets you. I wish it could be a happy ending every time."

Rain accepted the juice and checked the bandage over her needle's poke. "I wish no one ever needed this place at all."

Marta nodded and then pulled the door shut against the sight of a woman, now quietly weeping, walking past them under her husband's protective arm.

When Rain returned home after a stop for breakfast and a newspaper, she checked the clock and groaned. Eleven o'clock. She knew by now that the lab results took at least until 2:30 to come back. Then she'd get a call on her cell, but until then she faced hours of waiting in a quiet house.

Her cell phone rang. She startled with a conditioned panic response, despite her higher brain functions realizing there's no way she could get any news yet.

She glanced down and saw her parents' house number. She let it roll to voice mail rather than face whatever fake drama there was now. Since Brock had endured one frightening but ultimately harmless febrile seizure, Fawn had become a master of paranoid panic attacks, which for some reason they felt compelled to share with Rain, as if she were the only one capable of searching "green poop" on WebMD.

Rain walked to the bathroom, and on entering, sighed with irritation at the used-up toilet paper roll. TJ was getting so absentminded lately, forgetting to gas up the car, neglecting to pay the credit card bill until a second notice and late fee. Maybe this was how the pressure of fertility treatment was getting to him.

Or maybe he was just getting lazy in his thirties about those small acts of courtesy like changing out the toilet paper.

Rain reached under the bathroom sink for a spare roll, and a box drew her attention.

A pregnancy test.

They often came in sets of two. Here was the one left over from the box she'd bought in that last fit of optimism, months ago now.

Another conditioned response — had she

become Pavlov's dog? — she had to pee. Badly.

She could get her answer right now. Thanks to modern science and Dr. Gould, she knew down to the exact hour when sperm and egg met — plenty of time had passed for her body to start churning out hormones if one of those sperm really had burst through this time, if the cells had been dividing all along.

Images danced in Rain's head of what those early embryos looked like, as she'd been shown by Dr. Gould way back when during an orientation meeting. Then she remembered the drama of that last test. It was unclear, and there had been giddy joy, then the crush of failure. She'd vowed only to trust the final, definitive blood test answer. Just a few hours, she told herself. She could make it a few more hours.

She ran to the kitchen and buried the test deep in the garbage, under the dregs of last night's dinner.

After going to the bathroom — feeling oddly victorious that she'd done so without peeing on a stick — she picked up her cell phone to call her mother back. She had to get out of the house before she lost her goddamn mind.

■ ■ ■ ■

An hour later, Rain pulled her VW Bug up to her childhood home, where the door stood wide open in the January air, despite their heating bills, despite the presence of an infant in the house who could catch a chill.

Gran would have said, "Close the door, you weren't born in a barn!"

"Hi, Mom," Rain called, stepping over Dog, who raised his head an inch or so, but did not rouse himself to greet her. Rain glanced down at him, sprawled like a dog-shaped throw rug on the floor. "Ingrate. I took you to the vet when you ate all Fawn's candy. And you barfed in my car."

"Mom!" Rain called again. "Ready for the mall?"

Angie appeared, barefoot, wearing a denim miniskirt like it was summer 1987. She was yawning and applying lip gloss at the same time.

"Did you just get up?"

"Yes, and what's it to you? Hi, honey. Fawn!"

The last was directed to Rain's sister, who lumbered down the steps at being summoned.

Rain flinched away, not meaning to, unable to help her body's physical response to the sight of her single, younger sister and the bald-headed baby she carried in one arm. Rain thought, *Support his head!* But she said nothing out loud, knowing it would only cause a fight and make Fawn even more determined to let little Brock's head flop all around. Once Fawn had shouted at her, "I'm his mother! You're the aunt," making it sound as if she'd meant "ant," a tiny pest.

"What?" Fawn said now, rubbing her eyes with her free hand.

"Want some lunch?" their mother asked. "There are toaster waffles in the freezer."

Grandmotherhood had not improved Angie's cooking skills.

"Your dad's upstairs; can you check on that computer again before we go?" Angie said, scratching an armpit. "Ricky!" she bellowed now, so suddenly Rain jumped. "She's coming up!"

Rain climbed the steps, avoiding the one that felt splintery and unstable beneath the faded stair runner, and found her father in the room that used to be hers and now served as some kind of office or library or workroom or storage room. In any case, it had a computer, which at the moment wasn't working.

"There's my computer guru," Ricky said, smiling so wide she could see his missing eyetooth. Rain pretended not to notice, but she always did, as soon as she was old enough to realize most people's parents in her town had all their teeth.

"Hardly," Rain said. But she was the closest thing her parents had to an expert on hand, and what she knew, TJ had taught her.

"It's running so slow I don't know what all is the problem." Ricky stood up, his lanky frame nearly filling the space under the eaves where he'd crammed the old plasterboard desk.

Rain clicked around to start defragging the hard drive, something she could have explained on the phone in about ten seconds, truthfully.

"How are things with Mom?" she asked, eyes on the screen, though there was nothing she really needed to see. Her father was like a skittish mutt sometimes; direct eye contact spooked him.

"You know. Up and down."

Rain fought the urge to smile at this. Up and down was one way to put it, all right.

Angie and Ricky Davidson believed in free expression to the point of ecstatic kisses in the living room or thrown plates in the kitchen. As of now they both worked at Walmart. Which Rain thought might have been a bad idea, considering Angie could barely stand Ricky when they were in the same house, much less at the same job.

"But anyways. How's my girl?" Ricky asked, and Rain smiled.

"Just fine, Pop."

She'd once started to confide in her parents about trying to get pregnant, but that only launched Angie on a rambling speech about how she needed to "stop trying so hard" and "let it happen." Then speculation that perhaps TJ was "firing blanks."

"There, that should do it," Rain said. "Don't touch this for a while, okay? Just let it run. It will come up with a little box when it says it's complete, then hit 'OK.' I'm going to the mall with Mom."

"Make sure she doesn't take out a second mortgage to buy baby clothes."

"You got it. Love you."

Rain headed for the stairs. As she passed the door across from the landing, it swung open to reveal her brother, Stone, pale and thin as a sapling and nothing like his namesake. He was rubbing sleep from his eyes. "Hey, sis, can you help me with —"

"Call me later, okay?" she called over her shoulder, as she ran lightly down the steps, thinking at this rate she might never get out of the house.

Rain squeezed her sister from behind as Fawn smeared her toaster waffles with peanut butter, patted Brock on his fuzzy baby head, then she waved at her mom, who was perched on a kitchen barstool on her cell phone.

"Are we going, or what?"

Angie nodded and carried on her phone conversation as she followed Rain out to the car, then as she went back inside again for something she forgot. Waiting for her mother as she warmed up the VW, Rain recalled her childhood friends' breathy envy the few times they'd come to the house and saw how little her parents cared what she did or where she went. "Wow," they'd say, "you're so lucky."

Be careful what you wish for, she'd answer back, but only silently, already figuring out that to get along you have to go along, letting everyone believe what they wanted to believe if that made them happy to do so.

As they pulled away at last and Angie finally hung up her phone, Rain noticed in her rearview mirror that her mother had left the front door wide open.

■ ■ ■ ■

Angie strolled along next to Rain in the mall, nibbling a soft pretzel and chattering on about some reality show. Though Rain knew Beverly and Layla were both working, and she was not likely to get caught shopping when supposedly sick, her old schoolgirl impulse was to keep looking around for a truant officer or some such thing.

Rain was barely listening. She'd hoped that her mother would be a distraction, hoped that by getting her out of the house she'd have some alone time with her away from Fawn and the baby. On their best days, when Angie wasn't fighting with Ricky or sleeping off a party, they used to enjoy hitting the mall together. It had been Angie who convinced the teenage Rain to get a second ear-piercing up in the cartilage part of her ear. It had hurt like fire and gotten infected and Rain let it close up again. But in that moment they'd been women together, aligned in confederacy of hormones and gender.

Today, she'd chosen a stupid place to escape from thoughts of a baby. It was midday in a shopping mall, right after Christmas, and the place was crawling with mothers pushing strollers and dragging toddlers along to spend gift cards. She should have called Alessia instead and gone to get a pedicure. But then, Alessia was a walking reminder of fertility herself, now that her belly was round and cute.

Angie seized Rain's arm, her ragged red nails scratching Rain's skin. "Oooh! Let's go in there!"

Gymboree.

"Oh, not now, Mom . . ."

Rain pulled back, feeling like a recalcitrant toddler.

"Wait out here if you want, but I've gotta get in there and pick out something for Brocky."

Rain slumped with resignation and followed her mother in.

She gave in to temptation and checked her phone for the first time since deciding to go out. She'd refused to let herself check the time all through lunch, and until now in their wandering she'd not once looked at any type of clock. She'd even removed her watch before driving to the house to pick up Angie.

Two thirty.

Rain felt her armpits tickle with sweat at the mere notice of that time.

Angie was at the boy clothing, gushing

over something with trains on it. Rain wanted to tell her why it was so hard for her to be there, wanted to flee, wanted to bury her face in the pink layette before her and sob.

But Angie wouldn't get it. She had never understood Rain's anxiety, invoking "live and let live" and "give it time" as her favorite meaningless expressions, though she herself felt free to have a screaming conniption fit over someone eating the last of her favorite cereal if she so chose. Rain closed her eyes, pictured her beloved grandmother, and imagined herself sitting at her worn, wooden kitchen table, saying, *Oh, Gran, can this finally be it?*

Her mental Gran only smiled and patted her hand.

She wanted to text TJ, even though he wouldn't be able to answer, just for the simple act of reaching out to him in her anxiety and distress. It's what a wife was supposed to do, after all. They were supposed to lean on each other, like two sides of a triangle. Wasn't that one of the strongest shapes in architecture? Rain had read that somewhere.

Babies were everywhere in this Gymboree. In carriers worn on a mother's chest, in slings, in strollers and in baby seats.

Angie squealed and held up a blue pajama set with puppies on it. Rain gave her a tight-lipped smile and a thumbs-up.

A toddler in front of her dropped his stuffed clown toy on the floor. Rain bent to pick it up and hand it to him. The mother turned in that moment and snatched the toy away from her son. He reached and wailed, flexing his fingers.

"It's been on the floor, it's full of germs, and he'll put it right in his mouth," the mother said in the clipped tones of the irritated and superior. She was digging around in the diaper bag slung on the handles of the stroller, finally coming up with a snack cup of Cheerios, which appeased the little boy.

Rain shrank away, back to her mother's side.

"How's this one?" Angie said brightly, holding up a tiny three-piece suit.

"Seriously? For his formal diaper changes?"

Angie frowned. "How did I give birth to such a spoilsport?"

"Yeah, that's me. Everyone's favorite killjoy." Rain fingered a price tag. Hardly stuff Angie should be buying on her salary.

"I'm kidding. Lighten up."

"You think she'll be okay?" Rain blurted.

"Fawn, I mean. Can she really do all of it alone? I mean . . . ?"

Angie cocked her head at Rain. "Oh, she'll be okay. She'll have moments where she'll want to throw him out the window, all mothers do, but she won't actually do it."

"You wanted to throw me out the window?"

Angie was back to ogling baby clothes. Little socks this time. "Sure! All three of you. Sometimes at once," she chirped. "But I'd just shut myself in the bathroom and cry instead and come back out and carry on."

"Wow. That's . . . inspiring."

Angie put down the socks and turned to Rain, flipping her long, permed hair out of her face. "Sweetie, there ain't no sense in telling fairy tales about being a mom. It sucks sometimes. Sucks hard. And it never stops. Even when the kids sleep you're just on call. Someone might start barfing anytime or wake up scared. God, I remember one time Stone walked in on your daddy and me having sex. I was up there riding him like a cowboy —"

"Mom!"

"I'm just saying you're never off duty. Never. Even now, I've got Fawn and Stone still at home, and now Brock."

Rain suppressed a smirk at her mother's self-sacrificing tone. Angie never bothered much with rules or supervision. It's not like she was running a military school. Though, Rain had to allow, she was attentive in her way. She was known to join them in a spontaneous game of hide-and-seek or coax them into building a fort out of couch cushions. She once started a shaving-cream fight when Ricky had bought a case of the stuff on sale.

The next day, just as likely, she would shoo them away from her all day so she could talk on the phone to her girlfriends or give herself a home perm.

Angie continued, "I'm just saying, it's not like a Hallmark card. And if all mothers go around saying it's the best thing ever and it's one hundred percent wonderful every minute, then it will just make everyone feel like shit for being normal. Am I right?" She addressed this last to a young mother with a newborn dozing in a front carrier, holding the hand of a toddler wearing head-to-toe pink.

The young woman scurried away, and Rain cringed — for the hundredth or maybe thousandth time — for how her mother looked to outsiders: a middle-aged woman wearing the hairstyle and clothes of her prime — curly perm, shoulder pads, and all — smacking gum and issuing her pronouncements to the people around her whom she assumed were there to be her audience.

Her phone!

Rain fled from the store and stopped next to a fake tree, in view of a carousel full of children going round and round.

Dr. Gould's number glowed up at her from the display. She froze in the last moments of not knowing, then slowly raised the phone to her ear, screwing her eyes shut like a frightened child.

24

Morgan warmed up with some scales while staring at her phone, which she'd balanced on the edge of the music stand. Her bow angled wrong, and the resulting squeak bounced all over the empty school band room. She slumped over her instrument.

School had begun again, which provided an agonizing mélange of pleasure and despair. She could see him every day, but he was in the front of the class, pretending she was no one. The classroom felt foreshortened, as if the few rows of kids between them represented miles of unassailable distance.

She'd stopped visiting him after school. He'd told her to stop; they had to avoid any appearance of unusual connection.

Their time together was extremely limited now. They were both in school all day. Most evenings he was at home and unavailable, and she herself had the drudgery of homework to slog through.

She'd hit upon a way to communicate safely, at least. She'd written in a simple code on the back of her homework and dared to send him a cryptic text about the code, knowing he'd be clever enough to figure it out.

Translated, it had said this: *Call me after school, 3 o'clock.* She figured he'd have a classroom or an office to himself by then, or maybe he'd be on his way home in the car.

It was ten after three, and the waiting was agony. But there was something exquisite about the agony, knowing what awaited her.

Twice they'd met up in the practice room. She had relived those stolen moments countless times, especially the second time, which was more gentle and slow. And afterward they'd gotten dressed — it was cold in the room — but lain back down in each other's arms, using their coats as pillows, and talked like a regular couple might about what movies and music they liked. They'd seen a lot of the same movies, in fact, due to the movie nights with Morgan and her mom. Dinah always tried to expose her daughter to the classics of her own generation. Morgan had thus impressed him by quoting *The Blues Brothers.*

"It's 106 miles to Chicago, we got a full

tank of gas, half a pack of cigarettes, it's dark . . . and we're wearing sunglasses," she'd deadpanned.

"Hit it," he'd answered, and his delighted laughter fell like warm rain on her skin.

The phone rang. She gave a quick glance around the empty band room and picked it up.

Without preamble, he said, "What's going on?"

"Are you alone?"

"In my car."

Morgan's shoulders relaxed. At last they could talk freely, though she had to keep her voice down because band room acoustics could make even a quiet statement ring loud. "This is killing me not to see you. I mean, to see you but to have to act like we're nothing to each other."

"I know," he said, in the same reassuring tone he used with kids struggling over their homework. Lately he'd just been marking her own work all with an A whether she'd gotten the answers or not. She noticed because she flubbed a couple on purpose to see what would happen. He continued, "I had an idea the other day."

A delighted shiver ran through Morgan from her fingers inward to her core, and she curled her toes inside her shoes. "Yeah?"

"My brother is on vacation this week, Barbados or something like that. He asked me to look in on the house and water his plants."

"Oooh," Morgan replied.

"Think you can get away Saturday night?"

Morgan's breath was so shallow she feared she might faint dead away off her chair, her cello clattering to the floor. She gripped the instrument's neck to steady herself and cleared her throat. "Yes. But how will we meet without being seen?"

"I'll give you the address. His car has a big garage. If you park inside, no one will even know anyone else is there by a quick glance. I'll watch for you and open the garage. I better hang up. I'll text you the time and address. But don't text me back unless you absolutely have to, like, if you can't make it, just text 'never mind,' no other details."

"Got it."

"Gotta go. I have to get home."

Morgan hung up and was swamped with giddy excitement. She wanted to put her cello down and run ecstatic laps around the edge of the band room and screech until her throat was raw.

Instead, she tackled the concerto with an exuberance she'd never felt before.

The music rang in her ears and her fingers tripped lightly across the strings, her bow skating over the instrument, drawing the notes out into the air. Too bad her solo competition wasn't here right now, in this room. She would have nailed it.

The best part of their plan was that it was almost entirely risk free. An empty house! No chance of a barge-in. And her mother never questioned her evening plans. Dinah would have been horrified to learn her smart, wise daughter had spent New Year's Eve drinking keg beer at a drunken party and walked a trashed Britney back to her house where they snuck in through a sliding door. They both had hangovers in the morning: Morgan's was minor, Britney's was epic. But Dinah never questioned her, not even when someone tagged a picture of Morgan on Facebook with a plastic cup in her hand amid the crush of people, and it popped up on her profile. Her mother had not noticed it on Facebook, or it had not registered as cause for concern, at least not compared to Jared's new pothead tendency.

Morgan had untagged the photo and then scolded the kid who posted it via a private message. Some kids could be so careless.

Morgan yawned as she pulled open the local library's door, yesterday's giddiness over her upcoming romantic weekend already dulled by the heavy shroud of insomnia. Her nightmares had even begun to pick up in frequency.

He was starring in her nightmares now, something that unsettled her waking hours more than the old dreams ever had. In the latest, he pinned her to the floor in a passionate embrace, until she dissolved under him, disappearing completely.

She nodded to Kat, the librarian, and went to hang her coat in the break room. She had two hours of shelving and general assisting to do as part of her National Honor Society volunteering quota. Since she liked to read, the library had seemed like as good a choice as any.

Kat blocked her path coming out of the break room. "Oh, you have some help today! And he's cute, lucky you."

Kat was about thirty. She dressed in funky clothes out of vintage stores and used little-girl-style hair elastics with the big beads on them. She seemed to love to encourage Morgan to flirt with the teenage patrons checking out graphic novels.

As Kat led the way, Morgan muttered, "Live vicariously much?"

Morgan was rubbing her eyes — they felt

so tired, almost gritty — and nearly bumped smack into Ethan.

"What are you doing here?"

Kat blurted, "Oh! You know each other. Fabulous. Morgan, show him what to do to help us with the shelving. Then maybe you can help me organize this craft for preschool hour tomorrow." Kat scurried away, no doubt imagining young love blossoming in the stacks.

Ethan said, "I get extra credit in government if I volunteer."

"You don't need extra credit in that class. A monkey could pass that class."

"Oooh-ooh, ah-ah," Ethan said, sounding not at all like a monkey.

Morgan laughed and felt her embarrassment ebb. Just a touch. "Seriously, though? This is getting all stalkery. You've gotta knock it off."

"Then answer my texts. Call me once in a while. Don't shun me for something I can't help."

Morgan flushed. "That's not the problem. Okay, now listen, since you invaded my territory here, you have to work."

Morgan explained the procedure and Ethan listened very seriously, as if she were explaining the secret to life, the universe, and everything.

They pushed the wheeled cart over by the little kid chapter books. As they began work, Ethan said, "So let's do something Saturday. Wanna go bowling?"

"Can't."

"Oh, plans with Britney? Where you guys going?"

"No, not her. Some orchestra friends."

"Yeah? Like who?"

"Geez, what's with the twenty questions? You going to follow me there, too? Hide in the dark and leap out of the shadows?"

Ethan glowered and shoved a book harder into its spot than necessary. "Christ, I was just asking. And I'm fine by the way, thanks for your concern about how I've been doing all these months of your silent treatment."

"Did you come here just to make me feel bad? I said I was sorry."

Ethan stopped, a book in his hand, and tossed his shaggy dark hair out of his face. "Actually, no. You didn't."

Morgan felt hot tears pooling behind her eyelids and fought to keep her voice steady. "Well, I am. I've missed having you around."

Ethan slammed a couple of books and then looked at Morgan fully. "Hey, hey. C'mon, I didn't want to upset you. Geez, don't do that. You know girl tears are like kryptonite to guys."

He folded her into his arms. Morgan stiffened, remembering their last embrace, but she made herself accept his kindness. He really was being just sweet, and at least, since he was gay, she could be sure this guy had no secret agenda.

They jumped apart at the sound of a throat clearing. Kat was leaning around the end of an aisle. "Hate to break it up, guys, but if I'm going to sign your form for volunteering, there should be more shelving and less snuggling."

Kat waggled her fingers, giggling.

Ethan chuckled, and Morgan joined him, wiping the dampness off her face. She sniffed and intoned, "Librarian matchmaker misfires wildly."

Ethan finished for her. "Film at eleven."

25

Morgan pulled out of her driveway and had to force herself to breathe so she wouldn't pass out at the wheel.

Though the occasion felt momentous to her, the lie required to make it happen was pathetically simple. A brief, "Hey, Mom, I'm gonna spend the night with Nicole, okay?" And she was off to — dare she think of him this way? — her boyfriend's house. Her lover's house. Morgan giggled out loud.

Nicole was an orchestra friend she'd drifted away from in senior year. But it was believable enough she'd spend the night there. To Dinah, anyway. And unlike Britney, whose mother was friends with Dinah, Nicole's mom and her mother never even saw each other. Nicole's mom, in fact, commuted to Royal Oak to work, and no one ever saw her in town at all, hardly.

Morgan motored away from her house and indulged herself in a giddy squeal. She winced as her old car's buzzing exhaust messed up her sophisticated rendezvous.

All she would have to do was check her phone now and then for texts or calls from her parents. They'd have no way of knowing where she really was when she answered.

Morgan had committed his directions to memory, so she drove with confidence, while being careful not to speed.

She felt briefly self-conscious about her old beat-up Chevy in the fancy neighborhood, then reminded herself that no one would be paying attention, not really. Her car was just another car on just another street.

She pulled into a long driveway that ran down a hill, the garage mercifully out of the view of the road. The garage opened just as planned; he must have been watching for her. This gave her another delighted shiver.

Once the garage door closed behind her, she squealed again, unable to help herself. She'd done it! She was inside and unseen. She opened her car door to see him standing in the doorway of the garage, a big gorgeous smile on his face.

"Hey, handsome," she said, stepping out of the car in her skinniest jeans and a shirt she'd unbuttoned down to her cleavage on the way over.

"Hey, yourself," he'd said, appreciating her body from top to toes.

It took all her willpower to saunter over with a sexy swing in her hips, and not fling herself into his arms in one ecstatic leap.

The candlelight made him look like a movie star.

This time, there had been no frantic clutching on a cold floor. He'd ushered her inside and showed her a table set with two plates, and candles lit. Jazz was playing from somewhere. She couldn't see any stereo or speakers. Maybe rich people had ambient sound they could pump anywhere in the house.

The music-from-nowhere made the whole thing feel even more like a movie.

As he'd served the pasta, Morgan had worried aloud over making a mess. He'd assured her that he could clean up so well they'd never know the difference, and the wine and dinner he'd brought in himself. He couldn't cook, he admitted sheepishly, so he'd ordered from Amici.

Now they were still sitting in the chairs at the corners of the table, the crumbs of dinner and dessert still scattered on the tablecloth.

Morgan toyed with the stem of her wineglass, something she'd seen women do in movies. She'd had wine before, but it was always some awful fruity stuff that made her queasy, and only in plastic cups. This red had a strong and difficult flavor but that made it easy to sip slowly, and with each sip she'd acclimated to the acrid boldness and was detecting the berry flavor underneath. Eventually, she was able to drink it without even a shiver, like a Frenchwoman or some other species of sophisticated adult. He'd refilled her glass with what she imagined was an admiring smile.

So far they'd been talking about his college days. He'd been telling her about a guy named Bill, famous in college for his ability to eat the hottest chicken wings, handfuls at a time, without taking a single sip of beer or water.

He leaned back in his chair — the picture of elegant cool, like George Clooney — and said, "So where are you going to college?"

That yanked her back to her actual life, to the e-mails she got in the same week from both Central Michigan and Boston U accepting her as a student, and how all she could do was file away BU's in her "save" folder, because she couldn't bear to look at it, couldn't bear to delete it. She shook her head and sipped the wine.

"I don't want to talk about that. I'd rather talk about . . . travel. Where would you go, if you could go anywhere?"

For a moment — so quick it seemed like déjà vu, something she wasn't even sure happened at all — his smile turned into a sneer. "You mean if I were fabulously wealthy like my brother?" His face relaxed in the next instant. "I wouldn't waste my time baking on some bland beach. I'd explore some part of the world. Japan, or India. An African safari. Something like that."

Morgan sat forward then, nodding. Yes, go on!

He winked at her. "With a fancy, civilized hotel and a huge, soft bed waiting at the end of the day. What about you?"

She tossed her hair back — it was itching her face — and for a moment she wanted to brush her hair in front of her cheek again. But she did not. She made herself leave her hair alone and face him, scar and all.

"Actually, I think first I'd want to explore our own country. We're so lucky to have so much variety here, you know? I'd take an epic road trip. I'd go east first, to New York. Then work my way to California and north to Oregon. It would take months. I'd keep a journal, and take pictures, write poetry . . ."

"Oh, you write? I didn't know that."

Morgan flashed on her poetry notebook, hidden under her mattress. "Nah, not really. I was just rambling."

"That's interesting," he said, regarding her with one hand on his chin. "I would have guessed that most girls your age would say something like Paris or Hawaii."

"I'm hardly a girl," Morgan replied, tossing her hair in what she hoped was a flirtatious way.

"Come here," he said now and held out his hand. She took it and let him pull her from her chair.

He walked her into the living room in front of a fire full of wispy dancing flames, tugging her gently down to sit.

"I don't understand why I feel this way," he said, his eyes on hers. He clasped both her hands and ran his thumbs softly over her fingers. "But I do. You make me feel like a hero, you know that? Like I could run to California and back. Like I could conquer anything and anyone, and it's all there in your face. I thought I had that with . . . I thought . . ."

Morgan held her breath. She did not want to talk about his wife. Did not even like thinking the word.

He cleared his throat. "I wish I could

make you promises. But I don't know what tomorrow holds. I don't even understand today, right now."

She exhaled and squeezed his hands. "You don't have to understand it."

"But can you live with that? That's what I need to know. I can't promise you what will happen between us. I can't promise how often I'll be able to see you. Or how long."

A gasp escaped Morgan before she could help it. "How long?"

"That's just it. We can't proceed as normal, like an ordinary couple. It may feel natural to us, but . . . it's not that simple. Do you follow me?"

Morgan nodded. Of course. She was not a naive child, after all. She could not expect him to abandon everything he had and run off into the sunset with her. She set her jaw against the growing lump in her throat.

He scooted forward on the floor. Morgan began to feel deeply cold, despite the warm fire and the humming furnace.

He said, "I need you to not make demands on me is what I'm asking. Because I don't know what I can do, or when I can do it. If you can't live with that, I understand and we'll stop this now, before anyone gets hurt . . ."

Morgan held herself still, considering what

was worse: having just one piece of him, or nothing at all.

He moved in closer to her, and she thought he was going to kiss her lips, but he tilted his head and instead kissed her neck, then moved up to her earlobe. Almost involuntarily she tipped her head, opening her neck to him, her hair falling away from her scar, which he then kissed in a succession of soft pecks.

He moved down her chin then to her chest. She tilted far back such that she almost fell, so he caught her from behind and kissed his way down her chest to the first button on her shirt, which he unfastened with his one free hand.

Without understanding how, she was suddenly in his arms, and he was standing. She felt drowsy and light-headed, and light in body, too, seeming to weigh nothing.

He started to walk her toward the stairs and then he stopped on the first step, asking her in a hoarse, strained whisper: "Are you okay with this? All this?"

She found she had only the strength to nod and reach her arms up around his neck as he bore her up, up, up the stairs.

Morgan startled awake and almost cried out, then in an instant remembered where she was, and who that was sleeping next to her. A smile unfurled over her face.

The four-poster bed was impossibly soft and roomy. She could stretch every which way and still not hit the edge. She rolled to her side, facing him, and sighed. The hall light was on, and in the soft glow through the open door, his arm outside the sheets was in silhouette. She could trace with her eyes the definition of his bicep.

Maybe she should drop his class. There was no way she could sit in there every day, not now. She would combust right in her chair if she had to hold in the memory of this night and all the places he'd touched her. They had done it what, three times? Four? She wasn't sure, the memory was fuzzy, as if seen through a scratched lens. She just remembered feeling wonderful and ecstatic, over and over.

Had she taken her pill?

Morgan sprang upright. She normally took her pill when she brushed her teeth, and she could instantly tell she had not done that. They'd just crashed out in the sheets together after a while.

Morgan had to urgently pee, too.

She slipped out of bed and padded through the semidarkened house, feeling her way. She was afraid to turn on many lights.

Some night owl could notice the lights were on late with his brother on vacation.

Morgan found her bag by the door where she'd come in and then took it back upstairs to the bathroom. As her sex haze faded, she was starting to notice her head felt sore, and she had a funny taste on her tongue.

In the bathroom's soft nightlight glow, she ripped open her makeup bag and found her pack of pills. She relaxed at the sight of the empty pill slot and suddenly remembered she'd taken one dry before she'd even entered the house, figuring she might be too distracted to remember.

Thank goodness she'd convinced her mother she wanted them only to "regulate her period" when she started dating David. Dinah may have suspected the real reason, but if so, she'd apparently taken a pragmatic view and faked ignorance, and for that Morgan could only be grateful.

After a trip to the bathroom, Morgan realized she hadn't checked her phone in hours. She'd set it to vibrate and left it in her pocket, then as they tore off each other's clothes it would have landed on the floor in her jeans.

Morgan crawled around on the floor in search of it, her heart pounding harder with each second. What if something terrible had happened at home? What if Jared had a seizure? What if her dad had a heart attack like old Mr. Adamczyk . . .

What if her mother couldn't reach her phone and decided to try Nicole's house directly?

With quivering hands she read her messages. All from Britney, and one from Ethan. None important.

Her head felt swimmy and achy again. She wanted to search for some Tylenol somewhere but didn't want to wake him and didn't want to rummage.

She pulled herself back into the vast, soft bed and snuggled next to his warmth. In his sleep, he slipped a heavy protective arm over her, and she closed her eyes to revel in its weight.

But sleep never came.

Somewhere in the vast house a grandfather clock chimed the passing hours, torture for an insomniac who didn't like to think about the sleep she was missing.

In a cruel twist, the nightmares she would have avoided, being awake, taunted her conscious mind, as their images popped up again and again, especially the new variety with her being crushed or consumed by him. . . .

Him. She could no longer even think his

teacher name.

Morgan turned from side to side, her nerves increasingly jangly with anxiety, her mind exhausted from the effort of pushing aside her creepy dreams.

It was nearly nine o'clock when he awoke at last.

Morgan was in the kitchen, washing and drying dishes and setting them carefully on the counter. She'd already taken a shower, and then dried the shower with a towel, then carried the towel into the basement where she'd dropped it in a pile of towels in a basket.

Her skin was starting to itch, being in someone else's house, especially as daylight poured in through the tall, east-facing windows, their filmy curtains doing little to stem the flood of morning sun.

Her head was still pounding, but she didn't dare make coffee, not wanting to make the mess worse. For all she knew they were coming home today. She'd never asked.

So when he finally appeared, she felt at first relief, a great *whoosh* of it that almost took her right down to the floor, tired as she was from only having dozed for a couple of hours.

"Hey," he said with a gravelly morning voice. "You didn't have to do that. But thanks."

He started rummaging in the kitchen. In making coffee, he scattered the grounds on the counter and she flinched. He said, "Ah, don't worry. I'll clean it. They're not back until Monday. And I'm not expected home right away either. I was out with my college drinking buddy last night you know."

He winked at her and then came over closer. He set down his mug, cradled the back of her head in his large hand, and pulled her toward him.

His morning breath was terrible; the inside of his mouth was coated with goo, it seemed like. His whiskers were scratching her lips. She tried to return his kiss with enthusiasm, but she wished to hell he'd have brushed his teeth first.

He released her head and sat down at the table. She hadn't put away the wine bottle yet, not knowing what to do with it, so it glowed green in the bright daylight that filled the room. Looking at it now, in front of him, she realized the bottle was empty. Had they gone through the whole thing in such a short time? She couldn't remember him drinking hardly any of it.

"How did you sleep?" he asked.

"Oh, fine. That bed is heaven."

He looked at her over the top of his mug. "It was last night."

They both froze at the sound of his ringing phone, sitting right where he left it last night, on the kitchen counter.

He walked over to take it, already seeming to tense. He answered it and turned his back to Morgan.

"Hey, hon. . . . No, just woke up. No, I'm feeling fine. . . . Yeah, not too much, Bill's not that wild man he used to be. . . . Oh yeah? Well, that sounds cool. . . . A surprise, huh? Nice. I'm not forgetting an anniversary, am I?" Here he laughed with that deep chuckle that gave Morgan shivers. ". . . Good. Okay, sweets, gotta dash so I can get cleaned up and home. . . . Love you, too."

Morgan was frozen with her hand on a dishtowel. His banter sounded perfectly casual, and worse than that, genuinely warm and sweet.

He hung up the phone and turned back to her. His face looked downcast and sad. "Sorry."

Morgan leaned against the counter and began to fold and unfold the dishcloth.

"Look, I'm gonna have to hurry up here and get home earlier than I thought." He stared at the floor a second. "Shit, that means I'm going to have to run those sheets through the wash later, I guess. Guess it's good you started to clean up, eh?"

He started roughly stacking the dishes and shoving them away in cupboards. He gathered up the takeout containers and the wine bottle and knotted them in a trash bag by the door to the garage. He removed the tablecloth and shook the crumbs into the trash.

As he was doing this, he wasn't looking at her, just rushing frantically. So she joined him in trying to put everything back the way it had been, by adjusting the throw pillows and pushing in chairs. She followed him upstairs and to the bedroom. The cornflower blue sheets were already half torn off the bed; they had to have been pretty vigorous. Morgan frowned and wished she could remember the details better; a night like this would have to last her a while. It's not like his brother would go on vacation every week.

He stood with the sheets in a ball in his hands. "I guess if I can't get this done I'll tell them I took a nap here or something. Or I spilled something on the bed. Ha! You could say that."

He stopped and pecked her forehead. "Thanks for your help. Do you need anything before you go?"

She'd been looking forward to breakfast together over the table, having a conversation about how they would meet next, how much she enjoyed the night. Maybe more talk about travel.

His arm was around her, and he was walking her down the stairs. He handed her the overnight bag by the door leading to the garage and then did a visual sweep of the open-plan dining and living room area, the wadded-up sheets still in one arm, braced on his hip. "We covered our tracks pretty well, I'd say. I'll throw these in the wash before I shower, throw them in the dryer by the time I'm out, and tonight when I come back to 'water those plants' again, I'll stick them back on the bed."

He grinned at her — the picture of satisfaction — as if he'd filled in the last answer of a difficult crossword puzzle.

"I'd say we done good," he added with a twinkle.

"Sure we did," she mustered, trying to match his enthusiasm. After all, he was right. You couldn't tell anyone had even been there, and his bedsheet plan would work fine. For her part, no one had contacted her with any emergencies while she was gone.

It was all going exactly according to plan.

He leaned in for a kiss, and this time she dodged his morning breath but covered by tilting her head to kiss his neck next to his Adam's apple. A groan rumbled in his throat, and he briefly grabbed her hair.

Then he released her. "Bye, I'll get in touch when I can." He opened the door, and she stepped into the chilly garage.

One word rang in her mind as he swung the door shut behind her: *dismissed.*

26

Rain arranged the gift on the center of the kitchen table, next to TJ's favorite dessert: pineapple upside-down cake.

It was a plain white box with an extravagant yellow bow: a riot of curls covering nearly the whole top of the box. Inside were two things: a silver rattle, the type meant to be engraved as a keepsake, and a cotton bib that read WORLD'S BEST DADDY.

She'd planned to tell him that day at the mall, figuring school must be out by then, but when he didn't answer his cell phone, she changed course. This was too huge to be announced on the phone.

She was then going to tell him at home that night, but then he seemed so distracted and a little curt with her. That didn't seem right, either. She was going to tell him Friday, but then his buddy had swooped into town and TJ was going to go hang with him in Royal Oak Saturday night and go drinking, so she figured maybe Sunday was the day, provided he wasn't too hungover.

Since he'd sounded so upbeat on the phone in the morning, Rain felt at last this was the perfect time to tell him all their dreams were coming true.

Her ears pricked up at the sound of his car pulling into the driveway.

She had rehearsed this moment so many times. In some of her daydreams, she'd shown him the two lines on the pregnancy test and they'd danced around the bathroom together, whooping with glee. In others, she'd told him while they were cuddled in bed and they'd held each other, then made love carefully, befitting her delicate state.

The back door opened and she relaxed a couple of degrees, not realizing she'd been nervous. TJ had a cheerful, upright posture. His hair was slick and wet, and she could smell the soap all the way across the room, a fresh, almost minty scent that oddly reminded her of his brother, Greg.

"Hey, beautiful," he said, eyeing the package. "To what do I owe this pleasure? I've been racking my brain all the way over here about what occasion I missed."

"Not at all. You didn't miss anything. You definitely did not."

He cocked an eyebrow and settled into

the chair across from her. Rain sat on her hands to keep from ripping open the box for him.

He clowned by putting the ribbon on his head, and then as his fingers pushed aside the tissue paper, her every nerve screamed.

He picked up the rattle and blinked several times, looking at it like a monkey in a zoo regarding a strange piece of fruit.

She prompted him by picking up the bib and handing it to him. His mouth fell open, and he looked up at her, bafflement written in the crook of his eyebrows and slightly narrowed eyes.

"We're going to be parents," she told him, smiling hard, as if for both of them.

"Are . . . are you sure?" he asked, the bib and rattle in each hand, that stupid bow still on his head.

"Yes, of course I am. The doctor confirmed it with a blood test. It's true this time. No early home test, no faded second line. And I'm late. No period, either. Look." She pulled down her v-neck shirt. "Even my boobs are swelling up already."

He put down the bib and rattle carefully in the box, as if they were products he found unsatisfactory and intended to return. He closed the cardboard lid. "I'm . . . stunned."

She reached across and grabbed his arm.

"Aren't you happy? Please be happy . . ."

"Give me a minute," he blurted, and took off upstairs to the bathroom, leaving Rain to curl up alone in the kitchen chair.

When TJ came down an hour later, Rain was on the couch with her laptop in her lap, signing up for baby websites. The latest gave her a due date in September and told her that her child was the size of a kidney bean.

There were message boards, too. Virtual coffee klatches where mothers-to-be could vent about morning sickness and ask each other embarrassing questions. If she were the type of person to do such a thing, she could have posted, "My husband and I are expecting a baby after years of infertility and months of treatment, and all he can say is 'give me a minute.' I want to throw him out of the house and make him sleep on the porch. Is this normal?"

But instead she'd ordered some yellow onesies from Baby Gap.

TJ stopped in front of the couch, his head drooping in his classic hangdog posture. He clasped his hands in front of him. "Sorry," he mumbled.

Rain tried to say something conciliatory. She only managed to put the laptop on the coffee table and face him with folded arms.

Gran's advice was ringing in her ears: "The key to a successful marriage is to forgive, every day if you have to, and move on."

TJ dropped down to his knees next to the couch and took her hands in his. He stroked the back of her hand with his thumb. "Somehow I'd convinced myself it was never going to work. I'd accepted that. So this was just a shock."

"But treatment was your idea this time. I thought you were still . . . on board."

"I wanted you to try again because you wanted it. But I'd lost faith, honestly."

"So you were humoring me?"

He shifted in his awkward, crouched posture. "You could say that, I guess. I didn't think of it that way. I thought of it as giving you what you wanted because it made you smile."

"I suppose that's a better reason than competing with your brother." Rain chuckled as if she were kidding.

He stared at her abdomen then, still flat as ever, for now. He lifted the hem of her T-shirt and stared, as if he had x-ray vision and could actually see the embryo. Then he laid a hand gently there and breathed, "Wow."

Rain bent forward and grabbed him by the head, pulling him up on top of her, where she held him against her and relaxed at last. He was still on board with her after all. With both of them.

He snuggled up with her on the couch, wrapping around her like a vine. They barely fit this way, and it was almost comical how they were smooshed together.

TJ said, "Can't wait to tell my brother when he gets back from his tropical paradise."

"Oh, let's not tell yet."

"Why not?" TJ sat up from her a bit, wrinkling his brow and cocking his head to one side.

"I just . . . it's early and the first few weeks there's always a chance . . . that something could go wrong. I wasn't even going to tell my mom yet."

Rain knew the minute she told Angie that her mother would clear out the baby aisle at Walmart buying stuff. And if something did happen, she couldn't bear to even imagine the agony of all those baby things around. Not to mention having to untell everyone they'd told.

She could feel TJ's disappointment in the stiffening of his posture. After a moment, he untangled himself and stood up.

"I'm sure you're right," he said, sighing. "It's all very logical."

"Hey," Rain said, reaching for his hand and using it to brace herself as she stood, facing him. "It's our secret for now. That's kind of fun, isn't it? To have a secret?"

A strange expression passed over his face. He gathered her in tight and kissed the top of her head. "Sure it is."

27

Dinah snapped her head up from her final review of the Planning Commission papers — well, it should be final, nearly final, only she kept thinking of reasons to look them over again — to see Morgan coming in the back door shortly after 10 A.M.

"Wow, you're early for a slumber party night."

"I didn't sleep very well," Morgan mumbled. "Where's Dad?"

"He took the boys to Mass. He thought Jared especially could use it. I just wanted some peace so I could reread this stuff for my meeting. Are you sure you're okay, honey?"

Morgan rolled her head around. "I've got a headache something awful."

Dinah paused, tapping her pen against the documents, narrowing her eyes. "So. What did you and Nicole do last night?" As she said this, Dinah turned to her laptop open on the table next to her and made a few discreet clicks while Morgan went to get some coffee from the machine.

"Oh, you know, just watched a movie."

"What did you watch?"

"Um, actually it was TV. *Real Housewives, Teen Mom.* Stupid stuff like that. Mainly we just talked."

"Just talked? You didn't dip into the vodka or something?"

"Jeez, Mom, I have a headache. I said I didn't sleep well. You know how it is sleeping somewhere else."

"Sorry. Yes, I do know. I've gotta ask, you know."

Morgan massaged her neck. "I need Motrin and a nap. Anyway, don't you worry about me, Mom. You know good old Morgan."

Dinah stood up to hug her daughter, then dug around for some Motrin out of her purse. "You don't have to do everything right, you know. I love you no matter what."

Morgan downed the Motrin and went upstairs. "Thanks, Mom. I love you, too. Hey, we still on for a chick flick tonight?"

"You know it. I've got *Something Borrowed* all queued up for us."

Morgan gave her a wave before yawning dramatically and dragging herself upstairs.

Dinah frowned, then retreated to her laptop and opened up Facebook. Nicole was a friend of Morgan's, so just maybe her profile would be visible. . . . There. Last night she'd posted, "So much fun just watching TV with friends and just hanging out! I'm gonna miss you next year, Mo!"

Dinah smiled. She shouldn't have doubted her superstar daughter.

That evening, mother and daughter sat in front of a romantic comedy about — what else? — getting married. Dinah's favorite movies always had a wedding dress in there somewhere; talk about escapist. So it shouldn't have surprised her when Morgan asked, "So, Mom, tell me about marriage."

Dinah almost choked on her popcorn. "Why do you want to know? No one's proposing to you, are they?" and continued silently, *Like I know anything about it, anyway.*

"I'm just wondering what makes a person stay married. And what happens if you fall out of love? What happens if one of the people falls for someone else?" In the movie they were watching, in fact, it seemed clear the handsome leading man was engaged to the wrong woman.

Morgan picked at the popcorn bowl instead of looking right at Dinah.

"Honey, are you worried about me and Dad? Because we're doing just fine. We still love each other very much."

Morgan waved her hand. "No, I know that. Let's say . . . it's a friend. I don't want to say who, so don't grill me. Not someone you know. This person's parents got married, but they're having problems. The wife doesn't seem to love her husband anymore, and he's found someone else, someone who does love him. Should people like that ever tough it out? Or should they split up?"

"Whew. Deep thoughts tonight." Dinah tipped her head back on the couch, trying to rally her tired brain to be Wise Mother when all she'd been prepared to do was giggle at a Kate Hudson flick. But as she knew well from the twins, those pesky "teachable moments" could pop up anytime.

"I knew this one couple where the husband cheated on the wife. They made up, eventually. I don't know if it was love though, or if the affair was just about sex."

"I think it's love," Morgan said quietly, eyes fixed on the television.

"In that case, if it's really love with someone else, their marriage is in big trouble. But most of the time? When people think they've fallen in love with someone else, they're really just trying to escape from their problems. Like living in a fantasy. Grass is greener and all that stuff." Dinah curled up and turned to face Morgan. "I guarantee if they married the new person, it wouldn't be long before they'd be fighting over the mundane stuff like termites and plumbing and the kids, too. That's just the fact of it. Marriage is hard." She saw Morgan frown, as if this was somehow news to her. "Not romantic, but it's true, honey. Some people never really grow up, and they think that the first blush of passion is something they deserve to have, constantly and forever. Those types will never be happy, no matter how many pretty young things they run off with, who won't stay young, anyway."

"But what if they married the wrong person, like, by mistake, the first time? And the new one is actually the right one, for real?"

Dinah shrugged. "I guess anything is possible. I'd be surprised if a relationship that started with cheating and lying would work out, though. Don't you think?"

Morgan was fingering the popcorn and had stopped eating it. Still staring at the TV.

"Hello? Earth to Morgan? What's wrong? You seem way too invested in this conversation for just some friend's parents."

Morgan shook her head and smiled at Dinah. "Oh, it's nothing. Just thinking about these things, you know, as I get older and I think about getting serious. Someday, in the future. I mean, how do you know when it's a real, forever thing, then? If it's so easy to be confused by the 'first blush of passion'?"

"You know how I knew? When I imagined your dad and me growing old together. Sitting on a porch swing, covered in grandbabies. All wrinkled and fat and gray. Us, not the babies." Dinah laughed. "And that felt like the most wonderful thing in the world."

Morgan rolled her eyes and slouched. "How romantic."

Dinah shrugged. "It was to me. You asked." After a pause, she could not resist asking again, "No one's proposing to you or anything, are they?"

"Hardly. It's not like I have boyfriends lining up out the door."

"That's because high school boys are morons. You wait until they grow up a bit. Then they will be lining up for you. You watch."

Morgan seemed to flush a little pink at this. She said, "Whatever, Mom," but she was grinning.

Dinah smiled at her girl and nudged her playfully with her shoulder. How many mothers were so lucky that their daughter talked to them about things like this? Sought them out and spent time just hanging out?

Dinah allowed herself simply to feel lucky for once, to stop questioning, worrying, and just enjoy this small precious moment.

28

On the good days, Morgan's cello seemed alive to her; like a friend, or more accurately, like a loving pet: responsive to touch and attention, never judgmental, ever present.

Other days, like this day, in her room with her solo, it seemed like the actual object it was. A bulky hollow chunk of wood that could only be coaxed to produce music with just the right stroke of the bow, the precise placement of the fingers.

Morgan felt tears sting her eyes as her fingers once again collided with each other like a highway pileup, and her bow squawked across the string. She carefully rested her bow on the stand and set her cello carefully on its side, biting down hard on a surging desire to snap her bow over her knee.

Though, she thought as she lowered herself shakily to the side of her bed, being fiberglass, the bow might not break anyway.

She'd known a solo would be hard, out there alone with nothing between her and the judges but her instrument and the music stand. But she'd given in to the conductor, Mrs. Allen, and her wheedling to try a solo, for just this last competition, in honor of her last year in orchestra. After all, next year in college she would not be playing, in fact she probably would not even take her cello; it would be far too bulky in a shared dorm room.

Morgan sat back on her bed and massaged her aching hands. Her temples throbbed now that she was prone, and she closed her eyes, savoring the notion of sleep. But she hadn't yet done her homework for the afternoon; she'd decided to practice first because the boys weren't home yet. They always whined when she practiced the cello. Even with her door closed it was pretty damn loud, even if she clipped the mute to the bridge to try and dull the ringing sound.

She stared at her phone, praying for him to text her. She picked it up and thumbed through the old texts, rereading the precious few he'd been able to send.

Miss you.

All clear with house.☺

Will have house to self Fri night.

That last text had driven her to distraction. It was nearly Valentine's Day and while all her friends were carrying on about the Snow Ball and who they were taking, and what they were wearing, and whether they would be getting flowers and chocolates . . . she couldn't share in any of it, not even to pretend to be interested in anyone. The secrecy had begun to unsettle her. The ease with which he ignored her in class — while she sat in her chair almost exploding, she felt so pent-up — was making her feel queasy.

Then came that message about Friday night. It had taken her three tries to text back, she'd been shaking so hard.

Of course she'd agreed to come, although . . . It was one thing to play house in his brother's mansion, but his own home? And how could he be sure she wouldn't come back unexpectedly? Did she really want to be in their private space?

But the rehearsal rooms were now full of college students actually rehearsing. Morgan herself never had a bit of privacy anywhere. What else was she going to do?

Screw him in his car, or a crappy hotel room, like some kind of prostitute?

They'd made the arrangements very late one night, the glow of Morgan's phone setting her sheets alight as she huddled under the covers — late-night texting being specifically forbidden in her house — making her think of when she was little and was reading Harry Potter after dark with a flashlight until the wee hours. That seemed like a hundred years ago.

Morgan was going to drive to the mall to meet him. He'd said his neighbors were too nosy to risk her just driving up.

They were putting one over on everyone, and sometimes this made Morgan feel powerful indeed.

She heard the back door slam and her brothers bound through the door. The Elgar piece tumbled off the stand just then, bringing her back to the present problem. She couldn't seem to play the damn thing anymore.

Morgan was beginning to realize she'd have to cultivate another variety of lie. Barring a miracle improvement on her part, she'd never be able to go through with a solo performance, even if she scrounged up a real live last-minute accompanist. Then she'd have to make up some reason why not. Food poisoning, or a migraine.

This thought made her heart swell with a surprising burst of nostalgia and sadness for a rather pathetic end to her high school orchestra career. This definitely wasn't how her senior year was supposed to go.

Morgan felt like standing on the lunch table and telling everyone to shut the hell up.

They were all so . . . loud. Even though they were also all texting — a form of talking already — they were also talking over each other, shrieking "No!" and "Shut up!" out of surprise over some stupid revelation about something. There was no quiet corner to escape to. So she stuck in her earbuds and started the concerto playing, hoping maybe the music performed beautifully by Jacqueline du Pré would jar her back to being able to play it like she used to.

She listened, and picked the tomatoes out of her salad-bar lunch, and as such didn't hear Ethan until he manifested as a shadow over her shoulder.

She jumped and yanked out her earbuds. "Oh, you. Sheesh, you startled me."

"What's up?" he asked, turning a chair around and straddling it backward.

"Nothing."

"Wanna go to Snow Ball with me?"

Morgan quirked an eyebrow by way of response.

"You're my friend," Ethan replied drily to her unspoken smart remark. "Plenty of boy-girl friends go to the Snow Ball. It would be fun. I'll wear the stupidest bow tie I can find and buy you a corsage as big as a softball. We could sit in the back and make fun of the bad dresses."

"I don't want to do that."

"Are you already going with someone?"

"No."

"Then why not?"

"I just don't. It would be too weird."

"Why? Like I said, we're friends."

She glanced around behind them. No one was paying any attention. "I don't wanna be part of your pretending."

Ethan flushed pink, and his jaw tightened. "That's not why I asked. I wish I'd never told you."

Morgan glanced back down at her salad and pushed it away. "Sorry. I shouldn't have said that. But I just can't. I don't want to go be surrounded by couples right now."

Ethan frowned. "Why not? It's not still David, is it?"

She waved her hand. "No, no. It's just . . ."

Morgan paused. Could she really? The pressure of holding it in was harder than she ever thought it could be. And if anyone understood about secrets . . .

"I'm seeing someone."

"Yeah? Bring him to the dance, then."

"I can't." Morgan stared at the fake woodgrain of the cafeteria table.

"Why not?"

"He doesn't go here. He's . . . older."

Ethan leaned in and whispered, so close to Morgan's ear his lips almost brushed her scar. She could feel Ethan's breath in her hair, which made her think of *him* and his brother's house and she shivered. Ethan was asking, "How old?"

She made herself face him. "Old enough you can't tell a single soul what I just said."

Ethan's expression grew hard. "That doesn't sound good."

"I don't need you to judge me."

"I'm just saying that any romance you have to hide and sneak around about . . ."

Morgan jammed her phone and earbuds in her backpack, standing up abruptly and giving Ethan one last, eyebrow-raised look.

Really. He should talk.

She'd almost made it out of the cafeteria when she heard her name shrieked at the same time as Britney grabbed her hand. She yanked her over to the table where she sat with some girls from the band: flute players mostly, pretty girls whose giggles sounded airy and high, just like their instruments.

"Hey! Let's go to the movies Friday night. Then we can go get a coffee or something."

The girls looked at her expectantly. With Morgan standing and the rest sitting, faces raised, they reminded her of baby birds, twittering and all.

"Can't. I have plans."

She walked away quickly, knowing the bell was about to ring. She heard running feet behind her and cringed just as Britney caught up to her and snagged her elbow. Morgan fought her urge to yank away. Britney was such a touchy-feely kind of a girl, and that had really started to annoy the ever-loving hell out of her.

"What's up your ass? You too good for us or something?"

What if I am? she was tempted to blurt. "No, I'm sorry. I'm just busy, like I said. I am way behind on practicing for solo and ensemble."

"But you can't rehearse all night. Come out after!"

"I can't. I'm not feeling well lately. I think I'm getting my period or something. I'm just really tired."

Britney yanked Morgan to a full stop in the hall. Kids crashed into them from behind and cursed them out. Britney towed Morgan off to the side. "You're not pregnant, are you?"

Morgan started laughing, and she was so tired and loopy from the previous night's suffocation dream that she thought she might keep laughing all through calculus, Spanish, and the drive home. Finally she stopped. "I'm tired. Just old-fashioned tired. Anyway, I'm not dating anyone, remember? You ought to know, right?"

Britney and David supposedly weren't boyfriend and girlfriend, but they seemed to be together an awful lot, even so.

"Not dating anyone that we know of, anyway. Maybe you have a secret lover," Britney said, but it was clear from the toss of her hair as she spoke that it was just something to say, a joke of a notion so ludicrous it wasn't even worth sounding scandalized about. She gave Morgan a quick hug and made her promise to come to another movie sometime soon, and she nearly skipped away down the hall.

Friday couldn't come soon enough, Morgan decided, as with effort she peeled herself away from the wall and trudged off to class.

Friday evening, leaning on the side of her

Chevy in the mall parking lot, Morgan checked her phone. Right on time. But no sign yet of his car. She was just standing there in her ballet flats and miniskirt, goose bumps prickling her legs.

It was freakishly warm for February, but not so warm it was miniskirt weather. She wasn't supposed to be standing around, though. She was supposed to be picked up by now, in his warm car, on his way to his house. She had a change of clothes in her backpack, and Nicole was lined up to be her cover story, complete with fake Facebook update later. They'd even taken a cellphone picture together that Nicole would later post. As far as Nicole knew, Morgan was dating a twenty-one-year-old college student in secret because her parents would have thought he was too old for her. Nicole thought that was terribly romantic and was all too happy to help. Not to mention, Morgan let Nicole copy her calc homework every morning as a show of gratitude.

There. She recognized the car. Though she couldn't yet see the driver and didn't want to approach a stranger. She was already feeling naked and exposed, standing out in the open. . . . Finally she exhaled, not realizing she'd been holding her breath.

He'd rolled down the passenger window.

"Going my way?" he asked, and winked.

"I am now," she replied, and hopped into the warmth of his car as he pushed the button to roll the window up again.

She reached over to peck his cheek, but he moved back.

She sat back, feeling herself blush, and stared at her hands.

"Sorry, it's just . . ."

"I know," she said quickly.

"And, um, there's something else I have to ask. I need you to, like, slouch down or something. The seat reclines with a button on the side."

"Oh," was all she could think to say. The mechanical whirr of the seat reclining reminded her of the dentist's office. Finally she was low enough to be underneath the window view. She rested there on her back, staring up at the car's beige interior, not wanting to look at him from this humiliating position.

He didn't speak, either. They rode in silence with something unspoken growing between them like a balloon filling to the point of breaking.

Morgan was arguing with herself.

How dare he! You aren't some whore.

But be realistic: This could ruin him. That's why it's so powerful, isn't it? The fact that he's risking everything to be with you?

He could make it right. If he wanted to be together, he could leave his wife and in a few months see you properly. There would be no need for hiding like a criminal.

Morgan turned toward the passenger door, feeling the blood drain from her face. Her stomach turned over, and a wash of dizziness crashed over her.

"I'm carsick," she finally said. "I'm afraid I'm going to be sick."

"Just a couple blocks," he said, his voice gritty with strain. She heard a noise as he cracked the window. Cold outdoor air swirled into the car, of little help to her. "Breathe deeply," he said sharply. Like a command.

He doesn't want the mess, Morgan realized. How would he explain that? And obviously he had no notion of pulling over, or allowing her to sit up.

Morgan tried to breathe as he ordered, not wanting to throw up either.

Finally, the car stopped. "Hang on," he told her, and he hopped out, leaving her flat in the passenger seat. She heard keys rattling nearby, and then he popped the car door open and held out his hand. "Coast is clear. Quickly, get inside."

She felt shaky as she stumbled out of the

car and up some cement porch steps. He almost threw her across the threshold and she stumbled, grabbing a kitchen chair for support as he slammed the door behind them.

"Aaah. Now we're alone," he said, his voice blooming with relief.

Morgan sank into the chair, wanting to feel relief herself, still feeling sick, still reeling in fact, as if she'd been on an ocean voyage.

He was locking the door behind her and busying himself with something by the kitchen counter. She swept her eyes across his home — *their* home. There were afghans and framed photos of nature scenes, and seashells on shelves. The room had a disarray about it that was homey and familiar. Not unlike her own home, Morgan realized. She looked down at the faux-wood dining table.

"Here," he said, handing her a jelly glass filled with ice water. "Take little sips. I'm really sorry about that."

"I hated that," Morgan blurted, taking a sip and then pressing the cool glass to her cheek. "Like I was something disgusting to hide away."

She finally raised her eyes to his. She almost gasped. His eyebrows were lowered, his stare hard. "We cannot be seen together. Do you know what that would do to me? What that would cost me? Do you know what risk I'm taking having you here at all? In my house?"

"I'm sorry, I didn't mean to make you mad . . ."

"I mean, if my wife found out, the school . . . my whole world would be over."

The queasy overheated feeling was leaving her, and Morgan felt then as if she were growing colder by the moment, freezing slowly from the toes up.

"But . . . you said . . ." Morgan tried to remember his exact words from the night at his brother's house. Something about being patient. But didn't that mean waiting for something good in the future? "I thought . . . after graduation . . . I know this is . . . unusual, but you feel it too, don't you? That it's special? Meant to be? Won't they all find out sometime that . . ."

He raked his hands through his dark hair roughly, staring down at the table.

Morgan's heart thudded, and the chilled feeling spread to her limbs and fingers, and she began to tremble. "You . . . love me. Right? Don't you?"

He jumped up roughly from his chair and grabbed her close, covering her mouth and neck with urgent kisses. He began to caress her with one hand in her hair, the other roaming all over her back, and inside her skirt. She was wearing a thong and when he discovered it, he groaned into her mouth as they kissed. He picked her up, doll-like, and much as he'd done before, he carried her up the stairs.

"No," she said, panting. "Not in the bed . . ." *Not your wife's bed.*

In the bedroom, he set her down on her feet then lifted her again, facing him. In moments he'd hoisted her up, pressing her back against the wall, and pushing her skirt up and out of the way.

"I love you," he breathed into her ear as he crushed her hard against the wall. "I do love you."

She tried to say she loved him too, but she could barely catch her breath.

They ended up on the floor again, next to the bed. He'd fetched a spare blanket, and she was resting her head on his muscular arm, her leg thrown over his. The warm, languid feeling was back, all the earlier car-sickness and nausea nearly forgotten.

And he'd said he loved her.

She sighed deeply, feeling emptied out of all her stress, care, and worries, which now seemed minute and petty indeed.

He kissed her temple and whispered, "I have to get up for a minute. Sorry." She reluctantly moved her head and allowed him to rise. She followed the progress of his naked, strong body across the room to the bathroom and smiled. Then she rolled to her side.

Her eyes landed on a pair of women's slippers, under the bed.

They were moccasins, lined with puffy fleece, the kind that you would wear after a long day, on a cold night, watching TV, snuggled up next to your husband. Morgan turned to her other side and saw, sticking out of a dresser drawer that was not all the way closed, a piece of silky ivory cloth trimmed with lace.

She sat up, aware suddenly of how naked she was, and she snatched up the blanket around her chest. On the wall across from her, the wall where just moments before they'd been having sex, was a wedding photo. She hadn't noticed it, though it must have been just a few inches from her head.

The bride was wearing a simple white gown fitting close to the body until the hips, where it swept away, ending in a small train. It was an off-shoulder gown, exposing her delicate collarbone. The bride's bouquet of white tulips drooped down, loose in her hand as she gazed up at her new husband.

And he, the groom, the man who'd just nailed Morgan against the wall, was staring with fierce, wild love at his bride, a half smile on his face like he could hardly believe his luck, one arm wrapped around her waist, pulling her close.

The bathroom door opened, and he came back into the room, following Morgan's gaze.

"Don't look at that," he barked.

She dropped her eyes to the blanket, wondering suddenly if he and the wife bought it as a couple, strolling through Bed Bath and Beyond with their fingers laced together.

He said, "Maybe it was a mistake to be here." He pulled on his underwear and jeans roughly, as if he had somewhere urgent to go.

"Don't say that," she replied. "It wasn't. I . . . I'm happy to be here with you."

He stopped dressing, slumped a bit. "I know. It's just . . . too hard. Worlds colliding. It was just convenient was all. She'll be back early though, so . . ."

"Early? Early when?"

"Early in the morning. She's coming back first thing."

"I thought . . ." Morgan realized she'd assumed another overnight visit, when he'd only been referring to the evening.

"I'll take you back to your car in a little while. Want a snack? I've got some wine," he said, dressing again, pulling on his socks, a shirt, an old baseball cap. He started handing her clothes back to her.

"Um. Sure, I guess."

She dressed and started running through her choices. She'd told her mom she'd be gone all night. She could claim to have come home sick, but this also meant getting Nicole to adjust their story, and what if she couldn't reach her? What then?

"Shit," he muttered, as his phone vibrated on the nightstand. He snatched it up, and Morgan watched him pale as he read the screen.

"She's coming home tonight. Like, now."

"Oh, no."

"Hurry up! She said she's not feeling good, and she's coming home right now. I have to get you out of here and straighten this place up."

Morgan was throwing on her clothes now, taking three tries to get her arm into her sleeve. "Where is she driving from?"

"Lansing, so it won't take her that long. She was at some book signing for some yoga dude, and I thought she was going to stay the night in town with Beverly . . . shit."

He started jamming the blanket into folds. Morgan tried to help him, but he yanked it away from her. "Go find your shoes and meet me by the back door."

In a matter of minutes they were driving off into the evening. She'd started to lower the seat, but he told her not to bother, it was dark out anyway. He drove fast and hard, taking sharp corners that almost threw Morgan into the door. He pulled up next to Sears in the mall parking lot, away from any parking lot lights, and looked at her pointedly, hitting the "unlock" button.

Morgan looked back at him and opened her mouth to say something, but he cut her off. "I have to get going. Quick, before anyone sees us."

She hopped out and slammed the door just in time to watch his car pull away with the flow of traffic, leaving her standing alone, exactly as she'd been just two hours before.

29

Rain wasn't sick. She was feeling fine. She was feeling, in fact, far too fine. She had been praying for morning sickness, for fatigue like other expectant mothers talked about. Her breasts were even less sore than before. She had snuck into the bookstore's bathroom to squeeze them. They felt completely normal.

She then suffered something in the bathroom stall at the book signing that she could only describe as a panic attack: She'd slammed her fist into the wall behind the toilet hard enough to bruise her hand and screamed silently in such a way that turned her throat raw.

Rain left the bathroom stall trembling and convinced the baby within her had disappeared. She texted TJ that she was coming home and made her apologies to Beverly. Fortunately they had driven separately.

By the time Rain had gotten onto the

highway, reason had started to edge its way back in, and she understood, in her higher brain functions, anyway, that she had not lost the baby just because she wasn't vomiting.

She might have to quarantine herself from pregnant women, Rain thought, as a light mist started to fall — in February? — and she flipped on her windshield wipers. There had been a pregnant woman next to her at the book signing, opining about how miserable she was with heartburn, how pregnancy was such a trial and she wished she could hire out someone to do this part of the job. How she'd thrown up so much in the first trimester she'd subsisted on ginger ale and saltines. That's what started it all.

As the woman carried on this way, Rain's hand drifted to her flat stomach, and that's when she was overcome with the urge to squeeze her breasts and check for soreness. And she went to the bathroom and did just that, and she found none.

Rain tried again, in the darkness of the car. Still fine.

As she drove, she tried to recover the joy she felt when the nurse gave her the news. Rain had known the moment she'd said, "We have the results of your pregnancy test!," because the nurse's voice had an unmistakable brightness reserved only for good news. It had come like a burst of sun, the kind that hits you in the face when you drive out of a tunnel.

The joy had quieted some as she tried to find the perfect time to tell TJ, and then it receded like a tide going out in the face of his muted reaction.

Since then she'd begun to feel numb. Not depressed, nor joyous.

"Why can't this just be normal?" she shouted into the car's interior.

The only answer was the slapping of the wipers and the spitting of rain on the windshield.

When she walked back inside the house, she found TJ looking flushed and frantic, coming down from upstairs.

"What's wrong?" she asked.

"Nothing. I'm fine. Just worried about you."

He came forward to hug her, but his embrace was quick and stiff and he released her quickly. His hair was damp and he smelled like soap. He said, "Can I get you something, honey? Some tea? You said you're sick?"

"More like tired," she said. "Did you take a shower?"

"I was bored so I worked out on the elliptical and got all sweaty."

"Oh. Okay. I feel a little sleepy, I might turn in early."

Rain walked upstairs, conscious of TJ following her. She was impatient then with his hovering, making her wish she'd stayed at the hotel in Lansing with Beverly rather than come all the way home.

At the doorway to the bedroom she paused, and he bumped into her from behind. "What gives? Can I have some space?"

"Forgive me for being concerned about my pregnant wife who came home sick from a trip," he barked. "What if you passed out on the stairs or something and broke your neck?"

Rain pinched the bridge of her nose. "Your kindness is so overwhelming."

"What does that mean?"

Rain's armor was already worn thin and brittle. Her emotional fortitude to carry the burden for the both of them as a couple had eroded as well, and she almost relished this rare moment when she couldn't help herself: "Yell at me a little more so I'll feel even better."

He stomped down the stairs, leaving Rain bracing herself in the door frame. She heard his angry progress through the kitchen, heard a chair get slammed against the table or the wall, and then heard more pounding down another flight of steps to the basement. As Rain tried to breathe slowly to steady her pounding heart, she heard the *whoosh whoosh* of the elliptical.

Odd, she thought as she peeled off her pants and rooted in her dresser for a nightgown. Normally he wouldn't do the elliptical twice in one night. His knees were in bad enough shape from his old track-star days that even the smooth oval action would be too much after a time.

She dropped her cotton nightgown over her head and in the act of turning back the sheets on the bed, she paused. Something felt off-kilter in the room.

It was a scent, something vaguely floral with a dash of citrus. She frowned and scented the air again like a wild animal.

Her phone chimed from the pocket of her jeans, now crumpled on the floor. She stretched down to pull it from the pocket. Two messages: one from Beverly, hoping she felt better. And a picture from Fawn of a smiling, drooly Brock with the message, "First tooth!"

Rain dropped the phone back on the floor, where it landed with a quiet thunk.

■ ■ ■ ■

In the morning, Rain still felt fine. Her jeans still buttoned with no strain or effort.

She approached the bathroom with the same old infertility cocktail of fear laced with anticipatory sadness bubbling up within her.

She stepped into the bathroom and steeled herself. She sat down, looked down, and gasped.

Blood.

Not much, but more than a speck. A dirty reddish brown. Rusty, almost.

Her head swam. Despite last night's panic and despair, somewhere there had been a shred of optimism. At the sight of blood she found herself somehow — improbably after all that failure — shocked.

Rain peed, found a panty liner. Washed her shaking hands. In the mirror a ghost of herself stared back. She whispered to her paling reflection: "Spotting is normal. Some spotting is normal."

She lowered herself carefully to the edge of their bed and dialed Dr. Gould's after-hours emergency line on her cell phone. She knew the clinic would be open at least part of the day on a Saturday: A woman's eggs and uterus didn't care about weekends, and timing was everything.

She left a message with a bored-sounding nurse, and then she put the phone carefully down on the rumpled comforter next to her and put her face in her hands.

She didn't look up when she heard his footsteps.

"Babe?"

"Yeah," she said through her hands.

"What's wrong?"

"I'm bleeding."

She didn't look up from her hands, not daring to see if he seemed concerned, or frustrated, or even angry.

Instead she felt him settle next to her and wrap his arms around her. She allowed herself to be pulled close. "Is it . . ." he ventured. ". . . bad? Is it, I mean it's not . . ."

"I don't know," she said, staring across the room now at the blank pale blue wall. "I called."

He squeezed her. "I'm sorry I was such a dick last night. I'm stressed out. But that's not fair to you."

He turned her to face him, and she finally met his eyes. They were red rimmed, and the whites were run through with cracks of red like rivers on a map. He had shaved at some point, but hurriedly, so that his face was reddened and he had a nick near his jaw. She reached up with her thumb and pressed the dot of blood, wiped it away. His eyes welled up, and he pulled her in tightly. "I'm so sorry," he said. "I don't want to lose you. I can't lose you. Please don't let me lose you."

"Why would you lose me?" she said, half muffled by his T-shirt and tight squeeze. "I wouldn't leave you over one snappish remark. I'm not my parents who split up every other week."

"I don't deserve you," he said.

"Yes, you do."

"Trust me. I definitely do not."

Whatever he might have said next was cut off by the ringing of Rain's phone, lighting up with Dr. Gould's number.

Rain lay back on the vinyl cushion, her eyes trained on a small screen facing her. Ultrasounds at this early stage were no simple affair of a wand over the top of a swollen belly. "Transvaginal" they were called. Uncomfortable was what they were.

To her right, in a chair with her pants and underwear folded neatly in his lap, was TJ, also staring at the screen.

Dr. Gould was silent. A clock ticked in the room, and dull voices murmured outside. The waiting room had been busy, full of women with creases across their foreheads or nails bitten to the quick. Rain had looked away from the Success Wall of baby pictures.

"Ah!" Dr. Gould said. "There. Look . . . see that tiny flashing motion? That's a heartbeat. Baby is just fine and snug. A little spotting is perfectly normal, but I'm glad you could come in and we could check to put you at ease."

The screen winked dark as Dr. Gould concluded her work and held out a hand to help Rain sit back up.

"Now," she continued, "the spotting is harmless, but if it's alarming to you and you don't like to see it, you should put your feet up and rest for a few days. If it changes in amount, or turns bright red, or you feel cramping, you call me back immediately. But so far I see no cause for alarm and no reason to believe anything like that will happen. I'll leave you to get dressed and see yourself out. I have two IVF transfers this morning!"

Rain watched the door close behind the doctor and finally exhaled. She had been braced since that moment in the bathroom to be told it was all over, and now that there had been a reprieve — they'd seen their baby, even! Tiny tadpole of a thing with a flashing bright heart — she felt confused, at loose ends. She was glad she didn't have to drive herself home; she might not remember how to start the car.

She finally remembered she was nude below the waist so she turned to TJ to collect her clothes. She did a double take; his eyes were shining, and a wet track of tears was reflecting the yellow overhead lights.

"Hon?" she said.

"I'm so happy you're okay. That everything's okay."

"That's nice, honey. I need my panties, though."

He chuckled and sniffed and handed her the clothes. Rain dressed quickly now, wanting to get the hell out of that clinic, which had made her dream come true but was a reminder of all she had to endure for something supposedly so natural.

As she made to leave, TJ clasped her hand and pulled her back. He did something so unexpected, she would have laughed if not for the earnestness in his face: He knelt down on one knee, proposal fashion. He hadn't even knelt when he actually proposed.

He took her hand in both of his. "I'm going to be better for you. A better husband, a good father. I swear."

Rain chuckled, uncomfortable now that they were hogging this room away from someone about to have a life-changing procedure. She tugged at him, but he stayed stubbornly on his knee.

"I mean it," he said, sniffing hard, more tears leaking out now.

"Okay, okay, get up," she said. "I love you, too, and we're all going to be fine." She snatched a tissue from a box near the room's sink and dabbed at his face. "Let's get the hell out of here and get a pizza." Rain smiled and cracked her first joke in weeks. "The baby wants pizza."

30

When Dinah would reflect on this moment later, what would strike her was how short-lived the feeling of relief had been. Intense, but gone so fast it felt unreal, that hit of *Thank God.*

She'd been in the kitchen, chopping vegetables for a salad when the doorbell rang. She muttered a curse and took the knife with her to the door, intending to get rid of the salesman or evangelists and return to making dinner. The kids were going to be home soon from their practices and studying, and Joe had promised to actually turn up at dinner and skip the hockey game, even though the Arbor Valley Tigers were unbeaten so far.

When she approached the front door and saw the police car in the driveway, she began to tremble.

She'd locked the deadbolt as was her habit, and she fumbled for agonizing seconds trying to get the door open.

Not one, but two officers were on her doorstep.

"Mrs. Monetti?" they'd asked.

She could only manage to nod.

"It's about Morgan. She's fine, but —"

In this instant, relief flooded in so quickly she almost dropped the knife on her foot.

"— we need to talk to you about something that's happened. May we come in?"

Dread collected in a hard ball in her gut as she led the way inside soundlessly. One of the officers firmly suggested she put the knife away as they talked.

Dinah rejoined them in her living room. One officer sat on her old, broken-down couch with the soft cushions and had to perch at the edge so he did not tumble backward. The other officer had pulled in a kitchen chair to sit across the coffee table from Dinah.

"Morgan was discovered with one of her teachers in his car."

Dinah said, "So what if she was in a car? Whose car?" It had been raining. She'd probably gotten a ride. "Where is she, anyway?"

"She's at the police station, Mrs. Monetti. She was in a state of undress."

This was the phrase that upended her life.

A state of undress. "What do you mean?"

The other officer cleared his throat. "She was not wearing any clothing from the waist up."

Dinah put her hands to her face. "So he . . . attacked her? Who?"

"She has indicated to us that they were having a relationship. But it's not clear at this time exactly what the circumstances are."

"Relationship? Which teacher?" she shouted, her voice shrill and painful to her own ears.

"A Mr. Thomas Hill. Her calculus teacher, as we understand. You should come down to the police station as well. Your daughter is not being charged with anything, but I imagine you'll want to speak to her and take her home once we've gotten her statement."

As Dinah tried to find her coat, keys, and purse, she was already failing to recapture her first feeling of, *Thank God she's not dead.*

"How is she?" she asked them, unable to find her coat where it belonged so she went without, braving the chilly February air. "Is she upset? Is she hurt?"

"She's not physically hurt," the first officer said, the one who'd sat on the couch, as he led the way to the front door. "As for upset, I'd say it's more like belligerent."

Dinah rounded the corner into a small room, nested inside a labyrinth of corridors all in a bureaucratic tan color. Morgan was sitting in a plastic chair at a table, arms folded tightly, her head tipped forward and her hair obscuring her face.

"Mo?"

Morgan rose and flung herself at her mother. "Mom! It's been awful! They're treating me like a criminal!"

"What's he done to you?" Dinah asked, holding her and stroking the back of her head.

"Nothing."

"Nothing?" She tried to set Morgan back. They'd given her privacy to greet her daughter, but the walls of this room seemed thin and hopeless for private conversation. She glanced around for one of those big mirrors like on TV with the cops on the other side. There was none. "They said . . . they said you weren't wearing a top."

"But he didn't do anything to me. He didn't hurt me."

Dinah tipped her daughter's chin to get a close look at her face. "Wait a minute. He took your shirt off, but you call that not doing anything to you?"

"He didn't take it off, I did. I took it off. I keep telling them, he didn't hurt me or abuse me or attack me."

Morgan looked right into her face with shining eyes and declared, "I'm in love with him."

Dinah said the first thing she thought of: "That's insane."

"It's not insane! It's just different. I know it got him in trouble. But we're in love."

"Is that what he said? Did he say he loved you?"

Morgan flipped her hair back over her shoulder, chin raised. She immediately pulled her hair back forward over her face, across her scar.

"Yes. He said he loves me."

"He couldn't possibly!"

"Because I'm a disgusting freak, is that why?"

"Because you're a kid! His student!"

"I'm almost eighteen! I'm mature for my age. Wise, remember?" She sneered. "An old soul?"

Dinah sank down into a chair and put her head in her hand. "Oh, my God."

"What's so terrible? The age of consent in Michigan is sixteen. He'll get in trouble at work, but we'll figure something out."

"You going to figure out his wife, too?"

Morgan lifted her chin a degree higher. "They're having problems."

"I'll say they are."

Morgan huffed. "I meant before, Mother. Problems that had nothing to do with me."

Dinah shook herself out of her stunned stupor, stood back up, and took her daughter by the shoulders. She felt Morgan stiffen under her fingers, like when she was colicky as a baby and she'd tried to comfort her, only to have the infant Morgan shriek and go rigid with fury. Until this very moment, that had been the most difficult part of parenting her beautiful, honor student daughter. The first four months.

"Mo. He was taking advantage of you. He said he loved you, he told you that stuff about his wife, so he could get you to take your clothes off in his car."

She yanked away from Dinah. "How do you know? You don't even know him."

"Is that as far as it went? Taking off your top for him?"

The cop's word *relationship* echoed in her mind like the ringing of a gong as time slowed down before Morgan answered the question with one hand propped on her hip and her chin thrust forward.

"Of course not. We're lovers."

■ ■ ■ ■

Dinah had been afraid she might have to handcuff Morgan and stuff her in the backseat, the way she reacted at the police station to being told that despite the age of consent being sixteen, it was a crime for a teacher and his seventeen-year-old student to have a sexual relationship. TJ Hill was about to be arraigned in court.

As it was, Morgan was not speaking, curled up in a ball on the passenger side of the car, glowering at the dashboard.

At the police station, she'd started screaming she'd been tricked into talking to the police; she threw a chair over (much like Dinah had at that long-ago notorious teacher conference), and Dinah had all but tackled her to keep the police from having to intervene. From within Dinah's viselike grip, Morgan had shrieked that she was not going to cooperate ever again, that they'd have to throw her in jail first.

After assuring the police that Morgan would not harm herself — she'd seemed that hysterical — she finally led her daughter out to the car.

And the curtain of heavy silence descended.

Dinah struggled to think of how to tell Joe. He'd already texted her, wondering where she was and why dinner was half finished in the kitchen. She'd replied only *something has come up, be home ASAP.* This was not text-message-type news.

Dinah turned over the events of the last hours in her mind, while struggling to remember to drive.

"We're lovers," Morgan had said, baldly, with something almost like pride, in fact. What bothered Dinah most was the verb tense. *We are lovers.* Not "we were" or "we made love once."

Dinah had been told to expect a call from the prosecutor with more details, as she certainly wouldn't be getting any more information out of Morgan. The police had quickly obtained a search warrant and seized her cell phone and computer as evidence.

"Why did you do this?"

Without even looking, Dinah could feel her daughter's fury radiating like heat off a summer highway. Morgan didn't answer.

"Don't get me wrong, he's the sick bastard, here. But why did you let him do these things to you? Why didn't you come to us when he first . . . approached you?"

She stopped at a stoplight and turned just

in time to see Morgan yank the door open and jump out of the car.

"Morgan! Shit." Dinah punched the button for the hazard lights and leaped out herself, abandoning her running car, her purse, her cell phone, to chase her daughter along a grassy expanse in front of some office building. If any of the office drones chose to look up from their cubes, they'd catch quite an eyeful, Dinah thought, huffing along.

She caught up to Morgan and snagged her elbow, causing her to stumble briefly. Dinah caught her, flashing back this time to her unsteady toddler days.

Morgan flung her arms up and stepped back.

"Approached me," Morgan repeated through panting breath, picking up the conversation as if she hadn't just leaped out of the car and run. "Like some molester with a van pretending to give me candy. I approached him, I'll have you know. Because your daughter has a mind of her own. Remember how damn smart I am? I got accepted to Boston U, by the way, not that it matters."

Dinah reared back. "Why didn't you say you got accepted?"

"Because what does it matter if I can't go?"

"Is this revenge on us? Because of Boston?"

"Yes, Mother, I screwed my teacher because you won't let me go to the right school. My God, you're brilliant."

Dinah clenched her fist until her nails bit the inside of her palm. Where had her Mo gone? She didn't even know this furious, haughty girl.

"You've ruined your life!" Dinah cried.

"What you mean is that I've ruined yours. You can no longer claim to be the good mother, now that all three of your kids are fucked up."

"This isn't about me!"

"Well, that would be a first, then."

Dinah felt hot tears on her face. "Just get back in the car," she said, hating the pleading in her voice, but realizing whatever control over Morgan she ever thought she had was long gone now. In carrying on an affair with a married teacher, Morgan had officially declared she no longer gave a damn what any of them thought.

"Whatever," Morgan spat, stomping past her.

Dinah followed behind, making sure Morgan was actually heading to the car, wondering what in the hell she would do if Morgan flagged down some other vehicle, a truck or something, and hopped in, disappearing forever. Nothing seemed impossible anymore.

Joe's face in that moment would be something Dinah would never be able to erase from her mind.

He'd gone pale, yet ruddy splotches stood out on his cheeks so starkly Dinah thought he'd broken into hives. Then his face gradually morphed from pained horror into murderous anger. Dinah was glad TJ Hill was nowhere in reach or there would be literal blood on Joe's hands.

Morgan had bolted out of the car before Dinah had even brought the car to a full stop, run upstairs, and slammed her way into her room.

Dinah had come in and ordered the boys to make a frozen pizza, then dragged Joe downstairs to his den. She made him sit in his swivel chair and then leaned on the edge of his desk and gave him the news that would devastate him beyond measure, and in that moment she felt her first burst of bitter anger at Morgan for putting them through this.

She scolded herself: *Be mad at the teacher.*

He's the aggressor here, no matter what Morgan believes.

"If he were here, I'd punch him until he was dead."

"I know" was all Dinah could think to say.

"How could she do this? I mean, literally, how was it possible . . . ?" Joe put his head in his hands.

Dinah looked up at the drop ceiling, running through the last several weeks in her mind. She had no timeline of events yet. She realized with a chill that it could have been going on for months now.

"We trusted her," Dinah answered. "We didn't check up on her comings and goings. If she said, 'I'm going to Britney's house,' we said, 'Okay, hon, have a good time.' Kids lie for each other all the time."

Joe murmured, "But she posted on Facebook about being with her friends . . ."

"So," Dinah answered drily. "So they made it up."

"Not Morgan. I don't understand how Morgan . . ."

"Me either. She denied it, but I think she's getting back at us for Boston."

"But . . . this? Of all the ways to rebel . . . You said he's being charged?"

"Right. Age of consent is sixteen, but there's an exception for teacher-student affairs. I guess Morgan told them all about it before she realized that part."

Joe groaned, now tipping back in his chair. "Oh, Christ. It's gonna be on the news."

"The cops said the news won't name her, she's the victim of a sexual crime, and they don't do that."

Joe snorted. "So what? This is Arbor Valley, and she's the assistant principal's daughter. Like everyone won't know in about five minutes. I'm ruined, you know."

"Joe . . ."

"I'm not gonna get the principal job. I'll be lucky if I don't get fired. A teacher-student affair under my nose, and it's my own damn daughter. This is it. The end." He threw up his hands. "All that money for grad school tuition. I might as well have set fire to it."

"That's what you're thinking about now? Your career? Money?"

"It's not all I'm thinking about, but yeah, it has crossed my mind that my career is over and since that means health insurance and our mortgage payment, you should be concerned, too."

"I'm concerned about Morgan, what drove her to this! How screwed up she is now, how screwed up she must have been all along. . . . We should take her to Dr. Kelly."

"Oh, yeah, because that shrink was so perfectly brilliant for the boys. Speaking of burning money."

"How dare you throw that in my face at a time like this! What do you propose we do then? You know she believes herself madly in love with him. She wants to run away with him. What if he doesn't get convicted? Because God knows she's not going to be a very cooperative witness. She could choose to run away right now and disappear forever. So what do you propose we do, chain her in her room?"

Joe stood up from his chair so fast, it spun in his absence. Dinah was seized with an irrational fear he was going to try something just like that.

Joe marched into the garage and grabbed something. Dinah tried to follow, but he was already inside the garage and back out before she could see what he'd done in there. He ignored her demands to know what he was up to, rushing past her for the stairs.

Joe strode right up to Morgan's room, past the boys who were gaping behind their pizza slices, no doubt wondering — with no small amount of glee — what Morgan had done to make their dad so angry.

He tried to open her door, and it was locked. "Morgan Jane, open the door."

Silence.

Joe sighed. Then he took that high school fullback's shoulder and rammed right through the door, the lock mechanism splintering the frame.

Morgan shrieked. She'd been on her bed, earbuds in. She clutched a notebook to her chest and her eyes were wide.

"You're scaring her!" Dinah shouted.

Joe took what he'd been holding — the electric screwdriver, Dinah could now see — and went to work on the hinges of her door without saying a word. He worked with the cool deliberation of a surgeon. One by one the screws of her door hinges fell to the carpet as Morgan and Dinah watched, dumbstruck. Joe then yanked the door loose and propped it in the hall.

He pointed the screwdriver at Morgan. His voice was cold and calm. "You can't be trusted with a closed door. No computer either, no phone, and no leaving the house. Period."

"What about school?" Dinah asked, panicky suddenly on behalf of Morgan, with part of her acknowledging the logic behind what he was doing.

Joe turned to her. "You think she's gonna want to go to school as soon as everyone gets wind of this? I'll talk to Principal Jackson." He turned back to Morgan. "You'll finish out the year at home. Like that Mayfair girl last year with the chemo."

With that, he walked back down the stairs.

Morgan's fury had not dimmed. But she was also silently weeping, her defiance now crumpled into sadness.

"Mom?" asked one of the twins behind her, sounding so tentative he might have been eight years old again. "What's going on?"

Dinah couldn't find the words to answer him.

31

Rain almost didn't answer the phone.

She was at home, soaking in the quiet within her own little yoga space. She had melted into *trikonasana,* and it was a good, satisfying stretch. Her breath was helping her sink deeper, her hips were letting go, and she felt like she could even put her head on the floor at this rate.

She'd been planning her next class with her beginning students, making notes between postures. She could do all these easily, of course, being among the first postures she learned way back in her college days. But she liked to walk herself through a class, anyway, to remind herself of the beginner's body.

Plus, she wanted to test how her pregnancy would affect her, if at all. Dr. Gould had merely cautioned her against complicated inversions and headstands that might cause her to fall, but otherwise said she could continue as she normally would, for the time being.

The shrilling of the house phone continued long enough before the voice mail was set to pick up that she resigned herself to answer, which she did with a curt, "Yes?"

She had to ask him to repeat himself; she wasn't even sure who was on the line.

She figured out it was TJ, but she could hardly divine his words. She assumed one or both parents were dead, or maybe his brother or Alessia.

She shouted, "TJ, I can't understand you! What's happened!"

"I've been arrested," he choked out at last. "They think I assaulted one of my students. This is my one phone call, you have to find a lawyer."

"What? Oh my God, where are you?"

"In jail! They're going to take me to court; I need a lawyer right now."

Rain gripped the phone hard so she wouldn't drop it. She wanted to say, *How do I know how to find a lawyer?* And ask, *How could they think you would do that?* But instead she said, "I'll take care of it. I will. Are you okay?"

His voice was abraded, hoarse, as if he'd been screaming. "I'm in jail; how do you think I am? They took my belt so I don't hang myself."

"Jesus."

"Baby, I'm so sorry."

"You didn't do anything wrong," she said, at the end of that sentence her voice rising up, becoming nearly a question.

"I didn't, I swear, it's all a misunderstanding; get me a lawyer and get me out of here."

"I will. I love you. It will be okay."

"I love you, babe. Hurry."

The phone clicked off. Rain ran to the kitchen sink and retched.

On the ride home in the car from the courthouse — the first time she'd ever been there, no doubt she'd be back again, who knows how many times — Rain realized that TJ's arraignment had supplanted her gran's funeral as her life's nadir, and as soon as she thought this, she realized with grim certainty that new lows would be reached. Soon, and often.

Rain leaned her head against the car's cool glass in the backseat, directly behind TJ, in the passenger seat. Greg was driving.

She'd known that to turn to his successful older brother might be viewed as a betrayal, but Rain had no idea how one goes about finding a crackerjack criminal defense lawyer immediately, much less how to pay that person, and then there was the question of bail money. She'd stood dumbfounded in her living room, the stinging of acid still burning her throat from being sick, and realized every moment she stood there motionless, TJ was sitting in a jail cell, depending on her to get him out.

So she called Greg, who swung admirably into action as if operating on a crashing patient. Somehow he knew just the lawyer they needed, and Alexandra Girard was called to the courthouse.

Rain cried, and Greg put his arm around her, when she realized she would not be allowed to see TJ before he was formally charged.

The courthouse audience had been sparse — the news hadn't gotten out yet, though as soon as it did, that would be the end of near-empty courtrooms for them — and he'd entered a plea of not guilty in a cracking, quiet voice. Greg took care of the bond without flinching, without waiting for Rain to have to ask.

Then TJ was allowed to leave, and in the parking lot there was a brief and awkward dance around the car as TJ said he couldn't possibly drive, and Greg and Rain moved at once to the driver's seat, then Rain and TJ both made for the passenger seat, and finally she just got into the back.

The silence rang loud in the car.

They pulled up their Toyota next to Greg's Saab in their driveway. Rain could see TJ sit up straighter in his seat and could nearly read his mind: *my hotshot doctor brother with his fancy-ass car comes to the rescue.*

Inside, they listened to an urgent voice-mail message from Principal Jackson, including his home number. TJ and Rain traded a look. He wouldn't be going to work the next day. Maybe never again.

Greg said, "Let's call the union rep tomorrow. They can't railroad you out of a job based on a girl's accusation."

The lawyer already had an appointment to come to their house to talk strategy.

Alexandra, or Alex as she preferred to be called, had warned them just before they left the courthouse about pretrial publicity. She said a reporter had been in the courtroom, scribbling away during arraignment. No TV cameras yet, but that would come soon enough.

The story could be online even now, Rain realized, as TJ went to the refrigerator and pulled out a beer, drinking half of it in a series of desperate gulps, right there in front of the open fridge.

"Do not speak to the press," Alex had

warned. “No matter how tempting, no matter how they goad you, no matter how friendly they act, because that’s a tactic, too. ‘I just want to tell your side’ ” — this she said in a mocking singsongy voice — “but do not believe them. They want to hang you out to dry, I guarantee it. Ignore all calls and knocks on your door. If you get ambushed, say ‘no comment’ and tell them to call me. Got it?”

Here in their bungalow, his beer in hand, TJ dropped down to the couch and stared forward, his gaze somewhere on the carpet in front of the television.

The phone rang, and Rain ignored it. She could no longer imagine a ringing phone bringing anything but more disaster upon their heads.

Greg strode into the room and sat next to his brother on the couch, squaring his body to face TJ. Rain sat on the adjacent stuffed chair, an ugly floral thing she loved because she’d inherited it from Gran. From this vantage point, she could see the rarely glimpsed fraternal resemblance. They both had that same firm, movie-star jawline and defined cheekbones, though Greg’s hair was fuzzier, lighter, favoring his mother in that respect. Greg was also a little heavier.

Greg broke the silence: “Why do they

think you did this? What evidence do they have?"

TJ ignored his brother and looked Rain in the eye.

"Swear you'll believe me."

"Of course," she answered automatically.

"She's troubled. She's very troubled and has a crush on me. I was trying to talk some sense into her, and . . ." He took a gulp of beer. "She started taking off her clothes."

"What?" Rain asked, grabbing the arms of the chair.

"Jesus," muttered Greg. "Where were you that this was happening? Not in the classroom."

TJ answered, still looking at Rain. "No." There was a long beat of time, during which she saw TJ's Adam's apple bob as he swallowed. "In my car."

"Oh, you goddamn idiot," blurted Greg.

TJ finally looked at his brother. "Thanks for the support, jackass."

"I just . . . How stupid could you be? You let a troubled girl with a crush on you get into your car? You could have saved yourself the trouble and tattooed 'pervert' on your chest."

"I was trying to avoid something like this! I wanted to talk her out of it gently! I thought, if I go to the administration with this, she could claim anything she wanted to get back at me. And no one would believe my word over hers."

"Why wouldn't they?" Greg asked.

"Now who's the idiot? Do you know what happens to male teachers who have even the slightest hint of anything inappropriate? I'm sure Dr. Greg has read *The Crucible.* Accusation is enough."

Greg persisted. "Still, this isn't seventeenth-century Salem. You said she's a troubled girl, if you'd just explain . . ."

"It's Morgan Monetti. Yes, my boss's honor student daughter. All she'd have to do is claim I touched her and make her eyes tear up and it's game over. We're not talking some pothead Goth girl, or some freak chick cutting herself."

Rain found her voice. "Why would she do something like that?"

"How the hell am I supposed to know? Now you know why I've been under so much stress. I've been trying to handle it without worrying you. How was I supposed to know she'd start getting naked in my car? And that the police would swoop in just then? I still don't understand how that happened."

Greg said, "Maybe she did it herself. Maybe she called in an anonymous tip or something."

"Why would she do that? It's not like this is going to be a picnic for her, either."

Greg shrugged. "You're the one who said she was troubled. Maybe she snapped. A good attorney can make that work, TJ, and Alex is the best. We'll get you out of this mess, don't worry. I better leave you guys alone now."

He stood up and crossed the room to Rain, bending to kiss her cheek. "Take good care of yourself," he murmured quietly. Loudly, he announced, "Call me if you need anything at all before the meeting with Alex."

With that, he swept out of the house. Rain moved to TJ's side and took his free hand. It lay limp in her grasp. He continued to gaze at the floor.

"I wish you'd told me," Rain said quietly.

He snorted. "What could you have done? You'd have told me to go to the principal and tell him about her crush. Think I hadn't considered that? Like I said before, all she'd have had to say is that I put my hand on her thigh or something and I would have been ruined. And now I am ruined, just like I feared, and worse. The maximum sentence is fifteen years! I might as well jump off a bridge and get it over with."

"TJ!" Rain jumped to her feet. "Don't you dare, don't even joke about something like that."

"Gallows humor," he intoned, slugging the rest of his beer down and smacking the bottle onto the coffee table.

"I don't care. I won't hear that kind of talk. You have a baby coming!"

"Some great dad I'm going to be."

"TJ, you've got to listen to me." She crouched down next to him again, trying to get into his line of sight. "Alex is a great attorney. She's going to get the truth out. It will be hard for a while, but we'll get through it and then we'll have this wonderful baby together. I can't have you feeling hopeless."

"Don't you see? It's only going to get worse." He started peeling the beer label.

"I know it'll be rough . . ."

"No, I mean the lies that will come out. Brace yourself to hear some crazy stories."

"What are you saying?"

"I'm saying that she has invented a whole fantasy relationship that never existed. She started talking crazy in the car as if we were really in love, like, mutually, as if I'd made her all kinds of promises. You realize she holds my fate in her hands. She can tell the truth and get me off the hook, or she can continue to spin this web she's started and take me down. One guess which she'll pick."

"Maybe she won't. Maybe . . ."

"Maybe my ass. Hell, I think she's convinced herself. If she takes the stand against me, I'm doomed."

TJ finally looked her in the eyes and took hold of her hand, running his thumb over her knuckles like he'd done so many times before. "If I go to jail and lose you, I don't know how I'll go on living. I really don't."

Rain squeezed his hand back, hard. "You won't lose me. I can't control the rest, but that much I can swear."

He smiled with sad eyes, then asked her to go get him another beer.

32

Morgan lay on her bed, eyes on the dirty-white ceiling, her earbuds plugged into an old iPod, with her Elgar concerto on repeat.

To think she used to feel trapped in the house, in the community.

No, this here was trapped. The door off her room, phone and computer taken by the police, under constant watch by Dinah who had hired an extra temp and was managing the Den primarily by phone so she could play warden.

She turned over onto her stomach and pressed her face into the pillow, emitting a silent scream into its fluff.

She hadn't meant to get him in trouble. Hell, she'd been so very careful.

But she just couldn't leave things as they were, with his last actions toward her being to bark at her to get her shoes, how he practically threw her out of his car in the mall parking lot. He'd driven off and left her standing there alone in a dark and remote corner of the lot, not even seeing if she got into her car safely.

He'd been so curt and bossy with her, but he'd also said he loved her. She could no longer stand the limbo and texted him that she was desperate to talk to him, that it was of utmost urgency.

They met in the same mall parking lot, where she hopped into his car, this time sliding down in the seat without being asked. They rode in silence to a park-and-ride lot next to the highway, which was deserted except for them. By then the cold car had warmed up. He left it running, unbuckled his seat belt, and turned to her.

"Okay, what's so urgent? You better not be pregnant."

"No! I told you I'm on the pill. No, what was urgent was . . ." She hated how high her voice sounded then, and she tried to pitch it into a lower register, to sound mature and worthy of him. "I need to know how you feel about me. Whether you truly love me, or whether I'm an inconvenient burden to you."

His expression softened. "I'm under a lot of pressure . . ."

"I know you are. I know it's hard. It's not easy for me, either, to sit there in your class and do my homework like all is normal. To know you go home every night and . . . Anyway, the point is that if I'm in the way, just say so and we'll forget it. I'll get over it," she said, cursing her quavering voice. "I'll carry on somehow, but I can't take the limbo. I can't take the harsh attitude and then five minutes later 'I love you' and then five minutes after that you throw me out of your house."

Morgan drew in a deep, deep breath, all the way to her toes. "Do you love me?"

He looked her in the eye, his expression calm. "Yes," he whispered, barely audible over the rush of warm air from the car's heating vent.

He leaned in to her, and she opened her lips to the softest, gentlest kiss he'd yet given her. His hand came to her face and stroked her hair gently back.

"You're so beautiful," he whispered, stroking her chin with his hand.

"Even with my scar?"

"I don't even see it," he said.

He kissed her again, then began leaving a trail of gentle kisses down her neck to her collarbone.

She hadn't wanted to do it in his car. It seemed too cramped for one thing, and also there was still daylight in the sky.

He began unbuttoning her shirt and part of her wanted to protest, to tell him no, not here, let's make plans, but they were running out of places to see each other, and they'd just had such a lovely moment . . .

By the time her shirt was off and bra unhooked, he was kissing the tops of her breasts, and she was carried away by a rising tide to float far above everything else. Until the banging on the window, and the shouting, and her own pathetic yelping.

Morgan burrowed her head under her pillow, wishing she could unremember the cop dragging him from the car and flinging him up against its side, the other officer handing her the shirt back, leading her from the car and wrapping a blanket around her as if she had gone into shock.

TJ had hollered something like, "It's not what you think!" but then Morgan couldn't hear anymore because they stuffed him inside the squad car, and a second car was there she suddenly noticed, and they stuck her in back of that one like she'd been arrested, too, asking her all along if she were hurt, what had happened to her.

She'd sat in vacant, idiotic shock until she got inside the police station. A kindly woman officer — or at least she acted kindly, to get what she wanted — asked

Morgan questions while she drank weak coffee with powdered creamer. At first, Morgan said nothing at all.

Finally, she realized she might as well just tell them. After all, they'd been caught together, and if she didn't tell them the truth, then they'd probably assume he'd raped her or something.

So she just told the nice lady cop that yes, they were lovers. Morgan answered all her questions, told the whole story as the lady with her red hair in a bun jotted in a notepad and nodded with an air of serene understanding. Morgan had felt so giddy and relieved at being able to tell it all out loud that, by the time the officer had left to go find her mother to come get her, she was believing it had all happened for the best. His wife would surely leave him now, she'd muddle through the last few months of high school, and then they could figure out what to do next.

After she talked to her mother, the red-headed officer came back, and Morgan wanted to know what would happen to him.

"He's been arrested and will be arraigned later today," she'd replied with that same serene calm as she'd listened to Morgan's story.

"Arrested? But I just told you I didn't do

anything unwillingly, and I'm over sixteen. I'm over the age of consent."

By the time the officer had told her of the exception in the law for teacher-student relationships, Morgan thought she might faint — or punch the officer in the face in rage.

In any case, she vowed right then not to say one more word.

"Stupid," she whispered into the still air of her room. "I'm so stupid." She shifted away from a damp spot on her mattress. She hadn't even noticed she'd been crying.

She had checked, after all. She wanted to make sure he would not get arrested. Yes, she realized that they always had to be careful, that he would tell his wife in his own time, when he could, and that he had to figure out how to keep his job. She never dreamed he would land in jail.

And what she still could not figure out, no matter how hard she thought about it, was this: How did they know? How did the police know to find them?

At first, Morgan believed it had been horrible bad luck, but the more she pondered, the less sense that made. After all, there were two cop cars on the scene at once. They didn't drive around in tandem as a matter of habit.

Maybe someone saw them at the mall. Someone saw a young woman get out of her car and into an older man's car and called the police. But so? He could have been a dad giving her a ride because her car battery died.

Her gut tightened at the sound of her mother's footsteps, audible over a soft passage of the concerto playing in her ears. Had to be Dinah, since the boys were at school and her dad was at work. Morgan had already finished her class assignments in the first two hours of this torturously isolated day, though she'd left the books and papers lying around so she could ward off any interference from her mother by claiming to be "studying."

Her mother tapped on the doorjamb, since her door had been removed.

"Let yourself in," Morgan quipped drily. "As if I had a choice in the matter."

"You have a visitor," Dinah said. Morgan wouldn't look at her.

"Gee, thanks, Warden. A reward for good behavior?"

"Do you want to see Ethan or don't you?"

"Yes."

She waited until her mother's footsteps retreated, then she took out the earbuds and cleared a space on her bed. She tucked away her poetry, which had been half hidden under her pillow.

But when Ethan came in, he sat at her desk chair. She never used that desk for anything, other than stacking her clothes on when she didn't feel like putting them away.

"Are you okay?" he asked. "Everyone's worried about you."

"Ha. I'll bet they are." Morgan tried to act like she didn't care, but that effort only lasted a few seconds. "What's everyone saying?"

"That Mr. Hill seduced you in his car and got arrested. Is it true? Did he?"

She snorted. "No. He didn't 'seduce' me like some perv. We were having an affair. He's the older man I mentioned."

Ethan boggled at her, a cartoon rendering of shock.

"Close your mouth before you catch flies. What, is that so surprising, that I could have a mature relationship?"

"Not sure I'd put it like that . . . I mean, what . . . why? How did it even start?"

"Did you come over because you're concerned, or because you want gory details?"

Ethan looked down at his hands, where he'd been twisting the silver ring he wore on his index finger. "I'm just trying to figure it out. It doesn't make any sense."

"Love never does."

Ethan looked back up at her. "Love?"

"What, do you think I'm a slut? Of course it's love. And don't you start sounding like my mother."

"So what are you going to do now?"

Morgan shrugged. "Finish out the school year in my room, I guess. My dad thinks I shouldn't go back."

Ethan grimaced. "You probably wouldn't want to. Some people . . ."

"Some people what?"

"Never mind."

"Screw you, Ethan. You can't start something like that and not finish it. You have to tell me. What."

"Some people hate you for getting him fired."

"He's been fired?"

"Not yet, but don't you think he probably will be? It's not like he stole some Post-it notes."

"They hate me?"

"Some people blame you. Or at least blame you equally."

Morgan marveled at her own surprise at this, and further, how it stung to hear. "Well, they should. We were in it together, after all."

"I might as well tell you before you hear it

somewhere else . . ."

". . . not that I hear anything with my phone and computer taken by the cops, and I avoid the rest of the house where the family computer is. I'm like in a little black hole, here."

". . . but someone defaced your locker."

"Defaced how?"

"They scratched it up."

Morgan shrugged. "Big whoop."

"With words. It says . . . Well, it says 'Die slut die.' Well, it did, until the janitor came out there to paint it over. But people had already taken cell-phone pictures of it."

"It said 'die'? Does my mom know that?"

"I don't know. It just happened today. Your dad will probably tell her."

"Stupid childish morons." She tossed her hair. "Whatever." But her voice was cracking. "Did . . . did my brothers see it?"

"I doubt it, because it was in the senior hall. But I wouldn't be surprised if someone texted them a picture. Or at least told them."

Oh, shit. She hadn't anticipated fallout for her brothers. Connor would be looking to bash some heads in. She prayed that he would never get any clue about the guilty party or he'd end up expelled and home all day across the hall from her.

"I cannot believe someone ratted us out. Who would do that? And why didn't they mind their own . . ."

Her voice trailed off as she looked at Ethan, who looked pale and fretful, worrying that ring around on his hand.

"Oh, my God. It was you."

"What? What was me? I would never say something like that about you."

"Not my locker. I don't give a shit about my locker. You called the police. You did this to me."

"No!" Ethan put his hands up like she'd threatened to shoot him. "I didn't even know!"

"You are such a liar. It makes perfect sense. I told you it was an older man. You already followed me to my library job that one time, so it makes total sense that you'd follow me to the mall just to see what I was up to. You saw me get in his car and you called the police on us."

"I swear, I didn't."

"Who else would it have been?" She was controlling her volume with great effort, not wanting to get Dinah up here. "No one else even knew I was seeing anybody at all, and you right away were worried about this 'older man.' Well, thank you for ruining my life. If you see 'die slut die' on my house or car windows or something, you only have yourself to thank."

Ethan stood up hard, knocking the chair into the desk. "First of all, it wasn't me. Second, even if it was, 'myself to thank'? How about you, who thought sleeping with your teacher was a great idea? Or him, for being a disgusting pervert who preys on a kid in his class?"

"I'm not a kid, and I was not his prey!" Now she was screaming, all control burned away in her anger.

Ethan was already heading out the door, and Morgan heard Dinah's running feet. But before he left, he turned back to say, "I wish I *had* been the one to call, so I could take credit for ending it. It was sick, Morgan."

She threw her iPod, but a second too late, so that it bounced off her mother's head as she rounded the corner into her room and Ethan stormed down the stairs.

33

June 6, 2012

"Tell the court what you saw when you approached the vehicle."

Dinah reached for Joe's hand and gripped it hard. He allowed her to do so but did not react even with the lightest squeeze in return. They'd heard the story before — Henry had been over this with them — but this was open court, with cameras rolling, shutters snapping. Since Hill had waived a preliminary hearing, this was the first time the gory details would be splashed out in public. She imagined all Arbor Valley with smartphones and tablets and computer screens glowing across riveted, gleeful faces.

"We found Miss Monetti and the defendant in his car. As I approached, they appeared to be embracing, but when I pounded on the glass with my closed fist, they separated from each other. Miss Monetti clasped her arms across her chest. She was naked from the waist up."

A murmur rippled across the courtroom. That was a detail that had not yet been in the press and would no doubt feature prominently in the news stories the next day.

The officer continued to relate the story. "She did not appear to be physically harmed. Officers Stone and McAllister secured the defendant, read him his Miranda rights, and I helped Miss Monetti from the car and gave back her shirt, and a blanket, since she was shivering."

"Did the defendant say anything as he was arrested?"

"Other than saying he understood his rights, he repeated three times, 'It's not what you think.' "

"How would you describe his demeanor?"

"He was sweating, pale, and shaking."

The prosecutor sat down and TJ Hill's attorney rose. Dinah swallowed hard and breathed in deeply, as though to steady herself for a blow. The last time this Alexandra had spoken, her daughter had been portrayed as an unstable aspiring Lolita, with poor TJ as the innocent, bumbling victim of his own charm and chiseled jawline.

Alexandra clicked across the floor in her heels. "Officer, you testified that you came upon Miss Monetti naked from the waist up."

"That's correct."

"So she was already topless when you arrived on the scene."

Topless! Dinah's stomach lurched. A stripper is topless. A prostitute is topless.

The officer agreed, regarding the attorney with a wary glint.

Alexandra said then, "So you did not see who removed Miss Monetti's shirt? Whether it was the defendant or the young lady herself?"

"No, I did not see."

"Could you see what the two of them were doing in the car?"

"They appeared to be embracing, kissing."

"Appeared. Could you please describe exactly what you saw, and only what you saw."

"I saw their heads close together. Close enough together they could only be kissing. Or giving mouth-to-mouth."

An uncomfortable laugh rumbled through the audience, and the officer let slip a small grin.

Alexandra's face grew severe, in the manner of a parent about to lay down some punishment.

"Let me ask you, was the windshield

fogged up that day?"

The officer frowned into his lap. After a pause: "Yes, I believe it was."

"So, leaving aside the speculation about first aid, can you tell me exactly what you saw, and only that."

"I saw two figures in the car, close together."

"Close together over one side of the car, or another?"

"I'm not sure I know what you're asking."

"Could you tell whether the two were together in the driver's side? Or the passenger side?"

Long pause. "I believe it was the center of the car. They had leaned together over the center console, over the emergency brake."

"So the defendant was not on top of her, and not in her seat."

"No, not that I recall."

"So, before you pounded on the glass, through the fogged windows, you saw that they were each in their own seats, is that correct?"

"They were meeting in the middle — embracing, or something — but yes, they were bodily in their own seats."

" 'Or something,' you said. But given the fog of the windows, could they have been only talking, perhaps whispering? Is it possible?"

The officer seemed to sigh, or maybe that was Dinah, projecting her desire for him to be on her side, help their case. "It's possible," he allowed.

Alexandra nodded, thanked the officer, and sat down with a cool, detached expression. Henry went through the motions of calling the other officer on the scene that day to the stand.

Dinah swallowed a spike of anger at the prosecutor. She'd begged Henry to offer a deal to TJ that he'd be stupid to pass up, anything to avoid exactly this agony. But Henry had been politely steadfast: TJ had committed a crime, in fact he'd violated a minor child under his influence. He wasn't going to offer a "gimme" over something like this.

TJ had been offered a deal, but it included jail time and a guilty plea. His attorney was holding out for no contest, and that had been the breaking point for Henry. "He doesn't want to admit he did anything at all wrong. He needs to be held accountable."

And now here they were, the gory details unfolding in front of everyone, for who knows how many days, all for an uncertain result.

Dinah had seen enough *Law & Order* to know that the evidence was thin without her daughter's testimony, and Henry had explained that Morgan's statement to the police was inadmissible as hearsay.

It would help if TJ himself broke down and confessed on the stand, but that seemed too much to hope for. Was the jury disgusted enough to convict on the scant evidence they had? So far, the community disgust as registered online, via gossip, and in letters to the editor seemed wide ranging: It applied to TJ, Morgan, Dinah herself, and Joe (especially Joe), even the teacher's supportive wife.

Of course, even if he was convicted, what did it really matter?

Morgan's innocence was still gone, her senior year still ruined, and more crucially, with her eighteenth birthday approaching, Morgan had all but announced her intention to bolt. Even if he spent time in jail for what he did, Morgan would fancy herself waiting for him. She'd even think it was romantic: the two of them, against all odds, not even jail time could stop them. She'd actually used the phrase "star-crossed lovers" in one of their fights.

Dinah had tried that one brilliant scheme to win her daughter back to her side, and it had backfired something awful.

No, whatever happened in court — and she prayed against the odds that TJ would be locked away for years — she'd already lost her daughter.

Rain clenched her hands together to keep herself from shaking. She sensed a bubble of awareness around her: Somehow, everyone had figured out who she was. She already had rebuffed the reporters who kept asking her for comment, but she felt their eyes on her, heard the scratching in their notebooks.

Beverly had wanted to come along, pleaded in fact, even offered to shut down NYC for the day, but Rain had rejected her pity, which was all she was getting these days from her boss and sometime friend. Beverly called it support, but Rain knew full well Bev thought she was stupid and blind for staying with TJ. Alessia might have come, but she and her loving husband were cocooned with their new little family, their absence easily explained away, saving Greg from the awkwardness of appearing in court to support his disgraced brother. Like Bev, he had become more and more impatient with Rain, since his own belief in his brother's innocence had eroded. He'd recently told her that her devotion was "admirable but foolish" and that she should save herself and leave him.

Rain had been horrified. How dare he?

And yet. Troubling images plagued her at night as TJ paced the house, racked with insomnia, and she lay alone, twisting in the sheets, wide awake. The story she'd been telling herself about her husband's "mistake" had begun to fray, and she could not admit the reason to anyone. In fact, there would be hell to pay if she told a single soul.

Morgan had practiced her cool mask of detachment, modeling it after that of Alexandra, the lawyer. Though she hated what the lawyer was saying about her to get TJ out of trouble, she had to admire the skill it took to tell a compelling story of TJ's innocence.

Whatever it took, Morgan kept telling herself. This was all so insane. This archaic law with its arbitrary rule that somehow because he was a teacher meant she could not be responsible for a decision to have sex with him. She could have chosen to give a blow job to a fifty-five-year-old gas station attendant in the bathroom and that would have been perfectly okay.

And what about Britney? How many different guys had she screwed when stupid-drunk on schnapps out of a plastic cup? But that was just dandy?

Morgan had made love with two men in her entire life, both times on the pill, both times only when in love, and somehow it had become this horrid crime.

Well, there was the wife. But that wasn't the illegal part.

Morgan bit her lip and tried to push the wife out of her head. It was easy to do when she'd never seen her. She was like a bogeyman then: invisible, yet obviously wicked. Morgan could see the effects of her coldness on the poor man and shake her head in disgust that anyone could treat him so poorly, so ungratefully.

A headache began to roll around like a billiard ball inside her head. She could feel the wife's presence without looking at her. In that way she was like a bogeyman still; the wife made the hair on Morgan's neck prickle with tickly fear.

Morgan glanced up to see TJ holding his temple at the defendant's table as the cops were being cross-examined. Their mutual headache reminded her they were in this together. Come what may.

34

March 12, 2012

Dinah sucked in a breath as she stepped out of her car at City Hall. She did this every time she was out in public these days, this intake of breath like she was about to dive deep underwater. Whispers and stares trailed in her wake, everywhere she went.

Whenever she felt guilty about keeping Morgan at home, and not at school, she'd go out and feel the vibration of lurid interest all around her and remember that she was doing the right thing, protecting Morgan from all this.

The poor girl was so isolated and disconsolate, Dinah had caved in and bought her a cheap phone that could text since the police still had her existing phone, though she announced that she would be checking her daughter's text messages routinely.

Morgan had only sniffed and turned her back, curling up on the comforter. Dinah had tried to embrace her, and her daughter's body had gone rigid.

Dinah stepped over melting, graying snow on her way into City Hall. It was eerily warm for this early in a Michigan March. She'd spotted a crocus in the garden when she bent to get the newspaper off the porch the other day. She'd brought the paper to the table and performed her now-daily ritual of scanning it for anything about the case. Since the initial arrest and first few articles questioning "How could the school not have known?" the official press coverage had ebbed as both sides prepared for trial.

The absence of formal news only seemed to increase the buzz of gossip like the rising pitch of swarming wasps. Dinah had heard from Kelly there was a Facebook page dedicated to "supporting" TJ Hill, but she hadn't had the stomach to look, not after the queasy horror of reading the anonymous online comments posted after each news story. The "slut" remarks were eventually deleted by some faceless (and slow) moderator, but what difference did it make? Can't unring that bell, ever. Morgan had not been reading them, so far as she knew, what with not having her computer anymore and not wanting to use the general family computer in the den.

Dinah stepped into the City Hall chambers and blanched at the full room. It had to be the Den. It was the only issue of any substance at all.

She did a quick visual sweep, trying to gauge the crowd. Supporters? Enemies? Neither? She couldn't tell. Too many faces.

She chose a seat front-row center, where there were plenty of seats. The rubberneckers seemed to prefer the back.

The buzzing fluorescents hurt her eyes. This was no grand Romanesque structure, but an economic, utilitarian City Hall. Other than the city's seal on the wall behind the commissioners' seats, and a couple of flagpoles, you couldn't distinguish this room from any other colorless meeting space.

She fidgeted through the routine parts of the agenda, wishing to hell she'd had Joe here for support, as she'd planned. But it was his turn to play warden at home.

They both feared that if they took their eyes off Morgan for even a minute, she'd drive off and disappear forever. They took nothing for granted these days.

Connor had been in two fights attempting to defend Morgan's reputation and was suspended for a week. Dinah had pleaded uselessly with Pete Jackson, citing extenuating circumstances — after all, there had been a death threat carved into his sister's locker! — but he'd been unmoved. Meanwhile, Jared had become more sullen and withdrawn than normal, and Joe had heard through the grapevine he was back hanging out with the pothead kids.

Finally, it was her turn to speak.

Her knees were trembling as she rose, and she had to clear her throat twice. The words of her printed speech — written with such pride and anticipation just a few weeks ago — swam in her vision.

As she began, her voice cracked, and she took a steadying breath. The microphone picked up her shuddering inhalation and broadcasted it across the chambers. The Planning Commission chair leaned toward his neighboring commissioner and whispered, eyes still on Dinah.

Her rising anger at their naked gossiping felt familiar and galvanizing, and she sailed through the rest of the pitch for an entertainment license for the Den, feeling proud and imagining applause, though of course there wasn't any.

Dinah's satisfied smile melted away as she saw the first person rise to speak in the public comment portion. It was Helen Demming, in a suit that looked like Chanel but couldn't be. No one spent that kind of money around here. Not even Helen.

Helen pursed her lips and began to speak in a steady, clear alto, just like she'd done at chamber of commerce meetings many, many times.

"I know the chamber recommended this project, but I must tell you it was not a unanimous vote, and the concerns I had then still exist and in fact have only grown. Mrs. Monetti has described for you a project intended for the safe enjoyment of our young people, and I laud her intentions. But good intentions do not always produce the desired result. As evidence, I give you the skate park, which now is chained and padlocked because of the vandalism suffered there. That was also a project approved with the laudable goal of 'something for the young people to do.' They did something, all right. They trashed it and spray-painted it and bullied away the kids who wanted to just have fun. How do we know the same kind of thing won't happen here? And I realize that Mrs. Monetti has a deservedly wonderful reputation for doing nice things for the teens of this town, but the license is attached to the business, not the person. Should she sell the business — and we have no way of knowing if she ever would in the future — the license goes with it. With a change of ownership, the Den becomes a raucous bar just down the road from the high school and close to a residential area."

Dinah scribbled rebuttals in her notebook. But after Helen sat down, person after person rose to raise this or that niggling question about parking or noise levels. One even wondered if the kids would be smoking outside and tossing their cigarette butts into adjacent yards.

Dinah scrawled in her notes: *A 25-foot "toss"? And these kids don't smoke!*

It was her turn again, and Dinah stomped up to the podium, slapped her notebook down, and raised her hard gaze to the planners.

She opened her mouth to begin, but then she read their faces.

Every one of them was staring at her with disapproval and mistrust. Except for that young Amy person on the end, who always seemed to be on the verge of fainting from the first sign of conflict and had filled the seat of a commissioner who retired midterm. Amy wouldn't even look up from her table.

"Never mind," Dinah said, abandoning her brilliant rebuttals. "I can read the writing on this wall. You know, I have done nothing but support this community and its young people. Could I have made more money catering to a crowd that had more money to burn? Sure. Could I have opened up a soulless, impersonal franchise? Naturally. But I did not, and it's because I care. However, you all here are holding something against me, against my family, that has nothing to do with my business and don't think I can't tell. You can talk to me all you want about traffic concerns, but I'm being punished for what my family is going through, something that is horrible but not my fault, and not my daughter's fault."

She heard a rumble at this behind her and turned around. "Don't you dare! Don't you dare act like she's not a victim."

The word *victim* rang through the air like a whip crack.

Dinah began to shake. She had felt this way before, most notably when she'd tossed a chair in that conference with that loathsome teacher who had condemned her twins to being rotten kids forever before they'd even lost all their baby teeth.

"Forget it." She seized her notebook, bent to pick up her purse and paperwork, and headed for the back door. She was halfway across the lobby when she heard running feet behind her. A kid with ill-fitting khakis and a horrible paisley tie was puffing after her. "Could you give me a comment for the *Daily* about what you just said in there? You're referring to your daughter, Morgan, and TJ Hill?"

"Go to hell," Dinah said. The moron actually shouted after her, "Can I quote you on that?"

She heard more running feet and fantasized about punching the little twerp, but she turned to see Kelly, Britney's mom and maybe her only friend left in the whole damn town.

"Oh. Hi." She kept walking toward her car.

"I came in just at the end; what was going on in there?"

"If you're going to talk to me, you're going to ride in my car because I'm not staying here another second."

"Just drop me back off to get mine when we're done," she said, and hopped in. Together they burst into the damp night.

They didn't speak again until they were blocks away from City Hall.

Dinah said, "They railroaded me, Kell. Helen saw an opening to sink this permit and she ran with it. And they all followed along like little lemmings. Or rats. Are lemmings a type of rat?"

"That sucks out loud."

"I don't get why they're turning on us. On us! And he has a Facebook page supporting him?" Dinah pulled over in front of Sereni-Tea because she didn't trust herself to drive, her white-hot anger taking over by the minute. "Why is he the victim?"

"I know. It's so totally awful. I guess most people think she threw herself at him."

"So what?" Dinah nearly shrieked, causing Kelly to flinch. "If she's got some kind of issue, we will deal with it, but he's the adult, and he took advantage. She's a child."

"Well, she's seventeen."

Dinah cranked around to face her as well as she could in her cramped sedan. "Don't you start. Don't you dare."

"Sorry, I didn't mean anything by it. I was just saying. Anyway, they don't all think it's her fault. Plenty of people are disgusted by him, too."

"But those same people aren't exactly heartbroken with sympathy for Morgan, are they?"

Kelly didn't answer, only looking down at her folded hands.

"Is Britney in touch with her? I got her a cell phone again since the police took her old one. I hated to think of her so isolated."

"I don't think she is."

"Not her, too?"

"She's just weirded out by it. She doesn't know what to think, now. She told me it's like she doesn't even know Morgan anymore. And everyone's grilling Brit for details all the time, at school. She hates all that attention."

"I bet."

"What does that mean?"

"Nothing. My default mode right now is 'maximum bitch' so feel free to ignore me. Okay, I'm calm enough to drive without wrapping the car around a tree. I'll take you back to the lot. You'll forgive me if I don't get out of the car, though."

"Of course," Kelly said, turning to look out the window.

At City Hall, Kelly stepped out hurriedly, with a quiet "bye." As the door slammed, Dinah fantasized about loading up the kids and Joe and a change of clothes in her car and taking off for somewhere. Anywhere.

Dinah walked into her house, unnerved by the silence.

To think she used to be irritated by the fighting and chaos! Now, the twins seemed afraid to make a sound and stayed holed up in their room, giving Morgan a wide berth should their paths happen to cross. Joe was sullen and dark, creeping like fog around the house.

Morgan wasn't speaking to anyone unless she absolutely had to.

She'd wanted to sob with relief when Ethan turned up on the porch that night, and then to have Morgan scream at him and throw her iPod . . . Dinah had a welt for days.

Morgan had raged that he had ratted her out, and though Dinah tried to tell Morgan she had no way of knowing that, privately she agreed he'd probably done it. Someday she would find a way to thank him. Horrible as the experience was to have it all public, who knows how far it might have gone?

Dinah put down her purse and went to Morgan's room.

Her daughter was curled up on the bed, where she always was these days, her earbuds in her ears, papers scattered around her like a moat.

Dinah sat down on the edge of Morgan's bed without invitation and rested her hand on Morgan's slim hip. The bone was sharp under her hand.

"I know you don't want to talk to us," Dinah began, reciting a variation on the speech she'd been giving since that first day the police showed up and Joe took down her door. "But I love you more than my life, and nothing that's happened has changed that. I'm sorry for whatever way I failed you, and if there's any way I can fix it now, I would do it, in a second."

Dinah paused and sat in the stillness, trying to decode the song leaking out from Morgan's iPod. It had become her game of sorts, as she waited daily for Morgan to respond to her. It sounded improbably like Dean Martin. She waited all the way until the song — whatever it was — stopped, and there was a pause before the next began.

She felt a quick dart of hope when Morgan seemed to shift under the light weight of her hand on her hip, during the pause between songs, but then she stilled again, and this time the sound that came out was loud and screechy.

She doubted Morgan could hear her, but she said it anyway, "I'm here when you're ready to talk," and squeezed her hip lightly.

There was the smallest motion as Morgan flinched under her mother's touch.

She stopped in next to check on the boys, who were in their room. Connor was playing some *Star Wars* game. Jared had a jigsaw puzzle half formed on a sticky mat on the carpet. It had been a while since she'd seen that old hobby resurface. Dinah had gotten so excited when he started showing interest in something not digital that she fairly buried him in puzzles until he groaned whenever he saw one.

"Hey, Mom," Connor said, grumbling as his ship or whatever blew up.

"Hey, Mom," Jared said, yawning and turning a puzzle piece around and around in his hand. His pant legs had bunched toward his knees, which looked hairier, more manlike, than she'd remembered.

She never could notice a milestone of growth without part of her winging back to the NICU and their sparrowlike bodies splayed under the bright lights, and her heart would blossom with wonder and gratitude that they'd survived at all.

Is it any wonder she was protective of them? Jared with this awkward, shuffling gait and Connor with his shifting moods and struggle in school? Neither one seemed to have an ounce of natural social grace, blurting into conversations and offending the other kid with some joke that in their heads was terribly funny.

"Can I talk to you guys for a minute?" Dinah asked.

Connor shrugged and put his game controller down. Jared glanced up, looking bored within an inch of his life.

Dinah sat cross-legged between the two.

"Are things okay for you? At school right now? Or are you getting hassled?"

Connor perched on the futon and pulled his knees up to his chest. "Well, I've told everyone if they say one word about my sister around me, I'm ramming their head into the wall. And I think they pretty much believe me, so no one says anything to me."

"Connor . . ." Dinah began.

Jared shrugged. "My friends are cool. They don't talk crap about her."

Dinah persisted. "But what about other kids?"

Jared shrugged. "There are no other kids. No one talks to me but like three people, so. No problem."

Dinah slumped, defeated. She knew they had to be aware of the whispers, pointed fingers from kids — even teachers — saying, "That's one of the brothers."

"I'm really sorry, guys," she said.

Connor scowled. "What are you sorry for? You didn't do it. You, like, can't control everything, Mom. It's like apologizing for the weather."

"It's a sympathy-sorry, hon," Dinah said, though it hadn't been, not really. Someday they might have kids of their own and know what it was like to feel responsible for their every move.

She sighed and got up to leave them. They closed the door behind her, and Dinah hoped they were confiding in each other, at least.

Downstairs in the office, she found Joe, flushed with his third beer of the night, laptop in his lap, with one eye on March Madness highlights. He was in an old sweatshirt, which strained across his stomach these days, and a pair of jeans that hadn't seen the light of day since their Internet came in through a screechy dial-up modem.

"How are things going with you," she asked, as he clicked something on the computer and made the screen go dark . . . too hastily, she thought. "What were you reading?"

"Nothing. Sports stuff."

The outraged crowd on the television groaned over something, the timing oddly comical to Dinah, because it sounded to her like not even the basketball fans believed Joe.

"You should really go up and talk to Morgan."

Joe snorted. "She won't talk to me. And why should she? I'm not exactly Father of the Year."

"You're right that she won't talk to you, but she has to see you try. She has to see that you care."

"Of course I care, she's my daughter and . . ." He cleared his throat and shifted on the couch, setting the laptop on the coffee table. "I'll go up later. I will."

She sat on the other end of the couch. "How is it at the school?" she asked quietly, looking down at her own sock feet, which she drew up next to her. She and Joe had barely spoken about Morgan after that first tearful night when they tried to determine when and where she had managed to have an affair under their noses.

"How do you think? It's horrible." Sounded like *hah*-rible. "No one will look at me. No one will talk to me. I told you already about that lovely conversation with Pete Jackson, asking how I didn't pick up on this. He was pretending to ask as a principal supervising an employee, but I knew what he really meant. How the hell didn't I control my own daughter?"

"That is such bullshit. It's not Morgan who needed controlling, it's that pervert teacher's dick."

"Some control over our daughter would have been nice."

"Don't you start, too."

"What? You think it wouldn't have been a good idea to check in on her once in a while when she said she was gonna be someplace? In hindsight, anyways? Geez, Dinah, not even you are that blind."

"Not even me? What the hell does that mean?"

"It means your whole life you have made excuses for all the kids. And until just now, it looked like you were one for three, anyway, with Morgan the perfect kid. But it doesn't look that way anymore."

"Oh, so this is my fault now? First, Morgan's exploitation was her own fault, and now it's mine? How about you? You worked with that teacher, you hired him for God's sake. You put him in that job, in that class. You mean to say nothing he's ever done in the past hinted at this kind of thing? No one ever complained he was overly flirty? He never showed inappropriate interest in a pretty girl before? And as for Morgan, I'm not the only parent in the house, or at least I'm not supposed to be."

"No, he did not have a history of fucking his students, or I think I might have thought twice about hiring him, darling. Thanks for the support. You know I could lose my job over this."

"Oh, stop thinking the worst," Dinah

blurted. "You always act like the worst is going to happen."

"The worst is happening! Right now!"

He slammed his beer down on the end table, and the dregs fizzed as if in protest.

Joe stomped past her toward the stairs.

Dinah stood up and started after him. "Joe, wait . . ." she began, though she didn't know what she planned to say. He made a shooing gesture with his hand behind him, as if waving off a wasp. Dinah slumped back onto the couch.

The laptop was in her line of sight. With shaky hands, Dinah started it back up and checked the browser history.

It was Morgan's Facebook page.

Post after post, people were calling her a slut, whore, and worse.

Dinah swallowed down bile and then she saw Ethan's name. He'd written: *Morgan is hurting and confused right now, and you people are all pathetic assholes.*

Underneath his post was a barrage of insults, and kids accusing him of being in love with her, and informing him of what she was doing with her teacher when his back was turned. Dinah clicked on Ethan's name and found that the abuse continued onto his page. She didn't see Morgan's other friends anywhere in the cyber assault, on either side . . . Not Kelly's daughter, Britney, supposedly so loyal; not Nicole, who had covered for her. Nicole's mother had in fact left Dinah a blistering voice mail about her daughter being interviewed by the police — interrogated, she'd claimed — so maybe Nicole had been forbidden from ever interacting with Morgan again.

Dinah went back to Morgan's page and noticed that many of the people posting had profiles created just within the last few days. Fake profiles, no doubt. She could click to report them, but the real kids could just create new fake profiles.

She was relieved Morgan hadn't been online to see any of this. Her last post, Dinah noticed, was the day before the rendezvous in the car when all she'd typed was: "So confused." Had Dinah looked? Had she even noticed her daughter's post and thought to ask about it?

How long had Joe been stalking his daughter's profile and wallowing in this garbage?

Dinah could fix this small thing, at least, if nothing else. She only had to try a few times to guess Morgan's password, and then she logged in as her daughter and deleted the profile. Morgan would just have to start fresh, sometime in the future, when all this was a distant, nauseating memory.

35

Rain couldn't stop touching the top of her waist, where it strained against her jeans. She was dimly aware of sitting in a lawyer's office, next to her husband, to discuss defending him against charges of a sex crime against his student.

That fact did not seem as real as the actual swelling of her belly, the first she'd ever experienced in all her years of dreaming up a baby. She was assuring herself again and again that the baby was indeed still there.

She did it so often that TJ interrupted Alexandra to ask sharply, "Are you okay?"

Rain clasped her hands and tried to bring herself back into the room.

Alex smiled tightly at Rain, by way of, "Let's move along, shall we?" and resumed her speech. "It seems the most difficult piece for us to address will be the text messages. You're going to have to explain these to me, TJ."

Alex looked down at the papers in her hands, elongating her elegant profile. Behind her, out the windows of the closest thing Arbor Valley had to a high-rise, Rain glimpsed ducks paddling in one of those fake office-park ponds meant to serve as both drainage and "water feature."

TJ cleared his throat. "I was trying not to set her off. Trying to let her down easy."

Alex tipped back in her office chair and tapped a pencil against her chin. "Doesn't sound like letting 'down' here. I mean, listen: 'Miss you.' Seriously, TJ? And 'Will have house to self Friday night.' Come on."

"Hey, I thought you were on my side."

"Of course. Which means I have to look at this like a prosecutor might, so I can punch holes in it. And I guarantee you, Henry did a victory lap around his office when these turned up."

Rain interrupted, "He feels bad enough."

"Feeling bad or good is not the issue here. It's not going to feel good to be on trial. I can't soft-pedal this if we want to win. Now. Back to the issue. TJ, if you're telling me that these text messages were meant to deflect her, and keep her from freaking out, that's what we'll work with. What I'm envisioning here is basically telling the jury you were stupid and naive but not a sex criminal. Again, not fun to hear, but unless you want to spend your baby's day of birth in prison and your life on the sex offenders list, you'll just have to live with it. Next issue," Alex continued, looking down at her legal pad. "Our cross-examination if she takes the stand."

"If?" TJ asked, seeming to brighten. "She might not?"

"I understand that she's not the most cooperative witness, based on courthouse gossip and reading between the lines of the police report; she had quite a story to tell at first, then she clammed up at some point. She's on the witness list, naturally, but her unsworn statement to the police is inadmissible hearsay. I'm actually feeling pretty good about this. If Henry doesn't call her, then his evidence is thin. If he does, I'll be able to rattle her during cross, and my bet is that her story will fall apart. I've seen this before, when witnesses, especially young witnesses, are confronted with the judge on the bench, the jury staring at them, the audience, the lights, the swearing on the Bible . . . She could very well go to pieces in front of us. I mean, she made up an affair; that's not exactly the behavior of a stable girl."

Rain felt like she was watching a lawyer on a television show. She glanced at TJ, and he looked stricken. Rain frowned into her lap. Wasn't this good news? That their evidence was flimsy?

Alex continued, "Honestly, I'm not sure why Henry is pushing to go to trial on this, unless it's some personal vendetta to hang you out to dry, or he's trying to score points to get elected next year. That plea deal he offered was a joke, given his so-called evidence. It will be painful going to trial, but this has got reasonable doubt written all over it."

TJ groaned as if in pain. Rain reached for him, but his chair was just a little too far away.

Alex dropped her severe tone and tilted her head. The effort to look sincere came off as preprogrammed. "Look, don't worry. The situation could change as we learn more. Hell, the girl could recant any day. Public opinion hasn't been kind to her, either."

TJ shifted in his seat and raked his hands through his hair. Rain stared hard at him, trying to understand why TJ had barely looked at her during the whole meeting.

On the way home, Rain felt so tired in the

passenger seat she thought TJ would have to pour her out of the car. And she was supposed to go to work now, and preach "ohm" and chakras to the neighborhood mommies in their cute yoga pants. Gran used to praise Rain for her strength, but Rain always knew better. Real strength is innate. What she had was a finely honed, oft-practiced ability to fake it.

Dizziness swam up around her and Rain cracked the window, as TJ drove white knuckled down the highway.

"Stop," she muttered, clutching her stomach. "Got to . . ."

TJ finally heard her, and pulled over, but it was nearly too late when Rain opened the door without getting out and vomited onto the side of the road. She fumbled for her bottle of water and TJ handed it to her. She was breathing into her abdomen, spitting out water, and working to steady herself before she fainted right out of the car. She felt the car rock and heard the road noise change as TJ got out of his side, and Rain was briefly afraid he'd walk off and leave her. Hitchhike away somewhere and vanish.

Alexandra had been prepared to argue that the baby was a reason TJ wasn't a flight risk, but Rain had asked her not to mention it in open court unless she had no other choice. She did not want her pregnancy, her innocent fetus, dragged into the gossip mill; she had already been strategizing courtroom outfits that might conceal her pregnancy without looking so much like maternity clothes. Billowy maxi dresses were in fashion; that was a help.

The whole blissful experience, so long hoped and prayed for — irrevocably tainted.

When her mother called to talk about a baby shower, Rain had laughed. Who would come?

TJ crouched down in her peripheral vision. "You okay, babe?"

And the dizziness receded. His presence alone seemed to ground her. She met his eyes, which seemed dark and shrunken in their hollows. He might have lost weight. All those insomniac hours on the elliptical, not to mention his diet had consisted mainly of beer since his brief jail experience, which he refused to discuss.

She cleared her throat and gave him a weak smile. It was time to rally for TJ. He needed her as much as anyone ever had.

Rain had almost shaken off her morning's experience — both the attorney and the highway sickness — when she crossed the threshold of NYC to find Beverly shooting her a look of kind commiseration that also bore a slight head tilt of pity.

Rain looked away and tried to pass Beverly to ready herself for her class.

Beverly blocked her path. "I'm worried about you. Let's talk. Please."

Rain, resigned, followed Beverly into a small room in the back of NYC that Beverly used for private lessons and small, three-person yoga classes for the teachers themselves. There was still a ballet barre and mirror from the building's former incarnation as a dance studio. Unlike the main studio, which looked out over a shimmering inland lake, this room had mirrors, and Rain was confronted with her reflection. Beverly was always saying she was going to drape the mirrors with cloth: Preoccupation with the physical form was a distraction from mindful practice, she liked to say.

Rain would have been thrilled with covered mirrors so she could look at something else besides the floor, Beverly's face, or her own reflection.

"I'm going to warm up," Rain announced, "while we talk. I have class soon."

"Sure," Beverly said, as if Rain had asked permission. "Maybe I will, too. Why not."

Rain took in a deep breath and exhaled through the back of her throat, *ujjayi pranayama,* and folded into a forward bend. Her hamstrings were tight. She rode the tide of her breath back upward, sweeping her arms out in wide arcs, meeting in a prayer position at her chest. She was facing the mirror, to avoid facing Beverly head-on. Her friend's forehead was wrinkled, and she was making pitying puppy-dog eyes. Rain tried to soften her own facial expression and felt her whole self relax. How long had she been walking around all knotted up like this?

Beverly was in tree pose with one foot against her other thigh, knee stuck out sideways.

"How are you holding up?"

"As well as can be expected."

"Forgive me for asking, but . . . What does TJ have to say about all this?"

Rain considered her answer. "That he was stupid for trying to handle it himself." Swooping down, Rain spoke into her own shins. "But he was trying to avoid this very thing."

"Handle what for himself?"

Deep breath in, rising up. "Her sick infatuation. He was afraid of this, and it happened. He said the other day he wished he'd gotten fat and homely like his college roommate . . ."

"Yes, the poor handsome devil."

The smirk in Beverly's voice grated over Rain's newly relaxed mind, and she tensed again. She abandoned the forward fold and stepped back into downward-facing dog, elongating her back, rear in the air. She spoke to the back door of the room, looking between her knees. "He's saying he's the victim of this girl's issues. Maybe she would have latched on to another teacher if he hadn't been promoted to calc. To think we saw that promotion as a blessing . . ."

"You mean to tell me, deep down, you really believe he didn't do a single thing wrong? Bless your heart, but really, Rain? It doesn't sound too likely that he's been a saint throughout all this."

Rain couldn't see Beverly, but the honey-sweet yet stern grandmother voice was the same voice she'd used to lecture Layla about being more careful with the cash drawer.

Rain lowered herself to her hands and knees with great effort and folded into half lotus, facing Beverly now, who towered over her in tree pose, having switched to the other side. "Of course I take him at his word. He's my husband and I love him, and I don't plan to cut and run." At this, Rain felt a tickle in her chest, like a guilty person who has just told a lie. But she wasn't lying;

she did believe him. Of course she did.

"They can't have just her word for it, though," Beverly said, her voice never losing its kind, wise-elder tone. "They can't charge someone on one person's say-so with no evidence."

"Innocent until proven guilty, Bev." Rain closed her eyes and felt her red anger spreading out from her heart chakra, as Bev would put it. She tried to breathe deeply, but her body foiled this desire, and the air came in and out of her upper chest, too quickly. She rested the backs of her hands on her knees as she might toward the end of class.

Beverly must have lowered herself to the floor as well, because her voice was coming from Rain's level. She seemed to speak even more quietly now. "Honey, the police found her in his car, in a park-and-ride lot next to the highway, miles from town."

"It was stupid of him, as I said. But he didn't touch her. And stop calling me 'Honey.' "

"Why did I hear that she was naked, then?"

Rain's eyes snapped open, and she brought her hands to her chest, as if protecting herself. "From the waist up only, and how the hell would you know that? That wasn't in the paper."

Bev crouched down and met Rain's gaze. "I just overheard . . ."

"Gossip, Bev? I'm disappointed in you. And please keep that little tidbit to yourself, unless you can't wait to run out and add to the rumor mill."

"I wouldn't do that to you."

"No, you'd just give me grief over this — as if I don't have enough already — while I'm trying to get ready for class."

"I don't want to give you grief. I just want you to think this through."

"She took her own shirt off."

"Is that his story?"

"It's not a story. I'm suddenly unwell, Beverly. I'm taking a sick day."

Rain couldn't manage to smoothly roll her mat, so she grabbed it up in chunky, awkward folds, ignoring Bev's repeating of her name in that same calm voice like some kind of hypnotizing mantra. Rain got all the way to the parking lot when she realized she was still barefoot. She drove home anyway, feeling the grit from the parking lot against the pads of her feet, trying to concentrate on that, instead of the image that kept slipping into her thoughts like a photo slide: TJ and the girl fumbling, half naked in his car.

36

Dinah walked into the Den with her daughter in tow. Janine was behind the cash register, and Dinah flinched at the shock of their bold public appearance registering so plainly on Janine's face.

It was a slow time, just before eleven. After the kid crowd and before the lunch rush. Dinah could not stand to be under house arrest another moment, so she declared it Take Your Daughter to Work Day and dragged Morgan out to the car.

Morgan, wordlessly, as she did everything lately, stomped through the center of the Den and made for the stairs up to Dinah's office.

Dinah had been sweeping the floor for ten minutes — Janine and the crew had gotten so lax in her absence, it was a mess of raisins and muffin crumbs — when she remembered the computer and Internet connection upstairs.

She slapped the broom against the nearest wall and took the stairs two at a time.

Morgan was in Dinah's wheeled office chair but pushed back away from the desk, her hands gripping the edge, like she was holding on to a precipice. Dinah couldn't see her expression behind that long sheet of dark hair.

"Honey . . ."

"I am not . . ." — the words were eerie in their calm and deep, almost growling, register — "his victim."

"What are you reading?"

"The so-called news."

"I should have warned you not to look . . ."

"Oh, why, because it might make me faint? Because you'd have to break out the smelling salts? And thanks so very much for deleting my Facebook, Mom. I know it was you."

Dinah winced. "You didn't see what they were putting on your page. It was horrible."

She turned to face Dinah at last. "Why do they hate me? What did I do that's so terrible?"

Dinah ran forward, crouched, and let Morgan tumble forward from the desk chair and lean on her. She let her daughter sob, and she stroked the back of her head as she had the whole of Morgan's life.

"Oh, baby. It wasn't your fault. You didn't mean any of this, I know." Dinah stepped carefully around any "victim" language.

"It's not my fault I'm young. I'm not as young as my years."

Dinah, having no response, only squeezed her thin frame, feeling Morgan's shoulder blades poke at her arms. In some ways, what she said was absolutely true. Morgan had been treated as someone older than her age her entire life. At least, since the twins were born. Serious toddler-Morgan would waddle over to Dinah with diapers or wipes or the burp cloths she needed. Little Mo-Mo even learned how to switch on the button of the vibrating bouncy seat if it stopped humming while Connor was in it and he started screaming. Barely out of diapers herself, she was already an apprentice mother.

Finally, Dinah ventured, "But can't you see that it wasn't right? He's married. And your teacher. It's not an equal playing field."

"We weren't playing. We were in love. Are in love."

Dinah swallowed against her desire to scream that it's just sick for a grown man to screw a teenager. "What makes you so sure?" she asked instead, unable to keep the sharpness out of her voice.

Morgan shoved back from Dinah, the chair's wheels catching on a rug and almost toppling. She jumped up and pointed at her mother, looking so eerily like her own younger self that a chill pricked the hairs on Dinah's arms.

"I'm sure because I just feel it. I just know it. And anyway, he just turned thirty, which is not much different than Granny and Gramps's age difference and she got married at what, nineteen? We had bad luck to meet when we did, the way we did! I have never felt this way about anyone before, ever. And he loves me, he said he did."

"Then why is he married? Why did he keep going home to his wife?"

"People make mistakes. He married the wrong person. Anyway, she stopped loving him when she couldn't have a baby. He was wrecked about it."

"Or . . . he's not telling you the truth."

"He's not a liar."

Dinah sucked in a galvanizing breath. "He told countless lies to keep seeing you. And he's lying now, telling the police he didn't touch you."

Morgan drew herself up taller, more rigid than ever. She seemed to Dinah lately like blown glass: inflexible but fragile. One sharp blow would mean a thousand tiny shards. "He's saying what he has to say to beat this stupid case."

Dinah uttered the words that had been swirling around in her mind since Morgan first admitted it was all true: "You lied, too. Again and again."

Morgan tossed her hair, then self-consciously pushed it back in front of her scar. "I can't stop thinking about him. I needed to see him. He needed to see me. I thought about him every second I wasn't with him. I had no other choice."

"That's not love, it's obsession."

Morgan's beautiful face crumpled into a sneer. "What would you know about love, anyway?"

"What the hell does that mean? I love your father."

"You tolerate him. Barely."

"Love isn't always fireworks and rainbows. Mature love is quieter, but it's there."

"Keep telling yourself that."

Dinah had lost her again. For a few moments, Morgan had let her back in, and now she was back to the sneering contempt. Dinah could see as clearly as she could read the headline on the screen behind her that it was all a front. She recognized it so well because she lived it herself. Dinah was always at her most furious when she secretly worried, many strata beneath her outrage, that she was, in actual fact, wrong.

Not having anywhere to storm off to, Morgan settled for flouncing onto the old thrift store couch along the far wall of the office, under the eaves. "Don't forget to lock the maiden in her tower," she said drily, and she shoved in her earbuds.

The headline that remained on the glowing screen was the first story that had hit the news, sending ripples of titillated outrage all over town: TEACHER ACCUSED OF SEX WITH STUDENT; ALLEGED VICTIM IN HIS CLASS AT AVHS.

Dinah resumed her cleaning downstairs in the weird stillness of the Den. That's when she noticed the ambient music had stopped, and there was no chatter to fill the space. In fact, as she leaned on her broom and looked around, there wasn't a soul in the place and it was nearly noon.

"Why is it so dead in here?" she asked, to no one in particular, but Janine answered.

"It has been for a while. There was a surge of business right after . . . I think people were coming in to see you." She hastily added, "To support you. Some people said some nice things. You know, chin up and stuff like that."

"Yeah, right. They were coming to gawk. How long has it been dead like this? Why didn't you say anything?"

"And do what? I thought about it, but what are you going to do? You can't force people in here."

"I could run a special or something. Put a coupon in the paper."

Janine cocked an eyebrow, and Dinah spat, "If you have a better idea, genius, let me know. If this place shuts down, you'll be out of a job, too."

Janine pressed her lips into a thin line and threw down the rag with which she'd been polishing the countertop. "You abandon me here to run this place without you, to deal with a bunch of temps and high school kids who are lazy and eating all the pastries, in the midst of this . . . controversy, and you're mad at me?"

"It's not you. I'm mad at the whole damn world."

"It's tough all around."

"I'll say," Dinah muttered, sweeping up her last crumb pile. As her anger cooled, she cringed to hear her own angry words echoing in her memory She turned back to Janine. "I'm sorry. It's not you, really. It's everything. I just can't . . ."

Dinah failed to finish her sentence. Can't what? It was too big to even name.

Janine shrugged by way of response, her jaw still tight, polishing the countertop much harder than necessary.

Kelly came in, haloed by a summer-warm glow on this bizarre March day in the weirdest spring of Dinah's life. "Hey, I just read the paper. I'm sorry."

"Oh, what now?"

Dinah's stomach lurched, and she whipped her head around, looking for a newspaper. Kelly offered it, her face looking pained, but Dinah thought she could detect a bright, thrilled gleam in her eye.

The headline read "LOLITA MOM" BLASTS PLANNERS OVER BIAS AGAINST PROJECT.

Dinah loosed a blistering stream of curses and stormed to the storeroom with her cell phone, shakily dialing the newspaper offices from the number on page two.

The editor on the other end sounded about nineteen years old and apologized profusely, claiming that headline was a placeholder, that he had already nixed it and told the staff to write something else, but it got late, and someone sent it to press without replacing it . . .

Dinah interrupted, "I should sue you for defamation. And supposedly you have this policy against naming victims of sexual assault? Well, by naming me, what do you think that does for my daughter's privacy? Why not mark her with a scarlet A? As long as you're using literary allusions to tear apart her reputation, college kid, what year did you graduate?"

The apologetic voice grew cool. "I hardly think that's relevant."

"Neither is Nabokov."

She punched the off button and lowered herself to sitting on a box full of napkins.

Lolita Mom. All her life of fighting for her children, trying to do everything by the book and in their best interests, and she was reduced to a sneering nickname in the local paper of record. Not to mention her daughter.

The door opened and Morgan peeked her head into the storeroom. Dinah nearly thrust the paper behind her to hide it, then realized her daughter would grab for it then. So she acted like there was nothing of note in its pages, just the weather report, stock prices. All that stuff she used to give a shit about before everything went crazy.

"Mom? Hey, I was just looking at the calendar. It's almost the twins' birthday."

Dinah put her head in her hand. "I know." That date on the calendar had been stalking her. She hadn't the faintest idea what to get them, how to celebrate, and had no energy to do so, then was immediately choked by guilt. She knew no other way to react to negative feelings about parenting the twins; after all, she'd prayed for their very survival and had sworn she would give anything for them just to be alive one more day.

How dare she be frustrated? For even a moment?

Morgan said, "So, we should bake them a cake or something, right? Put up some streamers and stuff? Balloons? Or maybe they're too old for that stuff."

Dinah finally looked up at her daughter's face. It was splotchy and pale from their recent fight, and there were pronounced blue smears under her eyes from poor sleep. But her expression seemed genuine.

"Yeah, that would be nice," Dinah replied, hating herself for not being able to keep the curious note out of her voice.

Morgan seemed to read her thoughts. She looked down at the toes of her pink ballet flats. "I just noticed the date on the calendar and feel bad that . . . this" — she waved her hands in the air around her head — "might overshadow their day. That's not fair."

"No, it sure isn't."

Morgan plopped down on the box kitty-corner to hers. Dinah knew she should get out there and get back to work. She had so few days in the Den that she had to make them count. But the law of objects at rest staying at rest was most compelling just then.

"I have an idea for what to get them, Mom."

"I'm all ears." Dinah hadn't the faintest idea. Every year she warred between what the boys wanted — digital stuff, video games — and what she wanted to get them: educational toys, books, puzzles.

"We should get them an e-reader or a tablet computer–type thing."

"An e-reader? For them? They just want to blow things up on their video games."

"Duh. I know. But if you got them a computer gadget with, like, books on it, maybe they'd like the books?"

"Don't those things have Internet? Not sure the boys are ready for that."

"They're on the Internet all the time."

"No, I mean privately. In their room, where I can't check up on them."

"Mom." Morgan was using her flat, weary, patient voice. "Mom, you cannot control everything."

"Obviously," she could not help but say.

"I'm just trying to help." Now her voice

was brittle with impending tears.

"I know, Mo-Mo. And it's sweet of you. I just don't know if JC are ready for that. Maybe next year."

"You haven't said that in a while. JC."

When the boys were very little, when there was so much to do to keep them healthy and safe, "Jared and Connor," or even "the twins," felt cumbersome. "JC" evolved from a shorthand Dinah was using in e-mails to Joe — back in the days of AOL — and it crept into everyday speech.

"Let's just say I'm more nostalgic than usual."

Morgan sighed and raised her chin slightly. Dinah could see where the makeup caked over her scar had started to flake. No matter how many times Dinah tried to tell her that fading, cakey makeup made it even more noticeable, Morgan would still spend several minutes, every morning, trying to spackle over her one physical flaw.

"So what are we going to get them, then?" Morgan asked, now bristling with impatience.

"I don't know. I'll think of something. Maybe a gift card, then take them shopping out at Best Buy or something." Best Buy, off down the highway, where no one knew who they were. Where Morgan wasn't notorious. Outside the little bubble of their small, gossipy town, no one cared about them. Unless somehow the case went viral.

Thinking of a tablet computer, and the Internet, and viral videos reminded Dinah that, really, their story was a few outraged forwarded links from being national news. She herself had clucked her tongue in shocked disapproval at similar nationwide stories of teacher-student affairs: like that one teacher in Florida, who eventually married her young lover. Or was it Alaska?

Dinah clutched her chest at the thought of TJ Hill as a son-in-law.

"I'd better get back out there," Dinah said, though the idea of staying in the cool, dark storeroom the whole rest of the day (month, year) was appealing. "Maybe I should take you home."

Morgan sighed roughly. "Back to my cell?"

"It's not like that. I'm trying to protect you."

"A little late, isn't it?"

"I mean from the aftermath. You saw what was on the computer today. You heard about your locker. Do you really want to walk through the halls in the midst of that?"

"Maybe it's worse because I'm hiding, ever thought of that? Maybe if I went to school with my head held high, they'd all get over it."

"Oh, honey . . ."

"Really. Yeah, for the first few days it would be like, all shocking and stuff, but then I bet they'd move on to the next thing. I think my not being there is making it worse. Plus I'm bored to death. You keep saying how I'm the innocent one. So why am I on lockdown?"

Dinah bit her lip, swallowing hard. The next words she said could make or break it. Morgan's face was hard to read in the dim light. "You are the innocent in the scenario between you and the teacher. Absolutely. You are not innocent in the lies you told to see him."

"I thought he manipulated me and abused me, therefore I can't be held responsible."

Dinah retorted, "I thought you were a mature woman and fully in control of all your actions."

Morgan jumped up. "I'll get my backpack and meet you at the car. I don't know why I bothered trying to talk to you."

Dinah jumped up, too, and blocked her path to the door, trying to catch her eye in the gloom. "Maybe we should see a family counselor . . ."

"No. And I will never speak to you again if you even try."

"Why would that be so awful?"

"Because if you drag me there, it's because you think I'm twisted and disturbed and I'm not. End of discussion."

"Morgan . . ."

Her daughter ignored her, charging away through the Den and up the stairs. As she heard Morgan's footfalls grow distant and more faint, Dinah felt her daughter slipping away like sand through her fingers. Morgan's eighteenth birthday and legal adulthood loomed like a day of reckoning in sunny July.

37

In Morgan's new favorite fantasy, he would scale the rose trellis and drainpipe under her window, knock on the pane, and spirit her away to California.

There they could dye their hair and change their names. They'd live in some run-down but romantic old house, picking up odd jobs and coming together at night as a couple, unencumbered by the world's stupid rules. Morgan would study when not working, saving money for college. They would take long walks on the beach and make love every night without sneaking around.

Her other, more grounded version, was that he would be found not guilty because what evidence they have was stupid and circumstantial. He and his wife would then get a divorce, and then he would take Morgan far away, to California, where no one has ever heard of them and no one cares how old they are. They get married on the beach and live out their days as a living example of the exception to the rule. Her mother writes every week to beg forgiveness for misjudging them. Fantasy Morgan — depending on her mood — graciously consents for her mother to come visit, where Dinah apologizes through hysterical, hiccupy tears, and Fantasy Morgan announces she is having a baby and allows her mother to feel her grandchild kick.

Or sometimes she just throws the imaginary letters into the imaginary roaring fire.

Yet, in reality, she was still in her tiny, doorless room, furtively scribbling poems and hiding the notebook under her homework.

Died and no one noticed
Because I was still smiling

All the while, she had to wonder why he hadn't tried to get in touch with her. Not even a message through some kind of intermediary.

True, that could get him in big trouble. But "big trouble" was always possible, and it didn't stop him before.

She rolled onto her back, staring at the thin crack in her ceiling for so long it almost seemed to move, slowly, like waving seaweed. She blinked several times and it was normal again. She thought of that story they'd read in AP English the beginning of this year about the lady going crazy looking at her yellow wallpaper.

She pondered what she'd said to her mother that morning. Did she really want to go back into the high school? At the time she thought she meant it, but alone with her own self and the moving ceiling crack and her own memories, she had to admit she was afraid to go back.

But to stay in her room another day was agonizing.

She texted Britney.

If I came back to school would you sit with me at lunch? Or are you too grossed out?

She put the phone on her chest and hated how much hung in the balance of her reply. Kind of like with him: how much she pinned her hopes on whether he could sneak a text to her.

Obsessed, her mother had said. Morgan remembered when Britney became all head-over-heels about this kid at another school she'd met while visiting her dad. When the guy hadn't called her, Britney was a bitch-machine. When he had, she was all gooey and sugary. Morgan had said all the supportive things a friend was supposed to say, but secretly she'd been disgusted.

Morgan sat up, her head swimmy with the sudden verticality. No. This was different. *He* was different. This was no idle high school crush. It couldn't be, because why would he — why would the two of them — have risked so much otherwise?

She didn't ruin her life for a crush. No way.

Her phone buzzed.

Of course. You're my friend and I'll stick by you. I'm sorry I haven't been in touch before. I didn't know what to say.

Relief gusted through her. She replied:

I know. It's really weird. I'm coming back to school, just decided.

Britney said,

Good, see you Monday.

Want to come over this weekend?

Sorry, can't, I have plans already. See you Monday, though.

Morgan frowned at her phone. Plans the whole entire weekend? Every hour?

She shook it off with her favorite phrase lately: "Whatever."

She cocked her ear to listen for approaching feet. Satisfied all was quiet, she reached for her poetry notebook.

Polished
Steel
A sphere
Cool and hard
Whatever you throw
Glances off, tangential and gone

Morgan found her mother at the kitchen table, papers and spreadsheets in front of her, her forehead in her hand.

"Mom?"

"Oh, hi, hon."

Her mother swept away all the papers and gave Morgan her full attention. Morgan bit her lip to keep from laughing. How often before all this had she approached her mother, up to her ears in Den paperwork, only to get half her attention? She'd listen to whatever Morgan was saying, going

"MMMm hmmm" while carrying on looking at her papers.

Her grandmother used to use an expression that had something to do with closing the barn door after the cows got out.

"I'm going back to school."

"Mo . . ."

"Don't call me that right now. You're addressing the senior in high school, who is not sick, and not suspended or in trouble, and doesn't need to be sitting at home. Maybe it's more convenient for Dad, not having to deal with me in the building, seeing as I'm all notorious now. You know what? I don't care. I didn't do anything wrong, and I deserve to finish out my senior year like normal. Graduation, prom, everything. Yes, Mother, I said prom. I don't have leprosy, you know. I can still go."

"I thought you were in love."

"I can go with my girlfriends. Lots of girls do that. It's, like, so 1950 to only go to prom if you have a date. I can still put on a pretty dress and go dance."

"I'll talk to your father about it tonight."

"Well, if you must, go ahead, but I'm going. If I have to hitchhike or walk or ride the school bus, I'm going to school."

Her mother sighed so deeply Morgan was surprised she didn't pass out from the exhalation. "Fine. But I'm driving you and taking you home. You are not taking the car."

Morgan felt a coil of tightness snake through her chest. "Why?"

"As long as we're being blunt here, we're afraid you're going to run away. You have made no secret of the fact that you consider yourself an adult in everything but legal age. You also had no trouble lying and sneaking around these last months. You want to subject yourself to school right now, that's your choice, but I want to know for sure that school is where you actually go."

"You think I'm going to sneak away to see him?"

"I think very little is impossible these days. What? I'm agreeing you should go to school. That's what you wanted, right? How you get there shouldn't matter."

"You're still treating me like a criminal."

"I'm protecting you, as long as I possibly can."

"A little late for that."

"So you've said. But I don't give up on my children. Ever."

For this last point, Dinah pointed a sharpened pencil at her daughter.

Morgan growled and stomped away to her room. She threw herself on her bed and tried to conjure up his face. It was getting harder to do as it had been weeks since she'd seen him, and she found it alarming how fast the specifics of him were fading. In a normal relationship, she could at least look at pictures. But they'd never taken any pictures together.

As she jumped up to search for her most recent yearbook to at least look at his school picture in the faculty pages, her mind looped itself back to the worn groove of the thought that occupied more and more of her mind: Had he given her up so easily?

38

A freakishly warm March faded into a stormy April, as Rain bought a maternity wardrobe alone, in a town far down the highway. For a few hours that day, Rain soaked in the manufactured joy of the employees who'd been trained to revel in each customer's pregnancy. The salesgirls had asked her if she were having a boy or girl and she said she didn't know. They squealed at the delight of an old-fashioned surprise. In fact, she'd declined to find out because she wanted out of the ultrasound room as fast as possible, the bleak reality of their situation contrasting with the blissful daydream she'd conjured for so long.

Most of that shopping trip, though, she could put aside her husband's impending trial, the fact that Gran was missing yet another milestone, the fact that she found her mother's presence unbearable, not to mention her sister's, who had appointed herself Mothering Expert and decided Rain was a drooling imbecile on the subject of infants. In that anonymous store with searing yellow-bright lights, she was able to forget that she had become an object of curiosity.

Work was no refuge. After her confrontation with Beverly, the atmosphere had become frosty with Bev's disapproval. Layla, as ignorant of such things as a panting puppy, chattered to fill the dead space between classes. She also happily picked up the slack when Rain was feeling too ill (reality: too tired and emotionally withered) to teach.

Some of those early classes had featured uncomfortable words of vague support from the teacher's-pet types, but as their comments were greeted by Rain's mute, still face, they gave up and withdrew. No one showed off their new bow pose achievement after class anymore.

Indeed, her classes had begun to shrink.

This April morning, she sipped her tea as TJ picked up fallen branches from the latest storm. It would have been the Monday after spring break, if such a thing had mattered anymore. He'd be gathering steam for the last big push toward the end of the year. He'd be worried about how his students would do on the exams: Too many good grades meant maybe he hadn't challenged them enough, but too many poor grades meant he was perhaps failing to actually teach them. And she would hold his hand through it. At the end of the year he'd be triumphant, looking back with satisfaction, as if he'd never really been worried.

Now, he spent all day in front of the television, or on the elliptical, or on the computer, though he'd been advised to take down his Facebook page and stay away from social media in general. Alexandra had cautioned: "Any comment you make that someone gets ahold of could be newsworthy, or worse, evidence. For you, it's 1999. It wouldn't be such a bad idea to unplug the Internet entirely."

Rain had been all for it, but TJ had balked. He wanted to keep up his fantasy baseball team.

The phone rang and Rain winced at the sound of it.

"Hello."

"Rain, it's Greg. Look, is he there?"

"He's out picking up branches, but I can get him . . ."

"No. It's you I wanted to talk to."

"Oh. Okay."

Rain's hip stung her. The ligament down

there had been twanging lately, as if someone was snapping it, rubber-band-like. Her doctor assured her this was normal. She folded into a forward bend, taking the phone with her. It seemed to help.

"So he can't hear us?"

"No, he's outside. What is it, Greg?" Rain had begun to understand why TJ found him so irritating. He'd grown so sanctimonious since all the trouble started, as if he'd never made a mistake in his life.

"We just learned something you ought to hear."

"Fine, what."

Her hair was brushing the floor; she'd neglected to pull it back. She liked the curtain effect; it was like being cocooned.

"Our neighbor saw the girl leave our house."

"What?"

Rain stood up so suddenly her vision swam with stars. She grabbed a chairback and lowered herself to a crouching position.

"He didn't think that much of it at the time, but he's absolutely positive he saw a young girl leave our house when we were gone on vacation. He assumed that it was someone housesitting at the time. But we were talking over the fence just now, cleaning up from the storm, and Alessia and I mentioned the vacation. He said it was good we had that girl to watch the house and we were like, what girl? TJ watched the house. Then we all looked at each other like, oh shit."

Alexandra had shown them the police report, where the girl stated that one of the times she slept with TJ was at Greg's house. It had pricked at Rain's consciousness: How would she even have known TJ had a brother who was gone to make that up? Until TJ reminded her how small Arbor Valley was in some ways, how her dad was assistant principal and thus their families knew each other, really, and how easy it would have been.

"Rain? Are you all right?"

"I'm here," she croaked out.

"I think he's going to go to the police."

"What? No! Talk him out of it!"

"Rain . . . It's only right. If it's true . . . Then we need to know."

"It's not true, it's not . . ."

"I wanted to tell you before your lawyer did. I didn't want to believe it either, but . . . look, Alessia wants to talk to you."

Alessia got on the phone. "Rain? *Cara,* I'm worried about you. Let me come over and take you out somewhere, please? *Per favore?* You never could resist my Italian, no?"

Alessia's voice was layers of pleading and teasing.

"Fine, okay," Rain answered, just wanting off the phone. She hung up without saying good-bye.

He'd been out with his frat brother, she was remembering now. He'd said he was going out overnight so he didn't have to drive home late and possibly drunk. She'd told him when he got back about the baby. And she remembered like a kick in the chest that he'd come home with wet hair. Smelling like Greg.

TJ had been banned from Facebook, but Rain was not. She went to her laptop and brought up Facebook, looking for this friend of TJ's . . . He still looked like a Belushi-style cliché of a frat boy in his profile picture. Rain scrolled back, back, back to January.

"Please," she whispered. "Please say you were with him . . ."

The pictures on that weekend were of the former frat boy at some open-air bar in the bright sunshine, face reddened either with sunburn, drink, or both, longneck brown bottle in his fist, giving the camera a thumbs-up with his free hand. Caption: "Miami!"

"Oh God," Rain said, closing the laptop

lid. A swarm buzzed within her, filling her brain with noisy, queasy revelation. Every odd pause in his speech, his distracted behavior, his fervent yet illogical defense, those text messages . . . She'd known about it all and yet had tamped it down inside her, just like in her childhood when she purposely forgot that Gran wouldn't live forever.

TJ came in through the door, sweaty and damp from hauling sticks. Rain yanked her hand back from the laptop and glanced away from him.

"What?" he asked her. "Are you okay?"

Rain swallowed hard. "Yes. Just fine. I'm going out with Alessia later."

He rolled his eyes and walked to the sink. "Oh, goody. You guys can talk about how perfect everything is for them."

Rain stood up and drew her shoulders back, standing as tall as she could. "Knock it off."

"Knock what off?" He was barely listening, washing his hands.

"Stop picking on Alessia. She's supporting me, and I really need that now. You don't get along with your brother, fine, whatever. But stop applying your disgust to her. It's not fair."

He started shaking his head as he dried

his hands, a smirk twisting into place. "Come on. Don't you see how she patronizes you? Both of them act like we're the poor relations who need helping, especially now. Don't encourage them. Text her and tell her you're not coming. We'll get some takeout and watch movies instead. We deserve to have a nice afternoon alone for once."

Rain set her jaw. "I made plans and I'm keeping them. We'll watch movies later, but for now I'm going to see my friend."

"What if I need you here? I . . . I don't like to be alone. With my thoughts running wild, worrying . . ."

She sighed, picturing him pacing the floor, imagining a future in prison, without her there to draw him out of the darkness. . . . She reached for her phone, preparing to text Alessia that it wasn't a good day after all, but her gaze landed on the laptop.

Miami. His friend had been in Miami.

She forced a smile. "I'll be back soon. It's only lunch. Love you," she called, and snatched her phone and purse off the table, dashing out the door before he had time to say another word.

Rain toyed with a red glass votive holder as Alessia groaned her pregnant bulk down into the booth across from her; she was due in mere weeks. They were at an Italian restaurant Alessia had always favored for its authenticity and lack of crowds. It was in Royal Oak, which Rain remembered with a jolt was where TJ had supposedly been the weekend he visited his fratboy friend.

Alessia ordered minestrone, so Rain did the same, not caring what she ate, only eating at all for the sake of the baby.

"This place is private," Alessia said, glancing up and down the length of the restaurant. Indeed, the booths had high dividers between them, and everyone seemed to speak in the same hushed tones. It was late for the business lunch crowd. There were few other customers. "I'm sorry to bring you here for this, but I didn't want to talk about this at home. Yours or mine."

"About what?"

For weeks now, Rain had told herself, *It can't get worse; this is the lowest point.* She was about to be proven wrong again.

"I understand if you hate me for not telling you before."

"Alessia, if you don't just tell me I might scream."

"TJ cheated on you. Before."

Rain rolled her eyes. "I know he slept around in college while we were dating. We weren't really exclusive and I've made my peace with that. He was sowing oats. Sorry to take the wind out of your sails, but that's old news to me."

"No. When you were engaged."

"No, he didn't" was all Rain could think to say.

"Greg saw them together when you were off buying a wedding dress."

"I'm sure there was an explanation . . ."

"How many simple explanations can there be? He was kissing her neck, Rain."

"So what?" Her voice cracked over the words. "Whatever, that was then."

"I'm sorry I didn't tell you. Greg and I talked about it, fought about it, actually. He convinced me not to. He said you were the best thing that ever happened to TJ and if we sabotaged it by telling you . . . He said you would save him. That you'd fix him. For all these years I thought he was right. You both seemed so happy . . ."

Alessia's eyes were misting up, and Rain wanted to slap her. How dare she be the one to cry?

She continued, "That's why I'm here. I should have told you then, and I'm telling you now. Greg says you are standing by him and I think it's a beautiful example of how loving you are. . . . But now with what the neighbor saw, and Greg said there are text messages. . . . And now I can tell you it wouldn't be the first time that he'd done it. I think you need a lawyer of your own."

"I don't know if you've noticed, but I'm pregnant. We are parents together no matter what happens. You think this will be simple? Just break up, like we're in high school? I give him his class ring and letter jacket back? He's gone crazy or something; he needs my help."

"You need your help. Your baby does. He's betrayed you, ruined your lives . . . not to mention what it's done to that poor girl . . ."

"That poor girl is a few months from eighteen."

"Rain, I love you, and your loyalty is amazing. But you have to open your eyes. You have to protect yourself, and the baby."

"Too late," Rain said, as the waiter appeared with their soup. "It's too damn late for that."

The waiter shrank away as if he knew that he needed to.

Rain said, "So is that why Greg has been around so much? Soothing his guilty conscience for not letting you tell me before?"

"He knows you need taking care of. That your parents are . . . eh . . . airbrains? Airheads. Forgive the phrasing."

"Sure, I'll forgive. Why not."

They toyed with the vegetables in their cooling soup, each pregnant woman shifting uncomfortably in the narrow booth. Rain allowed herself some hatred for Alessia: beautiful Alessia with a rich husband who only had eyes for her and never made a move not Grade A approved for appropriateness. Alessia's baby would have an intact, happy family and all the material luxuries possible. Her own baby would be the pitied cousin, the one in whose wake whispers would trail. *Did you hear about her? Such a sad story . . .*

Alessia coughed lightly. "What are you going to do?"

Rain sipped her cold water, and after a moment, she gave Alessia the truest answer she had. "My baby's father can't go to jail. I can't have my baby grow up with that."

Alessia nodded, glancing down at her own belly, her own baby-to-be. "I know," she said quietly, reaching across the table to take Rain's hand.

Rain let her take it and let herself go ahead and cry. She said, "I hated you for a minute there."

"Yes," Alessia said. "I know."

They finished their lunch in silence, and Rain wondered how she could go home and lie down next to TJ. Nor could she imagine what else she could possibly do.

When she got home, TJ was at the table with both hands wrapped around a beer bottle. He raised his eyes to hers and then she knew: Alexandra had called about the neighbor's statement.

Then TJ said just that. Alexandra had called.

Rain only nodded.

"It's going to sound bad," TJ said. "But I swear it's not true. Alex says it won't hold up well in court, that he only came forward weeks after the police first talked to him; it was at a distance, and he wears glasses. She says a few rapid questions will make him look like a confused old man. She thinks he only came forward now because he wants to be famous."

Rain nodded. It all sounded so plausible. She realized she should pretend like she didn't already know this.

"So what is it that this confused old man supposedly saw?"

"That the girl came out of my brother's house, while he was away on vacation. But it couldn't be true. I wasn't even there. I was at home, remember?" He leaned forward, veins in his head standing out, like he was straining to lift something. "I was at home with you, all weekend."

Rain swallowed. "That's what you told Alex?"

"Yes, because it's true. I'm sure you remember. It was when you told me about the baby."

Rain realized a jury might well believe him. He had committed one hundred percent to the truth of this. He might even believe it himself. "So she's going to expect me to testify?" The thought gave Rain a blast of hot panic.

"You'd only be a rebuttal witness if this guy makes it to the stand. She thinks the prosecutor might not even use him. In fact, she says if they do, it goes to show they're grasping at straws. Hell, it could have been somebody turning around in the driveway. Eyewitness reports aren't that reliable, she said. Plenty of room for reasonable doubt."

"Reasonable doubt," she echoed.

"Will you do that for me, honey? If you have to?" He jumped up from the table quickly, a little unsteadily, and Rain wondered how many beers he'd gone through in her absence. He'd taken to putting the empties away, rather than leaving them lying around. As if by putting them away neatly, she wouldn't notice how many there were when it came time to return them to the grocery store. He crossed the room and took her hands, then rested his forehead on the top of her head. "I'm so sorry to do this to you. I don't want you to have to do this, any of this. I'm so sorry I screwed up."

"You're innocent . . . ?"

"I mean in how I handled it. That I didn't just go to the principal right away. I'm so stupid."

Rain felt him crying into her hair. What was it with everyone else crying today?

"I don't feel well," Rain said. "I'm going to lie down."

She drifted away from TJ, his hands running down her arms and clinging to her hand just for a moment as she wandered away upstairs. She paused at the doorway and locked it; another first, she thought. Along with her husband being arrested, and wearing maternity clothes, she has also locked her husband out of the bedroom for the first time ever.

She curled up, on top of the covers, facing out through the window at the gray wash of sky. He was asking her to lie for him in court. There was no getting around this fact. He had also lied about his whereabouts on a weekend that he had Greg's big, empty house all to himself, and a neighbor saw a girl leaving.

He had cheated on her before, when she was wearing his engagement ring and congratulating herself that when it came time to settle down, he chose her. Her, above all the others.

This girl was half naked in his car. In his car! Miles from anyplace that made sense, off a highway overpass of all places.

She admitted to herself the secret thought that had been tormenting her since the beginning, stalking the edges of her consciousness like a predator in the dark, just outside a ring of firelight.

TJ was just not that stupid.

Something felt funny in her belly, and Rain gasped, and grabbed her swollen abdomen, wrapping her hands over her most precious treasure, the only pure love she had left in the world. There it was again. It felt almost bubbly, ticklish.

The baby was moving. She was feeling her baby move.

She lay on the bed, crying in anguish and delight, while a movie ran in her head of what should be happening just now: running to get her loving husband, telling him, celebrating, laughing at the feisty new life that would be the best of both of them.

39

Dinah was crouched in the warm spring sun, drawing her specials of the day in bright chalk on the display, trying to care about her dying business.

All she could think about was her children in that massive high school surrounded by cruel peers. Jared had taken to wearing all black and complaining his legs hurt more than usual. Connor was constantly frustrated that his voice kept breaking up and down. He sounded like a clarinet blown by a novice.

Jared had also taken to shunning Connor — no real reason, a fit of adolescent pique, Dinah figured — which caused more fights between the two of them. Connor, never one to take rejection well, would lash out as if he thought his brother was the worst person in the world. He'd given Jared a strong shove the other day, knocking him into the table and giving Dinah a terrified flashback to the fight that had broken the vase and scarred Morgan. It seemed to do the same to Connor; he paled and ran upstairs before Dinah could admonish him.

And then, Morgan, insisting on attending school, now, in the midst of this. She had reported that the kids were nakedly curious, asking her crude questions, like whether she blew the teacher in his car. She kept finding lewd notes in her locker, so she put tape across the vents on the inside of the locker door, so nothing could be shoved in.

Morgan would just reply, if she replied at all, "I'm not allowed to talk about it." This was the answer they'd coached her to give that night before she went back, during an anxious dinner in which neither Morgan nor Dinah ate much of anything.

Britney was supposedly protecting her, telling people off who were rude, eating with her at lunch when no one else would. Dinah tried to be grateful when Kelly reported this, but she couldn't shake the feeling that Britney enjoyed having a role to play in their drama.

Ethan came in to the Den once in a while, to let Dinah know how Morgan was doing, from what he could tell.

Joe got reports, too, though he wasn't supposed to, but normal rules seemed to be going out the window. So teachers would tell him throughout the day, "She seemed fine today, people left her alone" or "I had to send a couple jokers to Pete Jackson for hassling her outside the music room."

Joe told Dinah he needed the reports, but he hated receiving them. He could tell how much pity and schadenfreude was behind these missives. The other assistant principal, Kate, had taken to regarding him every morning with a sympathetic pout, asking sotto voce, "How are things?"

Dinah felt a shadow over her shoulder. She turned in her crouch to be greeted by Helen Demming. "Oh. Hello." She turned back to the board to continue with her chalk.

Speaking of schadenfreude.

"Hello, Dinah. I wondered if I could have a word."

"Go ahead. You'll forgive me if I keep working."

Helen pulled up one of the wrought-iron outside chairs and sat with her pantsuited legs crossed and her hands folded across her knees. "I was hoping for a bit of privacy, but I guess this will do. Not exactly a stampede of customers here." She laughed lightly, as if she were joking.

"What can I do for you?" Dinah asked

through a heavy sigh. She was done writing the specials and began adding little swirly designs to the edge of the board, to give her something to do besides looking up at that pretentious horse-face bitch. She'd had a flair for art in school, but didn't work very hard at it, since it was no way to earn a living.

"I was wondering if you'd ever consider selling the Den?"

Dinah finally abandoned the chalk and rose to stand over Helen. "What, to you? As you so carefully note, there is not exactly a flood of traffic."

"The location here is prime, and not just for high school kids. I think you have an untapped market here, for a more sophisticated customer."

"Thanks for the advice, now if you'll excuse me . . ."

Helen drew herself up to her full height, which was still shorter than Dinah, even in her heels. She was wearing platform heels even, Dinah noted with a suppressed grin.

"I'm serious, Dinah. We've known each other long enough, you can give me the courtesy of serious consideration."

"We've known each other long enough to be up-front about the fact we can't stand each other. And since you torpedoed my entertainment license I don't even feel the smallest inclination to pretend otherwise."

"You don't have to like me for a business deal to work. So much the better, really. It can be so awkward between friends."

"I'd be surprised if you know that from experience."

"Even I have friends, Dinah." She fished into her purse and withdrew a letter. "Read this over, consider it. That's all I ask. This place can serve kids just like it does now, but adults don't come here, have you noticed? Sure, a few moms with kids at midday, but the reason grown-ups don't come is that they're not welcome here. The kids don't want them here, it's obvious. You ever see an adult walk in there when it's full of teenagers? You can almost hear the groan. But for a business to be a success, long term, everyone should be welcome. Not just a select few. Anyway. Please, take this. No harm in looking, is there?"

Dinah snatched the envelope, folded it in half, and jammed it in her pocket. "Okay, I took it. Good day."

Helen clicked away in her heels, and Dinah fantasized about her tripping and crashing face-first to the concrete.

It would be a cold day in hell when she sold her beloved business to that hypocritical, scheming bitch. She'd rather torch it herself.

Morgan threw her backpack into the backseat of the car, narrowly missing Jared's head.

"Hey!" he shouted.

"Sorry," she mumbled, folding her arms and slouching low in the seat.

Dinah pulled the car away from the school, unable to rally herself to get on Morgan's case.

"Boys, I have to drop you off home. Morgan and I have an appointment."

"Appointment where?" Morgan asked her, slit-eyed.

"With Henry Davis."

"The prosecutor? Screw that, I'm not talking to him. This is all his fault."

Dinah ignored her and switched on the radio to hear a droll NPR announcer talking about the coming presidential election as the silence crackled between them.

"How was school?" she asked, her forced brightness grating to even her own ears. No one bothered answering.

Henry greeted them with appropriate sobriety for the occasion and excused himself for just a moment to talk with an associate in the other room.

Morgan simmered with rage in the seat next to Dinah, across from his desk.

Henry had called Dinah the night before, asking her to bring Morgan in. He felt he could persuade her to testify if he framed the conversation well enough. Dinah tried to tell him it was useless, that indignant rage was Morgan's near-constant state, but Henry thought if it wasn't her mother asking, she might reconsider.

In that phone conversation, he had mentioned the possibility of subpoenaing her with the threat of jail if she refused to cooperate and Dinah had exploded at him. He listened to her eruption, then replied patiently, "I wasn't going to do that to her. I was just letting you know what the options are." Dinah reminded herself she really should listen to a whole sentence before flipping her lid, as she told Connor at least three times a week.

Henry returned to the room and greeted Morgan with a tight professional smile. She looked away as if she were trying to melt a hole in the wall with her glare.

"How are you holding up?" he asked.

"Just fine when people leave me the hell alone. People including you. I've got homework and I don't want to be here. I'm not helping you."

Henry settled down on his desk chair. He looked at Morgan with the detachment of a psychotherapist. "If I subpoena you to the stand, you are legally obligated to testify."

Henry darted a look at Dinah. He was bluffing, but it still twisted her guts to hear it.

Morgan huffed. "Whatever. Even if I sit there on the stand, you think I'll help you with this farce and travesty?"

"A farce and a travesty. My, my."

She whipped around to face Henry. "Don't patronize me. I'm not some ten-year-old winning a spelling bee."

"You're right. I apologize. People don't take you seriously, do they?"

"No. They don't."

"And that's not fair. From what I can tell, you're smart as hell, mature and poised, and you have every right to be taken seriously."

Morgan tossed her hair, then readjusted it. She straightened her posture. "Yes. Also true."

"You think this case is about you being treated like a child, and that infuriates you. A child who can't make her own choices about whom to love, with whom she is intimate."

Dinah thought she might be sick.

He was scoring points with Morgan, though. She nodded, leaning forward now, slightly. Henry folded his arms, leaned back in his chair. "That's not the point, though, and that's what no one has taken time to explain to you. For that I apologize. It's our failing."

A teenager likes nothing better than an adult who eats crow in front of them. Morgan was loving this. Dinah wondered if TJ made her feel that way, too: adult, mature. But didn't Dinah? Hadn't Dinah in fact treated her too much like an adult, in the end?

Henry continued, "This is about a teacher who behaved inappropriately and failed in his duty to keep his student relationships solely in the professional realm. You are an unusual case, Morgan, in how sophisticated and mature you are. This is not the first case of this I've run across in my career, you know. Most times, the girls are in thrall, and being manipulated, and once the spell is broken, they feel the full damage of a relationship that's inherently unequal. You believe you are TJ Hill's equal, and in many ways you are, and in fact far superior. But he" — at this Henry thumped his desk with his index finger — "did not treat this as a relationship between two equal adults. He treated you as a side project. A girl who would run to his beck and call, have sex when it was convenient, to be put aside at will. What kind of representative of the people would I be if I stood by and let that behavior stand? If I said, 'Well, but Morgan Monetti is so mature, I'm sure it was just fine.' I can't do that and I won't. We're not trying to convict him of murder and lock him away for life. We want to hold him accountable for what he actually did, and only that. Because right now, he's lying, Morgan. This man whom you want to think treated you with respect is now saying you are lovesick and crazy and made it all up."

Dinah realized with a burst of dizziness that she'd been holding her breath. Morgan seemed to be trembling in her seat. She could almost hear her daughter's defensive shell crack. Dinah gripped her chair arms to stop herself from jumping up and down to say, *Yes, exactly, that's what I've been saying all along!*

Morgan had been looking down at her lap. Dinah watched her daughter take two slow breaths. In, out. Then she looked up at Henry, her eyes slitted and her chin jutted forward. "He's only doing what he has to because of what you all are putting us through. Why don't you let TJ plead, if it's just about 'accountability'? Offer his lawyer something light that keeps him out of jail, then, if that's all you care about? Nuh-uh, this is about trying to persecute him because you're all hysterical prudes who really do think I'm a child. You almost had me going there, Mr. Prosecutor. Well done, did you rehearse in front of a mirror?"

Dinah began, "Morgan . . ." but could think of nothing helpful to say.

"I'll be in the car. Don't forget, Mom: July 11."

Her eighteenth birthday.

Morgan swept out of the room, and Dinah felt cold in her wake.

At dinner, Morgan snatched up her plate and took it to her doorless room, ignoring Joe's demand that she rejoin the family. He muttered that her behavior was unacceptable until Dinah snapped, "So what are you going to punish her with? We're pretty much down to taking her behind the woodshed by this point."

In her head, banging like a gong, Dinah heard, *July 11 . . . 11 . . . 11 . . .*

The trial would probably be over by then. Henry thought they'd get a date in early June. "Just in time for graduation," Dinah had muttered. On her eighteenth birthday,

Morgan could pack a bag, get on a bus, and vanish, and there wouldn't be a damn thing anyone could do about it.

She had to do something, and something big, soon. Or no matter what happened to TJ Hill, Morgan was as good as gone.

40

Rain hated Free Class Week.

Beverly loved the people cramming the Namaste Yoga Center, buying trinkets and cutesy T-shirts with clever sayings; she loved the boost in class enrollment that always followed. She served free tea and cookies baked with organic ingredients and talked chakras to anyone who would listen.

But to Rain, it meant that many more bodies crammed into the studio, extra sweaty feet all over the store mats for public use, and a spike in nervous giggling about any reference to pressing the pubic bone to the floor in cobra pose.

And this time, this particular early May week, she felt sure that she'd get gawkers. People who'd figured out that "the teacher's wife" worked there. Her pregnancy was undeniable now in her yoga clothes, which she'd had to order special over the Internet. This should have been beautiful. She used to fantasize about it, in fact, what she'd look like with a graceful arch of belly. Used to be that she couldn't wait for stretch marks.

But now her baby would end up the object of gossip: *Did you hear his wife is PREGNANT?* They'd text each other, and type OMG.

When Rain walked into the full class, it was as bad as she feared. The room quieted as she strode in. Some of them were nakedly gawking. She'd put on a baggy sweatshirt on top of her yoga leotard, though she knew it would get in her way and overheat her, trying to keep her baby out of the rumor mill as long as possible. Even a sweatshirt wouldn't work for much longer.

Her mother had said on the phone last night, "Well, fuck them, then," but then that was her advice for all Rain's problems. Fuck everybody. Well, isn't that what got them into this mess? Rain arranged herself in a seated position on her mat, rooting down into the floor, reaching the top crown of her head up to the sky. That's how she always thought of it, extending toward the sky, not the ceiling. The sky was always there, anyway, and seemed a much better thing to reach for. Her neck stretched long and she sighed, grateful for the extra space in her spine.

As she began her *unjjayi* breathing to settle herself for class, she remembered hissing into the phone to her mother, who'd insisted she just give up and move back home, "It's not that simple." Leave TJ? Let him go to jail? Going through labor without TJ by her side? No matter what else he'd done, this baby was part of him, too. This baby that they'd hoped, prayed, and tried so hard to bring into the world, together.

God help her, she was planning to lie on the stand if she had to. She just couldn't abide him going away. Not now. The future would have to take care of itself.

She raised her voice above the chatter and slipped a serene smile into place. "Good morning," she began, "and welcome to all the new faces . . ."

When she spotted one person slip in and linger awkwardly, as the rest of the class trooped out, Rain thought nothing of it. This often happened during Free Class Week. Someone would be curious about yoga and feel the need to pepper her with questions. Often, Rain could send the person off to Beverly, who was better equipped to answer earnestly about the benefits to the lymphatic system and blood flow to vital organs.

Rain had forgotten to tell the new students to wipe down the store's public-use mats, so she set about with the spray bottle and towel to do the job herself. The chemical sting of the cleaner clashed with the smoldering incense cone still going in the burner next to her. She would usually light one at the end, for *savasana,* if only to drown out the sweat smell.

Yoga might be graceful, but twenty-five straining, stretching, barefoot bodies in a warm room for an hour did not smell pretty.

Rain found herself distracted by the lake outside. Usually she had her back to it, leading the class, and if she were walking through the room helping adjust postures, she was concentrating on the students. It was as glassy as a polished stone, unruffled. It seemed to be waiting and serene, knowing that no disturbance was so great that the water wouldn't again settle against its edges, achieving perfection of a level surface only possible in nature.

Rain shook her head. Now she was envying a lake. Good God.

Finally, the woman approached, as Rain wiped her third mat, crouched with her knees up around her belly, which was still shrouded — she hoped — behind her big gray sweatshirt.

She cleared her throat, and Rain looked up, attempting her serene smile again. "Hello." The woman looked to be in her forties, but trying to seem younger. Long dark hair, recently highlighted, fell in chunky layers. But more than that, this woman looked so nervous Rain wondered briefly if she were going to throw up.

Rain dearly hoped she wasn't one of those types who thought a yoga teacher was a therapist.

"I hope I can talk to you," she began. Her voice sounded slightly raspy and deeper than Rain would have thought. "I hope you will listen, for just a few minutes, before you react."

Rain stopped wiping, stilled now with the towel in her hand. "Who are you?"

"I'm Dinah Monetti." A pause while Rain's mind scrambled like radio static. "Morgan's mother."

Rain was crouched, so the best she could do was crab-walk away, toward the glass wall that faced the lake. She shot a look toward the class door, on the other side of the room. It was closed, and they were alone.

Dinah dropped down to sit. "I didn't mean to scare you. I'm not going to hurt you, goodness."

"You shouldn't be here."

"I know."

"You could get arrested or something. Witness tampering. Intimidation."

"I'm not trying to intimidate. But, yes, I know I could get in trouble. I'm desperate."

"What are you so desperate about?"

"My daughter."

"I don't want to talk about her."

Rain had her back pressed up against the glass. The morning was cool outside, and the smooth glass felt steadying. She sat cross-legged and resigned herself to Dinah's presence. She'd throw her out soon, or just leave herself. Dinah did not seem to be physically threatening, though her presence sent waves of adrenaline crashing through Rain's system, even so.

"I know you don't. Look, she thinks she's in love."

"I don't want to hear it."

"I'm going to lose her. She hates all of us for interrupting her . . . romance. She's all but announced her plans to run away the day she turns eighteen. I may lose her forever. She could get hurt out there; she's not as mature as she thinks she is."

"Why are you telling me this? And why should I care? Forgive me, but your family has played quite a large role in ruining my life."

"As yours has done to ours."

Rain stood up. If this nutcase followed her, she'd call the police, or she'd call Alex. She wasn't sure how exactly, but their lawyer would have a field day with this incident.

Dinah stood, too, and suddenly her face crumpled, anguished. "No, I'm sorry. I didn't mean that . . . I blurt things out without thinking; it's my biggest fault. If I can convince my daughter he didn't love her, I can get her back. I can help her see this for what it was . . . I can get her back. It's danger she's in, maybe not literally, as if she's hanging off a cliff, but she might as well be. If she runs away, someone is going to zero in on how vulnerable she is and . . . She'll be prey. Again."

"So my husband is a predator."

"I don't know. I don't know what went on . . ."

Rain knew she was lying. That's exactly what she thought.

"I don't know what you think I can do. You are nuts to come here, and if you don't get out in ten seconds, I'm calling the police and our lawyer and telling them you're trying to intimidate me."

"She's confused. My daughter is lost, and, and . . ."

And then the lady fell apart. Shaking and pale, she folded down on the floor, curling up like she'd gone catatonic. She was muttering to herself something Rain couldn't hear.

And just like that, Rain was in her place, for just a moment, and the compassion rushed through her as quickly as the adrenaline had.

"Okay. I won't call the police. I won't tell the lawyer you showed up. But you really have to get out of here. We can't be seen talking, and I can't help you, anyway."

Dinah sat back, cross-legged, and held her forehead in her hand. She said, in the voice of someone living through the despair of an idea that only sounded good in her head, "I wanted you to tell her that your husband loves you."

Rain laughed, looking up at the ceiling. Definitely ceiling, not sky. "Yeah, that would work out perfectly."

"I guess I thought, if she could see you, if you were real to her, and not just some story he told about a cold, loveless marriage . . ."

Rain drew back. "That's what he said?"

"That's what she told me. That you'd withdrawn from him and stopped loving him because you couldn't have a baby. Don't hate me, I'm just repeating what she told me."

Rain stepped back again, almost touching the wall, looking down on Dinah still folded up on the floor. "Don't hate you? You come here, to my place of work, stalk me, really, to accost me and demand that I explain to your daughter — who slept with my husband multiple times — that he really loves me, and not her. You're crazy."

"Not the first time I've been told so."

"Leave. Right now before I change my mind about calling the police. Don't ever contact me again."

The lady followed a winding, nearly drunken path to the door, almost crashing into the next free class people. One or two of them looked at her a little too long, and Rain prayed that none of them would recognize her.

Rain encountered TJ at home, and he rushed to her with a hug and offered to draw her a bath. His hair was wet from the shower, and Rain remembered the day she'd come home unexpectedly to find him behaving oddly, freshly showered at a strange time.

She nodded numbly to the offer of a bath.

TJ kept asking if she was okay. She nodded and pointed to her throat as if it were sore. "Talking too much," she said. And he made her tea.

Slipping into the bath, under the bubbles, Rain pictured the girl in her home, in her bed, maybe even in this tub. A wave of nausea rolled through her.

She imagined TJ raking his hands through his hair — his classic gesture of distress — as he confided in the girl, this child, about their infertility. Using the deepest pain of their marriage like a gambit.

The mother could be lying, of course.

But why would she? In fact, that was incredibly foolish of her to show up there. Rain felt sure if she told Alexandra about this, they could get the mother in some serious trouble. If the mother was stalking her, that wouldn't exactly look good for the prosecution's case. It would make the whole family seem deranged and unstable.

Rain rubbed soap bubbles across her itchy belly, which despite everything, made her smile. The baby would be born not caring about any of this. The baby would just love her; the baby would be ignorant of anything but love, and brief hunger, maybe. Sleepiness. Messy diapers. This was the simple world of newborns.

But the baby would grow into a kid, and maybe not be perfect. TJ had seen enough imperfect kids struggling through his classes. Kids with learning disorders and physical deformities. Kids whose parents died of cancer, who resorted to cutting themselves to cope. Kids who grappled with depression, even in the bloom of youth. A musician honor student who thought it was just fine to sleep with her teacher.

Even though she'd resigned herself that somehow, improbably, TJ had actually had an affair with a student, in her mind this girl was a beautiful temptress. A siren. In fact, Rain had given in one day to a sick curiosity and looked up her picture online, finding it in an old news story about some music competition, and her beauty had almost knocked Rain out of her chair. Not to mention the long, dark hair worn much the same way Rain herself wore it now — straight, side-parted, no bangs.

It's easy to hate beautiful girls, and so she did. TJ was going through something, and the girl saw a chink in his armor and charmed him. He was technically wrong, she would allow, but just a few calendar months was all that stood between TJ who briefly fell from grace, and TJ the sex offender. It was all a technicality.

The baby kicked her, and she rubbed the spot as if truly stroking her baby's soft skin. "Shhh," she said, soothing the baby or herself, she didn't know.

41

When Dinah saw the envelope, she assumed it was another attempt from Helen Demming to buy her business. The formal, neat cursive "Dinah Monetti" on the cream-colored envelope shoved under the door at the Den was perfectly in character.

"Bitch," she muttered, and picked it up.

Janine was off for the day, and so Dinah was opening the Den herself, just like when she'd first started and didn't have enough revenue to hire much help. She could afford just enough to hire a couple of minimum-wage kids to cover the hours when the kids got home from school. She would dash home for the boys and Morgan, help them with homework, cook dinner, and usually fly back to the Den to help close, not trusting the kids who worked for her to count out the cash drawer or do a thorough enough job cleaning.

It was usually one of the best parts of the

day, back then, having sent her employees home, having the whole place all shined up and spotless, ready for the next day's business.

Now she had Janine, and a few shift managers she paid a little more, but the place did not belong to them, and they never could pay it the same loving attention. Crumbs would gather in the corners, tables would get sticky. It never was a dump — Dinah would have knocked heads and fired people over that — but it wasn't the same. If only she could clone herself and have a whole Den-ful of Dinahs.

Dinah ignored the envelope as she set up the cash drawer, accepted delivery of the pastries, and brewed the first pots of coffee. She could stand it no longer, then, and sat at the couch near the fireplace to open up Helen's latest salvo.

In the deliberate, even handwriting of a child just learning cursive and wanting to do it perfectly, she read the following:

You may call me on my cell phone and we'll talk.

That night, for once, Dinah had not minded that Joe was out at a baseball game, cheering on the AV Tigers. She'd plied the boys with some extra TV time after they finished their homework and joined Morgan in her room.

Dinah had rehearsed her speech and swore to herself she would not deviate or blurt impulsively. If she did this wrong, everything could get much, much worse.

Morgan had her cello in place, her eyes closed and her earbuds in. The fingers of her left hand were flying over the strings, but her right arm held an invisible bow. She sometimes did this silent practice, if she felt her instrument would be too noisy for the household. Such a considerate girl; everyone had always said so, since kindergarten when she'd share her crayons, even while they were still pointy and fresh.

Dinah moved into her field of vision. Morgan's eyes stayed closed. She swayed with the music, and Dinah could tell from the sound leaking out that this was her Elgar concerto she was supposed to have played at solo and ensemble, accompanied by Mrs. DeWitt, who was replaced by a college accompanist who turned out to be fictional. An alibi of sorts.

In all that had been lost these last months — all her college applications accepted, for instance, which should have been cause for throwing confetti but now passed with only bittersweet acknowledgment and uncertainty — this competition had been shuffled to the bottom of the list. She could see Morgan mourning now for what she missed that day. It rent Dinah's motherly heart, but she also thought, *Good, maybe now she's starting to see what this cost her.*

Dinah finally touched her daughter's shoulder. Morgan gasped, and her eyes snapped open.

"What?" she yelled, and yanked out her earbuds. "It's so humiliating not having a door. You know, I never did anything wrong in here."

Dinah bit down her next thought, about how she was sending him text messages from this room, planning their assignations.

"Morgan, I have an idea. It's risky, though. Dangerous. And you can't tell anyone."

Morgan's eyes widened, and she dropped her indignation. She set her cello carefully down on its side in front of her desk. Dinah settled on the edge of her bed, and Morgan remained on her chair, though she scooted it close.

"I did something reckless. I talked to his wife."

"What? And how? How did you even . . ."

Morgan's breathing shallowed. Dinah placed a steadying hand on her daughter's knee, and for once, she didn't stiffen or flinch.

"I went to her work. But listen: This could get us in a lot of trouble, so you can't tell a soul. But . . . I think you deserve some answers, don't you? And he's not going to tell us the truth right now, maybe not ever. But I think his wife will."

"Why would she talk to me anyway?"

"Maybe she wants some answers, too."

"I'm sure she read the police report."

"That's not the same."

"What if she, like, tries to beat me up or something? I mean . . ."

"She won't. She seems like a kind soul, actually."

Morgan shook her head and sat back. "No. Forget it. Something's fishy here. She wants to trick me, to talk me out of testifying."

"You already said you wouldn't."

"But she doesn't know that."

"It's crazy, I know. Forget it. Never mind. I just wanted you to know the truth."

"Why would she tell me the truth anyway?"

"Why wouldn't she?"

"To keep him."

"Would you want to keep him, if he'd cheated on you with a teenage girl?"

At this, Morgan huffed and turned away, arms folded like a barricade across her chest.

Dinah slumped. It was a stupid idea. She'd risked the case against TJ and getting arrested herself, and it was all for nothing. She began to stand. "I'll talk to your father about the door. He was upset that day."

"Mom?"

"Yeah?" Dinah turned back at the doorway.

"Did you really do that? Go find her and talk to her?"

"Yeah."

"Wow."

"Yeah, well. Lot of good it did."

Morgan shook her head slightly and picked up her cello again.

Dinah was washing dishes when Morgan appeared at her side, rubbing her scar.

"Yeah, okay" was all she said.

Dinah dropped a glass back into the water. Warm soapy bubbles splashed onto her abdomen, soaking her shirt. "You sure?"

"Yeah."

"Very secret. Top secret. Not a soul else."

Morgan regarded her with the cool weariness of someone much older. "I can keep a secret just fine. But will she?"

"Yes, I believe she will. She could get in trouble, too."

Morgan looked down at the floor. "Mutually assured destruction. Learned about that in world history."

"It's worked so far. The earth is still here."

Morgan picked up a dishcloth and started drying, without being asked. Dinah wanted to cry. For the simple normality in this action, for all the normality that was lost, for this time that should have been special and precious. They'd gotten their pre-ordered graduation announcements in the mail just yesterday. It was another milestone they should have been relishing but instead struck fear into Dinah at the thought of her daughter graduating in front of everyone, having been publicly shamed. Even as the legally acknowledged victim, there was no doubt that there was shame clouding the air around her like mist. She knew there would be a cadre of parents and faculty who'd rather she just stay home and keep the scandal from marring such an event. God help her, if it had been some other girl, she'd probably have said the same.

Part of Dinah — a bitter shame of her own — wished they would stay home and hide.

Morgan said, her voice sounding small and brittle, "Why did he tell on me?"

"Who? Ethan? Maybe he didn't."

"Mom . . ."

"Okay, fine. Let's say he did. He told because he cares. He really does love you."

"Whatever, Mom, he's gay."

Dinah shook her head in a double take, then shrugged. "Well, so what? He still loves you."

"Mom? Hello? He loves dudes."

"Not all love is romantic. Ethan is a boy who cares very deeply. It must be really hard for him to be gay and not be able to care openly like that."

Morgan grumbled something, and Dinah had to ask her to repeat it. She finally said, louder, "I wasn't supposed to tell you. I didn't mean to."

"I won't say anything."

"Not even to him, to say, like, it's fine or something. Okay?"

"I won't, I won't. I promise. He'll come out when he's ready."

Moments passed when the only sounds were quiet splashing. Then, from Morgan: "It wasn't supposed to be like this. It's not fair."

"I know, baby. I know. I said the same thing when the boys were born so early." Dinah shook the water off her hands and put her arm around her daughter. "But things get better."

"Yeah. Things are so great that Jared drew a marijuana leaf in Sharpie on the inside of his locker."

"What?"

"Oh. Thought you'd heard."

"Not that one, no. How did you hear?"

"I checked on him in the freshman hall."

"You did?"

"You always want me to check on them. I never stopped. Mom, I'm supertired. I need to go lie down." And with that, she was gone, trotting back up the stairs.

Joe came in just as Morgan was going up. Joe made to talk to her, his arms opening for a hug, but Morgan tossed a curt "Hi" and retreated up the stairs. The pained longing in Joe's face made Dinah want to cry all over again. Instead she wrung out her dishcloth. She was so tired of crying, and it never accomplished a damn useful thing.

"Did they win?"

Joe snapped his attention back to her. "Yeah. Might go to State. Our pitcher did a damn near perfect game. It was something."

"How were . . . How were people to you?"

"Fewer pitying looks than normal. I think they're kinda getting over it until, well. Later."

Joe went on, "Ya know, I think Morgan

was right about going back to school."

"You should tell her that."

"Yeah, maybe."

"No, you should. We haven't given her enough credit."

Joe scoffed and leaned on the counter, looking at his shoes. "We gave her too much damn credit, doncha think?"

"I mean now. She's courageous to go back into that school."

"You're doing it again. Unbelievable."

"Doing what?"

"Putting everything our kids do in the best possible light, making them look perfect. With Morgan you were right most of the time, but you did it with the boys, too, and look where it got them."

"Where exactly did it get them? Okay, Connor got in a couple fights and Jared got suspended once, but . . ."

"There should be no 'but'! It's always with the 'but' with you! But they had unreasonable teachers, but Jared's legs hurt, but Connor has a temper. You know, I deal with parents like you all damn day at school, who come in there and never want to admit there's ever a problem with their angels; it's all someone else's fault."

"I can't believe you're blaming me for this."

"I'm blaming the teacher! That Hill, I'd crush his throat if he were in front of me now. After I put his balls in a vise. But you are so quick to look on the bright side and you have to admit that for once, there is no goddamn bright side. Our daughter slept with her teacher, is planning to run away, and we will all be humiliated again in June when the trial starts."

"Maybe we can ask Henry to reschedule for . . ."

"The trial date is not the point!"

"So what is the point? Tearing me apart because I don't feel bad enough already?"

Joe slumped and crossed his arms. "We all feel bad, Dinah."

"But you seem to think I should feel the worst of all. I'm doing my best; that's all I've ever done."

"Me, too."

"So why are we at each other's throats? Why aren't we in this together?"

Joe kept staring at his shoes. Dinah thought his refusal to look at her might be the very worst part. "We are. But what do you want? Want me to lie and act like I think everything we ever did was perfect? What good would that do?"

"Can't we at least get through this before you pick me apart? All across Arbor Valley people are tearing me apart, and I can't believe I get it at home, too."

"Believe me, I'm no saint. I'm not saying it's all on you."

"But it's me who 'coddled' the kids."

"Well, yeah, Dinah, it was you. But I wasn't here, as you're always pointing out, so it's not like I'm some big hero."

"So if you'd been here to supervise me, it all would have turned out perfect." Dinah tossed down the dishcloth. "I'm going out for a walk. I need a break."

"Oh, come on . . ." Joe said, the words drawn out with irritation. He stayed where he was, not making a move toward her.

Dinah went right out the door without her phone or purse. If anything fell apart in her absence, Joe would have to deal with it all himself and see how easy it was to be the parent performing triage all the time.

In the driveway, as Dinah shuffled into the spring dusk, already muggy with impending summer, she thought if she'd detected one glimmer of genuine affection from Joe, she wouldn't have walked out. She'd have thrown herself into his strong chest and sobbed, like she'd done before they got old and tired.

She glanced back at the house, the windows aglow with warm light. The sight of her home looking so normal arrested her right there at the edge of their yard, and she stared at the scene, as the equal and opposite impulses to run home and run away rooted her in a kind of stasis.

42

Morgan kept sipping her bottled water, for something to do, trying to keep her hands from shaking, as her mother drove her west into the rural area surrounding Arbor Valley. Her mom was chattering to fill the silence — one of her most annoying habits — but today, Morgan didn't mind. She was telling her about how it used to be all forest here, hence the name when they bulldozed the forest to make way for the town.

Morgan's stomach turned when they passed a country club and golf course. He had mentioned it once, that night at his brother's house, talking about his hobbies. He'd said they'd spent a whole day out there, his brother bragging the whole time in subtle ways about his big house and fancy vacations, and how they went without a golf cart, so his knees throbbed, but he wouldn't give his brother the satisfaction of quitting before eighteen holes.

After another half hour, the car began slowing near a park entrance, and Morgan's blood rush sped up as the car slowed, then rumbled over a gravel drive, and approached a wood gazebo looking out over a still wetland.

Morgan had stayed home "sick" from school for this excursion, and Dinah had arranged for help at the Den to "stay home" with her.

So the park was deserted this midday in May. Except for a lone figure at a picnic table near the gazebo.

She did not look up right away as Morgan and Dinah got out of the car and approached; she seemed absorbed in the novel open in front of her. The first thing Morgan thought was that she looked so young.

Then she looked up, drew herself up straighter, and folded her book closed without marking the page.

Morgan and her mother drew to a stop a couple of yards away. Morgan looked at Dinah and watched her eyes dart back and forth. No one dared speak. The birds were loud in the human quiet.

She finally said, "I heard you have some things you want to know."

Morgan could only nod.

"Sit down, then."

Morgan felt her mom nudge her forward, and so finally she walked across the long grass — still damp from being in the shade of the trees — making her flats wet and tickling the tops of her feet.

She settled on the opposite bench of the table from her, slightly to one side. Dinah did the same, and together they made a triangle. *Isosceles triangle,* Morgan thought, thinking of math class, and him, and she had to grip the side of the table to keep herself from running back into the car.

It was too late now. They'd already crossed a line. In fact, just by agreeing to meet, they'd left that line far behind.

The wife spoke first. "My name is Rain. TJ is my husband. I've been thinking about what I'd say, and my first instinct was to apologize. But I'm not responsible for his behavior. So then I was thinking, this might be a terrible idea, and she might jump up and run away, or they might do something to me . . . By the way, I have pepper spray in my purse." At this she narrowed her eyes and set her jaw. "And I'm serious. I doubt you're totally insane, but I can't take that kind of chance. But since I'm doing this insane thing, what is it that I hope to gain? That's what my gran used to ask me when I was trying to decide what to do. To think about what I wanted to accomplish." She glanced down for a moment, then back up with a glare, straight at Morgan. "So this is the thing I have to know. How did it start? How did you go from a kid in his class to his . . . lover."

Her voice squeaked on that word, and Rain closed her eyes for a moment, taking a deep breath in through her nose and letting it out in a quick poof of an exhale.

Morgan wanted to die, right then, hoping she would just be struck dead by the hand of God at the picnic table.

She was so pretty, and young. Morgan had seen her picture more than once, but somehow in her mind she'd distorted the image to be someone old, cold, and dried up. Here was a woman not that much older than her, now in pain over . . . what happened.

This was not how the story went.

"Um. I mean. I guess the same way it always happens."

"Oh? This always happens?"

Dinah interjected sharply, "That's not what she meant."

"Mom, stop. I just mean, we just kind of were friends at first. We talked about stuff. I'd broken up with someone who was in the class. One time he took a call . . . well, from you, I guess. And seemed very sad."

"When?"

"Um. September. Maybe early October."

Rain nodded, her eyes down on the picnic table, as if she were watching this scene play out there.

"And . . . well, I'm sure you read about all this. I told the cops and they wrote it down. I'm sure someone showed it to you."

"Yes, I've heard the facts. This happened, then this happened, then this. I know where, and when, and approximately how often. But how did it . . . evolve? How does such a thing happen?"

"I don't know," Morgan whispered. "I don't know."

"That's such a line to cross. How does one even approach that line, much less cross it?"

Rain's gaze was up over Morgan's shoulder, somewhere in the trees behind her, and she seemed not to be directly asking Morgan anymore. Her expression was dreamy. Disconnected. As if she would start to float up from the picnic table and drift away over the pond.

Then she snapped her gaze back to Morgan.

"Did you ever do it in my bed?"

Dinah reached out to hold her daughter's hand. "You don't have to grill her."

"This was your idea," Rain retorted. "And if you want something from me, you have to give me something, too. And if you don't answer another single question, I want to know. Did you have sex with my husband in my own house, and in our bed?"

Morgan remembered being on the floor and seeing the wedding picture. How mad he was she'd been looking at it. She cleared her throat and replied, "Not in the bed."

Rain closed her eyes, and something like a quiver passed across her face.

She opened her eyes and spoke. "Your mother wants me to say that TJ loved me. That he can't be in love with you because he loves his wife. I have no idea what to think anymore, but you answered my question, so I'll give you this much. He swore on his knees to be a better husband to me. He was crying with joy when our baby turned out to be okay, after a scare, and he swore that he would be a good father . . ."

"Baby?" Morgan said.

At this, Rain rose from the table, revealing herself to be pregnant. Definitely and visibly pregnant. Morgan shot a glance at her mother. Dinah's jaw was dropping open in shock, too. How had her mom missed that detail?

"When?" Morgan finally gulped out.

"Not that it's your business. Since January. Are you satisfied with yourself?"

Dinah rose, too. "Now wait, I didn't want you to tear into her . . ."

Rain wheeled on Dinah. "What did you think I would feel like, when confronted by the girl who slept with my husband?"

Dinah put a protective hand on Morgan's shoulder. "She's just a kid!"

"Not just a kid. Not hardly."

Dinah croaked out, "That's not fair."

Rain snatched up her book. "None of this is. Not a damn bit of it. This was a stupid idea. Don't contact me again or I will call the police."

She ran with more grace than Morgan would have thought possible to a car on the other side of the gazebo, which Morgan recognized as the one he'd been driving when she got into the car with him that frigid December night, and they'd kissed, his mouth tasting of beer and breath mints.

On the drive home, Dinah muttered to herself about it being a crazy idea, and wrong, and begging Morgan's forgiveness, repeating about ten times that Rain had been in a baggy sweatshirt and she hadn't noticed the pregnancy, had been just as shocked . . .

"We can't tell anyone we did this," Dinal said, thumping the steering wheel.

"Mutually assured destruction," Morga muttered.

"Not mutual for her. All she'd have to d is look at the judge with those big blue tear eyes and talk about how we, like, accoste her or something. Of course, I have the no she sent with her cell number. Oh, that right. I have the note." Dinah exhaled shaky breath. "That feels better. But still . we can't tell . . ."

"We won't. No one will." Morgan felt su of it, though she couldn't say exactly ho Rain was so very calm. Unlike her ov mother, who had set them on this cra path. Morgan's stomach cramped. S curled up in the seat. Why had she hers agreed to it?

Because she wanted to hate her, tha why, she admitted to herself as soon as s thought it. She wanted to see a mea spirited, cold fish of a woman who wo be nasty to Morgan and then she'd f certain that it had been a miserable m riage and he'd never go back to her . . .

But . . . he'd sworn his love to her. S was pregnant with his baby. Picturing belly, picturing him on his knees weepi made her chest hurt as if she were drowning.

He'd sworn to be a better father, and a better husband, but there'd been some problem with the baby, and then he'd been relieved. Maybe that's all it was, relief. Morgan herself knew that kind of relief, when something you love is almost taken from you, and in the shaky aftermath you'll say anything. One of her earliest memories was of being mad at the baby brothers who kept her mom away so often — so mad that she wished they'd never come home from the hospital. Then she felt worse than horrible and promised to God to be the best little girl anyone had ever seen if he would just keep her brothers safe.

A new tenderness bloomed for him now, having nearly lost something precious, and how strongly he reacted. Of course in the heat of that emotional moment, he would feel powerfully moved.

Yes, they were having a baby, but the baby had been her number one project, and in fact, Morgan was remembering now, they were doing treatments with a specialist. She remembered him complaining once, he "wasn't even in the room" when his wife was trying to conceive. It was a detail she'd shoved out of her mind, the notion of his wife and syringes or test tubes and all that.

Rain had agreed to meet for a reason, and Morgan straightened in her seat, realizing that the wife must have had a very specific agenda: convince Morgan to give up on him; that's why the dramatic belly reveal from behind the table.

Dinah said, again, "Are you okay, honey? I'm so sorry I put you through that. I didn't know she'd react like that, though I should have. Stupid."

"No, I'm fine," Morgan said, smiling now and smoothing her shirt. "It's obvious."

"What is?"

"She's losing him. I can see it all over her face."

Dinah pulled the car to the shoulder, rock ing Morgan in her seat with the abruptnes of the swerve. "No, honey, that's not th sense I got at all. She was saying how h was on his knees and swearing . . ."

"You don't get it, do you? She's despe ate. That's why she agreed to this stup idea, so she could plant that seed of dou in me, so I will give up and leave him alo forever. But I know this for a fact: He risk everything for me. Why would he have do that if he just wanted to get laid? Sex is ea Love is hard. Love is worth risking eve thing for."

Her mother put her head on the steering wheel. "Oh, God."

Morgan patted her mom's shoulder. "Say, you want me to drive? You seem upset."

Her mother only shook her head, still braced on the steering wheel, so Morgan shrugged and leaned back in the seat, picturing that night he carried her up the stairs to the bedroom, telling her she was beautiful.

43

Rain stopped the car at a rest area just a mile down the highway, unable to believe she could walk into the house with TJ there and act as if all were normal — even the bizarre standard of normal they had these days.

She parked facing a grassy swath with a picnic table in the center and let her eyes unfocus, feeling herself go inward, to her baby. She rubbed circles over her little one and in doing so calmed herself.

In that first moment seeing her, Rain had felt a spasm of revulsion. Not at the girl, no, at TJ. Because she'd seemed so very much like a girl indeed, not the womanly seductress she'd envisioned. Somehow, in fact, she could see now she'd conflated the perky and supple Layla from work with the girl in question.

She'd noticed that scar and hoped it didn't register on her face, the surprise of it, and she immediately wondered what had happened and how this girl felt about it, then she wondered what TJ had said about it. He'd probably been very sweet.

There was a falling-away sensation to it, like shingles off a rotting roof, her increasingly strained love for her husband, as she confronted this young, scarred girl whom he'd slept with.

Girl maybe, but child not exactly.

"Not in the bed," the girl had said, at least having sense enough to look ashamed of herself. But that was the line this girl had drawn? Not at sex with a married teacher, not at kissing, not at making out, not at inappropriate texting, not at flirting . . . No, her big moral stand was that she didn't screw him in their marriage bed.

Where then, the floor? The shower? The couch?

Rain opened the car door, hung her head between her knees, and breathed shallowly over the parking lot, trying not to vomit.

TJ needed a psychiatrist, not jail. What would jail do for him, anyway? The idea of locking him up with murderers and rapists and drug dealers, where they would beat him to death the minute they smelled vulnerability, which they surely would, if he were locked away and had lost everything.

And where would she be? Squeezing out their baby coached by her bossy baby sister, while her mother chain-smoked outside.

And living where, exactly? Greg had offered to help with their mortgage, and with reluctance she'd let him, her yoga teacher salary pathetic against the weight of their debt and TJ on unpaid "leave" and almost certainly fired. But that could not go on forever.

Rain felt her stomach settle along with her resolve, dropping back into place just as it had been before this insane errand. She pulled herself in and closed the car door, hard.

Mission number one: Keep TJ out of jail.

Mission number two: Get him help. Save him from himself. Her baby needed a sane, stable father, and that's what they would achieve, whatever the cost.

TJ was not in the kitchen, nor upstairs, nor on the elliptical. Rain drifted through the house, each step making her heart pound harder. She saw his cell phone idle on the kitchen counter.

The car was here. He'd been a runner way back when, though he was supposed to take it easy on his knees these days.

She walked to the back door, into the

yard, and drooped with the snap of released tension: There he was. He was covered in grass clippings, his shoes stained green, and at the moment, a patch of sod and weeds was growing by his feet as he tugged away great handfuls of brush from along the back fence.

It had once been a patch of daylilies that had become overgrown with weeds from the field behind the house. Neither had had the energy to cope with yard work.

He yanked with ferocity. In fact, as she drew closer, she heard him actually growl.

She stood far enough back not to startle him as she said, "TJ?"

He startled anyway, stumbled backward, and tripped over a branch. Rain reached forward reflexively. His face was pink and sweaty. He laughed without mirth. "Ha. Clumsy me."

It took him a long time to right himself, and Rain felt a pang of sympathy.

Then she noticed him swaying in place, like one of those old toys with the rounded bottom that would never fall down.

Rain put on a smile. "Hi, honey. I didn't find anything I liked." She'd claimed to have been searching for nursery wallpaper. "You look like you've been working hard."

"Something to do," he muttered. Then he

scowled at the ground, like the grass had wronged him, and kicked at it. "Greg called. Had their baby."

"Oh," Rain said, not bothering to sound jubilant, though on some distant plane she was happy for her friend and in-laws. "Everything is okay, I assume?"

" 'Course it is, for good Dr. Greg. All perfect, what else?"

Rain put her hand on her hip. "We should be glad our niece is perfect, TJ. Does our perfect niece have a name?"

"Marjorie." TJ said it at first through a sneer, then he shook his head a little and repeated it, this time sweetly, with a sad smile and watery eyes. "Marjorie."

His gaze landed on his shoes, stained green. "Oh, crap. Ruined."

"Oh, it doesn't matter. They're only shoes. Now these can be your yard work shoes."

He nodded vaguely, his head bobbing like a buoy in waves.

"Why don't you come in? You can finish this later. Have a nice hot shower, and I'll make you some pasta."

He didn't move, but Rain took his hand and led him inside as she might a small child, and he allowed himself to be led exactly where she wanted him to go.

Rain boiled some tortellini while the

shower ran for a long, long time.

She shredded parmesan, and in this simple, caretaking act, she felt more peaceful than she had in weeks. This was what she was meant to do, care for her family, which for now included TJ and a baby. For better or worse, she'd sworn before God and everyone. Well, here was the worse. Stability had been the great gift of her youth in the form of Gran, and she would give that gift to their baby. She could be the anchor for her new family as she was from her family of origin. Being "the stable one" was hard, but what of it? It felt competent and strong, too. In fact, she felt nearly powerful now, having the fate of her family firmly in her grasp.

TJ emerged, damp and somber, if not sober. He walked to the fridge as if pulled there like a compass point, but she intercepted him. "I'll get you some water," she said.

He nodded again, that vague bobbing, and sank heavily into the kitchen chair.

She placed the pasta in front of him. "Honey, I wanted to tell you something."

He met her gaze. His eyes were swollen and red.

"If you need me to testify that you were here, of course I will do that for you. I want you to know I'm on your side. So you can be strong, knowing that, can't you?"

He smiled sadly, then even that wan attempt dried up and blew away.

She excused herself upstairs, while TJ ate the pasta with the grim determination of an inmate. Rain shivered and shook off the image. Upstairs, she called Alexandra.

When she got their lawyer on the phone, Rain said, "What's wrong? Has something happened? He's behaving so strangely today."

"Strangely how?" Alex's voice had a sharp edge of warning to it.

Rain related the manic yard work, the vague attitude, the listless responses. She left out the drinking.

She could hear Alex tapping something, her fingers or a pencil on the desk. She replied, "I've seen this before. It's normal to be depressed when facing something like this. It's like grief, I've found. People grieve for what used to be. It's a genuine loss. Even after we get the verdict we want, nothing is ever quite the same for having gone through this. Sorry to be so blunt, but I believe in truth. Be gentle with him, and positive. And if he's drinking, try to stop him. The last thing we need is for him to engage in some drunk dialing or posting erratic things online, or who knows what? Drunk driving, God forbid."

"Of course."

"And Rain? I really think what you're doing is so commendable. Lots of wives with even a hint of anything like this would have run for the hills. The devotion is touching."

Rain said good-bye and hung up and walked down the stairs. Her stretched hip ligaments pinched painfully, though she wasn't huge yet, but when she reached the landing and found TJ in front of the yellow glow of the TV set, curtains drawn, she forgot the lawyer.

On the TV screen was the Den. Dripping red spray paint blared "SLUT" and "WHORE" across the white clapboard of the front of the bungalow. The large picture window had been smashed in, so that the name of the place was no longer visible. A bland TV reporter was recounting the facts of the damage and that the owner, Dinah Monetti, could not be reached for comment, and husband, Joe Monetti, an assistant principal at Arbor Valley High, had declined to comment when reached at the school.

The reporter then launched into backstory as the wind tried in vain to disturb her sprayed-stiff hair: "Dinah Monetti's daughter is the seventeen-year-old girl prosecutors say had an affair with Arbor Valley teacher TJ Hill. His trial on a charge of third-degree criminal sexual conduct is set to begin June 6. Prosecutor Henry Davis released this statement: 'This vicious and hateful crime shows a deep misunderstanding of the case before us. I have confidence that this isolated incident does not reflect our community, which has a reputation of caring for young people, not attacking them at a vulnerable time. The Monetti family has suffered quite enough already, and the police will investigate thoroughly and bring the vandals to justice."

The phone rang again, and Rain knew without having to look it would be Alex. She handed the cordless to TJ, walked out into the backyard, and sat on an old lawn chair on the small patio, the sharp scent of torn weeds still hanging in the air.

She put her face in her hands and stayed like that until TJ ventured out of the house.

"Babe? That was Alex. She said what happened at the Den is bad news."

"No shit," she replied, enjoying, the tiniest bit, the shocked look on TJ's face at her casual and unusual curse.

44

As long as she lived, Dinah would regret making Morgan answer the cell phone.

But she didn't like to talk on the phone while driving, certainly not with her hands shaking on the wheel, thinking of the stupid risk she'd taken to meet the teacher's wife, and all for naught, for her daughter to somehow be ever more convinced the bastard truly loved her.

So the phone rang, and when she could see it was Joe, she told Morgan to answer it, not thinking fast enough to give her daughter a ready lie for where they'd been when they were both supposed to be home.

She'd heard him blare right out of the phone into the car, "Where the hell are you? Let me talk to your mother. Now."

Morgan had looked sick and greenish, and even more so when Dinah had to tell her why Joe was calling.

Now, facing the damage with the insurance agent taking pictures, ignoring the reporters trying to talk to her, Dinah mapped out her course.

There was a time when Dinah would have balled up her fists, pushed up her sleeves, and vowed to come back better than ever. She'd have applied the same "never say die" attitude she had always deployed with the boys and their challenges, with founding the business in the first place, and she'd have been right in there, sweeping up glass and hiring architects to expand the place, in fact, destruction be damned.

She stepped around the shards and pushed open the door. A chill air from the damp morning swirled around the café tables, and Dinah believed it would never feel warm again.

She marched up to her office, where Helen Demming's envelope stared up at her from the recycle bin at her feet.

Dinah spent most of that day on the phone. Morgan remained holed up in her room, having seemingly become genuinely ill after their morning's errand and having seen the damage to the Den. Morgan had insisted on seeing it for herself, telling her mother she'd only imagine something worse, anyway.

In the end, Dinah had conceded and driven her past it, reasoning it would be on the news anyway. "Oh my God," Morgan had squeaked out. At home, she'd taken the steps two at a time to her room.

When the police asked Dinah if she had any enemies, she'd cocked one eyebrow and said, "Other than the obvious?" Their serious veneer never cracked as they waited for a genuine answer. So she sighed and dutifully told them about that hoodlum Justin kid who'd knocked over a chair and coffee table at her place, not believing they'd ever be able to prove it was him, or even whether she believed it was him. She also mentioned Helen Demming's desire to buy the Den, but as much as she couldn't stand that hoity-toity bitch, she also couldn't imagine her with red spray paint in hand, or interacting with unsavory types to arrange for the vandalism. No, Helen would sooner take her out via capitalism and politics, the more public the better.

The police promised to increase surveillance at their home.

Henry called, apologizing as if on behalf of all Arbor Valley. Never mind, Dinah told him. Not your fault.

Dinah stood up and stretched in the kitchen. She had a little time before the boys got home, so she fetched the electric screwdriver from the garage and walked upstairs.

"Morgan. Come help me here."

Morgan picked her head up off the pillow as if she barely had the strength. She spied the tool in her mother's hand and cocked her head.

"Come hold your door. I'm putting it back on."

"Why?"

"Because I feel like it. And I can't hold it myself. So get over here."

Morgan approached the door, holding it in place, while Dinah pushed the screws in with a satisfyingly loud whirr from the screwdriver.

"Mom. Your phone."

Dinah paused and took the phone out of her pocket. She saw who it was and took the call. "Yes. Yes, I think that's a fair price. . . . I appreciate you not trying to gouge me. Considering . . . Of course . . . Send the papers over to the house."

She clicked off, sticking the phone back in her pocket.

"Mom?" Morgan asked. "Fair price for what?"

Dinah bent down for a new bunch of screws. "I'm selling the Den. Morgan! Hold the door, I don't have enough screws in yet."

"Why, just because some asshole trashed it?"

"Not just. Lots of reasons."

"But . . . you love that place."

"I did once, yeah. You know how some things you just know? That you don't have to reason out, because you just know it so completely? It's less like a realization than like you discover a fact that's always existed." Dinah paused to drive in another screw. Then she began fiddling with lining up the next screw just so. It seemed to take all her effort to get the point of the screwdriver into the slot. "I poured so much of my energy into that place, believing it was somehow going to make me special. It was supposed to be my trophy. Entrepreneur by day, Supermom at night. You know, I think I even believed it made people like me. But in the end, it was just a place that earned some money and sucked up too much of my attention away from my family. It was just a place, after all, and I don't want it anymore."

"But . . . you're just upset because of today . . ."

"No. It's been coming. I didn't realize it until now, but it's been coming."

"What will you do?"

"I don't know. Okay, you can let go, now."

"You didn't sell it to that old bitch, did you?"

Dinah smirked. "Now, that's not nice." It had been a direct quote from Dinah, as she'd ranted about Helen Demming at dinner the night of her offer. "Anyway, nope, I sold the license and fixtures and equipment to my landlord. He might open a hookah bar. That'll get 'em all lathered up."

Morgan laughed a little, but her eyes were wet.

Dinah tilted her head and put down the screwdriver. "Honey? I'm sorry, are you upset about the business? I didn't think you cared that much about it."

Morgan tucked her chin down. "I don't know. I don't know what I feel. Everything's just so crazy."

Dinah pulled her daughter close. "I know, baby. Totally crazy."

"I'm sorry."

Dinah answered reflexively, "It's not your fault."

"Well." Morgan pushed back, straightened up. She was looking away, her face knotted in a grimace. "Well, yeah, it kind of is. I keep saying he didn't force me, and he didn't."

Dinah's heart thudded. Another opening for reason, another chink in her fortress glimmering with daylight. “I know.”

“We love each other, we really do; that’s what no one gets. I didn’t ruin everything for nothing, or because I’m a stupid kid, who didn’t know better . . .”

Dinah bit her lip against her retort.

Morgan said, “You don’t believe me.”

“I . . . I would like to believe you . . .”

Morgan turned away and flounced back down onto her bed. “Thanks for my door back. Could you close it, please?”

The dinner table conversation about the Den hadn’t gone well. The boys were surprisingly upset. Connor went so far as to slam his door upstairs. Jared just fiddled with his glasses and asked where they were going to work when they got older, sending another crack across Dinah’s heart to think that was the only future he saw for himself.

Joe had stared into his plate of chicken, muttering, “It woulda been nice to have a conversation about something like this . . .”

He didn’t finish the thought, instead letting a black cloud seethe out around him, blanketing the dinner table and silencing any more chatter.

The kids finally scattered to their rooms. Morgan must have been reveling in a door again, and the boys had papers to work on.

Dinah threatened them with computer grounding if she heard one electronic noise from up there not related to homework, and Joe beckoned her to the basement home office before she'd even washed a single dish.

"Come on down here. I have to talk to you."

Dinah descended the three stairs to the sunken den, feeling her guts climb into her throat.

Joe turned around without sitting down. "They offered me early retirement."

Dinah blinked and reared back. "What?"

"You heard me. They want me gone, so they offered me retirement and promoted Kate to principal. They're gonna fill Kate's old job with some brownnoser from the middle school with no experience and not even replace me. 'Course they're saying it's all budgeting and shit and making it sound like a good thing. So it woulda been nice if you'd at least called me for five minutes before cutting away half our income stream."

"Hardly half, but anyway, we'll work it out," Dinah said, clenching her fists to stop her hands from trembling.

"We'll frickin' have to, won't we? With tuition bills coming, assuming Morgan doesn't run away, that is. Lovely." Joe collapsed onto the overstuffed sofa. “What did we do to deserve this?”

“We don’t deserve it. Bad things happen to good people all the time. I guess it’s our turn.”

Dinah settled on the other end of the couch with extra care, as if Joe were some fragile object she could break by jarring him.

He muttered, staring at the floor in front of him. “You coulda asked me about the door, too.”

“It was time, Joe. She’s suffered enough and deserves her privacy. We shouldn’t be punishing her. We should be helping her.”

“She lied to us.”

“Kids lie. Don’t tell me you never lied a day in your teenage years.”

“Not like this. About this.”

“No shit, Joe, but look at it from her point of view. She was in love. They were Romeo and Juliet as far as she was concerned. Hell, pursuing true love is practically noble to a teenage girl.”

“True love,” he sneered.

“Hey, I’m thinking like Morgan, here.”

Joe curled forward and put his elbows on his knees, his head in his hands. “How are we gonna get through this trial?”

Dinah scooted over next to him and put her arm around his broad shoulders. Her hand barely reached to the other side of him. "I don't know. But we will. Because we have to."

"Why doesn't that bastard just admit it? Plead guilty and get it over with," Joe muttered into his hands.

"That I can't tell you."

Dinah flashed to the tiny, angry teacher's wife with her round belly. She wondered if TJ wasn't hoping for some divine intervention to get him out of the mess. Or he could be the type of criminal who believed his own lies. Maybe he'd edited his own memory and truly believed her daughter to be crazy, because that was the only way he could face his wife.

Dinah squeezed her husband again. "We'll get through it. In the scope of a whole life, this will be a blip."

"Blip?" He laughed, equal parts scorn and exhaustion. He sat back, this time wrapping his arm around Dinah. She curled into his side, under his arm, feeling as safe as a grown-up ever could while her life spins out of control.

"Sure. An awful one. But a blip."

"Did I ever tell you I love you for being an optimist?"

"Yes. But say it again."

"I love you for being an optimist. Because

personally, I think we're doomed."

Dinah chuckled, bleakly, then settled her head over his low, thrumming heartbeat and closed her eyes.

"Yeah. Maybe so."

45

Morgan paused with her hand on the car's inside door handle and adjusted her mortarboard again. The hairpins tugged her hair. She growled with frustration and yanked it off, tossing the hairpins on the car's floor and setting the stupid hat back on her hair, where it would slide around, no doubt, but would be the least of her worries.

She could feel herself in the middle of a bubble of watchful anxiety. Her lanky brothers were crammed in the sedan's backseat next to her, and they were uncharacteristically quiet. The back of her parents' heads bore a listening-but-trying-not-to look of a slight turn toward the back.

The whole remainder of the school year she'd felt like a specimen being observed and noted, a rat in a maze. And this night, what should have been her night of celebration, it would only be worse.

She and her parents had gone in circles

for hours one night debating whether to even attend. Dinah was angry about the Den's trashing and the community silence about who had done it ("Maybe they don't know," her dad had ventured, and her mom had snapped back, "Bullshit, somebody knows but it's like the goddamn Mafia"), and she wanted to boycott the graduation as a form of giving Arbor Valley the finger.

But they were also planning to recognize Joe and the other retired faculty for their years of service, and in the end, Morgan decided that it couldn't be much worse than prom. She didn't want to skip her graduation. I mean, what were they going to do, boo her? Catcall? Screw them then, she'd said with a toss of her hair and a jutted chin that was all bravado.

But now in the car, her hand on the door and her family silent and pretending not to stare at her, she'd changed her mind. They should have stayed home.

However, here she was, in her godawful mustard-yellow cap and gown, with the crease lines because she hadn't unfolded it until that night, and her white NHS sash and honor cords, and she finally thought, *Well, hell, I've gone this far.*

She shoved open the door. "Are we going in or what?"

A television van was in front of the school. Her mother said softly, "Oh, no."

Joe said, "It can't be for us. They're just covering graduation in general."

Connor piped up, "They never have before."

Jared chimed in, "Shut up, moron."

Dinah reached around Morgan's shoulders, but Morgan shrugged away. "Mom, don't. Just be normal, because this is a normal thing, okay? I'm graduating, that's it."

"Hugging you is normal," she retorted in a small voice, but she folded her arms anyway.

They all walked past the cameras trying to act casual. Morgan wanted to look down and away, but she froze her face in a flat expression and walked on as if she was just another nobody, which was really all she ever wanted to be.

The current of graduates and families swept them along the hallways to the fieldhouse. The stormy weather report had forced relocation of the ceremony inside, which promised a stifling few hours. Morgan already felt her armpits growing sticky. When she considered she could have been at home with a bowl of ice cream and the television, she wondered what the hell she was trying to prove.

It came time for Morgan to join the line of graduates who would march in to good old "Pomp and Circumstance." Last year, Morgan had played the cello for that procession and looked on with envy at those graduates done with high school and childhood at last, still feeling pangs for her recent breakup with David.

This time, she stood in alphabetical order between Peter Miller and Linh Nguyen. She wondered where Olivia Nelson had gone. They all held their names, spelled phonetically in case of confusing pronunciations, written on index cards, so the faculty announcing the names wouldn't have to rely on the grads staying in exact order.

Linh smiled shyly and looked down. Peter acknowledged her presence with a briefly raised chin and turned away to talk to Lauren Lucas.

The chatter around her grew louder, but everything began to sound muffled, like she were hearing it through a shroud.

She sucked in a deep breath and looked up at the ceiling in the hallway. Almost over. All of it was almost over. The trial date had just been set for next week Wednesday — Morgan realized that must be why the cameras showed up, to get graduation footage at Arbor Valley they could play behind the reporter talking about the trial — and in any case it would all be over, and before long she'd be eighteen and it would finally be concluded, for better or worse.

Morgan had already nixed her mother's plan to have a charade of an open house. "Who would come?" Morgan had snapped. Dinah had stuttered around about grandparents and cousins and Morgan said they could have a cookout at the house for family but she wasn't having an "open house" where kids would parade in and out of the notorious girl's yard . . . or worse, like the prom.

Morgan looked down at her black flats, borrowed from her mother because all her shoes clashed with the awful sickly yellow of the girls' gowns. She had suggested to Britney that they all go to the prom in one big group, and Brit had blinked at her twice with wide eyes, then chirped, "Sure! Why not!" She was pretty sure Britney and David were sleeping together by then but she didn't much care; she just didn't want to be left alone on what was supposed to be a fun night, and she knew all their friends, including Nicole, and the flute-playing girls, were going, whether they had dates or not.

She'd suggested, at lunch one day, sitting

next to Britney, that they all try to wear the ugliest dresses they could find, just to be ironic and funny. They'd all laughed, said it was a great idea. Morgan had gone to thrift stores until she found some floral bridesmaid horror from 1991 or something, with a giant bow on the butt . . . and she was the only one who had actually done it. Everyone else wore the prom fashions you'd see in *Seventeen* or on mall mannequins.

Brit had stared at her and when Morgan demanded to know why everyone hadn't gone along, she'd whisper-hissed at her that they'd only laughed at the idea, not committed to actually doing it.

No one talked to her at the dance itself. Half of them had gotten tipsy before they even showed up, having snuck off somewhere to pass around some vodka. Her dad himself, in his role as dance chaperone, had tossed out Courtney and Justin, calling their parents to come pick their drunk asses up.

Once in a while, one of her friends would say, "Hey, how are you doing?" and then rush off to dance or giggle with someone else before listening to her answer.

Ethan had been across the room with some girl Morgan didn't know. He'd made as if he might want to come talk to her, so she turned away and crossed her arms.

After an hour, without telling any of her girlfriends, she called her mom to come get her. Britney would later swear the problem had been Morgan's, that she'd been prickly and unapproachable. Morgan allowed that she'd been in a bad mood, but she didn't deserve shunning. Britney made a big show of apologizing and Morgan let it go.

Morgan looked up and saw a TV journalist across the lobby. She gasped and turned to the wall. They might be trying to catch her on camera, though she knew they technically weren't supposed to, based on their own stated policy, since she supposedly was a "victim." But they might sweep the middle of the line of students, hoping to catch the "M" names.

She felt a nudge in her side. It was Linh who whispered, "They're gone."

Morgan smiled back. "Thank you," she replied in her own whisper, and she wondered why she'd never talked to Linh before, all these years.

"Pomp and Circumstance" began, and all the mortar-boarded heads snapped up from what they were doing. A few girls emitted giddy squeals.

Beginning of the end, Morgan thought.

She and Linh didn't say much during the

ceremony, though they did share an eye roll for one of the valedictorians, Conrad Jansen III, pronouncing their class one of "innovation, inspiration, and intelligence." He sounded so much like his uncle, the state senator, Morgan assumed his uncle had written the speech.

Morgan stiffened during Pete Jackson's remark about a "difficult" year in Arbor Valley. She could well imagine her mother getting really pissed off about that.

She wondered suddenly what Britney was doing, if she was giggling, or what. What she'd be saying if they'd been allowed to sit together. Britney was probably relieved she didn't have to. Though maybe she would have enjoyed the reflected attention, just as she seemed to in the hall, walking with a protective arm around her, playing the role of Caring Friend to Suffering Friend.

And what was he doing tonight? On a night when teachers dust off their own silly mortarboards? Was he bringing his wife ginger ale and crackers? Was he leaving her? Was he talking to his attorney? Was he afraid of jail?

Was he thinking of her?

Her row of students rose and began the march to the podium at last. Her mortarboard was slipping again, and she adjusted it.

Despite Pete Jackson's order that no one cheer until the end, for all, there was a smattering of rebellious applause for each name, sometimes gleeful hoots and whistles. Some moron had brought in an air horn. Morgan began to panic about what would happen after her name.

She turned to glance over her shoulder at the door behind her, next to the bleachers. She could bolt now, throw away her name card that was damp with sweat. It's not like they handed out the real diplomas anyway, here. Those would be mailed home.

Only that would be worse, wouldn't it? The Runaway Grad. They'd be able to track her progress, hear the slapping of her shoes across the floor for several yards before she actually escaped.

It was Peter Miller's turn. Off he went, leaving the empty expanse of the stage in front of her to cross.

Her chest was heaving under her gown, and stars were sparkling at the fringes of her vision. *God, don't let me faint.*

She never heard her own name, rather felt Linh poke her in the back. She crossed the stage at first with her head down, but then she raised her chin, remembering she came here because she deserved her graduation, if nothing else; she had earned this with her grades and studying and hard work; she was a good student, still. She always was.

There was applause. Polite, restrained, as in golf. She heard one "Woo!" from a guy, not able to tell if it was sarcastic, a form of catcall, or if someone was genuinely happy. Ethan? One of the twins? No way to tell, and then she was in front of Principal Jackson.

"Good for you," he said quietly, with a wink so fast and subtle she might have imagined it. He gave her hand an extrafirm shake.

"Thank you," she whispered back, and she concentrated on getting off the stage without falling, as she imagined the entire Arbor Valley community exhaling, having endured that moment together.

Walking along the side of the seated graduates, headed back to her row, she glanced at the crowd, with scant hope she'd actually see her family.

Then she spotted the twins, who were leaping up and down like jackrabbits, waving their arms. Connor whistled with his fingers. Morgan waved and flushed at once, and Dinah and Joe yanked them down in tandem.

She waved and mouthed, *Thanks, Mork and Dork.*

Much as they drove her crazy most days, she would truly miss them once she turned eighteen and got the hell out.

46

June 6, 2012

Rain knew she should eat, for the sake of the baby, but here it was, lunch break in her husband's trial, and she could no sooner eat a meal than she could run the Kentucky Derby.

TJ seemed encouraged, happy, even, by the morning's proceedings. He had a weird bounce in his step as they walked to the car, escorted by their attorney, who shouted comments to the press while Rain tried to pretend she was not aware of being photographed.

Alex led them to a small conference room in her office, which was close enough to the courthouse they could get back quickly. She'd ordered sandwiches so they could eat in peace and privacy, without having to be hounded by the press or gawking public. "In the home stretch," she'd said. "Hang tough."

Home stretch. The metaphor seemed appropriate for TJ, who was pacing with athletic energy as Alex pulled the door shut.

"Did you see her sitting on our side of the room? She's not on their side. And without her . . . And, man, Alex just took apart that cop on the stand, didn't she? I think we're gonna beat this," he said, tucking into his sandwich with gusto. A piece of onion had fallen off and was clinging to his chin. Rain was primed to wipe it off, but part of her wanted to slap it off, too.

She put a piece of pasta salad in her mouth and almost choked on it. No eating now. *Sorry, baby,* she thought.

"Beat this, and then what?" Rain managed to ask.

TJ smiled. "Then we sue to get reinstated at work, if they don't just do it, which they should, because I'll be innocent."

I will be innocent, Rain echoed in her head. Not that I am innocent, but I will be. Because the court said so.

"I meant, then what for us?"

TJ smiled. "Then we go and have this baby and resume our lives."

"What if we don't?"

"Don't what?"

"Don't beat it."

TJ tossed down his sandwich. "Seriously?

This is the first time I feel positive in weeks. I don't need you turning on me like that prick brother of mine, who believes his old-ass crazy neighbor over his own brother. We are so done with them, by the way. Never speaking to them again, ever. And that includes you and Alessia. Done." He brushed his hands together, bread crumbs scattering across the lacquered table.

"But we have a niece now! Little Marjorie! And they're paying our mortgage . . ."

TJ shoved back from the table and folded his arms. "Oh, good for him. He's just doing it to feel superior. He gets to hold something else over me. Believe me, he's giggling like a little girl when he writes that check. Why are you doing this to me, now? Huh? I'm on trial here, and my career is in ruins because some little slut is in love with me."

Rain drew back. She saw, in her mind's eye, the images of that red-painted word across Dinah's business. Her imagination pulled up an image of him having sex in their bedroom with this girl — scarred and young and damaged.

Rain rose. TJ looked up at her, still stormy and glowering. She'd seen that face of his so many times before: chin jutted out, eyes narrow, a crease between his brows. And right on schedule came the next phase. A flick of his eyes to the side of the room accompanied by a slight sigh. This was his shift from "angry" to "wounded." He folded his arms and slumped slightly, dipping his chin toward his chest. He'd gone into "sad little boy" now. This was Rain's cue to drop to her knees next to him, squeeze his arm, and apologize for upsetting him.

Yes, this was her cue to apologize. Even after all he'd done — to her, to the girl, to all of their lives — it was her apology to make in the world according to TJ Hill.

Rain thought, *This is my forever.* She'd earlier thought the trial was the "worse" in "for better or worse" but now she could see that wasn't so. The "worse" would be the collective years of this. She would be forever cautioning their child not to disturb or upset Daddy, not take anything to heart, Daddy was just having a bad day . . .

And when Daddy did snap at them, or sulk, or withdraw into his own emotional stew, Rain would still have to apologize, and she would not be alone. She pictured now a little girl in pigtails, saying "Sorry, Daddy, I didn't mean to be loud," and trying — like Rain had, countless times — to catch his gaze, to be assured her apology was worthy, and that the balance of their household on the fulcrum of his mood would once again right itself.

These were the rules of their household, as laid down by her husband and upheld by her own tacit participation, rules allowing him to cheat on her with a teenage girl, turn their lives inside out for public ridicule, ask her to lie under oath to save him, then demand an apology from her with not even a whiff of awareness that a single part of the problem lay with him.

Rain grounded her feet, pulled her shoulders back, and rooted herself to the earth as she'd done so many times in class. She laced her fingers across her stomach and said, "No."

"What?"

"I said no."

"No to what?"

"I will not testify you were at home. Because you were not."

His bravado melted away as the color drained out of his face. "No, baby, come on, I didn't mean to get upset . . . ." He clasped his hands like he was praying, or literally begging.

"You never mean to get upset, but you always do. And then I am the one who has to bring you back. I'm not doing it anymore."

"I don't understand . . ."

"I know you did it. As soon as you tried to convince me that you were at home when you were not, you knocked out the last brick of my faith in your innocence."

"You don't believe me?"

"Of course I don't. And you don't, either. If you'd stop the posing and the defensiveness for five minutes. It's time to plead guilty."

"I can't, they'll send me to jail . . ."

"So they will." At this, Rain's voice shook, so she clenched her fists and pictured him with the girl, as portrayed in the police report. On the rehearsal room floor, in his car, in their own house. "And you deserve it."

"You want me to give up?"

"I want you to admit what you did. I want you to stop putting that girl, her family, me, all of us, through this hell."

TJ frowned, his eyes starting to dart, panicked, as if police were going to bust down the door and haul him away right there. "Why do you care about her, anyway? Since you're so convinced she screwed me, a married man."

"She's just a kid. When we got married, she was wearing a training bra."

"You wouldn't do this to me . . ."

"You did this to you. And not only that, you did it to me."

Rain left her husband and her lunch behind, and she strode away, tears of rage making stinging tracks down her face, on her way to Alexandra's office.

Rain would have found Alexandra terrifying if she were the one in TJ's chair. Rain stood along the far wall of the room, leaning with her tailbone resting on the wall.

"Jesus H. Christ," Alex had blurted when TJ confessed that the reason he wanted to change his plea was because he was, in fact, guilty. Then, "You are an idiot."

Alex had been standing, Amazon-like, with a wide stance, hands on her hips, in formidably tall shoes.

Then, abruptly as if someone had cut her marionette strings, Alex dropped into a chair across from TJ. Their uneaten lunches remained on the table between them. Alex pushed them aside with her lips curled in mild disgust.

"New plan. I'll call Henry, ask the judge for a recess, and try to keep you out of jail. We'll explain your earlier plea and story as fear based, and now you've come to realize the error of your ways blah blah blah. At least you did this now and not when you were on the stand or after you'd testified. Talk about eleventh hour."

She rose, and to Rain she suddenly looked old. The makeup around her eyes was caking into furrows she hadn't noticed before. "Not that it matters," Alex asked, through a weary sigh. "But why now? Why this sudden attack of conscience?"

TJ did not reply, only looked across the table at Rain with wounded, sunken eyes.

Alex shrugged. "Well. I'm going to my office to call Henry and the judge. Stay put until I come back for you."

Rain checked her watch. She wanted to drive away and disappear. She wanted to drive to Gran's house and have her be there, give her a hug, bake her cookies, and put her to bed with a book. She even would have preferred driving to see Angie and Ricky and Fawn and the baby and ask Stone to play his acoustic guitar like he used to when they were kids, singing the sweet Simon and Garfunkel tunes she loved, just to humor her, because he hated them.

TJ broke the silence. "You should sit. You'll make your back hurt."

"I don't feel like it."

"I'm really sorry," he said, the words coming out thick and slow, as if he had to force them through layers of muck. He turned in his chair to face her. "I didn't mean for any of this."

"I'm sure you didn't."

"I . . . She . . ."

Rain almost shouted, "Don't bother," but stopped herself. She was curious to hear what he'd say.

He cleared his throat, hard, twice. "She tempted me. I swear, she was the one who . . ."

"Stop," she said then. "Just don't."

When he spoke again, minutes later, as Rain watched the geese in the fake pond outside, his voice was lower, and tired. "She thought I was a hero."

The geese continued to spin their lazy ovals. The air-conditioning kicked in, filling the dead air with a white-noise rush Rain was grateful for. She walked closer to her husband, who sat slumped at the conference table, head in his hands. "And that made you happy? That was what you wanted?"

He looked at her with a genuine tenderness she hadn't seen in a long time, hadn't even noticed when it disappeared. Right now, he wore the same look in the wedding picture in their bedroom. Rain remembered that day, and how beautiful everything was, and how she hadn't known it in the moment, so caught up she was in the order of events and whether her stockings were itchy and whether her veil was falling off.

As she looked back at the ruins of the person she used to love best, she vowed to recognize those moments when they happened. Be present in the moment, Beverly was always saying.

TJ finally answered, "At least I didn't feel like a failure."

Alex strode in with a sheaf of papers and a grave expression. Rain said, "And how do you feel now?"

47

Morgan had fled to the bathroom at lunch, not knowing where else to hide from reporters.

She knew they weren't supposed to name her in the paper, but they'd been bugging her parents and the prosecutor for a comment. Over lunch, it was only a matter of time that one, or maybe all of them, would start hounding her.

She had slammed her way into a stall, slipped the lock into place, then plopped down on the toilet lid, pants up, head in hands.

People came and went, using the other stalls, not noticing she was in there the whole time.

She caught bits of gossip floating over the stall door.

"She looks so young."

"I can't believe she's sitting on his side."

"That must be killing her parents. Can

you imagine?"

Then later, a new pair of women. "What do you suppose he was thinking?"

"He wasn't thinking. Except with his dick. Hey, did you notice? She looks like his wife."

"Creepy."

"You said it."

The door of the stall was a dull polished steel, an attempt to foil graffiti. Morgan could see a muddy reflection of herself. She could almost see this blurry image morph back and forth from herself to his wife. His wife, Rain, who was having a baby.

Morgan had snuck a peek at her just before the lunch break, while turning around and pretending to be fishing for something in her purse. Rain's hair had been falling around her face as she drooped forward like a wilting flower. She was alone — a barrier of empty space existed around her even in the crowded court. Then she'd shifted in her seat and looked up, brushing her hair back from her face. Her hand was shaking.

Then Morgan remembered the beautiful bride in the wedding picture on the wall, how he practically rammed her through the wall having sex right there, the slippers under the bed, the nightgown peeking from the drawer, getting dumped off in the parking lot like a hooker.

Rain did look like her, that long sweep of dark hair. They were both thin. Of course, Morgan had that scar. Maybe that's in the end why he was still with his wife . . . Morgan was damaged.

All morning, she'd kept trying to tell herself that the lawyer would say anything to get him out of trouble, that's all. He'd smiled at her; he loved her. This was all just a game to get this over with, without him going to jail . . .

At the price of this painful spectacle with her family at the center, her mother's business trashed and in fact ruined forever because her mother had sold it. The boys in trouble at school because Jared fell in with the potheads, and Connor getting in fights for her sake.

Her whole life she never wanted to cause trouble — all she ever tried to do was stay out of the way — and here she caused the most trouble possible, short of going to jail herself.

She knew he was going to testify soon. He would get up and tell his version of a story with her starring as a crazy Lolita, with her mother sitting right there in court. He would say these things so he wouldn't have to go to jail, wouldn't have to admit he'd done anything wrong. He was going to serve her up on a platter to save his own ass, truth be told. She'd been telling herself it didn't matter. She just wanted him out of trouble, whatever it took.

But as she listened to those people tell lies about her in front of her family and the whole town, she'd begun to wonder why he couldn't have just admitted it. To protect her. To protect his wife. She'd been squeezing her hands into fists all morning, as if she could hold on to the memories of being with him, of being in love. But like water, it was all running through her fingers, faster the harder she gripped.

Morgan jumped off the toilet and slammed her way out of the stall, sprinting back toward the courtroom and asking the first uniform she saw where to find the prosecutor.

Henry nodded on his side of the desk in a small conference room somewhere in the back of the courthouse. Morgan had just explained to him that she would testify if he needed her to.

She didn't want him to ask why, because she couldn't have answered with any kind of logic. A rhythmic headache was pounding behind her eyes, and she just wanted it all to be over, so she could be somewhere else, someone else, with normal problems.

Morgan's parents were sitting behind her, looking at her askance with wary hope. It made her sick to see their expressions, so she focused on the prosecutor's reassuring calm with his lightly folded hands and smooth voice.

"I am very glad to hear this, Morgan, and not just because I'm glad you feel able to tell the truth under oath. I'm glad because it looks like you won't have to."

"What do you mean?"

"I mean his lawyer just called to say he's changing his plea to guilty."

Her mother shouted, "Oh, thank God," at the same moment her father demanded to know why.

Henry continued, "I can't say why, and I don't much care. I got the impression from reading between the lines of his attorney's phrasing that his wife may have had something to do with his sudden honesty. But this is still important that you've said this, Morgan, because we have some more leverage now. I guarantee you the number one thing on his mind is staying out of jail and off the sex offender registry. His lawyer will act like we're desperate to get a guilty plea and hold out for a slap on the wrist. Now, we can hold his feet to the fire with your willingness to testify."

"But . . . I mean, I want to say what really happened. I want to be honest. But . . . does he have to go to jail? He didn't hurt me, I swear. He never forced me to do anything."

Her eyes filled up, and she put her fists to her eyes, trying to force the tears back in, muttering, "Dammit."

Henry pulled a handkerchief out of his pocket and handed it across the desk. Morgan almost laughed through her tears at his gentility. He probably proposed to his wife on one knee, too, and danced a waltz at his wedding.

"The hurt doesn't have to be physical or obvious," Henry said, with the gentle tones of a father talking to a young child. "He did something he should not have, and it has affected you and your family greatly, in many ways, not just the obvious ones, and in some ways that might not become obvious for a long time."

"I loved him," she said into the handkerchief.

"I know you did," Henry said. "And to my mind, that's just about the very worst part."

He looked up from her, addressing her parents. "The judge will recess for the afternoon, and Alexandra and I will start to hammer out a plea agreement. I suggest you all go home, the sooner the better, because as soon as court comes back into session and the judge recesses the trial, the reporters are going to swarm. They'll want a comment. I'm not going to comment, and I'm sure Alex won't, either. That'll leave you three to pester. There's a back door out of the courthouse. Joe, I suggest you bring your car around. I'll escort the ladies through the building."

Her dad stood up and went right out the door without a further word. Morgan rose to her feet, staggering slightly with the swimmy sensation in her head, not having eaten any lunch. Her mother caught her elbow. She tried to hand the handkerchief back to Henry, but he waved it away. "No, no. I have plenty. I buy them in bulk."

Henry walked them out of the building to the back lot, through the employees' entrance. Before he opened the door, he cautioned, "And don't answer the phone for any number you don't recognize. If any press ambushes you, send them to me for comment."

With this he swung open the door. Morgan had this heady notion of feeling like a movie star for just a moment, dodging pa-

parazzi. With a darting glance around, worried about reporters who might guess where they were, she trotted to the car, which was idling near a big garbage bin. She stopped at the door to the car, happening to look up.

There he was. Performing a similar maneuver, helping his wife into his car, the very same one where they'd been together when the cops banged on the window, when his warm hands had been fumbling with the button on her jeans . . .

Their eyes locked for a moment, then he looked down with no change in expression. Like she was no one.

She'd asked to be allowed to eat in her room and was granted this permission. Her parents were now behaving gingerly around her, and she both hated it and was grateful all at once.

She'd seen this before, with Connor in a mood, or for Jared if someone had teased him that day about his palsy.

Morgan ate her bowl of plain white rice, all she'd wanted, all she could stomach. She was cross-legged on her bed, listening to nothing but the click of her fork against the bowl. She tried to remember feeling loved by him, because she certainly had. She knew she had.

She pulled out her poetry notebook and looked over some of what she'd written.

Crackling, sparking
Dangerous they say
But heat is warm and
Life
Burning away all that is old dead dry
~
Crush me till
I'm flat, gone
Part of you
What I want
Part of you
~
Thought I was so good before
Dead more like it
But the dead are
No trouble at all
Quiet, obedient, still
~
Does the music box dancer
Twirl 'neath the lid?
Or is there
No room
In the airless dark
So she waits
For the hand to
Split the black with

Brief harsh light

~

Lift me up throw me down
Spin me round and round
Spread me out crush me small
Seize me when I sprawl
Stroke my skin brush my hair
Do whatever you think fair
Just never
Let
Go

Morgan frowned. Reading them back now — she didn't typically read her poems again, just set them free in the pages — they sure didn't sound like verses written by someone happy in love.

She checked her e-mail on her phone and saw a message from someone she didn't recognize. Henry's warning echoed in her mind, quickly overrun by trampling curiosity.

It was a random free e-mail account, from a Teresa Jane. Her breathing sputtered as she remembered that was his code name in her contacts of her old phone.

It was good to see you on my side today. I can't tell you how good. I now hear though that you are prepared to testify if

I don't change my plea. You know I never hurt you, I never made you do anything you didn't want to do. You're almost eighteen, as you said to me many times, you're not a child and don't deserve to be treated like one.

We can't have a future if I'm in prison. You hold my fate in your hands.

You are so special to me.

She felt a sinking sensation, but not scary or sad. It was comfortable and soft, this settling back to a familiar space. She entertained a delicious flush at a memory of him lowering her onto his brother's big soft bed. A future, he'd written.

A gentle knock on her door. She tucked the phone under her pillow.

"Yeah?"

Her mother slid in through the door, and she carried a bowl of ice cream. "Dessert?"

Morgan shrugged. She accepted the cold bowl in her hands, trying to make sense of what she'd just read.

"Mom?"

Dinah sat on the bed next to Morgan, but not too close, she noticed. "How do you know when someone loves you?"

"When you don't have to ask that question."

Morgan rolled her eyes. "Just like that, huh?"

Her mother shrugged. "Why should it be harder than that?" Then she leaned forward and put her hand on Morgan's knee. "I hope you have never once doubted that I love you. No matter how mad you ever got, no matter how mad I got."

Morgan shook her head. "No. I didn't."

She noticed that her mother's gaze had caught on something. Morgan followed it down. The poetry.

Dinah cocked her head. "May I?"

Morgan shrugged. Just that morning she'd been prepared to sit in a public courtroom and talk about sex with her teacher. Letting her mother read her poetry could be no worse.

Dinah pulled it toward her. Morgan spooned the cold blandness of her vanilla ice cream and waited for the freak-out.

Dinah leafed through it with a serious crease in her forehead, but silently. Occasionally she blinked rapidly and drew back the tiniest bit.

Once, she read a few lines aloud, in a reverent tone tinged with bafflement.

". . . bursts the seam of the sky, . . . setting alight the whole golden world."

When she set the notebook down, she

looked up at Morgan and said, “I never knew . . . These are good, Mo.”

Her ice cream had melted into soup. Morgan set the bowl on her desk. “I thought you’d be like, weirded out. Some of that is kind of weird.”

Dinah shook her head. “It wasn’t so easy to read the ones about . . . all of this, lately. Him. But that’s different. . . . I wish you’d shared them before.”

“It would have felt weird. Plus . . . you always make such a big thing of everything. I didn’t want a big deal out of it.”

“Like what big deal?”

“Oh, you know, like buying me writing magazines and clipping out poetry contest entries, and researching which colleges have writing programs . . .”

Her mother frowned, and Morgan could see her effort in reining back in what she wanted to blurt out.

Her mom bit her lip, and said, “I try to be supportive . . .”

“I know, and it’s better than, like, condemning it. But it’s too much. It’s suffocating.”

“Sorry.”

“No, don’t be all sad and that. I’m not mad. I’m just trying to explain.”

“I know you are. Wish you’d said so before . . .”

“Would you have listened? I don’t know if you’ve noticed, but you’re a little stubborn.”

Dinah smirked down at her own lap. “Like a whale is a little big.”

Her mother was quiet then for a minute, and Morgan sighed into that quiet. She realized how seldom it was they were ever just together in a simple way. Like when they weren’t having a fight, or talking about the boys, or her mom was trying to have a big old “mother-daughter moment.”

Finally her mom spoke, and Morgan tried not to roll her eyes; of course she couldn’t just be quiet for five minutes. “Hon, can I ask you? No pressure, I’m just thinking. What do you want to do? When all this is done?”

“ ‘This’? The trial?”

“Yes.”

Morgan rested against the wall behind her and considered.

What popped up now in her memory was that look, in the courtroom parking lot. No, it wasn’t a look, even. Their eyes had met, but he might as well have been looking at the garbage bin for all the emotion that was there. She could have chalked that up to the presence of his wife, not wanting to get caught looking, but she was inside the car.

His wife could not have seen his face.

All these weeks she'd suffered alone, cut off from everyone, cut off from him, and he'd never tried to reach her. Even as she was called filthy names on the Internet, as someone carved a death threat into her locker, as her mother's business was trashed, as his lawyer stood up and described her like an unhinged, desperate slut . . . He was silent and let it all happen, all to save his own ass. But only now, as he realized she held the key, in his last desperate attempt to stay out of jail, he reached out and what did he do? Did he even ask how she was holding up?

"Mom, I have something to tell you. He e-mailed me just now. Him. Mr. Hill."

Dinah jumped off the bed, and Morgan could read the signs of fury in her clenched fists, forward leaning posture . . . Then she shook herself like waking from a dream and sat back down. Her mom put the bowls on the floor and hugged her. "We'll call Henry in a minute. I'm so sorry this happened to you. So very sorry I let you down."

Morgan pushed her back, firmly, but she hoped not roughly. "Mom. You have got to stop doing that. I'm a person and I make decisions. Stupid ones, I guess, but I make them. Me. And so do Jared and Connor.

We're people, not puppets."

"How did you get so wise?"

"Yeah. Really fricking wise."

Dinah leaned in for another hug. Morgan could smell her mother's shampoo, and she breathed deeply, realizing that someday she'd miss this smell. At college, if she ever managed to go, or on her own somewhere, or . . . someday when her mom would be gone. She made a mental note to buy the same kind, wherever she went, whatever she was going to do, when "this" was at last all over.

48

And just like that, it was over, and Dinah exhaled, as if she'd been holding her breath for months now. She tipped her head up as if she were in a grand cathedral to thank God for this, though her gaze rested on flecked ceiling tiles instead of stained glass.

And then she promised herself to start going to Mass again.

TJ Hill had stood up in court with his lawyer, changing his plea to guilty as charged.

Excited whispers had swelled through the courtroom, and the judge tapped his gavel twice. The judge had asked him if he was sure. Then the judge had asked — his long, severe face the very picture of indignant irritation — why the sudden change of heart.

TJ Hill had mumbled so quietly that the judge demanded that he speak up.

"I was in panic mode before." He shifted from foot to foot. "That's all I can say."

The judge tipped back in his large judge chair, tented his fingers under his chin, and observed, "Quite a long panic, I'd say. Bond remains in effect, and you will report for sentencing on June 26." The sentencing was part of the plea deal, however, and thus a formality. Dinah had already been briefed: three years in prison, though with time off for good behavior he could be up for parole in a little over two years.

Another crack of the gavel and that was it.

Dinah squeezed the hands of Joe on one side, and Morgan on the other, and they stood up almost at the same instant. Henry turned around with a jubilant smile, reaching over the barrier to shake Joe's hand. Dinah leaned over for a hug, too. Morgan hung back shyly, her curtain of hair falling around her, and Dinah sensed the burst of a flashbulb and she knew what would be on the front page the next day.

They hung back while TJ filed out of the courtroom, trailed by his lawyer and a phalanx of press. After that crowd had surged past, Dinah locked eyes with Rain, across the aisle. She'd sat on his side of the room, but she had not followed him out. They traded a look, but that was all.

For all anyone knew, they were strangers,

with every reason to hate and distrust each other.

Henry was speaking now to Morgan, so Dinah looked back to their tight circle. He said, "I'm proud of you that you turned over that e-mail to me and didn't give in to his manipulation. That was very brave."

Morgan wouldn't answer at first, then she said something very quietly, in Henry's direction. He whispered back in her ear and gave a sad smile to Dinah.

"Let me walk out with you," Henry said. "They'll want a comment from someone."

"May I?" Dinah said. "It's all over now, and we can't hurt the case or anything, right?"

Henry frowned. "As you wish. But whatever you say could be in 48-point type tomorrow and repeated on the news in a constant loop. You do get a victim impact statement at sentencing."

"I'll be fine."

And so they walked out of the utilitarian courthouse onto the plaza, where benches no one ever used flanked a flagpole and a memorial to Arbor Valley's veterans.

The reporters moved like one organism from TJ and his lawyer over to the four of them and began shouting questions. Henry answered first in the practiced, dignified cadence of one who had given many, many interviews.

Joe made like a statue. He'd put on his stern assistant principal face and shielded Morgan under his arm. Morgan looked down at the ground, letting her hair form a barrier between herself and the rest of the world.

Dinah cleared her throat, not listening to any particular question, and their attention turned to her. They crowded around — about five of them plus a couple of cameramen, Arbor Valley wasn't that big — but there were enough that for the moment, they screened out everything else in her view.

"We're pleased at the outcome, but not how long it took for TJ Hill to tell the truth. I also want us as a community to stop and think about what it means to be a child. Teenagers today act very jaded and sophisticated, don't they? Without ever saying it out loud, we all know they have sex, and they drink, and smoke, and use credit cards and interact online, hold jobs, watch TV shows where the actors are having sex with everyone all the time, and all the other things we as adults do every day." Dinah sensed their fidgeting, noted one snappily dressed anchor lady checking her watch. She rushed her speech a bit. "We have let them grow up so fast that I can see why it's tempting to say a seventeen-year-old is the same as an adult. It's only a few months, right? What difference does it make? But I dare you." She pointed at them, addressing the press specifically, who would carry this story to the town, who would portray their family. "Think back on the things you did, when you were seventeen and thought you were immortal. Consider just one reckless thing, and now imagine that you didn't get lucky and come out unscathed. Imagine instead that the absolute worst happened, and not only that, everyone knew about it, and wrote about it, and commented on it in a public forum, and that the public forum where everyone commented will be preserved forever and ever in some kind of digital archive. The law knows, the court knew, where to assign blame for this exploitation of a child who has not yet matured into the person she's trying to be. I only wish the rest of you had been as wise."

There was a beat of silence as scribbling went on, and jockeying of cameras, as the reporters with shining, ravenous eyes were plotting their follow-up questions.

Dinah took that opportunity to forge through the lot of them as if they were no more than long grasses in a field. They parted in front of her, and with her family in tow, Dinah marched unimpeded to their car.

"He's right there," muttered Morgan from under Joe's arm. Joe stopped, and they all stopped.

Joe turned to face him. TJ was across the plaza with that slick lady lawyer. Joe bellowed in his best assistant principal voice, but with his accent in full glory, "Don't ever go near my daughter again, you fucking low-life pervert!"

Henry squeezed Joe's arm with a small, warning shake of the head. Joe stopped before any specific threats were spoken out loud.

TJ was already scuttling away, head bowed as if under fire. Dinah noted with a cocked eyebrow that Rain was walking to a different car.

Good for you, Dinah thought. *You go, girl.*

It was night, and the eleven o'clock news was coming on. The kids were all in their rooms, supposedly asleep, but probably not. Anyway, the next day everyone was going to the beach. Joe and Dinah had decided on the way home. They all deserved some stupid family fun with Popsicles and beach volleyball and Lake Huron, miles away where no one knew them.

The laptop was open with the newspaper story on it. It wouldn't be in newsprint until the next day, but the online version had come up merely a couple of hours later. TEACHER PLEADS GUILTY TO SEX WITH STUDENT read the headline. Dinah had been both happy and queasy.

Dinah and Joe were in sweatpants in the den, each with an open beer. They clinked bottles. "To justice, at last," Dinah said.

Joe grunted.

The TV anchor intoned an introduction to the story with the guilty plea, then said, "And there was an interesting reaction from Joe Monetti, the girl's father, and just retired assistant principal at Arbor Valley High, where Hill had been teaching."

The camera cut to Joe in all his raging glory, though his f-bomb was bleeped.

"Way to upstage me," Dinah said, chuckling.

"Yeah. That had been pent up for a while."

"You sounded like Tony Soprano."

"I wish. He'd be in a suitcase in the woods."

"Now, now."

"Nah, I know. A guy can dream, eh?"

The clip of Dinah only showed her saying

that she was happy with the result but not how long it took. "Sheesh. They cut out all that great material about kids growing up too fast."

" 'Course. It was too long for a sound bite. Now, if you'd cursed him out . . ."

The newspaper had buried her comments, too, only a few words and a clumsy paraphrase, way toward the end of the story.

Dinah stretched. "Now what? I feel like for months I've waited for this, and now it's over, and I just feel . . . hollow."

"I'm out of a job, you're selling the Den. We've gotta figure out what Morgan's gonna do next year, poor kid."

"She got accepted everywhere she applied."

"She wanted to go to Boston," Joe said, his voice dreamy with memory of a time when college tuition seemed to be their only Morgan problem.

"Yeah, poor kid. Wish we could have said yes. Coped with the distance. Loans, scholarships, maybe . . ." Dinah said.

"I don't think it would have solved everything . . ."

"Yeah, I know. Not that simple. Nothing ever is."

Joe took a long pull of his beer and nodded solemnly.

"I have an idea, though," Dinah said. "It's sort of crazy."

"Hell, crazy is the new normal. I'm all ears."

"Wait . . ." Dinah had glanced at the laptop and hit "refresh" on the story, idly, not really thinking, when the comments section lit up with reactions. She smirked and handed Joe the laptop. Together they huddled over it, reading.

Hooray! So glad to hear that he came clean and justice was done. About time. Now we don't have to worry about him getting his job back and preying on other students. — Avfan32

Just goes to show that a handsome face doesn't make him a nice guy. — Bert

I hope he goes away for a long, long time. Sick bastard. — Anonymous

I don't believe it. I think he just plead to make it go away so he can get his life back. All it takes is an accusation and you're life is over, people. Think about it. — JJ862

JJ862: What the hell is wrong with you?

The cops busted them together and she wasn't wearing a top. That's not innocent behavior. Maybe you like to screw young girls, too? Does it hit close to home, pal? Plus, learn to use proper grammer. It's your, not you're.

Joe sputtered laughter into his fist. "I love it when people correct someone's grammar and then spell grammar wrong."

Dinah skimmed the responses. Other than the mysterious JJ862, the comment thread was full of indignant outrage against the monstrous aggressor TJ Hill. "You know, just by sheer numbers, at least some of these people had to have been saying nasty things about Morgan before. Or they were at least silent while everyone else was."

"Mob mentality," Joe said through a sigh. "As old as the hills."

"Now everyone will say they knew it all along. I'd bet the house on that." Dinah snapped the laptop closed. "Whaddya say we get the hell out of Dodge?"

"What?" Joe rubbed his temples and yawned. "Dodge?"

"Not exactly. Arbor Valley. Let's get the hell out of here."

49

"Don't do this," TJ said, tears making tracks down his face, as Rain packed a suitcase with maternity clothes only, now that her belly was too big to hide, now that it no longer mattered. "You can't leave me now, before the sentencing, when they'll haul me off to jail. Jail, Rain! They're going to lock me up!"

Rain stepped past him into the bathroom and put her face cream and basic makeup into her travel case.

"Look at me!" he shouted and seized her upper arm.

Rain froze in the act of putting mascara in her bag. TJ was behind her in the mirror. She gave him a look through their reflections that made him let go abruptly, as if she'd grown too hot to the touch.

"I'm sorry," he said. "I'm sorry, I didn't . . . I didn't mean that. I didn't mean any of it. I need help, something's wrong with me."

At this, Rain cocked an eyebrow at him through the mirror.

"It was like a spell or something," he said. "She cast a spell . . . No, that's not what I mean. I know, it's my own fault. It was like I was trying to go back in time, to when things between us weren't so complicated . . ."

Rain went back into the bedroom, put the travel case in her suitcase.

She walked into the little yoga studio, which she'd always assumed they'd turn into a nursery, her yoga practice moving to wherever she found space and time, in the nooks of her new motherhood. She crouched in a squat and the baby punched, as if objecting to the tighter space. She smiled and rolled up her mat, affixing the carrying strap.

TJ had followed her. "Maybe that doesn't make sense. I don't understand it either. But it was so different with her, and we never talked about fertility, or babies . . ."

Rain stood up suddenly at this and braced herself on the wall. She noticed that TJ had not moved to steady her. He was looking down, still spinning his tales.

Rain pushed past him again, back up the stairs, her calf muscles already tired from last night's practice with Beverly, during which each woman had apologized to the other and a tentative peace had been established.

While rolling up their mats, Rain had strained that peace by announcing her intention to quit. Beverly was taken aback and at first thought Rain was resigning in a fit of pique, but Rain finally explained she was tired of faking an earnest interest in chakras. She just liked the stretching, the strength, but the rest of it was all an act for her. She'd said, "I'm tired of acting."

Beverly had nodded and asked a version of the question TJ was asking now, "But what are you going to do?"

Upstairs again, TJ was facing away from her on the bed, face in his hands. "You're going to stay with my brother, aren't you? Mr. and Mrs. Perfect." He sounded about ten years old, and Rain wondered if he realized that. *Not likely,* she answered herself right away.

Insight was not one of TJ's gifts. Never had been, really. Maybe not a gift of hers, either, since it had taken her this long to figure it out.

Rain added a newly purchased journal to the suitcase. She'd decided to dedicate her journal to the baby from this day forward and to write only things the baby might want to read someday. No doubt, eventually, she would have to explain to her child whatever truth there was to tell about his father. She could already imagine herself choosing words like *terrible mistake* and *he was not himself,* phrases that she'd been hearing from TJ for days, now. But she wanted all this — however it was told — to be a pebble dropping into a pool of happy warm memories. Ripples would occur but then fade and smooth out again. This was her constant prayer, second only to the health of her baby.

Rain walked around to the bed where he now sat. She removed her ring with some difficulty; her fingers were pudgy with excess water. The band left a reddened imprint. She held it out to him in her fingertips.

He looked up at her, saw the ring, and choked out a sob.

Her heart folded in on itself like burning paper. Just days ago, she'd walked into a courtroom prepared to lie under oath to save him.

TJ ignored the ring in her outstretched hand and stroked the side of her belly. He pulled her into the circle of his arms and laid his head on their child.

Rain lifted her free hand to stroke his hair.

"I love you," he said, his voice resonating through her body. She pictured their baby turning toward the sound. "I always did. I never stopped. I was just . . . I didn't mean it, I need help . . . Please help me through this . . . You hold my fate in your hands . . ."

Rain snapped herself up rigid.

The evening after the trial recessed, TJ's lawyer had come to the house, waving a piece of paper, sputtering with angry disbelief that TJ had ruined any hope of a favorable deal by e-mailing Morgan. When Alex smacked the paper down on the kitchen table and shouted at TJ that he could be facing charges of witness intimidation, Rain had pulled it toward herself and read the printout. *"You hold my fate in your hands."*

Rain stepped back, breaking the embrace. He still would not take the ring. Rain regarded its delicate circle. She flung it across the room, where it bounced with a thin *tink* off the vanity mirror above the dresser.

She scooped up her suitcase and yoga mat and descended the stairs.

The suitcase was heavy, but not backbreaking, and she was feeling rather spry. In fact, Rain was grateful to be trailing the suitcase behind her, because it provided a barrier between herself and her increasingly desperate husband, whose feet were now stomping down the stairs.

"I demand to know where you're going," he said. "You have to tell me; I have a right to know where you're taking my child."

This gave Rain a chill — another glimpse into the future.

She was halfway to the door when he snatched the suitcase out of her hand. Rain hitched her purse and yoga mat higher on her shoulder and stared at him. He was panting as if he'd run a distance.

"I won't let go of this."

Rain shrugged and turned toward the door. Greg would pick it up for her if she asked. Hell, the cops could come get it.

He shouted, his voice wild and cracked: "I'll kill myself! I swear, I'll take all the pills in the house. I'll slit my wrists. I can't go on alone . . ." He was gripping her suitcase so hard Rain felt a flash of worry he might swing it at her.

Rain stayed near the door. She reached into her purse and removed her cell phone, dialing a number she'd used so often these last months. "Greg? This is Rain. Your brother says he's going to kill himself. You might want to check on him. . . . No, I'm not at the house." She raised her eyes to meet her husband's. "I don't live there anymore."

She clicked off the call and dropped the phone back into her purse.

TJ, his mouth dropped open, his skin white but for red smears of flush on his cheeks, had dropped her suitcase handle. She stepped closer, picked her suitcase back up, and walked out the door.

Brock bounced with his whole little body, every ounce of him glowing with glee and joy over something as simple as peekaboo. Rain closed her eyes again, scrunching them up tight, then gasping as she flung her eyes open, eyebrows up, mouth wide. He let out a gleeful shriek, and Rain had to grip him hard under the arms so he wouldn't fall right out of her lap.

Angie was boiling water for tea. It was Lipton decaf, not any kind of fancy tea like Beverly might give her, but Rain was grateful for the gesture toward preparing something she liked. Stone was in another kitchen chair, fiddling with his guitar, picking out chords.

Fawn exclaimed, "Oh, let me do your hair! Can I do your hair? Please?"

Her sister clasped her hands under her chin, and Rain chuckled. "Sure, why not."

Fawn was attending cosmetology school at night. Stone, saying not a word, played the opening strains of "Beauty School Dropout" from Grease.

Rain sputtered laughter, and Stone winked. "What?" Fawn demanded, musicals never having been an interest of hers.

"Here you go!" sang out Angie. "I put an ice cube in it to cool it off for you a bit."

Angie traded tea for Brock, swinging her grandson high over her head. Fawn had disappeared up the stairs for her supplies.

Rain wondered, while blowing on her tea, what the odd feeling was, and then named it: surprised contentment.

She'd fled this house as a teenager, going to stay with her steady, calm Gran. After college, she'd lived in dumpy apartments, then married TJ, never even once considering coming back here to live.

And yet, here she was. Dog plopped his heavy head on top of her foot. It was like wearing one giant fuzzy black slipper.

Fawn clattered down the stairs with her arms full of curling irons and rollers and hair elastics and spray, and Stone switched to thrumming the bleak chords of a horror movie sound track.

"Shut up, buttface," Fawn retorted, but mildly, barely paying any attention, as she set about pulling a brush through Rain's long hair.

"When was the last time you cut this mess? Your split ends have split ends."

"My beauty regimen hasn't exactly been a priority. What with my husband screwing a teenager and all."

Stone quit strumming, Fawn quit brushing, and Angie quit tossing Brock.

Rain knew she should probably lighten the awkward moment she caused, but instead she sipped her bitter tea, too tired to do all the work anymore.

The door opened, and Ricky loped in, breaking into a grin. "There's my girl! There's all my kids. Damn, if this don't make me happy." He strode across the creaky floor and planted a kiss on Rain's cheek. He smelled like the aggressive strawberry air freshener he used in his car to cover up the cigarette smoke. "I'm sorry as hell for the reason, but I'm so glad you're here."

"Me, too, Pop," she replied. "I am, too."

Fawn had resumed brushing. "If I ever get my hands on that asshole, I will twist his head off like the stem off an apple."

"I never did like him," pronounced Angie, now bouncing Brock on her shoulder and pacing the small kitchen.

Rain frowned. "I thought you said I was lucky to have him."

"That's before I actually saw you when you were married to him. You were lifeless."

"Lifeless?"

Ricky took up the thread of conversation while Angie tickled Brock's chin. "Yeah, you were always fussing over him so much you barely paid any attention to yourself."

"Like this hair," Fawn interjected. "Not gonna cut it just now and get hair all over the floor, but promise you'll come to class with me tomorrow and I'll trim it up. Maybe some soft layers? Bangs, even. You've got the face for it."

"Forget the hair, go back to lifeless. And if I was lifeless, why didn't anyone say anything?"

"I did, once," Fawn said, and Rain felt the heat of some kind of curling iron behind her. "And you bit my head off. Said you guys were just tired and I was judging and anyway I was one to talk."

"I said that?"

"Yep. I remember the quote. 'You are one to talk.' Cuz I was still dating Davy."

Rain bit her lip as she remembered Davy, a dropout who had several DUIs to his name.

"I'm sorry."

"Well, you were right about Davy, anyhow, as it turned out. No big whoop."

Angie said, "Hey, Ricky, can you go change this little stinker?"

Ricky shrugged. "Why not? C'mere, mister . . ."

Angie plopped down across from Rain. She was wearing a denim miniskirt and a red tank top. She was kicking a plastic flip-flop halfway off her foot and popped a piece of gum in her mouth. "Nicotine gum. Finally quitting, if you can believe that. Hon, we did try to say stuff a couple of times, but we gave up quick when we could see how deep you were in. We figured eventually you'd come around."

"Took long enough," Rain muttered.

"Well, if I'd had any idea it would have taken all this, I might have made like that guy in *The Graduate* and screamed from the choir loft," Angie said, to which Stone began picking out the melody for "Mrs. Robinson."

Rain's tea had cooled too much to drink. Her head was warm from whatever Fawn was doing back there. "I'm surprised you all want me back here, if I was so lifeless and defensive."

"Honey, we knew it wasn't about you." Angie put her hand over Rain's wrist. It shocked her that Angie's skin was looking papery over her ropy veins. "You've always been the perfectionist in the crowd, and we knew you wouldn't give up just because we said so. You'd have to learn it on your own."

Rain closed her eyes and let her head relax into Fawn's rhythmic pulling and curling. One thing she'd forgotten, all those years since she left this home, so glad to put the turbulence and noise and squabbling behind her, was the forgiveness. Angie and Ricky may have thrown plates, but they would always forgive each other. And they were forgiving, too, in the sense of forgiving a bad mood in each other as well as themselves. These people couldn't carry a grudge any more than they could carry a car.

Rain contrasted that with Gran's exacting, black-and-white morality, and for the first time, she felt something less than idolatry for her grandmother.

"Mom? Did it hurt when I moved in with Gran?"

"Oh, like hell, it sure did," Angie replied. "I cried for days."

Ricky was coming down the stairs with Brock. "I can vouch for that. I offered to drag your ass back but Ang said no."

"I'm sorry," Rain said, putting her hand over her baby, imagining what it would feel like to have that child choose to walk away from her, long before adulthood.

"Don't be. I knew you needed it."

Stone started singing and strumming a Rolling Stones refrain, "You can't always get what you want . . . you get what you need . . ."

Angie wheeled on him. "Oh, for Chrissake, knock it off!"

But she was grinning, and so was Stone, and indeed so was Rain herself, marveling at the simple pleasure in a smile that was genuine, not an act to lift up someone else, someone all too happy to be lifted.

50

Morgan spotted him in the park and sped up to a trot. His hands were stuffed in his pockets, and he was looking down as if trying not to appear like he was waiting for anything in particular, least of all her.

But it had been too long, and she could no longer spare the extra ten seconds to amble as if she were too cool to hurry.

She flung herself at him. He seemed to resist her affection, and who could blame him?

"Ethan, I'm so sorry."

He seemed to relax only by one degree. Morgan snuffled into his shirt: "Teenager ruins life, friendship, career, and family. Film at eleven."

Ethan hugged her back at last. "Hey, it wasn't so bad. It's not like you burned down the house."

Morgan chuckled and set him back at arm's length. "Probably only because I didn't have any matches."

He began to walk, and she joined him. They were on a bark chip path on the perimeter of the park. Joggers flew past them, and the June breeze through the leaves sounded like muted applause as they passed.

"Are you okay?" Ethan asked.

"Yeah. I'm okay, I guess. Mom says I should probably see a shrink. I don't want to, but it will make her feel better so I probably will."

Ethan shrugged. "Couldn't hurt. Ask him how to come out of the closet for me. It'll be like, buy one analysis, get another one free."

"Haven't talked to your parents yet?"

"I think they know, and that's kind of the worst part. We're all just waiting to see who cracks first."

"Tell them in the car so they can't run away or something. Just go, 'Hey, let's stop for ice cream and oh, yeah, I'm gay.' "

"I actually considered taping it on the back of my mortarboard. 'Hi Mom, I'm gay.' "

For a few more steps they walked in silence. Ethan put his arm around her shoulders. "I can still do this, right? Because we're friends?"

"Sure." Morgan slipped her arm around his waist and leaned into him. Her heart didn't pound with excitement, and for this she was glad, not only for having gotten over her crush, but for the fact she could be this close to a man, this affectionate, and have it mean nothing more than what was obvious.

"What are you going to do now?" Ethan asked.

"This is the hard part. What I have to say now."

"Oh, great."

"We're moving to New Jersey."

Ethan stopped, which forced Morgan to stop and look up at him. "What?"

"Crazy, right? But my mom is selling the business, and they made Dad retire. The boys don't particularly like the school anyway. My dad has relatives in Jersey City. My uncle is a landlord and he's going to let us rent one of his houses for cheap until we get on our feet. I'm going to earn some credits at CCNY and if I do well enough maybe I can transfer to Boston U. Or somewhere else, I don't know. I'm not sure it matters so much anymore that I get away. I'll already be away."

"Damn."

"It's an adventure, right?"

"I would have thought you didn't have the

stomach for much more adventure."

Morgan grimaced. "I know. But look, what does Arbor Valley have for us anymore? From the twins born early and almost dying, my scar, now all this that happened . . . I'm gonna miss you like crazy, but the rest of it . . . And look, you're going away to Purdue anyway. We have Skype and we can text a million times a day and IM and everything."

"And Facebook."

"God, no. I'm boycotting Facebook. I don't need to sprawl my life out there for commentary anymore."

"I hear you."

They walked a few more steps, heard some more running feet, and paused while a couple blew past them, bark chips scattering as they zoomed past.

"So," Ethan said, "do you finally believe me that I didn't rat on you? Or did you just decide to forgive me?"

A flash of heat reddened Morgan's face. "Sorry. I feel like I should wear that on one of those signs, you know? That advertise businesses? 'Sorry everyone, for everything.' "

"I didn't mean that . . ."

"No, I know. I believe you. You'd be honest with me if you'd done it. And I wouldn't blame you if you had, anyway."

"Would you blame Britney?"

Morgan stopped so fast she almost tripped. "Oh my God, it was her?"

"I almost didn't tell you because you're friends, and I usually don't get in the middle of friends. But she's told a few people that it was her who found out and told the cops. She sounds almost proud." Ethan wrinkled up his face. "It's kinda sickening, actually."

"That bitch. I should have guessed."

"You were all set to forgive me for it."

"Because you would have done it out of love. She did it to be the center of attention. Or at least, that's what she's milking it for now. I mean, why else tell anybody at this point? When it's supposed to be over and I want to move on?"

"Guess she waited until after the trial because she didn't want to be called to the stand."

"For all we know she's making it up. It was anonymous, right? It could have been just a random stranger who saw me get in the car with a man and thought it looked suspicious."

Ethan wrapped his arm around her again and squeezed. They ambled on. He said, "I'm sure you're sick of it, and I'll never ask another thing again after this, I swear. But I can't stop thinking about this one thing."

"Fine. Go ahead."

"Why? Why him? You're a pretty girl and could have dated anybody."

"And you're such an expert, right?" Morgan had tried to say it playfully, but it came out with a sharpness that made Ethan pull his arm away.

He jammed his hands in his pockets. "You know what I mean."

Morgan folded her arms across her body as if she were chilled, though it was one of those honeyed early summer days that you try to remember in the dead cold of winter. Her mother had asked, so had Henry the prosecutor, so had kids at school who were bold or ignorant enough. She asked herself, many times since that day in court, what it was that made her briefly lose her mind.

"I don't really know. I think I liked who I was in his eyes."

"Who was that, then?"

"Myself as the adult I wanted to be. Grown up, wise, beautiful."

"I think you're all those things. So do lots of people."

"I didn't say it made sense." She stopped on the path, and he stopped ahead of her. The sun was behind him, and she stood in his shadow, shielded from its brightness. "You know? My mom keeps saying, Henry the prosecutor, everyone around me keeps saying I was a victim, manipulated, whatever."

Ethan put an arm around her shoulders, but Morgan shrugged it off. She continued, "But I feel really bad. I don't want to say it out loud, because I don't want to hear my mom go on about how wrong he was and all that, and he was responsible, whatever. But . . . Ethan, I feel awful. He was married. There's gonna be this baby, now, whose dad will be in jail . . . I didn't mean for that . . ."

"I know you didn't. Everybody knows you didn't mean that to happen."

"What the hell is wrong with me? And don't say nothing, because, yeah, obviously that's not true."

"Could I say anything that would fix it? Short of turning back time? I would if I could. You know that. So would your mom and dad."

"So would he, no doubt."

"No doubt. What's wrong with *him*? Now that right there is a good question."

Morgan shuddered. "I bet he was using me to have time-travel sex with a younger version of his wife. Did you see how much she looks like me? All that long dark hair." She grimaced.

Ethan reached behind her and gathered up her hair. "Ever thought of changing it?" He cocked his head this way and that. "You look so pretty this way. When people can actually see your face."

Morgan's first instinct: shake her hair away from him, pull it back across her face. She made herself freeze. She made herself look him in the eye. "Hey," she said. "You free for an hour or so?"

Ethan let go of her hair. "Considering you're moving, like, a thousand miles away? I'm free anytime you want."

51

This time, Dinah held her daughter's hand, and this time, Morgan let her.

Joe's warm hand was on Dinah's knee.

Behind her, of all places on the prosecution's side of the courtroom, were Gregory Hill and his pretty wife, their new baby dozing in her arms. Behind them sat Rain, next to an older woman Dinah didn't know. Maybe her mother.

The defense side of the courtroom was full mainly of gawkers and press.

TJ Hill looked like hell, and Dinah felt a reflexive maternal jolt at seeing him, unshaven, haggard, and pale. She turned to glance behind her. Rain's face was cool and still as a frozen pond. She was knitting.

Dinah wondered if she should call Rain after this was all done. She had yet to thank her for whatever it was she said or did that convinced her husband to at last give up his lies. And she suspected with a maternal hunch — that is, believed for certain, no proof required — that seeing Rain on that day at the wetlands, with her pregnant belly and obvious heartache, helped weaken the fortress of indignant outrage that Morgan had thrown up around herself. That had been a desperate gamble for Dinah, not only legally, but in the sense that Rain, if she'd been a conniving sort, could have done or said anything at all, just to hurt the girl who'd invaded her marriage.

One thing Dinah had learned about parenting the twins is that her hunches were unerring. She only had to remember to pay enough attention to notice them.

The judge gaveled court into session. Then it was time, and Morgan rose, smoothing her plain black skirt, and touching the ends of her newly shorn hair, which now just brushed her chin and set off her elegant cheekbones. Ethan had gone with her to the salon and convinced her she didn't need to hide behind her hair.

Morgan approached the podium between the two attorneys' tables, her smooth gait not betraying the fact she'd thrown up that morning or spent nearly thirty minutes trying on clothes, searching for the right outfit to tell the court, judge, and public what her teacher had done to her.

Dinah and Joe could have made victim impact statements as well, but they decided to afford Morgan the respect of speaking for herself.

Her daughter cleared her throat. "This is where I get up and say how Mr. Hill ruined my life. I'm supposed to talk to you about how, because of him, my mom's business got trashed with spray-painted slurs about me. How I missed days and days of school because I couldn't bear to walk the halls, how there was a death threat on my locker, how prom and graduation were an ordeal and should have been joyful. And all that's true, but that's not really the problem. See, people think I hated myself before, and that's why I let a teacher seduce me. That I have really low self-esteem because of this scar right here. But I had friends, I had a boyfriend before, a normal one. I did well in school and knew my parents loved me. It doesn't make sense, I know, but do people who get in trouble ever make any sense? Anyway, it's now, that's the hard part. When I remember my senior year, I'll remember being dumped off in a dark parking lot alone because his wife was coming home too early. I'll remember him unbuttoning my shirt in his car and then telling the police and the court and everybody that I'd taken my own clothes off because I was lust crazed and bonkers. I'll remember being crushed against a cold tile floor and how it hurt my back but he didn't seem to care."

Dinah gasped and bit her fist to silence herself. Joe was squeezing her hand so hard she had to whisper to him to ease up before he crushed it.

Morgan continued, "I know that's shocking. But if I got up here and acted like everything was fine, it would just be more lying, and that's what got us all into this mess. But this last thing is important to say, too. He did not ruin my life. Because I have a lot of life ahead, and I will not be defined by these few months. I'm taking my life back, and I'm taking my name back, so that this is the last time you'll write about me in the paper until I do something amazing that makes my family proud. This is the last time anyone will ever call me a victim."

With that, she whirled around to go back to her seat, her cheeks pink, her eyes bright.

Scattered applause burst out from distant corners of the room, gathering strength like the rain does ahead of a storm.

Morgan tried to muster a smile, but instead she sat down heavily on the hard bench next to Dinah and let herself be embraced.

■ ■ ■ ■

Rain was clapping.

She hadn't expected to. She was going to sit in the back with her knitting, and Beverly's quiet serenity beside her. She'd planned to tell everyone "No comment" and then go back to her mom's house where Stone and her dad were assembling the crib.

Though she did not hold Morgan any specific ill will — at least, not much — neither did she expect to applaud the girl who had slept with her husband.

But the detail about being crushed against the floor had made Rain drop her knitting in her lap.

How many times had TJ taken Rain herself so roughly? Slamming her against walls, tugging her down to the floor, heedless of rug burn or bruising. Rain would bite her lip and let him, though she never enjoyed it that way. And she was a wife, a grown woman! He'd done the same to this girl, and why would Rain have ever imagined differently? Why did she somehow imagine that their lovemaking — when it sprang to her mind, try as she might not to think about it — was loving and romantic? It made Rain want to vomit, too, the idea of this young girl not only manipulated by him but tossed around carelessly for his satisfaction.

She glanced around at the voracious interest written in the wide-eyed faces of the crowd. Rain put her hands across her belly and considered how long she'd shielded her baby from a nosy, rubbernecking public, a luxury Morgan's mother never had.

So when Morgan declared herself a victim no more, Rain started clapping before she knew what she was doing. Even as she realized reporters would notice and comment, she kept clapping, and with each slap of her palms, scraps of anger swept away on the current of sound.

Morgan leaned into her mother. Applause? For what? She wished it would stop. She shouldn't have gotten up to speak. She should have let her mother handle it.

When she'd written the speech, she hadn't anticipated how it would feel to have said it all out loud. Now she felt as naked as she had in the rehearsal room, the doctor's house, his car.

She was also feeling more ashamed by the day. Each time she saw a baby, or a pregnant woman, she would remember that because of something she did — after all, when they first did it it was in the rehearsal room, her own idea! — some baby was going to be born into the world with a daddy in jail, and a criminal record as a sex offender. Some kid would have to grow up with that hanging over him, like, forever. And she'd heard that the wife had filed for divorce, too. The pretty bride who looked so happy in that wedding picture.

The applause was dying away, which meant soon she'd have to rise and walk out through all these people. She wished she could just blink and be back home, under the covers with her notebook.

There was something else. Something she hadn't said, she hadn't dared say, not even to her mother, or Ethan, or even to write down secretly on her blue-lined paper. Once in a while, even now, even after all this . . . she missed him.

Her mom squeezed her hand. "We'll show them, won't we? We'll show them what we're made of."

The judge was gaveling down the last snatches of clapping, but even he seemed proud, or at least pleased.

Then he put his serious face back on and sentenced Mr. Hill to three years in prison.

The bailiffs came forward. This was it. What

he had been bracing himself for since the first moment he leaned toward Morgan in his car that windy December night.

He slumped, almost relieved it was finally happening. His lawyer was whispering to him something about good behavior and parole, but TJ wasn't listening.

He looked over his shoulder as the bailiffs cuffed him. He caught his wife's eye, and she looked away. As well she should. His brother openly sneered, his eyes flashing fury as if Greg was the victim. Alessia flinched like she'd accidentally laid eyes on a monster, and perhaps she had, at that.

Alex was speaking to him urgently, but TJ heard her like one of those honking noises from Charlie Brown cartoons. Man, he used to love Charlie Brown. And Snoopy. Greg used to draw Snoopy to make him smile when they were kids, back when his brother loved him. Back when everybody did.

He'd have liked to have seen his mom and dad out there, but maybe that was for the best.

"I'm okay," he finally told Alex. "I'm resigned to this."

He said it because he figured they would want him to say that, because he didn't want to end up watched for twenty-four hours in a glass box. Anyway, it was true enough. He was resigned to it. All of it.

He took one more look toward Morgan as the bailiffs led him toward the door. She'd cut her hair.

She looked so beautiful.

P.S.
INSIGHTS, INTERVIEWS, & MORE . . .

About the Book

AUTHOR Q&A

What inspired you to write this particular book?

I saw a headline in my local paper that read: FORMER TEACHER ADMITS HAVING SEX WITH 17-YEAR-OLD GIRL. How could I not read on? But the most striking part of the story was how the young woman in question — eighteen years old by the time the court proceedings had begun — was seated on the defendant's side of the court. Not with her parents. This got me thinking from the parents' point of view, then from the girl's side of the story, and how different those two narratives would be. Not to mention what the teacher's wife would be going through.

So is this novel based on a true story?

No, I wouldn't go that far. I did follow the case in the paper, but those stories were not very detailed or numerous, and that case never went to trial because the defendant pleaded guilty. I don't know any of the private details, nor did I try to learn them. My version is completely made up, as is the setting of my book, Arbor Valley.

Where did the title,* The Whole Golden World, *come from?

This novel was known as "Book 5" at first. Then one day, driving to the YMCA for an exercise class, the weirdest sunset happened right in front of me. There was a sort of crack between the clouds covering the sky and the edge of the horizon, just at the instant the sun was setting. The light that poured out was astonishing. The setting was as mundane as you can get: a Home Depot, a defunct lumberyard, a railroad crossing. But the light was magic. As soon as I stopped the car I scribbled lines of poetry. I'd already had Morgan's character writing poetry in secret (that is to say, I was writing the poetry), and I knew I had to use this in the book. And so I did, at a pivotal point in the story, and the title comes from a line in that poem . . .

Do you relate to a particular character?

I relate to many of them in various ways. Rain, the dutiful yoga-teaching wife, is a peacemaker who thrives on stability and smoothing things over, making it her job to make everyone happy. That resonates with me. Dinah, the firebrand mom, tries so hard to parent perfectly that she sometimes goes overboard. My son is at the point where he sometimes dreads asking me a question because I'm prone to giving him an encyclopedic answer just for the joy of responding to his interest, not to mention a nerdy desire to cover all the bases.

As for Morgan, I never went through anything like what she did (thank goodness). But it wasn't hard to cast myself back to being seventeen and feeling like you have finally grown up and learned everything, only to have adults treat you as either an adult or a little kid, depending on what suits them at the moment. It's infuriating and unfair in the teenage mind. That quasi-adult, shape-shifting stage is a heady and dangerous time, though it's too hard to see that as an adolescent right in the thick of it.

Did you have a particular goal in writing this book or a point you were trying to make?

No. My books are often topical (I've written about breast cancer, blended families, and compulsive hoarding), but I don't give my novels an agenda, other than this: to make my characters understood. You don't have to like them, but I always hope the reader understands them by the end, even when they behave in ways that seem to be inexplicable on the surface. I approach all of my characters, antagonists included, with compassion. I don't believe my characters are extreme, even if their actions sometimes seem that way. None of them are so different from the rest of us.

READING GROUP DISCUSSION QUESTIONS

1. What do you think of Rain's loyalty to TJ for much of the story? How does her pregnancy affect her feelings toward TJ and the case against him?

2. Why do you think Rain believes so strongly in their relationship as the story begins, despite problems that were already brewing regarding his mercurial moods and their infertility? Was her steadfast belief in their marriage admirable?

3. Why do you think Dinah and Joe are so disconnected as a couple when the story begins? Is it common for difficult family issues to drive spouses apart?

4. How much responsibility do Dinah and Joe Monetti bear for what happened to Morgan? Would the story have gone differently if the twin Monetti brothers had

not been born with physical and learning challenges?

5. Why do you think TJ refuses to admit what he's done when the police finally discover the affair? Do you think he believes his own stories?

6. Why do you think TJ had a sexual affair with his student despite the kind of damage it would cause?

7. Do you think Morgan was manipulated into the affair? Or did she choose her actions of her own will?

8. Do the respective ages of TJ and Morgan affect their individual accountability for their affair? Does it matter that she's only a few months from legal adulthood when their affair begins? Does it matter that he's only twelve years older than she is? How much does it change the situation that he's her teacher?

9. Do age limits written into law — for drinking, military service, smoking, voting, consensual sex — make sense? Does their arbitrary nature make them problematic, or are they simply a practical and

moral necessity?

10. What does it mean to be an adult? And do either Morgan or TJ meet that definition?

About the Author

MEET KRISTINA RIGGLE

Kristina Riggle is a former newspaper reporter now pursuing her first love, writing fiction. Her character-driven novels have been honored by independent booksellers in the Midwest and Great Lakes regions, and her debut, *Real Life & Liars,* was a Target Breakout pick. She finds people of all walks of life fascinating, as in the old A&E *Biography* slogan, "Every life has a story." She's the fiction coeditor for the e-zine *Literary Mama* and has published short stories at *Literary Mama, Cimarron Review,* and elsewhere. When not writing, she can be found taking care of her two kids and dog, and squeezing in time to read whenever she can.

The employees of Thorndike Press hope you have enjoyed this Large Print book. All our Thorndike, Wheeler, and Kennebec Large Print titles are designed for easy reading, and all our books are made to last. Other Thorndike Press Large Print books are available at your library, through selected bookstores, or directly from us.

For information about titles, please call:

(800) 223-1244

or visit our Web site at:

http://gale.cengage.com/thorndike

To share your comments, please write:

Publisher
Thorndike Press
10 Water St., Suite 310
Waterville, ME 04901